T·H·E

INTERPRETER

Forge Books by Robert Moss

The Firekeeper
The Interpreter

T·H·E
INTERPRETER

A STORY OF TWO WORLDS

ROBERT MOSS

A TOM DOHERTY ASSOCIATES BOOK

NEW YORK

THE INTERPRETER

Edited by David G. Hartwell

A Forge Book
Published by Tom Doherty Associates, Inc.
175 Fifth Avenue
New York, NY 10010

Forge® is a registered trademark of
Tom Doherty Associates, Inc.

Library of Congress Cataloging-in-Publication Data

Moss, Robert
    The interpreter : a story of two worlds / Robert Moss. — 1st ed.
        p.   cm.
    Includes bibliographical references.
    ISBN 0-312-85739-X (acid-free paper)
    1. Weiser, Conrad, 1696–1760—Fiction.   2. Pennsylvania—History—
Colonial period, ca. 1600–1775—Fiction.   3. Frontier and pioneer
life—Pennsylvania—Fiction.   4. Indians of North America—
Pennsylvania—Fiction.   5. German Americans—Pennsylvania—Fiction.
6. Indian agents—Pennsylvania—Fiction.   7. Mohawk Indians—
Fiction.   I. Title.
PR6063.083I58   1997   96–32345
823'.914—dc20   CIP

First Edition: March 1997

Printed in the United States of America

0   9   8   7   6   5   4   3   2   1

This story is for my father
a Scottish soldier
whose love reached beyond death

*Men do mightily wrong themselves when they refuse to
be present in all ages and neglect to see the beauty
of all kingdoms.*

—Thomas Traherne

*We must assume our existence as broadly as we
in any way can; everything, even the unheard of,
must be possible in it. This is at bottom the only courage
that is demanded of us: to have courage for the most strange,
the most inexplicable.*

—Rainer Maria Rilke

*Whenever a knight of the Grail tried to follow a path
made by somebody else, he went altogether astray.*

—Joseph Campbell

CONTENTS

TENT PEOPLE

FALL, 1709

1.

It was hard to see anything through the fog that blanketed Blackheath. The world beyond the tent city of refugees on the high plateau south of London was reduced to the spikes of leafless trees, a distant spire and the hard, sullen faces of the Londoners who had gathered to yawp and jeer.

"A right highwayman's fog," observed a man who had perched himself on a heap of slag beside the gravel pit.

The fog swirled and lifted, giving a view of the German encampment. More than a thousand army tents, each big enough to shelter three or four families, had been pitched on the heath. Anger seethed among the sightseers as they measured the size of the alien colony. The aliens were Palatine Germans, fellow Protestants and allies in the war against France, who had come to England at the personal invitation of Queen Anne. These facts won the refugees little favor in the eyes of the growing mob. They were *foreign*, and hence inherently untrustworthy. They spoke a different language, ate different food, followed different ways. Furthermore, they were believed to be stealing jobs from native-born Englishmen, and to be carrying filthy diseases from the Continent.

"More of them every day," grumbled a woman near the front of the crowd. "Thick as flies on shit."

"Bloody maggots!" A man's thick voice took up the complaint, hurling it into the hearing of the Palatine boys who struggled with the canvas sheets of their tent as the oldest hammered pegs into the muddy heath.

"Weevils!" came another voice.

"Fecking foreigners!" cried a man called Roper, who had recently lost his employment as a meat porter, spitting out the last word as if it were the world's worst insult. A burst blood vessel had stained his left eye a hot pink. He exhaled stiff clouds of raw gin. He cursed harder when he saw one of the foreign boys present his posterior, scrabbling at the top of his breeches to moon the hecklers.

Roper saw a rock the size of his fist at the edge of the gravel pit and scooped it up.

"I'll show you respect for an Englishman, you German sausage," he vowed, lobbing the stone at the boy who was capering in front of the crowd.

A ragged cheer went up as the rock struck the side of the boy's head and he went down, gouting blood.

"Bugger off home!"

"He bleeds like a fucking pig, innit."

"Nice bit of German ham. Nothing like it," volunteered the barmaid from the Two Cushions, who had come out to Blackheath with her current swain for a Sunday lark.

"Plenty more where that came from!"

Flying high on his marksmanship, Roper did not notice how fast the mood of the tent people had changed. Until now—apart from the boy who lay bleeding on the grass—the Palatines had all gone stolidly about their business, affecting not to notice the buzz of the angry crowd. Some of them were gathered in circles, listening to Bible readings (if you could call it the Bible if it were written in any language other than the muscular English prose of the King James version, which Roper, though illiterate, would not). Some of the women were cooking over open fires, or hanging clothes out to dry. Some—like the boy who had fallen—had been putting up new tents, as if Her Majesty had not spread enough canvas for the loafers already.

Roper was deeply persuaded that the tent people had stolen his job, though it was a Lincolnshire man and no German who had inherited his apron. His ugly mood was shared by much of the crowd. Many of the men had come armed with cudgels, pitchforks and knives.

The Palatines were stirring, forming ranks, jabbering in their own tongue, which troubled the uncomprehending English mob as much as their numbers. A tall, barrel-chested German moved among his people, a black-bound Bible in one hand, his other palm raised in a gesture of caution or admonition. He inspected the gash on his son's head.

"It is only a scratch," Johann Weiser told the tent people who flocked around him. "Scalp wounds bleed the most. Conrad, please go in the other tent. Greta will see to your wound."

"I don't need *her,*" the boy spat. When Conrad got to his feet, the hair that flopped over his forehead was matted with blood. More blood pumped from the wound at the side of his temple and streamed over his eyes, forming rivulets that ran down his chin and slopped over his chest. His shirt and breeches were already ruined.

Johann Weiser took his son by the upper arm, but Conrad wriggled free.

"Conrad!" a girl's treble protested as the boy dashed forward, wiping blood from his eyes with his sleeve.

"Will you look at this blood sausage?" Roper rolled his eyes and his belly in mock amazement. "Stuffed full of himself, is this one. Thinks he can take on a man!"

The meat porter balled his tremendous fist, ready to measure Conrad's length on the turf, which was rank with the excretions of thousands of persons—tent people and sightseers—who had no other conveniences. Close up, the German boy looked no older than thirteen or fourteen, despite his height and broad shoulders. The barmaid from the Two Cushions felt a pang of sympathy for what must await him from a man twice his weight.

As Roper swung, Conrad ducked to waist level and propelled himself forward, with such leaping velocity that his feet left the ground. The top of his skull drove like a cannonball into the pit of Roper's belly.

"Ah, Jesus and vinegar," Roper gasped, as he lost control of his motions and was flung to the ground with terrific force.

Conrad strutted around the hulk of his victim like a turkeycock, and kicked him in an uncomfortable place when, reviving, Roper went fumbling after a knife.

The mob seethed toward Conrad, bent on revenge for one of its own. On either flank, fights had already broken out between tent people and Englishmen. The handful of watchmen who had been observing the scene made themselves scarce.

Johann Weiser bulled his way through the press of people and grabbed his son by the ear. "*Unanständig!*" he growled. "This is disgraceful! This is not the way. *This is not our country.*"

"You were a soldier," Conrad protested. "A man has the right to defend himself and his own."

"Hear me!" Johann Weiser roared above the crowd as he hauled his son to safety. "You are not a man!"

"I just proved the contrary." Conrad smiled through the pain.

"Hear me!" his father repeated, with thunder in the words. "You will be a man *when I tell you that you are a man.*"

"And when will that be? When I bed a woman like my father's whore?"

The boy had vanished into the seething crowd before his father could mete out retribution that might have satisfied even the meat porter.

2.

Conrad ran blindly, away from the shouts and jeers and his father's wrath. He came to a high wall and scrambled over it, to find himself in rolling parklands where red deer grazed under the Royal oaks. When one of the Queen's deerkeepers came to chase him off, he ran north again, toward the Thames. He saw a curious tower-house set up on a hill. From behind one of its tall windows, John Flamsteed, the Astronomer Royal, briefly contemplated the panting youth before pulling the drapes against the strengthening sun and climbing into bed, having spent the whole night following the motions of the heavens through his long wooden telescope.

Beyond Greenwich Park, still heading toward the river, Conrad found himself in a warren of unpaved streets, no better than animal tracks between open sewers and low, mean huts. He stumbled over the stump of a beggar no older than himself, who turned his sightless eyes upward and croaked, "Alms for the blind."

Without calculating what he was doing, Conrad fished out the only money in his possession—a halfpenny given to him by a fine lady over the river in Regent Street who had allowed him to carry her purchases to her carriage because she liked his face. He dropped the coin in the beggar's filthy palm.

With his money gone, Conrad felt lighter.

Strange how we draw comfort from the plight of those who are worse off than ourselves.

"Bless you, young master," cried the blind boy, making off with remarkable speed and agility.

Ragged children flocked to Conrad, cawing and pecking like crows, now that he had established himself as a soft touch. A woman as round as a beehive oven shooed them away. A lean, blue-jowled man who had been following the scene with the hard eyes of a hungry wolf, puzzled by the contrast between Conrad's largesse and his bloody rags, shrugged and sloped off.

"Come with me, little one." The woman spoke in an accent Conrad could not place, perhaps from a country far to the east of his own. She pulled him through a narrow doorway into a tiny space walled by Hessian sacks and mismatched curtains. Despite the poverty of the surroundings, the stench of the neighborhood was kept at bay by an expensive aroma of spice and cologne. The woman brought a cloth and a pan of water and washed the caked blood and dirt from Conrad's forehead. She took ointment the color and texture of bacon drippings from a little tin and worked it into the wound with the ball of her thumb.

"You'll not bleed more today," she announced. "Unless you pick another fight with a butcher's mate."

Conrad narrowed his eyes, puzzled by the specific way the woman spoke to him of things she had—surely—not seen.

"We must speak of tomorrow and tomorrow," she went on.

When she took his palm, Conrad realized she was some kind of low fortuneteller, like the gypsies who had camped in the fields behind his father's vineyard until the duke's bailiffs chased them away.

"I have no money," Conrad told her.

"Does it think my sight is so dim?" the gypsy teased. She was not looking at the lines on his palm. Her fingers fluttered against his wrist.

"Tomorrow and tomorrow and tomorrow," she chanted. "*Ah.*" Her fingers tightened. "There she is."

"What are you saying?"

"She's there by the door. She loved you very much, didn't she? You were always the favorite. Liked blue, didn't she? She's wearing it now. A blue dress and a nice white bonnet. She smells nice, too. Like fresh-baked bread."

Conrad shivered and yanked his arm away. Every morning, when she was not tending a sick baby or nursing a new one, his mother would rise long before dawn to make dough and set loaves to bake in the big brick oven of his father's bakery in the market town in the valley of the Köpferbach. The warm, yeasty smell of newly risen bread would forever be associated with her.

"Didn't want to leave you," the gypsy woman continued, nodding to herself. "She's been with you in spirit since the hot fever came on her. Came out of her body before the breath left her, poor dear. Magda, is it?"

Magdalina. Conrad pursed his lips, determined to say nothing to confirm or deny what the woman was telling him. Maybe she was a witch. For all their Bible reading, his people had a deep belief in witches—good and bad—and their influence in the affairs of men and beasts. More than a few of the farmers and the farmers' wives around Gross Aspach blamed the failure of the last harvest on a wild horde—both dead and living—who rode the winds at night.

"Are you telling me you can see my mother here, in this room?" Conrad challenged the gypsy woman.

"I see her better with my eyes closed." The gypsy closed her eyes and rested her chin on her expansive bosom. "She says she's been telling you things in your dreams, but you forget when you wake up."

Conrad felt a stab of pain above his eyes, sharper than the dull ache of his wound.

"There is a name from a story. The name of a knight too pure for this world. He is on a quest full of peril and temptation. His name begins with a 'P.' "

Parzifal. It had been one of his mother's pet names for him, since he forever had his head stuck in stories of the Grail knights.

Whatever her motives, the gypsy woman was good—good enough to bring goosebumps. *Is she reaching into my mind, or is she truly talking to my mother?*

"If my mother is here—" Conrad faltered, shocked by what had already escaped from his mouth. The minister in his village, warring with the superstitions of his flock, had preached that the spirits of the dead lie at rest until the Day of Judgment, in some kind of divine coma, and that efforts to communicate with the dead are an abomination.

If my mother is here, then why?

"She loves you, child," the gypsy said gently, responding to the question he had left unfinished. "She wants to watch over all of you, and that is no sin, in God's truth. There is none among us that can do without watching over." She drew in her breath sharply, and put her hand to her chest. "There's more," she reported. "Not easy. Need to check. *Ah,* the pain! Need to let go—can't let go. Want to die, can't die, fighting to live."

The words came tumbling faster and faster. Conrad, scarcely breathing, hung on every one of them.

Though Conrad's English was almost perfect—he was a natural with languages, with a parrot's ability to reproduce dialect—there were things that he missed.

"What's that?" he interrupted, sensing something important slip by.

"Perch," she repeated. "You and your father were going for perch."

"Perch?" All that came to him was the image of a bird in a cage, swinging on a metal bar.

The gypsy made the gesture of flicking something over her shoulder, and a very different scene came flooding back. "*Barsch.*" He mouthed the German name for his father's favorite fish. They had gone fishing together, on a boat on a lake, cooking the fish at night over an open fire at their camp in the woods. A real expedition, two men in the wilds, a dream his father had long promised to fulfill.

A dream he killed.

"Something is not right," the gypsy was saying. "A woman who laughs too much. A woman with yellow hair. Another name from a story. Is it Gretel?"

"*Greta.*" Conrad did not hold back the hated name. "She is my father's mistress."

The gypsy released a long, sawing breath from the back of her throat. "Better," she announced, opening her eyes. "I think this is also why your mother stays behind. There is something unfinished."

Yes.

Conrad waited. When the silence had deepened between them, he said, "You spoke of tomorrow."

"I must check. I am not in charge here." She closed her eyes, going inward. Her voice shifted to a deeper octave. "You will walk where the earth is narrow. You will die and come back. You will see a battle in the face of the moon. You will be a peacemaker and a great interpreter in spite of yourself."

"I don't understand."

"To understand a destiny, you are required to live it."

3.

Conrad's interview with the gypsy brought back a memory he had never quite managed to suppress: the memory of the fishing trip he had taken with his father during his mother's final illness. It was supposed to be a man's affair. "Just you, me and Freddie," Johann Weiser had promised. "Freddie" was Conrad's younger brother Friedrich. Things had gone well enough, until the woman had turned up. Conrad's father had introduced her as an old family friend, and commented—too often—on the remarkable coincidence of finding her taking a rest cure alone at the little village on the lake.

This had been Conrad's first encounter with Greta Müller, the woman who now shared his father's bed. The heat rose in his face as he remembered how he had watched in hiding as his father and Greta sported in the water like puppies. The bold lines of the woman's body had been as provoking as full nakedness under the sodden, clinging shift.

Had they been lovers even then? *Was my father fucking Greta Müller while my mother lay on her deathbed?* It would be enough to set a ghost walking, if the gypsy spoke the truth.

Conrad's mind shifted to another scene, played out in Rotterdam the previous summer. Johann Weiser had wasted little time, after burying his wife, before packing up eight of his many children, the possessions they could haul on their backs and in little handcarts, and Greta, the "family friend." Conrad's father dreamed of a Promised Land in the New World. He had seen pictures of it in a book embellished with a portrait of Queen Anne that had been widely circulated among the little principalities of the Rhineland. America was shown in these illustrations as a beautiful, orderly country of fruits and flowers and waving wheatfields. In her Golden Book, Queen Anne promised the Palatines a release from the vicious cycle of war, famine and hot fever in the Rhineland: sanctuary in England, with the prospect of farms and freedom in England's plantations in North America. Johann Weiser burned to follow his vision of a land of milk and honey across the sea. However, his wife had not shared his passion. Magdalina pointed out that monarchs are less scrupulous than other mortals in fulfilling their promises, and clung to her native soil. "I belong to my valley," she had willingly conceded, "as a slice of bread belongs to the loaf."

Her sudden death had silenced these objections. Johann Weiser had led his little clan down the river valleys to Rotterdam in the summer of 1709, to sign on for the crossing to Dover on one of the Royal Navy transports Queen Anne had despatched to the Dutch ports. The occasion had been memorialized by a quill pen.

The scene festered in Conrad's memory, even worse than the scene on the lake.

Through the windows of a narrow, high-ceilinged room, in a high, narrow trading house, the sea had been lightly choppy, the water yellow with olive shadows. Conrad and his seven siblings clutched their possessions to their chests as they watched their father fold his great bulk to converse with the black-clad burgher who presided at the table with pipe and ledgerbook, comfortable in his rolls of fat. The Dutchman was van Toren or van Gent, one of the agents employed by Queen Anne to register the Palatine refugees and arrange their orderly passage to Dover. Or perhaps he was only a clerk. He affected the manners of a great man, and the true masters of Dutch commerce had little patience with grandees.

The Dutchman clucked appreciatively at Greta Müller's magnificent bosom, perhaps picturing her decorously disrobed on a Rubens canvas.

"My *wife*," Johann Weiser specified sternly, marking his territory.

The Dutchman scratched in his book.

Weiser, Johan Koenrat & vrouw & 8 k.

Conrad seethed, clenching his fists until his knuckles turned white. His little sister Catrina howled when the situation was explained to her. All the children knew that Greta Müller was not their father's wife. Johann's wife was buried in the cemetery at Gross Aspach only ten weeks before, together with the unborn child in her belly. Had the baby lived, it would have been her fifteenth. Johann Weiser was no slouch at fulfilling his marital duties. The Weisers were sturdy farming stock— though one branch of the family had produced ducal magistrates and corresponding airs—and knew in their bones that the fertility of man and beast and crops was related and that vigorous, healthy sex was part of the tribute man paid to the Earth. Not so long ago, sacred coupling at the turning points of the year had been a vital ritual among these people.

In his bones, Johann Weiser may have sensed that the loss of this ritual connection with the earth had something to do with the blight that had struck his beloved valley in the Rhineland. Three years of drought had killed the crops, while the mad duke of Württemberg salted the streets of his capital to give his mistress a pretend sleighride in the dead heart of summer. Johann had watched the vineyards he had planted with his own hands wither and die, despite backbreaking efforts to save them by carrying water from the fallen Köpferbach in leather buckets. As the grapes died, his wife had fallen into the sudden, violent fever that would not break. This double tragedy had shaped his decision. To sell for whatever he could get whatever he could not take with him—the bakehouse, the ruined vineyards, the parcel of land beyond the village—and move out with the children who were able and willing to travel, to claim the Queen's Bounty and the chance of a new life. And to take a new woman.

It is not good for man to live alone.

"A man needs to be mated," Johann had explained to his children. They had remained uniformly hostile to Greta. It was too soon after their mother's death, Johann recognized, for them to make the necessary adjustment. But there had been no time to prepare them, no room to let new feelings blossom. The moment of opportunity, the *kairos* time, was *now*. In a new life, in a new world, the children would surely slough off old resentments and accept Greta as their second mother.

Johann Weiser was right about the *kairos* time. He led his family on board the last Royal Navy transport that carried Palatine refugees from the Netherlands to England. The British government—shocked by the monstrous growth of the tent city on Blackheath—had already moved to ban further migrations from Holland; luckily for the Weisers, the news did not reach the captain of their ship before he set sail.

But Johann Weiser was wrong about his children, especially Conrad.

Each night under the canvas on Blackheath, Conrad listened to hot breathing and low gurgling laughter and half-throttled grunts and squeals from the corner where his father slept with Greta Müller, imperfectly screened from the children by an old blanket hung from two sticks. He tried not to picture what they were doing, but the images flocked at him. On his mean bed of straw, he felt himself plunge and churn among Greta's lush convexities. He feasted on her lips, on her swollen nipples. He smelled her sex. She smelled like runny cheese, like a full-fat brie sliding off the plate. Some nights, against his volition, he tensed and relaxed his body, falling into the rhythms of adult lust. His cock rose and stiffened until the skin was drum-tight and the brush of a fingertip, even a rough cloth, could make him burst. Night after night, he strained to hold back the demon seed. He did not always succeed.

Conrad would not make peace with Greta Müller, even after she got a wedding ring.

4.

Conrad's skirmish with the meat porter took place at the end of the seventh year of the reign of Queen Anne. There were at least fifteen thousand Palatine refugees in the tent city on the heath—a huge number in proportion to the population of South London at the time. They had come under the Queen's protection; her late husband, the Prince of Denmark, was a German-speaking Lutheran and Queen Anne—though a Stuart and a strict Anglican—was sympathetic to the Protestant cause. But the Palatines had become increasingly unpopular with Queen Anne's English subjects. For more than a year they had been coming and coming: in Royal Navy transports, in fat-bottomed Dutch merchant boats, in fishing ketches. Exposed to all elements, chilled to the bone, they were wracked by typhus, scurvy and the bloody flux. As the knacker men carted their bodies off to the limepits, black rumors thrived. The aliens (it was said) were the bearers of unspeakable pollutions. Every sickly child, every cow that gave sour milk, was blamed on them.

They were hated even harder as scabs who were stealing work away from true Englishmen. The greatest outrage—the source of white-hot, trembling rage among London's cartels of professional cheats and beggars—was that the Queen and her misguiding ministers had given these interlopers a license to beg in the streets of the capital. This had sparked gang war, fought with knives and knuckles and clubs. It threatened to produce a surge of mob violence that would shake the high and mighty across the river. Dukes and their mistresses woke with thumping hearts and clammy palms from dreams of being butchered in their beds. Such things had come at their kind from Blackheath before. The blasted heath had always been a hotbed of rebellion, a mustering place for King Mob. Had not Wat Tyler, a common blacksmith from Dartford, gathered a horde of a hundred thousand peasants and artisans here in Richard II's time? At the Court of Queen Anne, it was not forgotten that Tyler's rude army from Blackheath seized the Tower of London and held the capital in thrall until the tide turned and a Lord Mayor who had more than one use for a knife and fork skewered the Dartford blacksmith like a stuck pig. As the tent city on Blackheath grew and grew, and Germans fought with professional beggars and plain working men in front of St. Paul's, the Queen and her ministers heard the dragon stir.

Something had to be done with the tent people. Sending them home was a popular suggestion, and far from the least polite.

Sending them to the American plantations was a more pleasing idea, at least for the Queen. It would be seen as the fulfillment of a promise; like Johann Weiser, many of the refugees had crossed the North Sea in hopes of fortune and freedom in the American colonies. Sending them to America had the advantage of finality; no emigrant would willingly undertake to repeat the nightmare of the Atlantic crossing. As Protestants who had seen their homes looted and their women ravished by King Louis' dragoons, the Palatines could surely be counted on to form a stout bulwark against the ambitions of the French in North America. Since the Germans were known to be industrious farmers, they were likely to improve land values by carving wheatfields and orchards out of the American wilds.

This left open the delicate issue of who was going to pay to ship the Germans across the Atlantic and feed and supply them until they were self-sufficient. The treasury had been exhausted by the ruinous cost of the Duke of Marlborough's wars on the Continent. Everyone wanted to see the Germans gone but nobody wanted to foot the bill. It required an elegant charmer who knew the right people to come up with the solution. His name was Robert Hunter. He was a would-be playwright who counted Addison and Swift as his friends and tickled Mrs. Masham, the Queen's favorite courtier.

Hunter maintained that the Palatines could pay their own way, by contracting to make tar for the Royal Navy, in the pine forests of New York, until they had repaid the cost of passage and provisions. In an age of wooden ships, tar was a hugely valuable and strategic commodity. Since the Royal Navy had long been dependent on Scandinavia for its supply, Hunter's scheme had a patriotic ring. If his projections proved correct, the British Empire would not only be able to produce all the tar for its own shipping from the forests of New York, but would generate a tidy profit as the world's leading exporter.

Robert Hunter was not a disinterested party. In an age where no clear boundary was drawn between private interest and public service, Hunter planned to make his own fortune on the side. He had already used his ability to tickle Mrs. Masham to arrange his appointment as the next Royal Governor of New York. It was widely understood that the governorship was a license to pocket vast commissions from the sale of Indian lands. Her Majesty was known to be interested in the cause of American Indians; she had actually invited four of their chiefs to visit her Court, and they were said to be crossing the seas even as these matters were debated. The engaging Mr. Hunter made it clear, in his amusing way, that he intended to cheat the Indians *fair*.

Out of this stew of resentment, greed and xenophobia bubbled the first mass migration from Europe to the New World. Beyond the understanding of the players, this event was to change the makeup of America and mold the character of a new figure on the world stage: the *American*.

Conrad Weiser was thirteen when he joined Her Majesty's transport the *Lyon* for the wretched, protracted voyage to New York, a teenager tormented by raging hormones and fantastic visions. Yet already he was stalked by greatness. The shadow of Skycatcher fell over him, a memory of the future. Despite himself, he would be *sakowennakarahtats*, the interpreter, "he who digs up the words and plants them anew," a messenger between worlds. Despite the sweaty nights torn between desire for his father's mistress and ferocious hatred of the woman who supplanted his mother, he would grow to inhabit the larger identity that was waiting for him among a people he had never seen with ordinary eyes.

PART ONE

PROMISED LAND

✦

1710–1712

Truly, here are real savages by our standards; for either they must be thoroughly so, or we must be. There is an amazing distance between their character and ours.
—Michel de Montaigne, "Of Cannibals"

Ordinary people who know how to dream have many times seen that the dead appeared to them, just as they were in life. Therefore we believe that life does not end here on earth.
—Nalungiak, a Netsilik Eskimo

No one ascends from the underworld unmarked.
—*The Descent of Inanna*

CHAPTER 1

THE FOUR KINGS

1.

The Mohawk squatted on the padded seat of the open coach, his sinewy arms dangling between his knees, like a wolf, and waited for something to speak to him.

Hendrick, the English called him. To his own people he was Forked Paths, a war captain of the Wolf Clan who moved against his enemies in the way of the forest, where nothing is straight. But the crooked streets of London, still new to him, held traps and deceptions as deep as any Hendrick Forked Paths had laid.

He was not attending to the round, sucking mouth of the Englishman who sat facing him, with gold galloon on his courtier's coat and a great bush of powdered hair that was not his own, or the halting gutturals of the Dutch interpreter at his side, or the creak of the carriage wheels, or the squall of the lewd, strapping doxies who flounced about at the foot of the Haymarket, or the scrape of a busker's fiddle, or the scuttle of rats along the open sewers, or the screech of the gulls—salt birds, bitter birds—though the Mohawk could distinguish all these sounds, and a hundred more. To his wolf ears, the roar of the city was not a sea, or a wall; it was a forest where every bush had a name, every leaf stood apart, though in this cramped world of the Sunrise People so many were pressed together.

Hendrick was listening and looking for a guide, something that knew him, a cousin from the world of the *Onkwehonwe*, the Real People, on the farther shore of the ocean sea he had crossed in the white men's floating castle—for the raven that shows the path of the deer, for the wren that warns of witchcraft, for the hawk that sees beyond forests and

25

mountains. Hendrick found only the gulls and the fat, waddling pigeons, tamer even than the flocks of passenger pigeons that came with the spring melt into the Real World, so many and so helpless that a child could bat them off the branches with a stick or catch them in her bare hands. London pigeons reminded the Mohawk of the swag-bellied Englishman who sat opposite, his buttery face half choked by his neckcloth. Londoners smelled alike to Hendrick. They stank of meat that was born dead, of four-leggeds that lived to be butchered, not hunted, and therefore—alone among animals—had no home in the spirit world. Beneath clouds of claret and gin, civet and cologne, the courtier in the carriage reeked of dead meat and cow's milk, which was worse than poison to the Real People. Hendrick had once been persuaded to drink cow's milk in a Dutchman's house at Albany. It had made his ears ache and his nose bleed.

The war captain's clothes were new. He wore a flowing scarlet mantle trimmed with gold and a shirt of finest cambric over a long black waistcoat with matching breeches and stockings—black because the Court was still in mourning for the Prince of Denmark, the Queen's late husband. All four of the Indian ambassadors wore similar clothes. Their outfits were gifts of the Crown. Puzzled as to how Indian chiefs should be attired for a call upon Her Majesty, the Queen's advisers had sent them to a playhouse tailor who dressed the kings of the stage. The Indian ambassadors had improved the costumier's designs with touches of their own. Hendrick wore the *kahstowa*, the feathered headdress of his people, crowned with a shower of white feathers and bright turkey down. He carried a heavy, ball-headed war club weighted for his hand, carved and notched to recall the scalps he had taken from the French and the Bark Eaters, their native allies. He wore three pairs of earrings, posted in the holes drilled in his ears when he was still an infant on the cradleboard. His pipe-bag was slung from his broad shoulder, because man rides to the skies on a cloud of tobacco. Tied to his waist by a rattlesnake belt was the otterskin bundle that held the power to bind souls and to kill from afar, and the vocabulary of his dreams.

□

Londoners surged around the two coaches, goggling at the visitors from America. Some had seen Indians before—wild men exhibited in cages as circus novelties—or heard tales of Pocahontas. But London had never played host to Indian royalty until now. The fact that there were no titles of kingship in Mohawk country, and that the four Indians in the two coaches were not even traditional chiefs, was a detail omitted by the hack authors of broadsheets and ballads celebrating the visit. The illustrations that embellished these publications showed the Indian Kings in the raiment of medieval monarchs, with beards and crowns, or in the robes of the Magi, bearing gifts in gold coffers.

What most impressed the crowd was how *unlike* the pictures the Queen's visitors had turned out to be. They were awed by Hendrick's sheer physical presence. He was a giant by English standards, a tower of hard muscle rising nearly seven feet high. The Londoners were fascinated by the tattoos of his companions. Nicholas Etakoam, the Mahican, had a flight of thunderbirds engraved across his temple. John Laughing, a Mohawk from the Upper Castle at Canajoharie, was adorned with curving lines that resembled both the phases of the moon and the raking clawmarks of a bear. Brant Vanishing Smoke—who belonged to the Bear Clan—wore tattoos of huge, stylized claws on his wrists and forearms, as if the paws of his totem animal were resting over his own.

A wit in the street hailed Vanishing Smoke as the Illustrated Man. Prints copied from his official portrait by Verelst, the Court painter, would soon be used as advertisments for London tattoo parlors. The phases of the moon were incised in exquisite detail across his forehead. His features were fine and regular, but the dark bars across his lower face suggested the predator, as the wolf's markings blacken its jaws and draw its prey to the terrible, steady eyes that read whether the quarry is ripe for the harvest. Lunar disks or gorgets were tattooed between Vanishing Smoke's collarbones. His chest bristled with spearpoints and arrowheads. Strangest of all was the thing that seemed to be scaling his sternum. It looked like an armored aquatic bug, ancient and utterly alien.

The warriors of Kush had worn pendants carved in the shape of flies, modeling themselves on the kind of biting fly that would not leave off an attack until it was dead. What kind of warrior—what sort of King— sported a tattoo of an insect from an ancient era?

□

The coachmen pulled on their reins and swore at their horses. Hendrick rose from his heels.

"This is the longhouse of the English Queen," Abraham Schuyler informed the Mohawks in their own language.

Vanishing Smoke studied St. James's Palace. The building was the color of black river mud. He saw horse warriors in breastplates of bright metal, and helmets plumed with horsehair, which made them one with their mounts. He recognized something he knew, and smiled on them.

□

The Indians were escorted by three white men who had sailed from the New World with them. They were Colonel Peter Schuyler, his brother Captain Abraham Schuyler, and Colonel Sir Francis Nicholson. In an age

of war—the current one sparked by a dispute over the Spanish succession—everyone wanted a military title; Nicholson liked to be addressed
as general. Peter Schuyler, the first mayor of Albany, was the cleverest
of the three. He had made a fortune in the fur trade and used his money
to buy influence among the Indians. The Mohawks called him by his
first name, but rendered it as Quider, because it was hard for them to
get their tongues round the letter P. Abraham Schuyler had learned native languages the old-fashioned way, by sleeping with the women. As
Albany Dutchmen, stirred by profit, not flags, the Schuylers were not
automatic enthusiasts for the war policy that had brought the Indian
Kings to London, but would move with the prevailing wind.

Colonel Nicholson and his Scottish associate Samuel Vetch (who had
stayed behind in Boston) were the moving spirits behind this expedition.
Nicholson was an empire-builder who planned to deliver a series of
blows to the French that would knock them out of North America. He
knew that no European army could win battles in the forests of North
America without native allies. He hoped to achieve two objectives in
London. First, to convince the League of Five Nations (to which the
Mohawks belonged), via the stories the Four Kings would take home,
that the might of Britain was invincible and that the Confederacy should
scrap its official policy of neutrality in white men's wars and commit its
warriors to Britain's cause. Second, he hoped to inspire Queen Anne and
her ministers to stop dallying and despatch a fleet of warships and a
redcoat army to expel the French from Canada. Francis Nicholson had
brought the Four Kings to London to arrange a war.

□

His Grace the Duke of Shrewsbury, the Lord Chamberlain, hooked his
richly upholstered arm over Peter Schuyler's.

"I trust you explained to them about the *chairs*."

For an instant, Schuyler appeared at a loss. His mouth opened and
closed like a fish out of water.

"In case Her Majesty does the honor of asking them to *sit*," His
Grace prodded the Dutchman.

"Ah, the *chairs*." Schuyler took it in. "They are perfect gentlemen,
you know," he added evasively. "I have entertained them in my own
house many times."

He did not comment on what much of London had observed: that
the Four Kings from America shared a violent and inscrutable aversion
to all modes of seating suited to an Englishman's rump. Whether lolling
at ease in their lodgings in Covent garden, or on public display with the
Lord Mayor or the Astronomer Royal, they went to any lengths to avoid
arranging their hindquarters in the prescribed style. They sat on their
heels, hugged their haunches, or sprawled full-length on backs or bellies.

□

In the audience chamber, Hendrick took the plump hand Her Majesty extended to him, palm down, and squeezed it experimentally. He still found it strange that the English greeted each other by touching finger-tips. Real People took you by the upper arm, closer to the heart.

The elderly Stuart sovereign was small, round and heavy, sheathed in black cloth. Hendrick smelled powder, musk and thick red wine, sluggish as congealing blood. And the stale, cold stench of meat buried the whole winter in a cache beneath the snow, stored against the Starving Time before the birds fly back from the south. Hendrick smelled her dead womb, that had delivered only still-births, and babies born to die.

The Queen's lips fluttered. It would please her for the Four Kings to be seated.

Hendrick watched his companions bend backwards and part their meat on the chairs that had been placed before the throne. This was necessary, Quider had explained to them; if they sat on the floor in the way warriors are meant to sit, Her Majesty would mistake this for an insult. Hendrick compromised by staying on his feet. He was the Word Carrier for this delegation, the one charged to speak for all. He could stand without giving offence.

He addressed the Queen, in his own language, as his elder sister.

"*Aktsia*, what is now spoken by one mouth is shared by every heart. We are grateful we have come safely across the Great Water, which our grandfathers have never done. We have come to condole you for the loss of your husband, who walks the path of strawberries.

"With this belt—" he held up a string of wampum beads, which was accepted, on Quider's nod, by a Royal equerry "—we wipe the tears from your eyes, that you may see clearly.

"We remove the blockage from your ears, so you may hear clearly.

"We open your mouth, so you may speak clearly.

"And we open the passage from your heart to your mouth, so that henceforth you will speak only from the heart."

The Mohawk's cadences were waves, rolling one on top of the other, each extending the range of the one before. At his last words, Brant Vanishing Smoke and the other Indians gave a sharp, sudden yelp of confirmation. When Abraham Schuyler translated the words of condolence, the Queen put a hand to her heart.

The Lord Chamberlain looked daggers at Schuyler. This episode was not on the program. The exchange with the Queen was supposed to be confined to the reading of an agreed text, drafted by Schuyler and Nicholson, and responses to any questions Her Majesty might be pleased to ask.

Now Hendrick held up a belt that reached from his shoulder to his waist: eleven rows of white and purple beads, strung on strips of rawhide. Without wampum—the sacred shells of life—a man's speech is empty or (worse) a deception. The Lord Chamberlain intervened to claim possession of this curiosity. The Queen, motioning for him to give her a closer look, puzzled over the belt as if trying to determine where it might fit in her wardrobe.

The Lord Chamberlain scowled at Major Pigeon, the court soldier who had been charged with reading the prepared text of Hendrick's speech.

"Great Queen!" Major Pigeon piped, the queue of his tie-wig bobbing behind him. "We have undertaken a long and tedious voyage, that we might see our Great Queen."

"*Aktsia*," Hendrick resumed. "Our path is thick with blood and betrayals."

In his own tongue, Hendrick always referred to the Queen as his big sister. There was no servility in his speech, nothing of the subject. He spoke as a younger man to a slightly older female relative.

Hendrick made the promise Colonel Nicholson had schemed and dreamed for. He would recruit the Mohawks and their sister-nations to march with the English against the French. But he warned that there must be an honest exchange of services. The Queen must leash the sharpers who were thieving Indian land with fraudulent deeds, issued by cheating governors.

"Your traders are snakes who poison us with rum. If the beaver pelts we have brought them were piled one on top of the other they would touch the sky. Yet all we receive are a few rags that leave our backsides bare, and trinkets our women are ashamed to wear, and the hard water that drives the spirit out of the body."

Peter Schuyler shifted uneasily. He remembered Indians sprawled insensate at the door of his trading house after swapping the peltries from a whole winter's hunt for one night's oblivion.

If the English wanted the Mohawks to fight for them, Hendrick pursued, they would have to show more resolution than the previous year, when a small army led by Nicholson sat in the woods at the south end of Lake Champlain, chewed by horseflies and mosquitoes, waiting for a fleet and an army from England that had been promised but were never sent.

"Big Sister," Hendrick told the Queen, "we are ashamed that your white children in the Real World loll about all loose and bare before our enemies, like trade women who put their legs in the air for any stranger. We ask now that you furnish them with a small prick, and insert it between their legs, so they may begin to stand like warriors."

Abraham Schuyler was obliged to cover his mouth with his hand.

His cousin Quider, who had many faces, matched the impassive expressions of the native ambassadors without difficulty.

When Hendrick paused, Major Pigeon eagerly lisped another section from his text, utterly oblivious to how widely the Mohawk orator had diverged from the authorized version.

Apart from food, Queen Anne's ruling passion was the established Church. The crafters of the prepared speech had catered to this by inserting a passage in which the Mohawks made a prayerful request for an Anglican missionary to take up residence among them.

"Great Queen," Major Pigeon read from his text, "we have some knowledge of the Saviour of the World."

The Queen nodded her approval. She indicated that she would personally contribute to the costs of the mission. Her largesse would extend to the building of forts and chapels and the provision of two splendid sets of communion plate, one for the Mohawk mission, the other for a projected church at Onondaga, the capital of the League of Five Nations.

The Queen wished to know how the Mohawks—a people grievously exposed to the blandishments of French Jesuits, as well as the tricks and sorceries of pagan conjurers—had grown to such dutiful respect for the English Church.

"Big Sister," Hendrick responded, "we have been told by priests that your grandfathers killed the son of your Creator, but that he permits you to eat his flesh. Your Great Spirit is strange to us. He drove your First Man and First Woman out of the Sky Garden for eating an apple. Yet he forgives you for killing his son. The priests say that everything is made clear in a holy book. We hope you will send us a priest who can speak the truth of this book, and lift the darkness from our minds. We know your Great Spirit is strong, because he speaks in the tongues of cannon and sends white death among us on the wings of evil spirits that were never in our dreaming."

2.

Vanishing Smoke, Hendrick's friend and fellow ambassador, lay on his back on the bare floorboards, forsaking the alien softness of the bed, which was plumped up like a turkey's breast. The steady patter of rain on the slates outside the window of the tavern in Covent Garden matched the rhythm of waterdrums during the circle dances in his village. The beat was calling him home. Vanishing Smoke let his eyelids fall and woke into the dream.

I am lost in a thick wood. It is a forest of spars, not trees. I am flying low, so low my wings almost brush the men who are rowing a dinghy between the bigger ships.

Dead sailors twist in the wind, where gibbets crowd the edges of the docks. Crows are their visitors.

I beat my pinions, gaining height. Now I can see the fields and villages of the tame people laid out as a patchwork quilt, soft greens and yellows under the rain.

I taste the sting of salt water. I fly on with the sun behind me, into the night. The Thunderers are angry. I hear their deep-throated roar. It splits open the sky. Through the gaping rent they hurl hissing spears of white fire. As they plunge into the sea, the ocean boils and hisses; the waves crackle and burst into stabbing fingers of flame.

The heat parches my mouth and blurs my sight. I am dizzy. A savage wind knocks me off-course. I lose height and am nearly lost. Rallying, I catch an upward gust and ride it across a sky of burning sulfur.

At last the Thunderers slake their wrath and the light returns. I can see my shadow, an arrowhead skimming green water. The smell of the pines rises to welcome me back to the Real World.

It is a good time, in the Real World. I find my family gathered at the edge of the Floodwood River. Learning fom the beavers, our boys have made a dam of dead branches to guide fish into their nets. Our women are gathering herbs and berries. I find my wife, Redhawk. She is ripe with a new baby. Our daughter Island Woman—the one who came to us from the north, and was born to us in the ritual of requickening—is laughing with pride and joy because she has discovered something rare and powerful among the bushes. She holds it up in her cupped palms, turning it gently so Redhawk can look. The flower is ononkhwa. *Medicine. Island Woman was born with the medicine gift. She knows the language of plants, and she knows we must ask permission from their leaders before we take anything from them. She crouches now to return a pinch of tobacco to the earth and the plants in exchange for the medicine they have gifted her.*

It is good to be home among my own people, with sunlight speckling the brown river. I rest on the bank, under a maple, and watch the little ones sport for prizes of maple candy. My sap runs strong. I throw back my head, and feel the weight and thrust of my horns. Redhawk lies with me, eager and lithe. I see the girlchild who is quickening inside her, and she tells me her name.

The scene flickers and reforms. I am shapeshifting into another form. I cannot breathe. The air is heavy with smoke. The fireholes in the longhouse have been covered with sheets of bark, because of the early snowstorm that is beating down on the roof. My people are cold and frightened. It shames me to see my children shivering without blankets, without even a bearskin to shelter their nakedness from this unnatural winter. They are scrapping in the dirt, fighting with dogs for a knucklebone.

There is worse. I rush from firepit to firepit, demanding "Who brought this upon you? Who is to blame?" My wife's clanmother, Fruitpicker, is the only one who will look at me, and she returns at once to her own business, shaking me off like a bad dream.

Then I know horror. As I move through the longhouse, I see that my people are vanishing from this world. I find my wife's sister mashing a handful of dried corn kernels in her wooden mortar. Then she is gone. She does not walk out the door, or fly up the smokehole. She is simply plucked out of her space. For a moment, there is a hole in the world where she sat. When it closes, it is as if she has never been.

I see this happen again and again. My friend Mad Owl is squatted down, restringing his snowshoes when he, too, is plucked out of his world.

My people are dying.

I snatch up my firelock from the space below my sleeping shelf. I must bring meat and warm furs.

Outside, in a howling white desert, I cannot see my hand in front of my face. I hear the snap of muskets, and look for an enemy. It comes too fast for me. I fall under its crushing weight.

We roll together in the snow. I lie, limp and broken, beneath the immense white pine, the grandfather of all the forests, the Peace Tree of our sacred stories.

I see a Face in the tree. The Face is contorted with pain, broken-nosed, the mouth distended. It is red like sunrise and black as the end of the world. I want to escape from the Face, the kakonsa, *but the tree will not release me. The sticky mess that seeps from its skin, sliming my own, is not resin, but blood.*

In the forest around us, all of the trees reveal Faces in pain. They lean against each other at crazy angles. Shattered by the storm, their broken limbs dangle from slivers of bark.

The high keening of the wounded trees is more than my heart can bear. I suffer their pain more deeply than my own. In this moment, I see the ax-marks at the foot of the great pine, and know I have helped to kill it.

Vanishing Smoke sat up, his heart hammering, his skin clammy with cooling sweat. He squeezed his nose between thumb and forefinger. He blew vigorously, but without effect, until a sneezing fit began to clear the blocked passages. He wiped his nose with the back of his hand, which came away slimy with mucus and blood.

That's how it was: when you saw a Face, you got nose trouble.

Vanishing Smoke squatted in a corner of the room and buried his head in his folded arms. He had woken into the most difficult dream of his life.

He knew he must go back into this dream, to make sure that its message was clear. The dream world was the real world, and the meaning of a dream must be stalked in the night forest where it lives.

Vanishing Smoke lowered himself onto his back and lay like a corpse, with his mouth half-opened so his breath rasped lightly as it sawed between throat and palate.

He watched the light patterns form and reform behind closed eye-lids, and willed himself back to the places of fear in the dream—to the longhouse of disappearing people, to the forest of wounded trees. He was looking for a dream guide who would answer the questions that were drumming in his head. *Who is to blame? Can this evil be averted? Can the dream be changed?*

Maybe Fruitpicker would talk to him. Perhaps an ally who had not shown himself in the original dream would now appear to help him. The dream spoke of medicine power, so maybe the Bear, his clan animal and the owner of many medicines, would come to guide him. Perhaps his dead grandmother, who sometimes advised him in dreams, would speak to him now.

As he slipped back inside the dreamscape, it was his adopted daughter, Island Woman—a strange, solitary girl, slender as an aspen—who came to meet him.

You are to blame, she told him. *You sold us to the newcomers. That is why the trees are dying.*

Could the dream be changed?

Instead of an answer, he was shown another scene. He was dreaming the dream onward. He saw himself running across a firepit, wearing the Face of the Divided One. He saw himself quarreling violently with Hendrick Forked Paths, his friend. He saw himself descending into a cave deep in the earth. He saw death by fire and sword.

Shadow men flay my skin and roast my flesh in a slow fire. Are they men or spirits? They become crows that pick my bones clean.

I am a sack of bones, rattling in a sack on a woman's back. I have died and come up through the ground. I am going to be buried again, in the Feast of Souls, so my spirit will be freed to walk the path of strawberries and dance with First Woman.

I am told, You must die the second death, but not until you have saved what can be saved.

Vanishing Smoke came back from this dream of a dream with new understanding. He belonged to a dreaming people. He had been taught since early childhood that it is natural to see the future in dreams. And that if it is possible to see the future, it may also be possible to change it.

He recognized that, in his dream, he had journeyed into a possible future. Some of the evils that lay along his path might be changed through his own actions—for example, if he chose to separate himself from Hendrick and the men who had brought them to London. Some of the fearful things in the dream might be modified by ritual and self-offering, to appease the spiritual powers he had angered. This would require consultation with a *ratetshents*, a strong dreamer, to confirm whether the dream was a calling to join the Society of Faces and to follow the lightning path of the shaman. Other elements in the dream seemed to carry a kind of fatality: they could not be altered, only *chosen*. He had seen his own death, and felt sure it would come in a way he could neither avoid nor would *wish* to avoid.

He did not fear the death of the body. He was ready to leave it behind like his borrowed clothes. He knew that there is life after life, because his grandmother had come back in sleeping and waking dreams to tell him about it, and because his dreamsoul had flown to the spirit world. What is required of a man is that he should *choose* his death, as the sick deer or the lame moose chooses death when it looks into the eye of the wolf, as a mother chooses death to save a child.

These were not things to be discussed with Hendrick Forked Paths or the other Indian ambassadors. They had turned their backs on the old ways, and drowned the dreaming, night after night, in a torrent of liquor. Vanishing Smoke had run with them, fought with them, drunk with them for many seasons. Now he would be different, because of the dream.

□

He took to spending long hours apart from the others. In the streets of London it was hard to be alone, even in a borrowed matchcoat that hid the extraordinary array of tattoos that covered his chest.

In his mind, he returned to the Greenwich observatory, and peered at the stars again through Flamsteed's telescope, whose angle was adjusted by raising or lowering the barrel on the rungs of a tall wooden ladder placed next to a window in the octagonal room. He wondered where, among the distant fires, was the Sky World from which First Woman had fallen, to be caught on the wings of blue herons, before she danced the earth into being on the Turtle's back. Flamsteed, always indulgent with those who sought God among the stars, had told him of a Greek philosopher who taught that the immortal spirit in each human being comes from a star and returns to that star after physical extinction.

Vanishing Smoke remembered the counting sticks the clanmothers had given him to take on this journey. They had asked him to number the English, so the Real People would know exactly how many of the Sunrise People they had to contend with. Vanishing Smoke had broken the counting sticks, during the ride from Portsmouth to London. What could he tell his people? *That the Sunrise People are as many as the stars.* Even now, the Mohawks had learned, ten shiploads of newcomers from another country in Europe—relatives of the gaunt army of tent people the Indians had observed on Blackheath—were sailing to the Real World. If the English treated their own people like this, how would they deal with the Real People if they became masters of the world across the water? Would they kill the trees? Would the bear and the wolf still have room to live?

Vanishing Smoke passed his days alone, thinking and dreaming, in the upstairs room of the tavern on King Street. The upholsterer-proprietor, Mr. Arne (whose infant son would one day write "Rule Britannia") was troubled by the reclusive behavior of his guest, and informed the Palace that the Mohawk must be gravely ill, since he refused all nourishment except water and tobacco.

3.

The Palace decided that the three available Kings should be taken to see *Macbeth*, on the reasoning that one savage tribe can make sense of another.

A huge crowd had been gathering since noon outside the Queen's Theatre, in the Haymarket, because word had spread that the Indian Kings were coming. Watchmen cursed and sweated, beating a path through the mob with their long staves. Street women blew kisses and darted quick fingers in hopes of a souvenir—an earring, a feather, even a quick feel of one of the wild men from America. Hendrick Forked Paths (promoted to Emperor of the Indians in one of the latest broadsides) favored his audience with a wave that made his scarlet cloak swirl.

The scene inside the playhouse was dark and smoky as a Mohawk longhouse in winter. Tallow candles sputtered in sconces and ring-shaped chandeliers, hollowing the faces of patrons lucky enough to have secured front row seats on the spikes. These iron teeth projected from the lip of the stage, inserted by a thoughtful management to deter critical playgoers from attacking the actors. To Londoners, a night at the theater was still participatory sport. They wrestled to get in—more ribs than usual had been broken that Monday evening—and then they wrestled the players.

The mood of the audience was touchy. The fiddlers employed to soothe the crowd could sense it, and were scraping off-key. The program had been switched at the last moment (Shakespeare in place of Congreve, Mr. Wilks in place of Mr. Betterton because the popular Mr. Betterton was down with the gravel or the gout). The performance was late, and so were the guests of honor. To top it all, one of the Four Kings was missing. The handbills had announced, quite definitely, that the evening's entertainment would be graced by *four* woodland kings. Their dusky faces beamed from the woodcut under exotic turbans, tastefully framed by palm trees. The theater manager, Mr. Spate, had one of these flyers in his damp fist as he conducted three live Indians and their escorts through the stamping, shouting throng to the box he had reserved for them above the stage apron.

A piercing whistle was followed by a screech. "Oy! Where's the Illustrated Man then?"

"We paid for Four Kings!" someone else complained.

"Give us our money back!"

Mr. Spate's real troubles began when he had ushered the Indians into their box.

"Can't see 'em!" came a roar from the upper gallery, where people were clambering up onto the benches. "Put 'em up where we can see 'em!"

The patrons were shoving and jostling, trying to get a better view. One man tried to climb up on another's shoulders, and was angrily rebuffed. A fistfight broke out.

"Ladies and gentlemen!" Mr. Spate protested, teetering over the edge of the box. The manager's voice was no match for the hubbub. A missile whizzed past his ear and splattered against the wall, emitting a gaseous stink. Ominous points of color apeared in his pale, moist cheeks.

The manager flailed his arms at the orchestra, which chopped off the *Lillibullero* in mid-bar, and at his stagehands, who wrenched up the curtain to unveil a ghastly scene. Against a painted backcloth of a blasted heath, three crones reveled by a bubbling cauldron.

"When shall we three meet again,
In thunder, lightning, or in rain?"

The Indians inspected the stage witches with keen interest; these were familiar figures. Hendrick had once thrown the broken body of a hostile sorcerer down a ravine.

But the witches' incantations were swallowed by the uproar, which had spread from the gallery to the pit.

"Put the Kings up where we can see 'em, or there'll be no play!"

The curtain came down again.

"Your Mightiness—your Royal Arboreum," Mr. Spate fumbled, uncertain how to address a seven-foot king of the forest. "Would Your Grace deign to favor our patrons with a few words? It might steady them, so to speak."

A timely diversion made it unnecessary for Hendrick to respond to this petition. A brisk figure, strangely attired, bounded onstage and declaimed:

"Oh Princes who have with Amazement seen
So Good, so Gracious and so Great a Queen;

Who from the Royal Mouth have heard your Doom
Secur'd against the Threats of France and Rome
A while some Moments on our Scenes bestow.''

Hendrick's first impression of the speaker was of short, thick, hairy
legs protruding from under a checked skirt. The feet were splayed duck-
like, which was the way with white men who did not know how to walk
in the forest. The overall effect, nonetheless, was of a warrior tribesman
readied for battle. The actor wore a long feather in his cap, and carried
a killing iron half as long as his body and a round shield. Black eyes
glinted above a curling black beard. The actor's ferocious appearance,
and the force of his delivery, quelled the audience. The threatened
Doom burst with the thump of a coehorn mortar.

"That's Wilks," an equerry whispered. "He has the title role."

"The world's a stage!" Wilks rolled his baritone at the box. "Their
Majesties willing, let them be seated here, with us poor players, for all
the world to see."

The audience cheered this suggestion.

Chairs were provided—to Hendrick's mild disgust—and the Indians
were redeployed on stage, in full view of the audience.

The curtain went up, and Hendrick found himself inside a world he
knew: a world of ghosts and witches, of unrelenting women who drove
their men to killing, of flying heads and trees that walk. Hendrick shut
out the low mumble of the interpreter. Though the name of this grim
winter's tale of a mountain people was hard for him to pronounce, he
knew Macbeth and his enemies. They could have been Mohawks.

A resinous fog obscured the stage, the witches disappeared through
a trapdoor, a vengeful spirit haunted the Scottish king's banquet. At last
the actor playing Macduff marched across the stage in savage triumph,
holding up the plaster head of Macbeth.

Hendrick dug his elbow into Nicholas Etakoam's ribs.

"You see? The Sunrise People call us savages. But we take only a
small piece of skin and hair. This tribe takes the whole head."

4.

The Groom Porter was the member of the Royal household who was
charged with supervising all that pertained to one of the ruling addictions
of Queen Anne's Court: gaming. It fell to the Groom Porter to ensure
that the playing cards imported in vast quantities from the enemy,
France, were not marked, to regulate the stakes for a game of picquet
among the higher nobility, and to supply dice for the sovereign's own
table. This indispensable man was called on to devise fresh entertain-
ments for the Indian Kings and, in particular, to revive the low spirits of

Vanishing Smoke, who continued to sulk in his room and would not allow the finest doctors in the country to bleed him or administer enemas.

The Groom Porter prescribed an evening of sport at a superior establishment whose proprietor was well known to him. Though Vanishing Smoke looked halfway to the grave—the whites of his eyes yellowed, his tongue furred, perhaps by constant infusions of tobacco juice—Hendrick persuaded him to come. The evening began well enough, with a few bumpers in honor of the Queen, her Church Established, and the Indian Kings. Though Vanishing Smoke would not touch ale or claret, he weakened when the landlord began pouring brandy, which the Mohawks much preferred.

There were ladies in lisping abundance, all paint, powder and softness lapping over their low-cut crinolines. The Groom Porter knew how to show a gentleman a night on the town. Vanishing Smoke took no interest in the women, to the point where the Groom Porter wondered if the tattooed man might be another way inclined. But when steady drinking had reduced him to a semistupor, he allowed a dark-eyed slattern to perch in his lap.

The Groom Porter played marriage broker. Silver changed hands. The knob-nosed landlord, all smiles and scraping, supported Vanishing Smoke's slack body by the armpit and helped him to a room up under the eves.

Before Vanishing Smoke's clouded eyes, the room rolled and tossed like a ship's cabin in a storm. The woman twittered and squalled like a thieving bluejay, pecking his clothes from his body. Blue veins showed against her buttermilk skin.

"Let's 'ave a look at it then."

He gasped as she pulled his breeches away and gave his member a hearty tweak.

"Oh, Lord, such a homunculus! Black as sin, aren't we?"

Vanishing Smoke tried to shake her loose, but she got a tighter grip and rubbed until he stiffened against his will. Then she opened her jaws and slipped his organ inside, like an eel she intended to swallow whole. The tingling sensations were new to him and not unpleasant, but they warred with his nature, and he rebelled.

"You're a plain dealer, are you, golliwog?" she said, rubbing her gums. "Well, I give a gent just what he wants. You'll see why they call me Rattlesnake Bess."

She hoisted her petticoats and pulled him into her. "That's it! Oh, you're a goer, you is!"

If only she would stop the noise. Soon she was panting and moaning in a parody of passion. Her joints were well-oiled. She pumped him as if she had a fist inside, as if she were milking a cow. The sensations, as before, were pleasurable, but everything tasted sour. This was not how man and woman should lie together. With his wife Redhawk, and with hospitable girls in distant villages, at the time when the fires were re-kindled or the green corn stood tall, the act of mating took the partners beyond themselves, in the return of life to the earth. In these mechanical grindings, on this hired bed, he was less than himself. Despite the fog of drink and the penumbra of the room, he could see the whole scene clearly, as if he were floating under the ceiling in his dreambody, and disgust curdled inside him. To sustain his waning appetite, he tried to picture himself in woods scented with sweetgrass, making love to the music of the deerhoof rattles on Redhawk's leggings. The image only added to his disgust and homesickness. He broke free from the whore. A low wail escaped from his lips, rising quickly in pitch, lingering in a sad, pulsing tremolo.

"Blimey, you're a queer one. Is it a full moon tonight, then?"

Vanishing Smoke was at the window, craning out, seeking the Dog Star that escorts the evening star across the night sky.

"Must be the drink." Bess salved her professional honor as she ad-justed her clothes. "You boozers are all the same. Can't keep it up long enough to do a lady a favor."

Vanishing Smoke could not find the Dog Star. He had never felt more alone.

5.

The following night the Groom Porter offered the Four Kings a different kind of entertainment, to show them the stuff fighting Britons were made of. He escorted them to the bear garden at Hockley-in-the-Hole, to watch what was advertised as a Tryal of Skill. The Indians watched a Coventry man and a Berkshire man go at each other with backswords, falchions and quarterstaves. The Mohawks enjoyed the display, but were restless at not being able to enter the fight. One of the oddities of the English (they had observed) was that they paid to witness what any warrior does for his own pleasure. So, instead of running the deer or hurling a hard ball at each other's heads, the Sunrise People crowded onto narrow benches to bet on fighting cocks and hired gladiators who were careful not to draw too much blood.

The Berkshire man was declared the winner and Hendrick, seated in a place of honor beside the ring, consented to present the purse. There were shouts of delight from the audience as the next attraction was led in. Vanishing Smoke had drifted away, breathing noisily through his mouth. Now he revived with a start, rubbed his eyes, and stared.

To the blare of a trumpet, the master of ceremonies capered across the ring, brandishing a whip and a short sword, with a fiddler at his heels.

Following behind were two comical fellows in motley, who skipped about as they forced a brown bear to shuffle along between them on his hind legs by pulling on chains secured to an iron ring around his neck. The bear was small, compared to the grizzly Vanishing Smoke had hunted on his first winter kill. He was lean, but not like a Sticky Mouth just risen from his long winter sleep. This bear was wasting; he had lost his appetite for life.

A knot of enthusiasts gathered a few paces from the Mohawks. Vanishing Smoke looked at them. He saw squashed-nosed bullies and soft amateurs, holding their dogs by the ears. The dogs, like their masters, came in all shapes and sizes, from a nervous terrier to a slavering mastiff. A pink-cheeked butcher hovered in his white smock, ready to take charge of the leavings.

Vanishing Smoke made a damp, popping noise with his lips, inaudible to his neighbors in the clamor of the pit, and the bear raised up his dish face and looked at him. The bear's keepers were hitching his chains to a post embedded in the middle of the ring. Vanishing Smoke read the torment, and sudden hope, in the small brown eyes.

The Groom Porter nudged the interpreter. "Tell our Mohawk friend the money-droppers here never allow old Bruin to be killed. He's too costly an investment."

Vanishing Smoke received the translation without comment.

The trumpet sounded a tinny fanfare, and one of the fanciers loosed his dog. It was a thin, vicious mongrel with a patch over the eye, scarred from previous fights. With a survivor's cunning, it circled the bear, testing the length of its chain. Darting back and forth, nipping and snarling, it led the bear through a shambling circle-dance. Inch by inch, the chain shortened, until the bear was flailing about in confinement, his back hard up against the pole.

The bear raked at his tormenter, growling and champing his teeth. But again and again his claws closed on empty air.

Vanishing Smoke's fingers tensed, curving into claws.

"Go again!" the crowd roared.

More daring now that his victim was so narrowly confined, the mongrel whipped round behind the bear and made a running jump at his head. The dog's jaws clamped on an ear, ripping and shredding.

The bear hissed and shook his head violently, but the dog hung on.

The crowd screamed its approval. "That's a goer!" "That's a game 'un!"

Vanishing Smoke groaned and clutched his upturned feet. In that moment, the bear shook himself free. The mongrel bounded away, panting his achievement. His owner was beaming. He had a scrap of raw liver ready for a reward. The man with the mastiff moved forward; his turn was next.

But Patch, the mongrel, was a seasoned performer. He wanted to take his bow. He trotted once more in front of the bear, just out of range, mocking the captive.

A chuffing sound rose out of Vanishing Smoke's throat. He saw the bear look at him again, the eyes pink in anguish, out of a face now mired in blood and slaver. Then the great paws came down and the crowd gasped, because the clever dog had taken one bow too many.

The bear swept the dog up into his embrace, and sank his teeth into the mongrel's neck. He had to work his jaws to find the bone; his teeth, made for grinding tough roots, had been worn down by age and mushy food. Vanishing Smoke watched intently, champing his teeth.

"Patch got it wrong that time," a ringside expert piped up. "The bear had more chain than he reckoned with."

"*No*," came a voice edged with fear. "The bear shifted the bloody post! Look!"

The spectators gaped because, sure enough, the stout post that had survived a hundred of these contests had been dragged to one side.

The ringmaster must have failed to notice, because the trumpet sounded again, for the mastiff to take his turn on the dance floor. The bear barreled forward to meet him, bouncing the great post like a matchstick. With a single, sweeping blow, he hoisted the big dog high into the air. When the mastiff came down, his guts were spilling out of the rent in his side.

The mood of the crowd turned from amazement to panic. Only the Mohawks remained still as the spectators fought to get to the exits.

But the bear was not looking for a new adversary. He was looking for his kinsman.

To the horror of the Groom Porter, Vanishing Smoke rose from his place and padded into the ring.

He was singing a song he had known from the cradleboard.

> *Don't cry, little one.*
> *Don't cry, little one.*
> *The Bear is coming to dance for you.*
> *The Bear is coming to dance for you.*

He looked into the eyes of the bear. He spoke words that were song more than speech.

"Grandfather, I respect your knowing. Grandfather, I honor your courage. Grandfather, I ask your permission to free you from this life."

The bear opened his arms to the Mohawk, and Vanishing Smoke entered his terrible embrace. The great jaws were at his neck. The Mohawk reached for the knife at his waistband that was his own claw, and searched for Grandfather's heart. The Old Man gave it to him.

The Groom Porter was wild and spluttering, his wig hanging off the side of his bald pate.

Vanishing Smoke knew that what must be done could not be explained to the Sunrise People, who acted as if four-leggeds have no souls. They must be made to do what they did not understand.

He told Abraham Schuyler what was required. The interpreter was uncomfortable.

"Tell them," Vanishing Smoke insisted.

The interpreter turned to the Groom Porter. "He says that Grandfather—that is to say, the bear—must be buried on a high place, facing the sunrise."

Satisfied that his message had been delivered, Vanishing Smoke wiped the blood from his knife and rearranged the scarlet cloak about his shoulder. Grandfather would be born again, with the rising sun, into the Real World, which never dreamed of a bear garden.

CHAPTER 2

WEISER'S CROSSING

1.

While Vanishing Smoke danced with the bear, Conrad Weiser and his brothers and sisters were tossed like rag dolls between the decks of Her Majesty's transport *Lyon*. The Lords of Trade had insisted on boarding the Palatines who had signed on for America months before, to get them out of view of Londoners. The little fleet of ten transports and a man-of-war, the *Feversham*, had spent long weeks at anchor, or shuttling back and forth from Southampton to Spithead, waiting for favorable winds and reliable news of the movements of French warships and privateers. The salt beef and ship's biscuit were rotting before the fleet turned its back on English ports. Weakened by poor food, inactivity and airless confinement, many of the Palatines succumbed to scurvy and typhus. Teeth fell from rotting gums. Conrad was torn from his dreams by the moans and scratching of his neighbors. The smallest children died first. Conrad stood with Anna Eva Feck and her parents as they watched the body of her infant brother—no bigger than a love cushion—heaved over the side.

Johann Weiser gathered some of the Palatine men and lodged a formal protest to the captain about conditions on the *Lyon*. This was Conrad's first chance to play interpreter, since the official interpreter was with Governor Hunter on board the *Feversham*.

"We are not slaves," Johann Weiser told the captain. "We are free Protestants who have accepted the Queen's bounty, and we demand to be treated accordingly."

The captain insisted he was doing the best he could on the sixpence a day, per head, that the Lords of Trade had allowed him for their provisions, and that he was obliged to be frugal with the ship's stores, for there was no telling the length of the crossing.

The Palatines sought consolation in what Governor Hunter had promised them in the New World: forty acres of prime arable land for each family, and tools to till it. Forty acres was more than all but a few of them had owned in the old country. Johann Weiser told his children that they would plant wheat and rye and grapevines. "One day," he promised, "we will have our own mill and a bakery better than the one we had in Gross Aspach, and people will come for miles to eat the best bread in the colonies and drink our good Rhine wine. We will do better than survive. We will live as honest men are meant to live."

There was more than one catch in the contract. The brute issue of how many of the emigrants would survive to claim their bounty weighed on everyone's mind when the sky turned black at noon and the ships plunged and sawed through the first storm at sea. There were subtler snares, buried in the wording of the covenant each head of family had been required to sign before being taken on board. The covenant stated that each Palatine family would receive its forty acres of American soil,

as soon as we shall have made good and repaid to Her Majesty . . . out of the Produce of our labours, the full sum or sums of money in which we already are, or shall be, indebted to Her Majesty, by the produce of our labour in the Manufacture of all manner of Naval Stores on the lands to that end to be allotted to us.

Johann Weiser, a literate man who prided himself on his head for business, had noticed that the contract did not define "the full sums or sums of money" that the Palatines would be deemed to owe Her Majesty by the time they were decanted in the New World. There was not even a vague indication of how long the emigrants might be obliged to work at making tar for the Royal Navy before they were released from their debt. He had heard of indentured servants bound to work at the pleasure of others for three, five or even ten years. No fixed term of service was prescribed in the Palatine covenant, but might not the vagueness of the wording be abused to bind those who signed it for as long as any indentured servant?

He had made the governor's interpreter translate and retranslate the suspect clause, in the presence of a circle of his friends.

"You have a shrewd head on your shoulders, Johann Conrad," the factor had intervened. "But you fret yourself to no profit. Her Majesty has no wish to alienate the affections of you and your countrymen. She wishes you to live as her free subjects, as pioneers and defenders in her plantations. I assure you that in one season of making tar, you will discharge all your debts. I have reason to believe—" he added confidentially "—that her generosity will extend to presenting you with your farms on your arrival in New York, and that you will not be obliged to expend your energies on tar-making until you have your families safely settled."

Joachim Feck, who had been cheated by a duke in Württemberg, wanted to know why these things were not in the contract.

"What man in his sane mind puts all his faith in a piece of paper?" the governor's man had countered breezily. "A man's word is his bond, surely. I tell you what is in Governor Hunter's heart. Would the governor do us the honor of coming with us in person if he planned to treat us any less than fair?"

This exchange had not silenced all doubts. But Weiser and his companions had had enough of sleeping under canvas on Blackheath and sending their children to scrounge for charity in the streets, bate for the bile and bare knuckles of London gangs. New York was a world away, a thinly populated province—by all accounts—where three thousand Germans who had faced all the horsemen of the Apocalypse and endured could make their own terms, if it came to that.

So Conrad's father had put his signature on the covenant, and the other doubters followed, though one important detail remained obscure: the precise location of the Promised Land where each family would take up its forty acres. The factor had laughed off this concern. "The Province of New York is bigger than all the German principalities. Land is one commodity you will never find wanting." It seemed the Queen or her trusted men had a deed to a vast tract, granted by friendly Indians who would welcome the Palatines as their neighbors. The word Schoharie was mentioned.

By candlelight at night, in the bowels of their rolling ship, the Weiser family pored over a London map, embellished with pictures of crocodiles and palm trees, that located the place in Mohawk country, south of the river that bore their name. The word "Schoharie" sounded Dutch. No one told them—if indeed anyone knew—that the Mohawk word means Floodwood, and that the Indians gave it that name because, at its height, the Schoharie is the most violent river in New York, capable of bearing away whole groves of trees and any human habitation along its course.

□

While the Palatines were ignorant about the nature of their Promised Land, the Mohawks who ruled it were equally unaware that one of their valleys had been promised to outsiders. The matter was not discussed with the Four Kings in London. In any event, the Kings—who were no lords, let alone kings, in their own country—had no power to give away Mohawk lands. This required the consent of the whole people, especially the women who tended the cornfields and owned the village granaries. Individual land titles were unknown to the Real People. Their chiefs had been known to sign dubious deeds, when drunk, but these were just as often disavowed by them sober.

The Mohawks were still struggling with the newcomers' conception of property rights. For the Real People, the Earth was a Mother whose body could never be bought and sold. The right to use the land belonged to those whose ancestors were buried there, and to those who hunted and tilled the earth in balance with all the four-leggeds and bird tribes that shared life upon it.

□

In the stinking hold of the *Lyon*, while Conrad groaned with stomach cramps, and little Catrina hobbled back and forth to the bucket with the runs, Johann Weiser tried to sustain the spirits of his family with stories of the travails of the children of Israel on the road to the Promised Land. Johann looked more and more like an Old Testament patriarch, with his wild, matted hair, and the iron-gray stubble he had allowed to sprout, for lack of soap and fresh water. He recounted a favorite tale from the Book of Numbers, in which Balaam, the heathen diviner, encountered the Almighty on the high places of Moab.

"The prophet of Baal conversed with our true God, falling into a trance with his eyes open. It was revealed to him that the Chosen People, whom the Lord delivered out of Egypt, have *the strength of a unicorn.* He shall eat up the nations of his enemies and shall break their bones and pierce them through with arrows."

Johann's eyes flashed fire as he recounted this vision of a people as strong as a unicorn. He squeezed Greta, whose belly—Conrad noticed— was swelling beyond what could be accounted for by the vile shipboard rations.

Conrad moaned and turned his back. The mention of the unicorn called up an image that did not belong to the Book of Numbers. It was an etching by Dürer, glimpsed in an anteroom of the duke's palace when his father had business in Württemberg.

On the back of an immense, strong-thewed unicorn, a bearded satyr is carrying off a naked woman. He has seized her around the midriff, pushing her breasts up high. Her round thighs open as she kicks her legs. The horn of the unicorn juts at a steep angle toward the sky.

Conrad hardened against the coarse sacking of the plank where he slept. He tried to stop the features of the woman splayed on the unicorn's back from shifting into the greyhound face of Greta Müller, too narrow for the opulent body. *Is there no relief from this ache?* He tried to turn his mind to sacred things. When this did not relieve the ache, he began to itemize the discomforts of the journey, the grim death-toll of the emigrants—so many of them children—tossed overboard with no more ceremony than a few words from the Bible. The ache remained.

He squirmed at a cool touch against his neck.

It was little Anna Eva Feck, with a damp cloth.

"I thought it would help," she said shyly. The silver flecks in her blue irises made a pattern of stars, but Conrad did not notice.

"Nothing will help," he spat, turning his face to the wall.

2.

The tossing death of the voyage did not end even with the sight and smell of the New World—the clean, piny smell of virgin forests blowing across the bows. One of the transports was wrecked off Block Island, when the end of the journey at last seemed at hand.

The Four Kings, newly embarked on the *Dragon* with a hold full of gifts from the Queen and a regiment of soldiers in one of the escort ships, were still a month away from Boston Quay when the Palatine emigrants first set foot on American soil. They were led down the gang-planks to stretch themselves on Nutten Island, in plain view of the batteries and ramparts of the little city on Manhattan Island. A new tent colony sprang up like mushrooms as Governor Hunter discussed what exactly was to be done with the new arrivals with the leading men of the colony.

Putting the Palatines to work was a matter of urgency. The costs of the voyage had swallowed most of the 8,000 pounds the Whig ministry had allowed Hunter for his expedition. He knew there was little hope of getting more cash where that came from—less even than he knew since, while he had been on the high seas, the ministry had fallen and the new Tory government in London wanted nothing to do with his American schemes. The Palatines must go upriver *at once* and make tar.

Robert Hunter had not yet laid eyes on the interior of his province, but he learned within days that its thickets were partly of human making. He summoned the Crown surveyors to determine the exact location of the tar manufactory. To his amazement, he was shown maps on which almost the whole territory of the Hudson and Mohawk valleys was carved into huge tracts, the names of the patentees stamped on each one. To judge from the maps, there was hardly a garden plot left in the entire province that did not have an owner, or at least a pretended owner. In most cases, the lands so generously distributed by former governors— for appropriate bribes—had been neither settled nor cleared. The Earl of Cornbury, the Queen's cousin, had been especially free in selling off native lands to speculators; when not engaged in business of this kind, he was known to parade the battlements of Fort George, rouged and dressed as his Royal cousin. More often than not, the patentees had never clapped eyes on their estates.

"Does anyone actually *live* here?" the governor demanded of his surveyors. The sweep of his hand covered most of the province above the fur traders' town of Albany, at the head of navigation on the North River.

"Only a few Indian traders," Hunter was informed. "A rough lot. Mostly Dutch, and not choosy about trading with the enemy." The Indians themselves were not mentioned.

"Schoharie," Hunter experimented with the foreign word. "I am informed we may have clear title to lands at Schoharie, and they may suit our purpose."

The surveyors guided the governor's eye to the lines on the map that demarcated a vast tract known as the Mohawk Patent. Encompassing all of the Schoharie Valley, south of the Mohawk castle at Two Rivers, the patent had been issued by Governor Fletcher (who rivaled Governor Cornbury in his greed, though not in cross-dressing) to a group of speculators headed by one Nicholas Bayard. The lines on the map were not firmly drawn. They dwindled to dashes and dots and vanished altogether along the southern and western borders of the tract.

"It is hard to say where such a property might end. A man with a roving eye might carry it all the way to the sunset—" the chief surveyor tipped the governor a wink "—no offence to your honor, to be sure. You see, the boundaries on the deed are such things as a blasted tree, or a stone heap, or a carved stump under the hill, and one such might very well be mistaken for another."

"This is something of a hypothetical, is it not? For I was informed at London that the Mohawk Patent is vacant."

"Torn up by His Grace the Earl of Bellomont, sir, when he came in and the Indians told him they was robbed."

"Quite right, too."

"Tore up the deed in front of the Indians and danced a jig on it, too, if reports be true. Though Mr. Bayard and some of them other gentlemen still hold their claim is good."

"Are these people of substance?"

"Mr. Bayard, sir? You have naught to fear from the likes of him. Now, Mr. Livingston and Colonel Schuyler are different fish. But you'll have no dispute with *them*. Indeed, Mr. Livingston charged me to inform your honor that he waits upon your pleasure."

Hunter turned a searching glance on the pursy face, briefly wondering how deeply the chief surveyor lived inside this Mr. Livingston's pocket.

"So I was not misinformed. Schoharie it will be, then. What papers must I put in order?"

"You will need a new deed, sir. From the Indians. Seeing as how Governor Bellomont tore up and burned the old one."

Governor Hunter looked thunderstruck. "I was given to understand this land is free and clear!"

"No cause for alarm, sir. Mohawks will sign a new deed readily enough if you wine them and dine them right and give their women some nice presents. Mr. Livingston and Colonel Schuyler will get the old reliables together, you can bet London to a brick."

"I see. What kind of expense might be involved?"

"A thousand pound would cover it, I dare say."

"A *thousand pounds?*" Governor Hunter felt a headache coming on, and reached for the flat-bottomed decanter of Madeira. This—and how many more unexpected expenses?—would have to come from his own pocket. *I could go bankrupt before the Navy ever sees a barrel of tar.*

"Well, well," he recovered. "We must make a program. I suppose I will have to council with these Indians."

"At Albany, sir. That's how it's done. It's a pretty voyage, sir. A German gentleman told me it's like sailing along the Rhine."

"Very well." The dramatist in Robert Hunter brightened a little at the thought that the encounter with the Indians might be picturesque, even the stuff of a play that would serve the current fashion in London.

"If I might presume, sir." A sallow, hawk-nosed fellow who had stayed out of the conversation now spoke up.

"Mr.—"

"Bridger, sir. Superintendant of the Queen's Woods."

"Yes, of course. We shall have need of your special knowledge, Mr. Bridger."

"That's just it, sir. I was informed you'll be wanting to make tar and pitch for the Navy."

"Quite so. And masts. Mustn't forget the masts."

"Then I'm afraid you are looking at the wrong place."

"I don't follow."

"It's like this, sir. Pitch pines love a barren, sandy soil. From the samples we have seen, the Mohawk Patent is different altogether. The Schoharie valley is rich, loamy bottomlands. Lovely for farming. Not good for pine trees at all."

"Have you taken leave of your senses, man? There are pine trees everywhere in this country! I saw them from the ship."

"Not in the Mohawk Patent. Not the kind you want. Pitch pines are tricky."

Governor Hunter replenished his glass, not wishing to believe his ears. To have come all this way, at such risk and expense—to find his project burst like a bubble.

"I won't have it!" He banged his fist on the table. "I brought the damn Germans here to make *tar*, and that is what I will do! Who will show me the way?"

"Mr. Livingston, sir." The chief surveyor's smile was a touch too oily. "May I send for him?"

□

Robert Livingston did not know much more than Governor Hunter about making tar, but he had not become one of the richest men in the colony by missing opportunities. Livingston combined an adventurer's willingness to take risks with the Scotsman's ability to hold on to the gains. He was a contrabander of no mean skill, buying furs and silver stolen from New England by French Indians from the merchants of Montreal, bartering with French buccaneers in the lairs on Snake Island and Hispaniola. He had financed Captain Kidd's notorious venture in piracy. While Kidd was hanged at Wapping and strung for the crows to peck at Tilbury point, Mr. Livingston quietly sold off his share of the take to fencing masters (that is to say, master fences) and sent scouts to sniff out the treasure Kidd buried along the path of his final voyage from Hispaniola to Boston. Livingston's nose for a profit and his magic with a balance sheet would have allowed him to prosper in any commercial environment. He had doubled his chances in upstate New York by thoughtfully marrying into the local Dutch establishment. Alida van Rensselaer Livingston, the lady of Livingston Manor, might be no great beauty, but she was the daughter of the Patroon.

Robert Livingston could charm, when it pleased him, despite his long doorstopper of a nose and an accent that marked him—in priggish English ears—as a North Briton, closely related to the woad-wearing Picts.

Robert Livingston succeeded, with extraordinary speed, in making himself the desperate governor's indispensable lieutenant. He guided Hunter to virgin pine forests on the west side of the Hudson, so wild nobody had bothered to claim them. He sold the governor more pine-woods on the east bank of the river, on his own princely estates. Furthermore, Livingston undertook to supply all the needs of the Palatines while they worked in the tar camps.

"To serve a friend and Her Majesty's cause," he told Hunter, "I will demote myself to the station of commissary."

Governor Hunter, a novice in many things, was not so naive as to swallow this without chewing. A contract to victual the emigrants, like a contract to victual the army, was virtually a license to print money. A ruthless and imaginative man could pump up his commission to giant proportions, by padding lists, giving short weight and delivering inferior provisions. But such things were not mentioned among gentlemen.

Hunter was more interested in Livingston's hints that a fortune might still be extracted from the Schoharie lands, even if they were worthless for the purposes of the Royal Navy. Livingston escorted the governor on an inspection of the bustling traffic around Coenties wharf, to demonstrate that beaver pelts—the "soft gold" of the colonies—and naval stores were not the only avenues to riches in American trade. There was money to be made, heaps of it, by supplying Boston and Philadelphia and the Sugar Islands with flour and bread and peas. The Mohawk Patent could become one of the breadbaskets of the continent, given settlers who were hardy or foolish enough to brave the conditions of the frontier.

"Plenty of gentlemen have been willing to take a flyer on Indian land," Livingston told the governor. "Damn few have the stomach to *live* on it. Your Palatines could be just the ticket."

CHAPTER 3

ISLAND WOMAN

1.

The mists of sunrise whispered his name. At the joining of the two rivers, below the hill where the Mohawk castle reared its spiked palisades, a gauzy veil fluttered over the woods. To the west, where the Mohawk Valley was squeezed between the noses of two stone giants, the mist settled thick as snowdrifts, or the smoke of green firewood. The sun would burn all of it away before it had climbed halfway up the sky. Vanishing Smoke had taken his Mohawk name from a morning like this.

His family missed him. He had been gone from the Valley for many moons, and now summer was coming on.

His daughter Tewatokwas—Island Woman—led the file of Mohawk girls through the high gate of the palisade, along the narrow trail to the cornfields. The other girls were a little wary of this tall, sharp-featured twelve-year-old who had been brought back from the north to the village at Two Rivers by a raiding party several winters before. She was knowing far beyond her age, an old soul. She saw things before they happened. She used difficult words, some from the language of the Hurons who had raised her. But nobody questioned that she belonged. She might have come to the Flint People as a captive from Canada. But from the moment she had drunk strawberry juice in the sacred lodge and received the name of a Mohawk who had gone before in the ritual of requickening, she was Mohawk, and would be Mohawk until she died this life and beyond it. Her adopted father, Vanishing Smoke, born among the Mahicans, had become a Mohawk in the same way. This was one of the reasons why the Flint People, beset by many enemies, had survived.

They brought people from many other nations into their lodges and made them their own.

Redhawk, Island Woman's adopted mother, had fallen ill, so the girl was carrying her infant sister in a cradleboard on her back, supported by a burden strap looped around her forehead, to leave her hands free. When they reached the clearing, Island Woman hooked the burden strap over a hickory branch. The girl reached in her pouch for a twist of dried meat, chewed it quickly and regurgitated it, morsel by morsel, into the baby's mouth. Then she arranged the soft, dry moss that lined the cradleboard to make a comfortable nest. With food in her belly and her sister in plain view, the baby would rest content in the warming sun while the girls weeded the plot of corn, beans and squash with their digging sticks.

Daniel Talldeer, Island Woman's brother, had no patience with these proceedings. He was disgusted that his mother had ordered him to go with the girls, when he could have been fighting with the other boys or stalking game in the woods. At nine, Talldeer had already killed his first deer—an eight-point stag—and been honored with the traditional eat-all feast. So, while Island Woman and the other girls moved, singing and gossiping, among the corn rows, Talldeer slipped away into the sunless passages of the forest. He thought he might find some birds to bring down with his quiver of blunt arrows, but in his mind he was stalking real enemies— Abenakis from the Saint Francis mission, Flatheads—along a muddy river far to the south, where his uncle had died in battle.

Long-fallen trees powdered under the boy's light running feet. He saw the trail of a deer in pressed leaves and bent grasses, but the trail was already days old. He sensed a more powerful animal, and took cover behind a tree. He smelled his quarry before he heard it—the familiar, sweetish tang of the bear grease his own people used to keep off black-flies and mosquitoes in this season. But they were coming from the west, not the north (the direction of his village) and they were coming by stealth, avoiding the paths, marked by stone heaps, that joined the villages of the Confederacy.

A stab of fear brought all his senses alive. He fitted a blunt to his bowstring, angry with himself for leaving the flint-tipped shafts his father had given him when he killed his first buck at home in his mother's lodge.

He saw them now, jogging deftly around and over the tangle of fallen limbs and spreading roots. They were stripped and painted, their scalplocks daubed red with vermilion. The scout who was guiding them could have passed for a Mohawk, but wore a double-barred cross of silver, like the Mission Indians. The other warriors were darker and heavier than most of the Mohawks at Two Rivers. They moved in single file, but Talldeer knew they would not dare to strike so deep into Mohawk country without flankers.

The boy saw a flash of white among the green-black shadows. A newcomer was running with the strangers, running like one of the Real People, with his toes turned slightly inward, his elbows close to his sides. His skin was darker than Talldeer's, but he wore a black hat with a swan's feather and a flapping white coat with silver buttons. Talldeer had never seen a Frenchman, but he had heard his mother talk of the men in white uniforms who had come to Onondaga, the place of the Firekeepers, in the moons since his father had crossed the Great Water.

Now the boy's fear was no longer for himself but for the girls in the cornfield and the baby sister hanging from a tree in her cradleboard—especially for the baby, because war parties have no time to play nannies. He shuddered at the image of the raiders smashing his tiny sister's skull against a rock.

In his brief lifetime, Talldeer had never seen or heard of an enemy war party on Mohawk land, though he knew that war raged on all the borders of the Confederacy. Fruitpicker, the Mother of the Wolf Clan, said that their people lived in safety in their villages because of the wisdom of the chiefs of the Confederacy, who had made treaties with both the French and the English in the year Talldeer was born, and had vowed to stand neutral in white men's wars. The boy's father had told him a different story. Vanishing Smoke said the Real People's enemies were scared of them, now that they had plenty of guns and powder from the English, and strong castles on the south side of the Mohawk River. Whoever was right, something had changed, and a nine-year-old boy stood between a war party of French Indians and the girls in the cornfield—and a drowsy village where the men who were home were grayhairs or children or sleeping off last night's rum.

Talldeer made his choice by instinct, not calculation.

The boy waited dangerously long, until the Frenchman in his white coat was too near to escape being blinded or stunned—if no more—by his smooth-tipped arrow. When he released his taut bowstring, he did not linger to see whether his shaft had found its mark. He was off and running, away from the village and the cornfield. He heard the angry grunts of the enemy. He threw back his head and loosed a high, piercing howl. He hoped the sound would warn the girls in the cornfield, while drawing the raiders after him, in the opposite direction.

He ran as if his moccasins were winged, leaping more than trotting, like the time he had beaten the best runners of his age from the Upper Castle at Canajoharie. The enemy seemed to be a long distance behind, and he began to worry that he had not diverted them from their original path.

He slowed to yell insults into the woods. "You skulk in the bushes like girls! Are you caught in your petticoats?"

He tried to remember better insults he had heard his father use, especially on the nights when Vanishing Smoke had been drinking hard with Hendrick and the other Burned Knives.

He remembered a good one, and the effect it had on his father when his mother, enraged because he had smashed her Delftware plates during a drinking bout, had hurled it at him.

"*Iotkanisotsen!* May your fish rot right off!"

Talldeer giggled. You couldn't say much worse than that in Mohawk.

He picked up speed, racing westward, in the direction from which the invaders had come.

Then an arm of the forest reached for his throat, choked off his wind, and tossed him into a heap of fallen branches as if he weighed no more than a cornhusk doll. The boy clutched at his neck, gasping for air, and seared his fingers on the rawhide thong that had reduced him to a captive animal.

The raiders ringed him like enormous crows, mocking him with glinting black eyes. A dark giant grabbed at his hair, wound it into a rough braid, and pricked a circle around the top of his scalp with the point of his knife. The giant gave an experimental tug, and rocked with laughter.

"Too small to take home," Talldeer's tormentor chortled, in a language the boy could grasp, but that was not his own.

The knifepoint pushed deeper, and a thin stream of blood trickled down the boy's forehead. Talldeer bit his lip, forcing himself not to cry out. The first thing a Mohawk boy learned was never to admit pain.

The rawhide noose was loosened, and the man who had lassoed him stooped over Talldeer, examining his features.

"Kill me slowly, slave," Talldeer braved it up. "So I can show you how Flint People die."

The man leaning over him was the one with the French cross. His almond eyes were close-set and slightly slanted, over high cheekbones, like Talldeer's own.

He surprised and humiliated the boy by patting his cheek as if he were a baby, or a camp dog. Talldeer sank his teeth into the stranger's hand.

"Little wolfcub." The stranger cuffed him without force, ignoring the bite. "We do not have time to give you a slow death."

Though his accent was not that of the Valley—he turned Rs into Ls—the man with the French cross was speaking Mohawk.

The Frenchman in the white coat stood next to him, one hand on the trigger guard of his musket, the other favoring the fresh bruise above his collar left by the boy's practice arrow. Talldeer was disappointed that he had missed his target: the space between the eyes.

Since his first hunt, his father and uncles had drilled it into him that any day is a good day for a warrior to die. He still had his knife, the ivory-handled blade Vanishing Smoke had bartered from Hendrick Klock, at his trading post between the Mohawk castles. *I can take one of them with me on the Path of Souls,* he calculated. *And raise a howl my sisters must hear.*

His fingers were twitching toward the knife when he heard Island Woman's voice.

"Talldeer! Come to me *now!*"

His sister sounded as if she were merely calling him to the lodge for a bowl of corn soup.

As his hand closed on the grip of his knife, the stranger's fist clamped over it.

"*Aktsia!*" Talldeer yelled to his sister. "Run away! Run to the village."

But Island Woman stepped into plain view, walking calmly toward the circle of French Indians.

"*Kats kanaka,*" she repeated. "Come to me."

The man with the silver cross released his grip and pushed Talldeer toward his sister with a vigorous shove between the shoulderblades.

The boy ran, through the line of enemies masked with red and black paint, into his sister's arms. He fought to hold back tears, bitterly ashamed because he had failed her and yet felt safe in her embrace, even though death walked at his left shoulder, like the Mission Indian with the silver cross who clasped his sister by the upper arms.

"Little sister," the stranger spoke to Island Woman.

She frowned at him, trying to remember.

"Before you had lived four winters, you were our dreamer. But we did not listen."

☐

The scene returned to her, from her childhood among another people. In the deep of midwinter, after blizzards that piled drifts of powdered snow over slush and ice as high as the spikes of the palisades of the Huron village on the Bay of Quinte, her people had felt safe from raiding parties. But a messenger had come to Island Woman in the night, when she lay snuggled in the hollow of her mother's back, feet to the fire, under the warmth of a beaverskin robe. Behind closed eyelids, she saw his eyes pressed close to her own and shivered as his sleek fur brushed her skin. He was beauty and terror, this night hunter: shearing teeth and swaying haunches, eyes burning like ancient amber, moonshadows dap-

pling his black pelt. She was not afraid of him. The panther was urgent.
She understood she must go with him, without question, without delay.

She slid from her body without effort, as if she were merely slipping
out from under the heavy beaver robe. She hovered for a moment above
the firepit, looking down at the ring of sleeping forms, at the small bulge
of her own body joined to her mother's, at her big brother, Cloud Singer,
sprawled on his back. Then she shapeshifted into something lithe and
light and *fast*. As she rushed straight toward the bark walls of the lodge,
following her guide, she had the brief impression of something stretching
thinnner and thinner, like a membrane, until it burst open and she shot
out above the snowdrifts and across the frozen lake.

Panther led her to what she needed to see and report. On the southern side of the lake, enemy raiders had built humpies of skins and spruce
boughs. The spoonlike prints of their snowshoes stretched far away, toward the lands of the Confederacy. Island Woman saw the immediacy
of the danger. The raiders were already stirring, their faces masked with
black paint. They had rested without making fires, to hide their approach
from the sleeping village. They would pounce before sunrise, running
like wolves up the ramps of snow that had made the walls of Island
Woman's village useless for defense.

She heard the panther's hiss on the wind as she turned home to
rouse her mother. Her mother listened, but the men in the lodge were
heavy with sleep, drugged by the comfort of the fire. One of her uncles
growled that Island Woman was only a child, too young to know the
difference between true dreams and false ones.

Because she would not leave off, her mother had taken her, swad-
dled in furs, to a hunting cabin outside the village. It was there that the
Mohawks had found her, and carried her back to their own country.

◻

Since that time, Island Woman had never seen her Huron brother. Now
she searched the face of the stranger with the close-set eyes.

"Cloud Singer?"

"The blackrobes call me Antoine," her brother smiled at her. "Because I was lost and found, and their Anthony is a spirit who finds what
is lost."

"You have a brother," Island Woman explained to Talldeer, who
was struggling to follow this exchange.

The Frenchman came forward, speaking gentle words in the language of the Senecas, the Keepers of the Western Door of the Confederacy. Of the Five Nations of the Longhouse, the Senecas lived furthest
from the English, and closest to the French. They stood astride the great
falls at Niagara, commanding the approaches to the Great Lakes, and

ruled the jumbled tribes of the vast Ohio country as viceroys for the Confederacy.

The white coat was part of the dress uniform of a French officer.

But the man who wore it was not wholly French, Island Woman judged. *He is half ours, half theirs.*

"We come in peace," said the half-Frenchman.

He speaks from the lips, not the heart, Island Woman decided. But he was handsome, with a ready smile that sometimes reached the eyes, and he was no older than the boys who had been paying court to her in the village since her first moonflow.

"You have come a long journey," she told him, looking at his patched moccasins.

"I am called Wind Tree. I come from the house of my father at the Great Falls. I have walked the path of the Peacemaker from Niagara to Onondaga and into the land of the Flint People, to plant the Peace Tree."

The fine words evoked the foundation story of the Confederacy, but Island Woman was not lulled by them. This one prettied things up, but in his heart he was French. And the father he spoke of could only be Joncaire, the most dangerous of all Frenchmen.

"We know the kindness of Mohawks toward weary travelers," the half-Frenchman pursued. His eyes moved from the smooth oval of Island Woman's face to the slopes of her firm young body.

Tradition would be respected, if the French Indians truly came in peace. Island Woman asked the strangers to wait at the edge of the woods while she sent Talldeer racing ahead to alert the village. The old men and boys at the castle had already armed themselves, troubled by the sounds of skirmishing in the woods. A deputation that included Fruitpicker, the youngest of the clanmothers, and Two Minds, the oldest of the traditional chiefs, came to greet the strangers.

The younger children came skipping around Wind Tree as he walked through the gate of the fortified village, plucking at his white coat and his sword. The girls trilled birdcalls of welcome, because Senecas were family to Mohawks. Island Woman, sensitive at her age to any telltale signs of sexual interest, guessed which of them might have shared a sleeping mat with one of these visitors during a powwow or a seasonal visit to the trading posts near Montreal. Moon Shadow was a prime suspect in Island Woman's eyes. She rolled her eyes at Cloud Singer and Wind Tree. *That beaver would raise her tail for any man who has all his parts.*

Island Woman noticed that Fruitpicker was treating the new arrivals as honored guests. The clanmother led them to her own lodge—shared with Island Woman's own family and six others—and ordered fresh venison and bear meat brought for the huge pot of corn soup that was always simmering over the fire, ready to supply hungry strangers. The unbreakable rule of hospitality among the Real People was that you always feed travelers before you get down to business.

Fruitpicker stood broad and strong, with a wide, flat but ever-mobile face, dusted with freckles. Despite her girth, her breasts were high and firm and she moved with a jouncing, exuberant rhythm. She generated warmth and energy; Island Woman felt stronger in her presence. Before the newcomers came to the Valley, the village of Tiononteroken—Two Rivers—had belonged to the Wolf Clan. Since their world had been turned upside down, the three clans of the Mohawk (Turtle, Wolf and Bear) were jumbled up together. But though the Wolf Clan no longer owned Two Rivers, it was first among equals, like the Turtle Clan at Canajoharie, the place of the Pot That Washes Itself. This made Fruitpicker, the Mother of the Wolf Clan, an exceptionally powerful woman.

When the visitors had finished eating and put their cup-sized ladles away, Fruitpicker spoke to them, holding up her badge of office: a wampum belt with the design of a she-wolf suckling male and female figures.

"You resemble one of the Real People," she addressed Wind Tree. "But you come armed among us, in the clothing of our enemies, while the strongest of our warriors are away on the trail. This is not friendly."

The half-Frenchman held up his own belt: seven rows of purple and white beads, with the design of a European taking the hands of the Five Nations. He insisted that he came with an offer of peace, from his father, the French agent Joncaire, and from *his* father, the viceroy of New France, whom the French Indians called Onontio, or Great Mountain.

"We have heard that some of the Mohawks have been fooled by the twittering of evil birds. My father sees many looks away, and he has seen Mohawks of no consequence sailing to England to drink the hard water of the Sunrise People. He has sent me to remind you that in their wisdom, the chiefs of the Confederacy made a peace with Onontio, and that your brothers and sisters live in safety and comfort beside the French." He glanced at the Seneca warriors, and at Cloud Singer, called Antoine, with his blackrobe cross. "We know that the clanmothers and men of good minds of the Flint People are too wise to follow the example of a few drunken warmakers, and that you understand that the English come only to steal your minds and your lands."

This struck a chord with Fruitpicker and with many of the elders present, who had opposed the mission to London. But Fruitpicker was not going to expose the divisions among her people to a French spy who might also be a harbinger of war. She had lost two husbands and a son in wars with the French. Since the day, long ago, when the French first came to the Real World and an adventurer named Champlain fired his arquebus into a group of Mohawk chiefs, killing them through their wooden armor, the Mohawks had been almost incessantly at war with the Ax-Makers. If the Mohawks had not been supplied with guns and powder by the Albany Dutch and, later, the English, they would have been annihilated; this was the origin of their alliance with Britain. But the French were crafty and persistent, and their blackrobe missionaries worked tirelessly and selflessly among the Five Nations. Almost every Mohawk in the Valley had kinsmen who had moved to live beside the French, at the missions around Montreal, lured by the promises of the blackrobes to supply their needs in this world and the next.

Between the guns and the lies of the French and the English, the Real People walked a knife-edge.

Though still weak and feverish, Redhawk, Island Woman's mother, had hauled herself from her mat to listen to the visitors. She coughed when Wind Tree described the Mohawks who had gone to London as people of no consequence. Island Woman squatted beside her, waiting to see how Fruitpicker would deal with the half-Frenchman.

"Wind Tree is young to be a Word Carrier," the clanmother told him. "Does your father send you to us because you are his dark shadow? Or because he is afraid to tell his own lies to the Flint People? Is he afraid we will stroke him the way we caressed the French soldiers who came to kill us in the Starving Time?"

Wind Tree was shaken by the force of this attack.

"Mother," he responded, holding his anger in check, "my father has sent me so we may speak to each other from the heart, in the language of the Real People, without a white interpreter to change the words and put trees in our path."

Some of the Mohawks grunted approval for this answer. "You talk like one of us," Fruitpicker conceded. "What is your clan?"

"*Tawihstawihs.* Snipe."

Fruitpicker considered this for a moment. The Hill People—the Senecas—had eight clans, but the Mohawk had only three, and the Snipe Clan was not among them. Away from his own nation, a clan member could always count on the hospitality of members of the same clan, but a small matter of protocol arose here.

Fruitpicker poked the ground with her stick and announced her ruling. "*Sakkwatho.* Here, you are Wolf. Tonight, we will dream on your words. Tomorrow, you will speak with the council. But first, we will find out whether you and your brothers have learned how to dance."

2.

Talldeer whittled a hickory stick fiercely while his mother helped Island Woman dress in a chemise of midnight-blue calico, hung with silver brooches, for the social dances in honor of the visitors.

"Mother," the boy spoke to Redhawk. "If we dream everything before it happens, how come none of us knew that Wind Tree and his warriors would come today?"

"We dream everything before it happens," Redhawk affirmed slowly. "But we remember only *some* things. And dream visitors can be deceivers, just like ordinary people. It takes a strong dreamer to know the difference."

"Island Woman is a strong dreamer," Talldeer challenged his sister indirectly. "But she did not know what was going to happen. Even though she found a brother she lost many winters ago."

Redhawk looked at her daughter. The arrival of Cloud Singer, Island Woman's birth-brother, with the French Indians, made her uneasy. It might reopen old wounds and test new loyalties. It might remind Island Woman of things seen in the bloody snow, in the wake of a Mohawk scalping party.

"We don't know what Island Woman dreamed or did not dream," Redhawk said carefully. "She has not chosen to tell us."

Among the Real People, dream-telling was the first business of the day. But customs were changing. White men's liquor and the clutter of white men's thoughts were stealing the dreaming. Redhawk found herself increasingly afraid of what the night brought her. Since the sickness had crept into her bones, she had taken to spitting her dreams into the earth, and scrubbing their residue from her body, instead of telling them in the family circle. But Island Woman was an *atetshents*, one who dreams true.

"Last night I dreamed of my father," Island Woman spoke up. "I dreamed my father danced with a bear and was joined to him at the heart. My father is sick but this has given him strength to return to us."

"*Ah.*" Redhawk exhaled a long sigh of relief. Her darkest dreams had been of Vanishing Smoke, since he had left the Valley to cross the ocean.

And I dreamed I became two people. But Island Woman did not tell this to her mother. It might have foretold the coming of her Huron brother with the French Indians. Or it might foreshadow a rift in her own being, as deep as the split in the Real World.

3.

The deep rhythms of the waterdrums carried through the village, and Island Woman ran to join the young ones who were gathering for the festivities. She loved to dance, to see the sweat gleam on the faces and chests of the young men. She could dance until dawn and run, dancing, into the cold swell of the Floodwood River.

The lead singer shuffled around the council house, turning always to his left, sending up little puffs of dust from the floor of beaten earth as he chanted the high, whining syllables of the Standing Quiver song. This was an easy dance, just right to get everyone involved.

Cloud Singer bobbed up before her, handsome in a ruffled shirt with silver armbands, and she let her brother pull her into the snaking line. The drums throbbed deeper, joined by the rattles. Island Woman stepped faster, switching partners as the beat changed to that of a sprightly moccasin dance. She saw Moon Shadow latch onto her elder brother, swinging her hips. One of the Seneca warriors planted his bulk in front of her, sweat beading on his open face. The Frenchman's son, Wind Tree, made a comical roundabout to claim his place. She was embarrassed by his foreign, theatrical bow.

The half-Frenchman danced well. When they moved into a duck dance—one of Island Woman's favorites—he stayed opposite her as the line of women and girls rolled backward, like the river, in front of the plunging men. The men dipped their heads and swooped low, like aquatic birds on their prey. When the men raised their arms, the women's signal to bounce forward, Moon Shadow hooted a mating call. Clasped hands came down, and Island Woman was crushed against Wind Tree's chest. She felt his heart beating against her own, and her blood moved with its pulse. So close, the warmth and smell of this urgent male power.

The drums pounded, the men honked and quacked. Released from the snare, the women and girls danced backward inside the circle of male bodies.

He wants me, Island Woman recognized. Moon Shadow was right. A woman could smell it.

During a pause in the dancing, Wind Tree slipped away. He came back lugging a fat-bellied keg that required his two hands. He had picked up a varied following—young and old, men and women—who came jogging along at his heels, eying the keg thirstily.

"I hope the Mohawks have not become so English they have lost the taste for good French brandy," Wind Tree taunted as he broke the keg open with his hunting knife.

This drew shouts of protest. All semblance of order was lost as Mohawks thrust themselves forward, with ladles and cups, to get a first taste of the Nantes brandy.

Wind Tree offered Island Woman brandy from his own ladle. "*Snakira*. Drink."

She wrinkled her nose.

He drained half the ladle, to encourage her, and pushed it to her lips. She took a brief swallow, and felt the firewater burning a path to her belly.

"More."

She shook her head.

"More for *me*," Moon Shadow intervened, pressing between them. Moon Shadow was hot and flushed. Island Woman had seen her leave the dance with Cloud Singer and wondered if she had already led her brother out into the fields.

She felt a tug at her leggings, and turned to find Talldeer. "Our mother needs you," the boy said, his face hard.

"*Onen'ki'wahi*," she told the half-Frenchman. "That's it for now."

Wind Tree shrugged. Moon Shadow was already guiding his hand to her mouth.

Island Woman tried to make sense of the storm of feelings inside her. Wind Tree was young, and well made, and a guest in the village. It was no shame to want him, no harm to lie with him. But not like this, in front of the whole village, with hard water on his breath.

There was little sleep in the village after the drinkers had filled and refilled their ladles and kettles. A drunk came roaring through Fruit-picker's lodge, kicking live coals onto the sleeping mats, until the clan-mother rose with a bellow and laid him out with a blow from the two-handed pestle she used for pounding corn. After that, Redhawk rose from her sickbed and took her children to a place of relative safety outside the palisade. From the high path, Island Woman saw the pale blur of a cottontail among the elms. There were noises from the grove—snuffling and snorting, followed by a high yelp.

Island Woman's anger contended with jealousy, but turned darker when she realized that Moon Shadow had taken the half-Frenchman beyond the grove, among the roots of the Horned Tree. This was a great white oak that had withstood all the raging storms of the Floodwood creek. A pair of antlers was set between the limbs, like the living bones of a *royaner*'s headdress. A hunter or a shaman had placed them there, before the Flint People had built their new castle where the Floodwood joined the Mohawk River. The great oak had claimed possession, enclosing the antlers in its living timbers so they now seemed to be rooted in the tree.

Island Woman had sat with the oak, like countless dreamers before her, to share the deep dream of its heartwood. She had journeyed into the deep body of Mother Earth from its roots, and flown like a bird from its canopy. Childless women came to the Horned Tree for the gift of making. Was this what Moon Shadow was doing? The cackle of her laughter, harshened by drink, moved Island Woman to deeper rage. This was profanation.

I hate her. I hate him. I hate him.

4.

The formal encounter between the French envoys and the village elders started two days late, to give everyone time to recover from the effects of the brandy. Recovery, for some of the drinkers, meant a trip to Klock's grogshop across the Mohawk River to get a fresh supply of spirits. One of the lodges burned down the second night, and a Mohawk man lost an ear to his wife's teeth. The arsonist was not hunted and the woman went unpunished, because the Mohawks believed that a person could not be held accountable for his actions when he was drunk.

"A drunk gives over possession of his body to wild spirits," Fruit-picker reminded the women. "You can see them go inside him through the holes in his second body, if you know how to look."

Yes, Island Woman thought. *I have seen them. They are hungry ghosts, trapped between earth and moon, who try to feed on the living.*

The mood of the council was soured by hangovers and sore heads. Wind Tree reminded the Mohawks that the English were not to be trusted, which everyone knew. There was an edge of menace in his message; Joncaire warned that the French would descend on the Valley with fire and sword if the Mohawks sided with the English. The threats were not well received. The old ones remembered the French raiding parties that had fallen on the Dutchmen's town at Schenectady a generation earlier, and the army of Denonville, that had burned the Seneca village at Ganondagan, with its vast granaries, several winters earlier. But the French soldiers in Canada were a long way off, and most of the Indian nations allied with the French were blood-enemies of the Mohawks. The English lived close by, and if you could not defeat your neighbor, it was necessary to come to an arrangement with him.

Still, it was easy to agree to talk. There would be a grand council at Onondaga, the capital of the Confederacy, between the French and the Five Nations. Wind Tree offered a knotted strip of deerskin. Each knot represented one day. When they had all been untied, the conference would begin. The Mohawks would be there.

Listening to the leisurely, formal exchanges between the speakers, Island Woman was torn between her allegiance to her adopted people, and the childhood memories that returned to her as she watched Cloud Singer, her Huron brother, who sat with Wind Tree's bodyguards wearing his silver cross.

"Your father will know what to do," Redhawk promised her after the meeting.

This might be true, Island Woman conceded inwardly. But it was cold comfort. *Because the newcomers are not our worst enemies. We are destroying ourselves. If we lose the dreaming, and the paths to the spirit world, we will no longer be the Real People.*

CHAPTER 4

HOMECOMING

1.

The batteries on Copp's Hill and Fort Hill fired in salute as the *Dragon*
eased through the narrow passage into the deep waters of Boston harbor.
Colonel Nicholson and the Four Kings stood at the bow, drinking in the
scene: the slavers and merchant vessels tied up at the long wharf at the
foot of King Street; the fishing boats and ships of the line bobbing at
anchor in Nantasket Roads; the crowd along the docks, jostling Governor
Dudley's welcoming party with its drums and fifes; the well-fed man-
sions rising proud above them.

Boston was a fine town for a man with an eye to a profit or a frolic.
Since the Commmonwealth of Massachusetts produced little of its own
for export, Boston traders lived on their wits, pocketing fat commissions
as they bartered the wares of other colonies—and goods smuggled from
the French at Port Royal—for imports from across the seas. Down the
gangways came rum and sugar from the West Indies, manufactures from
England, salt fish from Newfoundland, and precious two-legged cargo:
African slaves and white indentured servants, who had sold their labor
(and often their lives) for a chance in the New World. Back went New
York flour and peas for the Sugar Islands, timber for the Navy, beavers
and minks for London hatters and tailors. All this coming and going
favored the industry of tavernkeepers, cockfight organizers, professional
ladies and Crown officers with preferment or licenses to sell. Down by
the Boston docks, a flotilla of well-rigged young ladies signaled the incoming fleet with lacy handkerchiefs and frilly knickers.

The sea-rovers and money men of Boston were making a fair bid to bury the dour Puritan origins of the colony, and in this they had the full blessing of Joseph Dudley, the governor. The government of Massachusetts was one of Dudley's family heirlooms, but he had found it an uneasy inheritance. His father, also a governor of Massachusetts, was a scowling Calvinist bigot in the style approved by Cotton Mather and the Saints of New England. The elder Dudley had croaked his last with a rhyming couplet in his pocket that defined his view of the family mission:

> Let men of God in courts and churches watch
> O'er such as do a toleration hatch.

Dudley the younger was made of different stuff. He had served the hated Andros as president of the council, fallen with his patron, and been shipped to England in fetters. Queen Anne had thought so little of the judgment of his fellow provincials that she had sent him back as governor. Since then, Dudley had lived in a state of declared war with much of his province. The Mathers damned him as an agent of popery and the devil; the assembly accused him of selling public office and conniving at illicit trade with the French; farmers and settlers, terrorized by French Indian scalping parties, cursed him for abandoning the border country. The memory of the massacre at Deerfield, six years before, was still fresh. French Indian raiders had slaughtered more than fifty of the settlers, men, women, and children, and led more than a hundred captive to the blackrobe missions in Canada. After six years of threats and ransom negotiations, the massacre was unavenged and many captives unredeemed.

Both Governor Dudley and his critics watched the return of the Indian Kings from London with lively interest, because it was widely believed that the answer to the Deerfield slaughter and the terror out of Canada lay here. Dudley was cheered by the sight of British redcoats on the decks of the convoy.

The pinnace was lowered, and Nicholson, the Schuyler brothers, and the Four Kings were rowed to the long wharf. The band struck up the "Grenadier's March" as Colonel Nicholson walked ahead of the Mohawks to shake hands with the governor. Nicholson was ill at ease in Boston. The year before, when the promised fleet from England had failed to appear and he had been forced to abort his projected invasion of Canada, rowdy Boston apprentices had yelled "Wooden Sword!" in his face. But now he had four hundred Royal Marines at his back, and a commission from the Queen to send an armed expedition against Port Royal, that nest of privateers.

Like Londoners, Bostonians gaped at the Mohawks, magnificent in their Court costumes. But the mood of the Boston crowd was less friendly. Too many people there had lost a friend or relative to Indian raiding parties, and had a hard time distinguishing one kind of Indian from another.

"Murdering savages!" someone hissed as Hendrick and Vanishing Smoke passed.

"The only good injun's a dead one!" yelled a philosopher in the crowd.

"Good God!" Francis Nicholson's Yorkshire temper was aroused. "These chiefs are going to help us beat the French! Do you hear me? They have been to London to see the Queen!"

This brought ragged cheers, and a shout of "God save the Queen!" from one of the officers, followed by a ripe, prolonged raspberry from an unidentified source.

□

As the claret passed around the governor's table that evening, it was agreed that, though the colonists were a factious people, the grand enterprise that had taken the Four Kings to London might pull them together. There would be no problem recruiting New Englanders for an assault on Port Royal, an isolated French outpost on the rugged coast of Acadia. "They will swim there if needed," observed Samuel Vetch, a canny Scots adventurer who was Dudley's partner in business and Nicholson's partner in strategy.

Vetch's ambitions extended to making himself the owner of the rich fisheries and beaver dams of Acadia. He was planning to lead the expedition in person and make himself the first governor of a new British possession. He had even hatched a name for it: New Scotland, Nova Scotia. The other white men at the dinner were sympathetic to his ambitions. Governor Dudley counted on claiming a viceregal share of the prizes, and winning popularity among his difficult subjects.

Nicholson had set his sights higher. He aimed to make himself governor of all Canada. In his grand design, the seizure of Acadia would help to rally the Five Nations to his cause by proving that the English were capable of winning a decisive victory over the French. In London, he had been promised a full battle fleet and seven regiments of British regulars for the invasion of New France. When they arrived in the spring, colonists and friendly Indians would rush to sign on for the larger endeavor. Striking by land and sea, the British forces would seize Quebec and Montreal.

"Within two years," Nicholson predicted, "all of North America will belong to the British Crown. I promised Her Majesty that I would make her empress of America, and I mean to deliver."

The Four Kings missed these remarks. The Schuyler brothers had thought it prudent to exclude them from a conversation that touched on such matters as the division of the profits anticipated from victualling the troops and delivering presents to the Indians.

In the absence of the Four Kings, Governor Dudley, who had been raised to think of Indians as savages beyond salvation, spoke freely on this subject.

"Every week, I have to listen to some cow-chaser's report that one of his relations has had his hair or his livestock taken by savages. The savages in question are often from the Jesuit mission called Sault Saint Louis."

"Caughnawagas," Peter Schuyler confirmed.

"Is it not true that these Caughnawagas are related to the Mohawks you escorted to London?"

"You are not mistaken. The Jesuits persuaded a Mohawk sachem to move to the mission at the Sault before the last war. Almost half the Valley Mohawks followed him. It is a matter that requires some delicacy. Mohawks will not willingly fight their cousins at the Caughnawaga mission, and the other way round. But they will fight each other's allies."

"I see. May I ask if you consider *your* Mohawks any less savage than the ones who have been terrifying half my province?"

"No less savage. But their savagery is not directed at us."

There was still something puzzling Govenor Dudley. "Colonel Nicholson has persuaded me, as he seems to have persuaded Her Majesty, that we cannot thrash the French without Mohawk allies. I have watched other Indians run away at the sight of a single Mohawk, here in the city of Boston. The Mohawks are surely a little people, greatly reduced in numbers by war and disease. How can it be that they are so greatly feared as warriors?"

Peter Schuyler glanced at his brother, who had wintered with the Mohawks and shared their lives.

"A warrior who has no fear of death—" Abraham responded, "—can do things that astonish other men."

"One warrior, certainly. But we are speaking of a whole nation."

"Exactly. Mohawk warriors do not blindly follow orders, like our soldiers. Each one thinks and chooses for himself. Yet, like ancient Spartans, Mohawk warriors are driven by common beliefs about what it means to be a man, and what a man must endure without complaining. But this is not the whole of it. The truth is that, though Mohawks are the fiercest of warriors, their women are even fiercer."

"You jest with me, Mynheer Schuyler."

"No, sir. The strength of this people is the strength of their women."

2.

Joncaire, the French Indian agent, stood in the shade of a conical hill
and took a swallow from the panier his Pani slave had filled at the creek.
The water was wonderfully cold but mildly salty. The Iroquois ate their
meat and corn without seasoning, which was still a hardship for this
nobleman of Provence, after all the years he had spent among the Indians. At least here, in Onondaga country, one could count on salt from
their springs and their bitter lake.

Joncaire stood at the edge of a green plain raised high above the
rippling sea of green hills that he and his little army had crossed. The
stream flowing from the salt lake carved the plateau like the lifeline
across the palm of a giant. This was rich, confident country: late strawberries grew wild, and the ripening corn stood as high as the Frenchman's chest. The elmbark lodges of the Onondagas were scattered
casually on both sides of their river, without defending walls.

The village of Onondaga did not look much like an imperial capital.
But despite appearances, it was a place of empire, capital of the League
of Five Nations—Mohawks, Oneidas, Onondagas, Cayugas and Senecas—created by a mystical being, the Peacemaker, and Hiawatha, his
interpreter, before the newcomers had entered the Real World. The
authority of the Confederacy extended deep into the rich Ohio country
to the west, and south to the rolling grasslands of the Susquehanna. The
Five Nations had destroyed or subjugated their neighbors—Hurons and
Mahicans, Cat People and Leni Lenape—and survived all the efforts of
the French and their Indian allies to break their power. In Joncaire's
opinion, it was the Confederacy of the Longhouse, more than the English settlements along the coast, that was the main obstacle to the dream
of a French empire in North America extending all the way to the China
Sea.

The Onondagas were the firekeepers of the Confederacy. They
lived without palisades because whoever attacked them would have to
face the fury of the Five Nations. They also had long ears and saw many
looks away. Joncaire knew that their spies had followed his progress all
along the shore of Lake Ontario, long before he entered their country
and cached his canoes.

The French agent watched the reception committee slowly gathering around the council lodge. It was a waste of energy trying to rush the
Indians; he lounged in the shade of an elm, while his Pani slave kept
the flies off with a whisk of horsehair.

Louis-Thomas de Joncaire was lithe and dark, his face sharp and
sudden as a hawk's. His white hair, startling against his sun-blackened
skin, was the gift of what he had lived among the Indians. He had just
turned forty. His earliest dreams of empire came from boyhood rambles

among the ruins of the Roman amphitheater at Arles, near the village of
Saint Rémi where he was born. His gold-laced uniform and the gorget
at his throat displayed his rank as an officer of the Compagnies Franches
de la Marine, the Sun King's colonial troops. Joncaire preferred to live
and fight in buckskins and breechcloth, like an Indian or a *coureur du
bois*. But he was here to parley, and in matters of diplomacy the natives
loved pomp and circumstance. He was heir to a minor title, and the
flunkeys who surrounded his friend Vaudreuil, the governor of New
France, addressed him as the Sieur de Chabert. The English had put a
price on his head. Reports from their agents referred to a sinister "Jean
Coeur" who worked tirelessly to turn the Five Nations against the English colonies, omnipresent but elusive.

Joncaire squinted into the sun to watch Charles le Moyne rooting
about in the charred remains of a log house. Young le Moyne was a
mountain of flesh. One day he would be the second Baron of Longeuil,
but he would pass for a meat porter or a publican. *It is in the breeding,*
Joncaire reflected. *Le Moyne's grandfather was a tavernkeeper at Dieppe. But
this is a country where a man can write his own pedigree.* What counted was
that Le Moyne had spirit and the Onondagas liked him. He ran with
them, danced with them, courted their women. The only way to win the
trust of the natives was to share their lives. It was a rare man among the
English, with their sneering, superior ways, who was capable of this.
That was why France could win the wilderness war for North America.
And Joncaire believed it was his personal destiny to ensure that it did.

He had been all of seventeen when he crossed the Atlantic as an
ensign in the marines, to find an army mustering on the island of Montreal. The viceroy of the day, the Marquis de Denonville, was sworn to
destroy the Senecas, the warlike people who guarded the Western Door
of the Iroquois Confederacy.

Ensign Joncaire was assigned to a company of regulars. Over lakes
and rivers, he moved with them to the landing at Irondequoit and on
along sunless forest trails, past breathstopping gorges, to assault Ganondagan, the great bark city of the eastern Senecas. They had found the
Seneca city deserted. Joncaire had been astonished by the huge bark
cylinders, stuffed with corn flour, and the endless fields of green corn
along the river. Denonville was furious that the enemy had flown the
coop. He ordered the Seneca farms and granaries burned. He did not
want even an ear of corn left for the rats to gnaw. The French army
moved for days in a fire haze that shut out moon and sun.

Joncaire had been ordered to take a file of marines to burn a small
village west of the Genesee. He walked into an ambush. His journey
ended at a village of the western Senecas where he was received by two
rows of women and children who went for him with stones and clubs
and fingernails. He survived the gauntlet to watch several of his men

die exquisite deaths. He was stunned by the stoic bravery with which his Huron tracker went to meet his death; the scout had not cried out, even as a nightmarish crone had gnawed his thumb to a stub, even when his flesh hissed under hot metal. When it was Joncaire's turn to perform, the best of his courage had been to wish for a quick death and to enter the circle of enemies singing a rough boatman's song.

His life had been saved by one of the Seneca women. She asked for the Frenchman's body to requicken the spirit of a son killed in battle. In a ritual in the Longhouse, they had laid Joncaire out for burial and raised him again with a new name. The young knight of Provence could not have guessed, in the first night of horrors, that he would live to find beauty as well as terror in the world of these people. In his seven years among the Senecas, he learned that the cruelty of the Iroquois—though real and indelible—was calculated. The Iroquois knew that the best way to subdue their enemies, while limiting the bloodshed, was to spread accurate reports of how they rewarded those who fought them bravely. Joncaire never forgot this lesson.

His greatest teacher was the sweet brown woman who moved like quicksilver, coming shyly one night to creep under his beaver blanket. She bore him four children, including Wind Tree, whom he had sent to the Mohawks to warn them of the consequences of following the Four Kings. When the French offered the Senecas an exchange of prisoners, Joncaire had not leaped at the prospect of going back to a white man's world. He had promised his Seneca woman he would return, and he had kept this promise. Now he summered on the island of Montreal, where his devoted French wife, Madeleine le Guay, presented him with a new baby each year. But he wintered among the Hill People, at Canandaigua or Seneca Lake, with his Seneca family. He planned to build a strong stone house near the falls at Niagara, commanding the western door of the Confederacy.

"They are coming, Father."

Wind Tree pointed with his lips. Joncaire saw a cloud of feathers burst from the village below. Soon he was ringed by Indians.

A plumed chieftain strode into the midst of the circle and tapped the earth with the point of his stick.

"Great Mountain, we are glad you have survived the dangers of the road, and come among us in good health. Our women have hung up all our kettles to welcome you."

Dekanisora addressed the French agent by the generic title the Iroquois had bestowed on the masters of the mountain-island of Montreal. Joncaire was glad to see that the Onondaga speaker was wearing the silver medal the Governor had presented to him at Montreal, though he did not doubt that if Dekanisora were meeting the English, he would substitute one of *their* medals. Dekanisora was a fine, fluid orator; the Onondagas always produced *les grands gueules*, the big mouths, of the Confederacy. Joncaire trusted this one as much as the snake he had killed with the butt of his gun on the last leg of his journey to the capital of the Five Nations.

The council assembled around a huge firepit heaped with a pyramid of logs. The Fire that Never Dies. Its smoke did little to deter the swarms of gnats and invisible punchins. Sweating in his uniform, Joncaire envied the Indians their bear grease and fish oil, which kept the insects off their skin. His message was addressed to the Five Nations, but Joncaire could see at a glance that attendance was sketchy. Besides the Onondagas, the only traditional chiefs were Oneidas from Kanowahale, the Place of Skulls. The few Senecas who had come, in addition to Wind Tree's bodyguards, were there for personal reasons.

The exchange of formal speeches, filled with the machinery of clouds and winds, consumed much of the day. The rituals of native diplomacy were no less elaborate than those of Versailles or the Chinese court. The real business was conducted at night, in more intimate sessions. Joncaire set up his tent at the edge of the village and invited chiefs and elders to visit him in twos and threes. Nobody left without a present: a small keg of brandy, a new kettle, a pound or two of black powder.

Meeting alone with the French agent, Dekanisora spoke harshly of the Four Kings. He called them self-seekers, bribed by the Schuylers and the English to sell their own people. "They speak neither for the Confederacy nor for the Flint People. They do not even speak for the village of Two Rivers."

"Tell me about the one the English call Hendrick."

"*Ochwistanorum hotoradhe*," the Onondaga spat. "Forked Paths seeks only money."

"He is reputed to be a great warrior."

"A warrior who kills women," Dekanisora rumbled.

The old wound has not healed, Joncaire noticed with pleasure. The Onondaga speaker had once been married to a Caughnawaga Mohawk, a woman Joncaire had personally employed as a spy. The woman was reputed to be a witch, proficient in the uses of poisons. When one of his brothers had died suddenly, Hendrick Forked Paths had blamed this woman—and clubbed her to death near Albany. The blood debt had been paid, with many fathoms of wampum, according to the Great Law of the Confederacy, designed to prevent vendettas among the Five Nations. But Dekanisora had not forgotten or forgiven. This was something Joncaire could use.

The Onondaga speaker turned his odd, twisted cane—the work of climbing bittersweet on a young hickory—between his huge hands.

"There is another who went to London," Joncaire pursued. "The one the English call Brant."

"*Jachte hatgachtwi*. Vanishing Smoke sees nothing. Once he was a

seer, but he is blinded by Forked Paths and the hard water. His wife is
a good woman, but he no longer hears her."

"These Mohawks are not alone. They have followers."

"Their followers are only Burned Knives, eager for rum and glory."

"Are there no Burned Knives at Onondaga? Did not warriors from
all the Five Nations march with the English to Lake Champlain last
summer? I watched you when you set your own seal to the treaty of
peace at Montreal. These Mohawks—Hendrick and Vanishing Smoke—
are working to uproot your Tree of Peace, and overthrow the laws of
the Confederacy. Is the voice of the Firekeepers no longer heard in
Mohawk country?"

"It will be heard," Dekanisora said grimly.

"Then these two Mohawks must be destroyed."

□

Alone in his tent, Joncaire stripped off his uniform and rubbed grease
over his face and chest in preparation for the homeward trek through
the woods. He felt the wind shift and swirl inside the canvas. A dark,
narrow-faced Indian with the heads of woodpeckers bobbing from his
headdress slipped inside the tent.

"Who are you?"

"Two Hearts, they call me." The sorcerer spoke in a metallic singsong that rode on a deeper burr of sound. Like two people—neither
altogether human—speaking at once.

"I believe I have heard of you."

"I can go where others cannot go. I can see many looks away and
kill with a thought. The hearts of your enemies are in my hand."

Two Hearts raised his left palm and curled the fingers inward.
Watching this, Joncaire felt an uncomfortable tightening around his own
heart.

There is power here, surely. But also madness and deformity. He saw that
the sorcerer's right arm was withered, his shoulders misaligned.

"I will have no parlor tricks," Joncaire said sharply. "What do you
want of me?"

"I will give you the bodies of your enemies. You will give me their
souls."

3.

Hendrick and Vanishing Smoke left Boston with nine packhorses loaded
with gifts from the Queen, and an armed escort of ten men supplied by
Governor Dudley, who hoped to avoid unpleasantness with colonists
who could not tell one Indian from another. When Colonel Nicholson
bade farewell to the Mohawks, he was in excellent spirits; the Massa-

chusetts assembly had voted to raise nine hundred militiamen to join his assault on Port Royal, to impress all merchant ships in Boston harbor for transport duty, and to supply his own table, for the duration of the campaign, with as much wine and fresh beef as he and his guests could consume. This last item was of no passing importance, in Nicholson's view. The Yorkshireman was firmly convinced that the state of the general's table reflected the state of the whole campaign. He was no less assured, as he watched the broad backs of the Mohawks recede into the distance, that when he met them again, they would come at the head of a great army of the Five Nations, awed by their tales of the invincible might of Great Britain, and greedy for more of the glittering prizes they were bringing home from London. It was true that Vanishing Smoke had seemed surly and out of sorts, but Nicholson attributed this to alcoholic poisoning, compounded by the effects of the sea voyage.

We made him a king. He will do what he is told. Or else Schuyler will find us a new king.

The Mohawks shed their Bostonian escort at Springfield, and parted from the Schuyler brothers at Albany, the Dutchman's town of stepped gables that fell down the hill toward the Hudson, inside its wooden walls. Peter Schuyler engaged a flatboat to ferry the bulk of the Mohawks' gifts upriver from Schenectady, the frontier trading post an hour's ride to the northwest, across dreary pine barrens. He offered his own team of horses to carry them part of the way, but Vanishing Smoke said he would go on foot to find his own canoe, and the others went with him. They had spent months in alien conveyances, in boats and coaches and litters; now they would travel their own way. Running through the woods, the Mohawks moved faster than their convoy had traveled on horseback along the road from Boston. It was high summer in the Valley and, even toward the river, the air lay damp and heavy as a hot bath. This did not slow the Mohawks. As his legs pumped and the smells of the forest crowded his senses, Vanishing Smoke felt his lungs open again.

In the Real World, a man can breathe.

Only one of the bark canoes they had cached at the mouth of the creek above the traders' landing was still intact. It would not hold the four of them, with their heavy packs. Hendrick Forked Paths wanted to hire another flatboat, but Vanishing Smoke had a different thought.

"I will go home in my own way," he announced. "Not as cargo for strangers." He wanted to make a new canoe, starting from scratch.

Impatient to get back to their families and show off their spoils, the others were inclined to leave him. He had been a drag on the party since he had fallen ill in London. But Hendrick knew that the four envoys who had gone to London must return to Two Rivers as a united group. There must be no hint of a falling-out, no rival reports about what had been seen and decided among the English.

So Hendrick, John and Nicholas Etakoam sat and smoked while Vanishing Smoke ranged the woods until he found a white elm that met with his approval. It was tall and sturdy, almost clear of branches on the lower part of the trunk. He shinnied up. As he climbed carefully down, he cut a deep vertical slit in the bark with his knife.

Etakoam came to help. The two Indians stuck their fingers into the crack. Circling the elm in opposite directions, they peeled off a big sheet of bark.

"You picked a good one," Nicholas commented, when he had inspected the sheet for holes and found only a small one that would be easy to patch.

They laid the bark on the ground, smooth side down, and placed stones on top to stretch the sheet flat. They planted sticks in the ground to frame the curved sides, and cut hickory staves for ribs and transverse support. They made bast from the hickory to tie the nose and tail of the canoe, and stuffed the chinks with fistfuls of crushed bark. They laid extra pieces of bark inside the canoe to strengthen the hull and stop up any leaks.

Even with four pairs of hands to help, the work took hours. Hendrick grumbled that all of them could have been home by now, feasting with their wives and children.

When the work was done, Vanishing Smoke thanked the elm and the hickory for their gifts, scattering a few shreds of tobacco among their roots.

He felt cleaner and stronger, to have made something, perfect of its kind, in the old way. Something that was not the gift of the newcomers. This was part of his homecoming.

□

They reached Two Rivers after nightfall. The riverbank blazed with torches. It seemed the whole village had come down to the landing to greet them.

Talldeer bounded and leaped around his father, jabbing at him with an imagined spear. Vanishing Smoke laughed and chased after the boy with his war club. He stopped short, because he felt an iron claw ripping through his intestines. His vision clouded. The scene around him fractured into a swirl of dots. He staggered, and had to summon all his will to stand upright.

He saw the wounded bear in the bearpit, opening his arms. His blood pumped so hard he felt as though it would burst from his ears.

His daughter, Island Woman, pressed herself against his body. As her face took form, he saw the fear and compassion in her eyes.

Redhawk took his upper arm and leaned her head against his neck.

"Come to the lodge," his wife breathed in his ear. "You are tired and need rest and medicine."

"Not yet." Vanishing Smoke's lips grazed his wife's forehead. He smelled sun and sweetgrass in her glossy hair. "There are presents to give out."

The cargo from the flatboat had been placed in the charge of Fruit-picker. The elders and clanmothers would decide in the morning how it would be shared out. Some things must be kept for the people at the Upper Castle at Canajoharie, and at the smaller settlements along the Floodwood River. But the goods the Mohawks had brought in their own packs in the two canoes were fair game for everyone. Two of the women were already scrapping over a bolt of bright red calico.

Vanishing Smoke unwrapped the bundle he had reserved for his own family. A new copper kettle, scissors, plates and linen for his wife; silver brooches and a new dress for Island Woman; a looking glass for the baby—who cried out and tried to kiss the face she saw reflected in the mirror. And a long pistol for Talldeer, who brandished it like an accomplished duelist.

"You will have powder and balls when you show me you can use it safely," Vanishing Smoke promised his son.

Hendrick's wife, Corn Carrier, squealed with delight over a picture in a gilt frame. It was a mezzotint of Hendrick in his London costume. But for the clan wolf lurking in the background, and the suggestion of woods behind, he might have been a character from a Shakespearian play.

Hendrick Klock, the trader from across the river who had given Forked Paths his white man's name, was called on to read the words under the picture. Klock grinned as he got his tongue round the sonorous syllables:

Tee Yee Neen Ho Ga Row, Emperor of the Five Nations.

Only a few of the Mohawks had the faintest conception of what the last phrase meant. There was a buzz of excitement as the villagers debated the meaning of the English words. Some of the voices became shrill and scornful. One of the women spat on the print. A long-haired elder paraded up and down, flapping his arms and crowing like a cock rooster.

Island Woman tugged her father's hand. "Did they make a picture of you too?"

Vanishing Smoke was embarrassed. He had been trying to hide his own portrait under his blanket, bitterly regretting the fact that he had brought it home as a souvenir. Island Woman snatched it from him, and took it to the fire, so she could make out the features better. Redhawk and some of the Wolf Clan women, including Fruitpicker, gathered to look.

Despite the odd garments, there was no doubt about the identity of the man in the print. He stood with his clan bear, and the artist had gone to great pains to copy all of his elaborate tattoos.

Fruitpicker whistled at Klock, beckoning the trader over to read the inscription.

Klock was uncomfortable, having watched Hendrick Forked Paths storm away from the people who were mocking his English titles. He looked to Vanishing Smoke for guidance, but the Mohawk remained completely impassive.

Klock cleared his throat and read:

Sa Ga Yeath Qua Pieth Tow, King of the Maquas.

"King of the Mohawks?" Fruitpicker echoed. "Since when have the Real People had kings?"

Vanishing Smoke stared off into the wall of darkness beyond the river.

"*King?*" the clanmother screeched and gave him a nasty poke in the ribs. "You let them call you king? I remember when you came to us, bare-assed and stuttering, and we took you in. No wonder you're sick!"

Vanishing Smoke did not try to defend himself. He had eaten Queen Anne's bread, and accepted the flattery of her countrymen without protest. It was right that his wife's clanmother should remind him what he was.

Though worried about her husband—whose weakness showed in the yellowish cast of his skin, the dullness of the eyes—Redhawk did not speak in defense of Vanishing Smoke. The clanmother was right. He had set himself above his people, a people who did not recognize kings. The chiefs of the Five Nations were not called kings but *rotiyaner*, or "men of good minds"; they were chosen by the clanmothers and governed only at their pleasure. They were enjoined to be walking sticks for the people to lean on.

It was Island Woman who spoke up, defending her father. "My father has never pretended to be something he is not. He accepted an honor on behalf of all our people."

"*Serihokten*," Redhawk hissed. "Stop the words."

Redhawk threw the portrait on the ground, and kicked at the frame until it splintered apart. She ripped out the print. Then she squatted in front of the fire and fed her husband's image to the flames.

Vanishing Smoke turned his back. Island Woman, sobbing, put her arm round his waist and guided him toward the lodge.

"What are you doing?" Talldeer asked his mother as she batted the flying cinders back into the fire.

Redhawk was leaning too far forward, eating smoke, trying to hide her tears from her son.

Fruitpicker ruffled the boy's hair. "Your mother is burning the sickness."

CHAPTER 5

THE DIVIDED ONE

1.

When she burned the picture, Redhawk took a part of her husband's soul, the part that had attached itself to Hendrick Forked Paths and the English.

She told him, "Now you will belong to yourself and your own people."

Weak and exhausted, Vanishing Smoke let his wife minister to him, and basked in the light and laugher of his children. The baby's gurgles and wet kisses made him smile in his heart. "We should call her New Smile," he told Redhawk.

A part of Vanishing Smoke had been missing for a long time. Now that Redhawk had burned the picture, it was gone for good, to be seen only in dreaming as something charred and deformed, something you would not want to bring into your house.

This left a gaping hole inside Vanishing Smoke. In the past, he had filled this hole with the spirits that drive a man to drink and into the killing frenzy of a warrior who shaves his head for war. They would come again, if this hole inside him stayed open. It was meant to be filled in a wholly different way.

He remembered a place of power. He had journeyed there often in his dreambody, when his dreaming was strong, and sometimes in his meat and bones.

Vanishing Smoke decided he must return alone, with both his bodies, to the place of power where the dream gates had opened to him in his youth and he had entered the deep dreaming of the earth itself. He had honored this experience in the extraordinary tattoo he had asked a friend to carve in the skin above his breastbone and blacken with gunpowder. This symbol, which mystified natives as well as newcomers, was a personal key to the dream gates, one he had neglected for so long that he needed to haul his sack of meat and bones back to the place where he had found it, and beg the spirits to permit him to turn it again.

2.

The place of this dreaming lay southward and westward from the Mohawk castle, on a high limestone plateau pruned by shearing winds. The old ones said that in the time when a woman led the Real People over a bridge of ice across the northern sea, this land was buried deep under the ice. The retreat of the ice sheet had pitted and gouged the earth, like the marks of the colossal bears and tigers who had walked here when the sun was young.

Soon after his family fled the Indian-killers and despoilers of New England to live among the Flint People, Vanishing Smoke had been drawn by a dream to this high, stony place. He had found the entrance to a cavern the Flint People had forgotten, though their ancestors had known it; flint arrowheads lay below the funnel mouth, a memory of hunters or warriors who sought shelter here many winters before the newcomers landed. Whatever the weather was like outside, it was always mild and temperate down in the cavern, inside the warm body of the Mother.

He washed himself in the stream before entering the tunnel. No one had disturbed the heap of spruce boughs he had placed to conceal the entrance he had found. He pulled them back in place behind him, disguising his trail. He was traveling light. He had brought only his medicine bundle, his pipe and tobacco, and ancient tools for making fire.

He moved into the twilight zone below the cave mouth, pushing back the veils that spiders had woven. Brown bats rustled like dead leaves. His way led steeply down, through narrowing passages that squeezed his broad shoulders. He was obliged to stoop, then crouch, then crawl on all fours like a baby as the roof dropped toward the floor of the tunnel. Before he was through, he was wriggling on his belly, wishing that it had not thickened since he came here as a youth, willing his aching bones to take on the rubbery pliancy of cartilage.

When he could stand again, he was greeted by the song of the hidden waterfall. He entered an immense chamber, lit by the moonglow of frozen cascades of flowstone. He shared these depths with salamanders and blind fish that never saw the sun. His way was that of life itself. At every bend, false passages with wide, easy openings tempted him from his path. Graveyard light carved spooks and monsters from protruding rocks. Vanishing Smoke did not falter. He remembered his way.

He entered the inner chamber, where the Stone Master stood sentinel over the hidden waterfall, on a ledge a hundred feet above a circling pool.

Vanishing Smoke threw off his deerskin cape and his breechcloth and waded into the pool, until the hard spray of the waterfall enfolded him.

Cleansed and exultant, he chanted the new song that burst from his heart and renewed his pact with the power that is within everything and beyond everything, the power of All That Is.

He made his self-offering:

I am only a weak vessel, given to temptation, full of error. But so far as this weak vessel may be charged and filled with Thy power and light, for the purposes of soul and spirit, to help and serve others, then let it be filled, according to Thy pleasure.

Waves of light-energy rolled through him and pooled at his heart. They brought a surge of pain and joy that burst the limits of his body and left it doubled over, shaking and sobbing.

Only in this way can a man know his offering is accepted.

Later, he crouched on a ledge of stone and coaxed flame from punkwood with his fire-drill. Deep in the bowels of earth, he sat with the fire and waited for the dream gates to reopen.

3.

Governor Hunter was troubled by the large numbers of younger children the Palatines had brought with them. Some had become orphans during the voyage and could only be a drag on the labor force he was sending to camps beside the Livingston estates. None of them were likely to be of much use when it came to clearing land and girdling trees.

The governor decided it would be prudent to limit the number of mouths that he would be responsible for feeding through the good offices of Robert Livingston. He announced that all Palatine children between the ages of eight and twelve would be hired out to work for private individuals in the province of New York, unless their parents could demonstrate that they were capable of earning their keep in the tar-works.

The orphans were already plucked and trussed, since the governor would allow no petitions on behalf of the children unless they came from the parents. The widowed mothers were scared and vulnerable and used (he supposed) to being ordered about by men; they would be too fearful of what might happen to their remaining children to put up much fight.

The opposition gathered around Johann Weiser. He protested when prospective employers from Jersey and Long Island arrived at the encampment and began inspecting likely children like slave buyers at an auction block. Even mild Joachim Feck, normally a man of few words, got mad when a New York grain merchant squeezed Eva's bottom and tried to get a look at her teeth.

But it was Conrad who jumped in. "Take your hands off her!" He gave the grain merchant a shove that knocked his hat off his head and set his wattles trembling.

"I'm glad one of our men has some balls," Dina Zeh spoke to her neighbor in a stage whisper. "Even if they are unseasoned."

Eva Feck looked at her young protector with adoring eyes. She was disappointed to observe that the admiring glances Conrad sought were those of the full-grown women.

"This is unconscionable!" Weiser spoke for all. "This is no part of our agreement."

"You signed the covenant," the governor's factor reminded him. "It clearly states that you will serve *at Her Majesty's pleasure*. No one is exempted on the grounds of age or dignity. Nor does it state that you are to be subsisted in any specific locality."

"If you steal our children," Johann said with deep anger, "you will pay for it. If Governor Hunter sets himself up as Pharaoh, he will share the fate of Pharaohs."

"I caution you, Mister Weiser. The laws against sedition are no milder in the colony than at London, and no less likely to be applied in their full severity in this time of common danger."

Weiser decided to defend his own children by lying about their ages. But Greta gave the game away. When the agent approached her separately, running through his list of the Weiser children, she disclosed that Georg Friedrich—Freddie—was just eleven. Certainly, Freddie looked no older, in the puppy fat that had somehow survived the journey.

When the agent ran down the list to Conrad's name, Greta said breezily, "Oh, he's twelve."

"I am *fourteen!*" Conrad shouted when they brought over the Long Island landowner who had agreed to hire Freddie.

His father confirmed that this was so—or very nearly so, since Conrad was approaching his fourteenth birthday—while Conrad scowled at Greta, convinced that her mistake was deliberate. The agent decided not to quibble. Bagging one Weiser boy was as much as could be hoped for, and Conrad looked fully capable of holding his own, with a woodsman's ax or a pair of fists.

That night, Conrad confronted Greta. "Why did you give up Freddie?"

"I was asked a question and I gave an honest answer. Would you have me lie?"

"I would lie any day of the week to save someone in my family."

"Would you lie for me?"

"You are not my family."

Greta screamed to Johann, "You see? The spiteful boy dares insult me to my face!"

"Greta—" Johann came over and put his arm round her shoulder. "Don't upset yourself. It has been a taxing day for all of us."

Why won't he stand up for us? Conrad lamented. *Why does he let her lead him round by the cock?*

His hatred deepened when he heard Greta tell one of the other women, "I say good riddance to fat Freddie. We have too many mouths to feed already."

And one more growing inside your belly. My father's bastard. Was it conceived before my mother died?

The rift within the family only deepened when Johann arranged a marriage service with a Lutheran minister who was in the city. While the family feud shadowed the Weiser's passage upriver, darker shadows overlaid it, like the wings of enormous war birds.

4.

Okwari came for Vanishing Smoke as he lay in the twilight zone between sleep and waking. He felt the gentle tap on his shoulder, and looked up into the great dish face.

The bear enclosed his hands in his huge paws and led him through a circle dance. Okwari took off his skin as a man might remove a garment, and indicated that Vanishing Smoke should remove his own skin. When they swapped skins, Vanishing Smoke saw they were joined by a cord at the heart. Okwari told him:

> *Burn sage for me and I will come to dance with you. Any who seek to do harm to those you love will learn the wildness of the Bear. When others come for help and healing, you will call for me and I will show you the cause of their pain.*

Vanishing Smoke roamed with the bear and relearned the secret language of herbs and plants. He noticed that his daughter, Island Woman, was already proficient at this art, more gifted than he could ever be, except when he saw through the eyes of Okwari.

Then Okwari brought him to a place like the edge of the world.

Vanishing Smoke saw a black river beyond a smoldering plain and a horned mountain that burned with dark fire.

I cannot go further with you, Okwari instructed. *You have come to the place where a man must walk alone in his bones.*

Okwari opened his great jaws. He devoured the man who was Vanishing Smoke and spat him out like a filleted fish.

Stripped of everything that belonged to him in the surface world, Vanishing Smoke was ready to meet his death.

The gatekeeper was waiting for him.

The gatekeeper asked, *What is the face of your death?*

Vanishing Smoke assumed the Face of the Divided One.

You may pass.

He crossed the slippery bridge of souls. He concealed his light from the Crusher of Skulls on the far side, who waits to devour the brains of the dead. He saw the villages of the unhappy dead, and the bridge of light to the higher worlds that is a consuming terror to those who are not ready to walk it.

When he came back to his skin, he knew the ritual he must perform to honor this vision, and the actions in the daylight world that must flow from it.

There was one thing that remained to be done in this place of power, before he went into the woods to find the Face of his death.

He scaled the slippery rock wall to the ledge where the Stone Master watched over the hidden waterfall. He gave thanks to the Stone People, then raised his arm to clasp the huge fossil embedded in the wall. A creature that had walked on many legs, and swum with fins and a fishtail, and faced its enemies in armor. A powerful being that had ruled when the sun was very young. Through his fingertips, through his skin, he remembered.

□

Vanishing Smoke went in search of the great white pine that had bled in his London dream. The tree found him. He stepped out of the shadows of the deep woods, and there it stood, in a shaft of sunlight.

He again made fire in the way of his ancestors, feeding the sparks that flew from the fire-drill with dry wormwood before he piled on twigs and fallen branches. When the fire was crackling away, he made his offerings—tobacco and dried leaves of red osier dogwood—and rubbed the turtle rattle he had inherited from his grandmother against the tree.

He spoke to the pine as a living being. *Everything is alive, everything is ensouled.* He asked its permission to take what he needed, for the fulfillment of his dream.

He sat with the tree for a time, slipping back into another time when the Real People had been divided against themselves and against spirit, and the Peacemaker had come with a song of healing to comb the snakes of evil from the minds of men.

I will put on the face of the Divided One to tame the spirit of death and division that lives in it. When I take this spirit into myself, I will lift it from the minds of my people.

"From you who stand here," he spoke to the tree, "I ask to borrow a small part of your living flesh, to guard and to heal."

He waited until he sensed the tree's agreement.

Gently, he stripped off an oval of bark and started carving the Face in the living tree, choosing a section of the trunk where the grain ran smooth. He worked with flint knives, scoring the features of the Divided One he had glimpsed in the dream.

He burned the edges of the Face away from the trunk with firesticks, scraping away with one of his stone knives to curb the spread of the flames. When his work was complete, he thanked the tree and carefully stamped down the embers of his fire. In time, the bark would grow back. The tree would again be whole.

He finished the Face at the camp he had made at the edge of a narrow gorge, where huge boulders sloped down toward a fast-flowing stream. He painted one side red, using the holy paint (made from hematite) instead of the traders' vermilion. He blackened the left side with charcoal. He fastened tufts of bear's hair to the mask with strips of woodchuck skin, and made a loop at the top to hold the tobacco ties he would use to feed the Face. He inserted bright disks of copper in the eye sockets. They shone back at him like mirrors.

Finally, he smeared the distended lips with corn mush and the eyes with crushed berries of the manroot, to quicken the sight.

When he blew tobacco smoke over the Face, he knew it was alive. His hands trembled slightly as he hung it from a branch, not yet ready to experiment with its power. He knew this power was two-edged: to heal and make whole, but also to rend and drive to madness anyone who abused it.

The wind sighed through the forest, shaking the trees. Above the treetops, along the sunset ridge of the world, low-flying stratus clouds did battle with the dying light. Vanishing Smoke wrapped the mask, red as sunrise, black as mourning, in a cornhusk sack, and turned his footsteps toward Two Rivers.

Death walked at his left shoulder.

CHAPTER 6

A COUNCIL OF BIRDS

1.

Governor Hunter sat in an elbow chair with his hat on his head, waiting for the Indians to settle down. They were arranging themselves in a half-moon on the boards the Commissioners of Indian Affairs had had laid across Handlaers Street, in front of the Albany town hall, because there were far too many of them to accommodate in the council room. All those waving feathers and vivid colors gave Robert Hunter the sensation that he had wandered into a tropical aviary. He reflected on whether he might be able to make use of this image, when he again had leisure to write for the London stage. *The Council of the Birds.*

Robert Livingston had claimed the seat at the governor's right hand. Peter Schuyler took the place at his left, and the two local grandees proceeded to vie with each other to claim Hunter's wandering attention. The thick-bodied men with nose-bobs were Senecas, Schuyler explained. The Mohawk warriors had cut off most of their hair, leaving a crest in the middle, but their chiefs and elders, who squatted in front, wore their hair long. Perched like a vulture in the center was the Onondaga speaker.

Governor Hunter recognized Hendrick Forked Paths, got up in his London finery, seated with some of the younger braves. A tattooed man—identified by Schuyler as Brant Vanishing Smoke—seemed to be keeping his own counsel, squatting with his eyes closed and his hands clasped around his knees, rocking on his bottom.

"The man is drunk," Livingston pronounced when Hunter asked what was wrong with the Mohawk. "It doesn't take much." He leaned closer and whispered, "It may serve our purpose as it has done in the past."

Lolling apart in the shade were some fierce-looking men who had plucked their whole heads, leaving only a topknot above the fontanel.

"A fine collection of hairdressers," the governor remarked. "Who are those prodigies under the poplar?"

"Caughnawagas," Schuyler informed him.

Hunter nodded. Then the import of the alien syllables came home. "Caughnawagas? You mean French Indians?"

"Quite so."

"But, good God—" The governor stared. "They are not *our* savages. They are King Louis' savages. I will have them arrested as spies."

"I would not recommend it, sir. For one thing, the Caughnawagas are related to the Mohawks, and we would not wish our Mohawks to take offence. For another, the Caughnawagas bring us information—" Schuyler narrowed his eyes a fraction "—and *other services* that are beneficial to both parties."

Robert Livingston weighed the value of telling the governor that Schuyler meant *trading with the enemy*. Albany thrived on it. There was not a merchant *handlaer* in the town, from the Patroon downward, who had not profited from the contraband trade in furs from Montreal. The Caughnawagas, free to come and go as they pleased in Mohawk country, were the prime couriers. Livingston decided that the pleasure to be derived from embarrasing Schuyler might be outweighed by the risk to himself; it was common knowledge in Albany that the lord of Livingston Manor had himself been charged with fencing French contraband.

Besides, the mere sight of the Indians from the Caughnawaga mission had thrown the governor into a visible state of agitation. "I do not see how I can be expected to discuss serious business with the Five Nations in the presence of French spies," Hunter rumbled.

Livingston motioned for one of his servants to give the governor a silver tankard of rum punch. It was infernally muggy down here by the river, and the governor had already announced that he found Albany water undrinkable; it tasted of vinegar, like Dutch salads.

"By my observation," Livingston volunteered in his soft Scottish burr, "no *serious business* is conducted with Indians in public. They are best handled singly, or in small parcels." He lowered his voice to add, "And may then be had for the cheapest rates."

Governor Hunter's face relaxed into an expression of superior insight. In the two months since he had taken possession of his province, he had found himself more and more dependent on the advice of this enterprising Scot, not least in finding a place to settle the Palatines and put them to work. His grand scheme for transplanting the German refugees had threatened to turn into his worst nightmare before Livingston had handed him a solution. Useful in this, Robert Livingston would no doubt prove equally useful in Indian diplomacy. Was he not Secretary to the Albany Commissioners of Indian Affairs? Livingston would never have made a go of it at Court, Hunter reflected. Not with that yellowed, ratty old wig, those drawstring lips and that nose off a conger eel. But the Scotsman had an eye for the main chance. And the governor recognized that, despite their contrast in style, they had something in common. They were both poor men's sons. The difference was that Livingston showed it, while Hunter did not. And that Livingston had made himself a rich man, something the governor had yet to accomplish.

Hunter sipped his rum punch, hoping that a key to fortune was to be found—as Livingston promised—at this conference. These Indian proceedings took an unconscionably long time to get organized. The Indians had kept him waiting more than a week since the day when the congress had been scheduled to begin. And each party of laggards dawdling down the hill past the fort expected to be saluted with cannon. Since he had presented his formal speech, the Indians had kept him waiting for another two days while they considered their reply.

"We do not speak all in a rush, like white men," the Onondaga speaker had the gall to inform him, when he despatched a message asking them to hurry up. "We always try to give you our best words."

"In dealing with Indians," Robert Livingston murmured, "one requires the patience of a eunuch at the court of the Great Turk."

Hunter liked the image; he would mention it in his next letter to his friend Dean Swift, whose mordant sense of humor would be of service here.

The governor grumbled, nonetheless. "If these savages want their presents, they had better get on with it." The new consignment of presents—a hundred firelocks, a thousand pounds of gunpowder, duffels, strouds and gewgaws, not to mention the expensive inventory of gifts for individual chiefs—was a sore point with Hunter. His predecessor had left the provincial treasury empty. He was already at loggerheads with an insolent assembly that starved the government and refused to pay his salary. A packet boat had brought news that there was a new ministry in London that declined to honor his bills. He was supporting the twenty-five hundred Palatines who had survived the crossing on his own credit. To top it all, he had been required to stand surety for the retail price of goods supplied by grafting merchants for Indians who did not even do him the courtesy of showing up on time to collect their loot.

The Albany Commissioners of Indian Affairs—as fine a collection of sharpers as Hunter had encountered anywhere—had solemnly assured him that if the Indians did not receive their bribes, they would go over to the other side. But who was going to foot the bill? Not the commissioners, nor the mutinous assembly. It was the governor's lot (so Hunter learned) to exhaust his own credit to pay for the defense of a fractious, self-seeking people, and to whistle his way to the poorhouse if Her Majesty's government refused reimbursement at the end of the accounting. With each day he spent in his colony, Robert Hunter felt himself sliding deeper into the quicksand of debt.

But he was not a defeated man. Indeed, he had risen in good spirits and might have stayed that way, had he not been obliged to swat at gnats in the sultry summer heat, with the choice of looking at painted Indians or the fort at the top of Junckers Street, a military abomination with yawning gaps in the palisades, put up on a site that could be commanded by any attacker who seized the crown of the hill. Governor Hunter had a plan. It was hardly less ambitious than the "glorious enterprise" projected by Francis Nicholson and his troupe of Boston adventurers. If Hunter's plan could be accomplished, it would not only secure his present fortunes; it would bring a deluge of future wealth and honors. The governor's confidence was riding high, thanks to business arrangements he had concluded the previous night, at an intimate supper with the useful Mr. Livingston. All that was required now was a private chat with the right Mohawks, people Livingston had promised to deliver.

Hunter savored Livingston's analogy with the eunuch at the court of the Great Ottoman. He flattered himself that he had turned a few ladies' heads at court. He did not propose to play eunuch with the Indians who made him wait until his backside was aching. He meant to roger them royally.

□

The governor sniffed at his scented handkerchief. The stench of Albany was pretty ripe, perhaps no sharper than London's, but distinctly more *rustic*. These July nights, the Dutch tethered their cattle in the streets, in front of their houses; in the mornings, a man could not walk the cobbles without playing hopscotch among steaming cowpats. Farm odors were compounded by the smell of the Indians, which reminded Hunter of gamebirds left hanging too long.

He was relieved to see that the Indians were finally ready to begin. The Onondaga speaker stood in front of the Five Nations, a large belt of wampum suspended from his shoulder, a bundle of memory sticks in his hand.

The name of this Onondaga word-carrier was Kaquendero. He had often enjoyed Peter Schuyler's hospitality, and Schuyler had suggested, discreetly, that he should replace Dekanisora—the famed Onondaga chief—as the speaker for this assembly, being friendlier to the English. The fact that the Indians had complied boded well for the conference, but was no promise of full success. As Schuyler had warned the governor,

the way of the Indians, in public councils, was to say what would please
their auditors.

Kaquendero laboriously repeated all the points Governor Hunter had
made in his own speech, adding diplomatic replies. He addressed Hunter
as Corlaer, a name borrowed from an early Dutch pioneer that the Five
Nations used as a generic title for the rulers of the New York Colony.
Through the Dutch interpreter, the governor heard the following:

"Brother Corlaer, some of our brothers have been in England and
have returned to us safe. Though they are from the Mohawk Nation, we
regard them as coming from all the Five Nations, as we stand united.
They have told us of the Great Queen and her power."

Schuyler nodded his head in approval. In private meetings with the
Indians, he had pressed for the inclusion of a passage along these lines. He
knew from his spies, and from Hendrick himself, that the Four Kings were
under fierce attack from their own people. This public endorsement, from
the spokesman for the Confederacy, would strengthen Hendrick's position. The Mohawk war chief was too useful a tool to have broken.

Governor Hunter beamed as Kaquendero proceeded to confirm what
the Four Kings had agreed in London, and more. The Five Nations
were willing to receive Anglican missionaries and English soldiers, to be
garrisoned in forts near the Mohawk castle at Two Rivers, and at Onondaga, the capital of the league. The speaker promised that the Five
Nations would close their doors to Jesuits and French agents, and forbid
their braves to take the warpath against the Catawbas who—though
blood enemies of the Iroquois—were friends of the English government
of the Carolinas.

"The warriors of the Five Nations will rest quiet near their homes,
ready to answer Brother Corlaer's call. So long as sun and moon shall
shine, and the rivers flow, we will hold fast to the shining covenant belt
that joins the Real People and the Sunrise People."

Governor Hunter doffed his hat. His aides passed out silver medals.

Despite the delays, the heat and the stink—and those plucked mur-
derers from the French mission squatting under the poplar—the governor congratulated himself and his advisors on a good day's work. But
the real business was just begun. Before going to bed, Hunter counted
on making himself master of a hundred square miles of Mohawk land,
if not more.

2.

Vanishing Smoke had brought his whole family to Albany, but his wife
and older daughter had no time for listening to speeches in front of the
town hall.

Redhawk and Island Woman had their own rounds to make: to the
neat Dutch house by the stone church, with a stone wall facing the street
and shingles of white pine, where Widow Veeder did a brisk trade in
furs; to Tobias Franck's store near the King's Tavern, where lounging
soldiers hooted obscenities at a pair of likely looking "squaws."

Island Woman bristled at the foul word. To call a Mohawk woman
a squaw was the same as calling a white woman a cunt; the word *otiskwa*
refers to the female organ. Her mother squeezed the girl's arm to stop
her from yelling back at the soldiers. They had more important work
to do than swap insults with ignorant men. They were here to gather
information—as was Cloud Singer, Island Woman's brother, who had
come with the envoys from Caughnawaga—and to keep an eye on their
own men. Vanishing Smoke was stronger, and clearer in his purpose,
since he had gone to find his true face in the woods, and he had
promised his wife that he would not drink with the white men in Albany. But Hendrick Forked Paths and the other Mohawks had made
no such promise, and there was no telling what they would do if they
got drunk. They were capable of selling the land from under the
village.

"Track them like wolves, watch them like hawks," was Fruitpicker's
injunction to the women of their clan.

Redhawk and her daughter would do this. But first, they would
trade. The Albany merchants were starved for peltries, because the war
had dried up the supply of furs from Canada and the Great Lakes. The
Mohawks did not have many furs to sell them. The beaver ponds in the
Valley had been exhausted for many winters past, and the botched expedition against Canada the previous year had prevented the men from
trading with the western Indians.

But Redhawk had a tidy stock of beavers, muskrats and martens to
sell, and she did not intend to dispose of them cheaply. Some she had
bartered from Senecas and Caughnawagas, in return for some of the
things Vanishing Smoke had brought home from London, or for goods
that Albany traders had advanced to her on credit. Some had been en-
trusted to her by Fruitpicker's brother, who had traveled as far as the
country of the Miamis, near the French outpost at Detroit, to bargain
for winter furs. Traffic in furs outside the town limits was illegal, according to the charter that gave Albany a monopoly on the trade. But
the Albany traders, from highest to lowest, flouted their own laws as
cheerfully as their soulmates at Montreal. Those who were interested in
a quick, one-time profit, preferred to barter with Indian men because
they could get them drunk and fix the scales and the terms of exchange
without protest. But those, like Widow Veeder, who were interested in
recruiting a stable network of suppliers and sub-agents for the long haul
preferred to deal with women like Redhawk, who could make sense of

the pictographs—and sometimes the figures—in the ledgerbooks, and
came back season after season when they were treated fairly.

Redhawk had heard that Tobias Franck was offering top prices for
furs, so she led Island Woman toward his store. Both women had packs
of furs strapped to their backs.

"How much for that piece of beaver, John?" yelled a redcoat lounging at the door of the King's Tavern. He had a beerpot in his hand, and
had patently downed a few more. The state of his hose and buttons
would have made a drill sergeant swoon.

"The squaws do it for free, innit. They love a bit of cock."

"How about it then, darling?"

He made a grab for Island Woman. The girl swung out into the
middle of the street to dodge him.

"Saving it for the gentry, are we? Come on, give us a feel."

The soldier ran up behind Island Woman and tried to shove his hand
between her thighs.

She rounded on him. If the redcoat had not been sozzled, the cold
fury in her eyes might have been enough to propel him back to the
safety of the tavern.

But he came on, groping at her high, firm breasts through the calico
chemise.

"*Tsitak!*" Island Woman spat. "Eat shit!" Then she kicked him hard
in the groin, moving with a dancer's speed and agility.

The soldier howled and hobbled backward, clutching at his injured
parts.

Redhawk placed herself between her daughter and the clot of
bloodybacks that had formed in front of the tavern.

"Come on boys," urged the friend of the man who had been kicked
in the crotch. "Let's teach the tarts how to be friendly."

"Not worth the candle, lad," Sergeant Buttress intervened. Native
women could be hellions. One of them had scarred his cheek for life.
Besides, the governor was in town and the troops had been ordered to
treat the Indians dainty. A misstep with a Mohawk girl could cost every
man present forty lashes.

"I'll get you next time, you bleeding cunt!" vowed the one who had
groped Island Woman.

Try it, Island Woman promised him mentally, *and I will drive your
soul from your body. If you have a soul.*

□

Inside Franck's store, Redhawk pinched the blue and red strouds the
trader got out to show her. This one was too coarse; that one, too light
in color. The wool used for Mohawk skirts and leggings must be midnight blue or crimson.

Tobias Franck groaned inwardly and hooked his spectacles over his ears as he opened his account book, to show Redhawk his crude drawings of the fifteen beavers she owed for trade goods he had advanced to her the previous season. Mohawk women were sharp bargainers, and this one was probably the toughest of the lot. She did not drink alcohol, she checked the weights and the quality of the merchandise, and she would argue prices until the sun came up again.

But Redhawk was reliable. The trader could always count on her for a good fat bundle of peltries in the spring, and sometimes even in the slack time in midsummer. Redhawk generally paid her debts, when the count was right. But today, Tobias was not inclined to humor her for long. He anticipated brisk business before the close of play. As soon as the Indians at Governor Hunter's conference had taken delivery of their presents, they would be running in here—and into every other grogshop in town that would have them—to barter for rum.

Trader Franck considered himself a fair man. He diluted his rum no more than others did, which was surely a favor to the Indians, who had no head for liquor. And he watered his grog with good Hudson River water and not his own urine, as Johannes Bratt (whose urine, admittedly, must surely be almost pure spirit) boasted of doing.

"Two beavers for one red blanket." Island Woman frowned at her mother. "That is not a fair trade."

"I can't help it if the price of furs is down," Franck defended himself. "It's on account of the war."

"You speak like a fox. There are less furs because of this war. So the price of furs should be higher."

Redhawk was the one Indian of Franck's acquaintance who had a clear grasp of how markets operated.

"Three beavers for two blankets," the trader compromised. He wanted her out of his store so she would not be present to offer advice to the thirsty warriors who would soon be begging him for rum. Redhawk nodded at her daughter. This was fair.

3.

The sun was down when Governor Hunter received the Mohawks hand-picked by Livingston and Peter Schuyler in private. They met at Schuyler's house, a mansion by local standards, though not by Hunter's. The governor found it comfortable but quaint, stuffed with Dutch curios, like the delftware plates that hung on the walls from hooks, the huge open fireplace jutting out into the middle of the parlor with only a hood to encourage smoke to go up the chimney, and the monstrous *kas*, a hold-all cabinet that reared up like a giant's coffin.

Schuyler had picked his cousin Abraham, in place of Lawrence Claessen, the conference interpreter, to explain the governor's wishes to the Mohawks.

The Mohawk delegation was small enough to be reliable (Hunter's advisers had promised him) while just large enough to be judged representative. It was necessary to include delegates from all three clans of the Mohawk Nation, because a recurring objection to previous Indian deeds was that the signatories did not represent the whole people. The Mohawks who had gone to London—Hendrick, John and Brant Vanishing Smoke—were obvious allies, men who could be counted on to return Her Majesty's favors. The Schuylers had dressed things up by inviting White Eagle, a traditional chief, or *royaner*, of the Wolf Clan, and a chief of the Bear Clan whose name was translated as The Rattler. Colonel Schuyler did not consider any chief of the Turtle Clan to be reliable in his business, so they made do with an old man of indeterminate status whose eyes flicked back and forth, the whole evening, between the liquor decanters and the heap of presents that had been cunningly deployed at the foot of the coffinlike cabinet. The presents included a hogshead of claret and several large kegs of rum, unopened—and hence presumably unwatered—since they had been shipped from Antigua.

Livingston and Schuyler played affable bartenders. As the liquor flowed, the Mohawks became more and more accommodating. Governor Hunter smoked a pipe or two with the sachems, gasping at the bite of their homegrown tobacco. Only Schuyler paid attention to the fact that Vanishing Smoke left his glass untouched.

"Are you quite well?"

Vanishing Smoke's eyes crossed his. No friendship there, Schuyler recognized. In London, when this Mohawk had set himself apart from the group, Schuyler had assumed it was simply because he was sick and hungover. But there had also been that crazy business in the bearpit. *It may be a vision thing. The wild men are strangers to us, however we dress them up. They will give up their names, their homes, their all for a dream or vision.* Schuyler briefly considered whether he had been mistaken to include Vanishing Smoke in this gathering. This was the last place in the colony where one wanted to have to contend with a dream prophet. He reminded himself that Brant Vanishing Smoke, the Indian King, was his own invention, and could be just as easily unmade. *To the extent that his own people listen to him, it is because we are behind him, with guns and money. Without us, he will vanish as swiftly as the morning mist from which he derives his name.*

The conversation turned to the Schoharie lands. Though by all accounts the territory was fertile, ideal for European-style farming, the Schoharie Valley below Two Rivers was thinly settled by a mixed population: Mahicans and Stockbridge Indians looking for respite from war and despoliation on the New England frontier, Mission Indians who had grown jaundiced with Jesuit hospitality. The chief of the most sizable village—a few lodges and cabins at the foot of Onistagrawa, Corn Mountain—had come down from Caughnawaga. The Mohawks claimed ownership, but few Mohawks would be displaced if the governor's scheme prospered and European settlers moved down there in force.

This was one reason Schuyler was optimistic about getting the governor's business concluded smoothly. Another was that, a full century after they had first encountered Europeans, Mohawks still had inordinate difficulty grasping the white man's concept of land ownership. As best he could understand them, the Indians believed that land rights are transient. Their women owned the cornfields they planted, as long as they tilled them. Their men had the right to hunt over certain preserves, and control the passage of others, but that right would expire if the hunters moved away permanently. In the native conception, no man could own the earth itself; he could only use it. The land could not be bought and sold, only borrowed.

So, when the Indians made their mark on deeds that gave white men absolute ownership of their lands, in exchange for a fistful of beads or a keg of rum, the natives went away laughing, because they imagined they had tricked the newcomers into paying for something that cannot be sold. One would have thought that the dispossession of the New England tribes—some of them already reduced to the condition of vaguing drunks and sellers of brooms—would have been an object lesson for the Mohawks. Perhaps the Mohawks, the terror of the New England tribes, imagined that what had been done to their blood enemies had no relevance to them. Perhaps it was simply that they had not yet been exposed to large numbers of white colonists moving beyond the walls of the frontier forts to hack farms from their woods.

The arrival of an army of settlers, with plows and fences, would be a bitter education for the Mohawks, and this was what Governor Hunter's plan required. Charges of fraud would follow, as day follows night. Therefore the transfer of the Mohawk Patent—disputed and burned once before—must appear in the legal sense (if no other) to be impeccable.

Livingston unscrolled the new deed of gift of the Mohawk Patent and raised an eyebrow at the governor, as if to indicate, *No time like the present.*

"Shall we, gentlemen?" The governor moved to the writing table and took up a quill pen.

The traditional chiefs looked uncomfortable. The old toper standing in for the Turtle Clan emptied his bumper and burped.

Hendrick Forked Paths squared his shoulders and moved decisively to the table to take the quill from the governor's hand.

"Good man."

Hendrick was starting to draw his symbol—his clan wolf gripping a death hammer—when Vanishing Smoke thrust himself into the center of the room and held up his hand for attention.

"I think if we sign this paper the newcomers will overrun our valley and eat the land as their cattle eat up the grass, until there is no place left for the bear in winter or the deer in mating time."

He spoke slowly and rhythmically. Hunter did not grasp the force of his words until Abraham Schuyler, stony-faced, began to translate.

"He says the earth is the body of his mother and cannot be sold."

"I would have you remind our friend," Hunter came back smoothly, "that what we contemplate is a deed of trust. Such an arrangement will regulate settlement, improve the land, and keep out the damned French. This will serve the interest of all parties, as we have explained in detail."

To which Vanishing Smoke replied: "I am sorry my brother kicks dust in our eyes, as if we are little children who cannot see beyond it. We have taken counsel with wolves, and talked with the winds, and we see more than he imagines."

Governor Hunter slammed the flat of his hand on the writing table when this was translated, spilling a few drops of ink.

"You chose these bloody people," he said, turning on Schuyler. "You sort them out."

The mood of the Indians had turned. Hendrick had set down his pen and turned his back on the deed.

"We have an arrangement," Schuyler reminded him gently.

Hendrick looked at Vanishing Smoke, and was shaken by the power he read in his eyes. They seemed to reach out like fists. The other Mohawks avoided them.

He shames me, Hendrick realized. *But only if I oppose him. There is nothing to be gained here today, only something to be lost.*

"We are grateful to our Brother Corlaer for his many kindnesses," Hendrick spoke formally. "We are glad he now admits that the Schoharie lands belong to the Flint People, since he has gathered so many presents to buy them away from us."

It took Hunter a long moment to puzzle this out. Schuyler was quicker. Things were shifting against the governor's plan with a vengeance. Hendrick had just told the governor that the old patent he had sought to revive was worthless.

"What is happening?" the governor demanded, impatient with the delays in translation.

Hendrick's bulk, against the door, matched that of the massive *kas* against the opposite wall. He said, "We will take counsel by our own fires before we receive the gifts of our brother."

Though a couple of his companions looked longingly at the un-breached hogshead and the kegs from the West Indies, they all filed out after him into the summer night.

"You picked these savages!" Governor Hunter stormed at Schuyler. "I was led to believe they were old reliables!"

"It's been a long day." Robert Livingston offered the governor a glass, and brought himself within the sweep of Hunter's guns.

"You are supposed to be Secretary of Indian Affairs, Mr. Livingston. You hatched this changeling. I want this matter attended to. *Do you hear me?* I will have this matter *seen to!*"

"You may count on it, sir."

□

The Mohawks left Albany without signing the governor's deed. What gave Hunter's advisers even deeper concern was that they did not even return to Schuyler's house to collect their presents. This, in Schuyler's experience, was unheard-of.

CHAPTER 7

DEATH OF VANISHING SMOKE

1.

Livingston saw opportunity in the governor's discomfort. The Schuylers had picked the Four Kings, and it was now seen that they had not picked altogether wisely. Far from turning Brant Vanishing Smoke into a pliable tool, the visit to London had turned him into an Indian agitator. There were reports that the change in his personality extended to matters of religion: that the Mohawk had joined a secretive order of witches and danced on live coals in a devil mask.

Governor Hunter had made it plain that he blamed Livingston, no less than Peter Schuyler, for the Albany fiasco. If anything, he seemed more vexed with Livingston than with the Dutchman, after receiving a swarm of complaints from Jean Cast about the quality of the food and provisions that were being delivered to the Palatines in the camps. It would not do to fall out of favor with the governor so soon in his tenure, and leave the prime source of patronage in the colony in the hands of other men.

Livingston saw a way forward. If he could rescue the Schoharie land deal, he would prove himself more valuable to the governor than his rivals, and more deserving of a princely share of the spoils. The first step must be to remove the Mohawk who had placed himself across his path. Brant Vanishing Smoke must be broken, in spirit or body. The origin of the attack must be well disguised. However deeply divided, the Mohawks would unite against any outsider who attacked one of their own.

There were ways of arranging these things. Joncaire, the French agent, had been seen at Onondaga, and his spies and runners were constantly coming and going throughout the territory of the Five Nations.

The governor had complained about the presence of Mission Indians from Kahnawake at the Albany conference.

"The attack must come from Joncaire. Or be seen to come from him," Livingston told the jowly, blue-shadowed James Mackie, his confidential agent. "Though Brant is an ungrateful brute, he went to London and was received as one of the Four Kings. It is already known that Joncaire put a price on their heads."

"It could be made to appear the work of a Jesuit poisoner," Mackie ruminated. "The Jesuits are known to be adepts in all the black arts. It is said the blackrobes at Kahnawake employ the Indians to gather manroot and wild hemlock for their experiments."

"Maybe so. But I would not have Joncaire forgotten in this business. Joncaire is known as a stone-cold killer, capable of all things. And his bastard son was lately at the Mohawk castle. They are known to use sorcerers. We might reflect on the virtue of similar tools. It is not clear to me whether the Indians believe in God, but they believe in witches as fervently as our late deluded King James."

"Do you want him dead then, or just given a good scare?"

"Or scared to death." Livingston toyed with the conjunction. "I wish the man removed from my path. I do not care how the job is done, so long as it cannot be attributed to us. If the pawprints of the French are on it, we gain a further advantage. The Mohawks will lust for vengeance. We will not have to go courting them to fight the French. They will be urging us to keep up with them."

"How do you want me to handle this?"

"Choose a go-between. Someone who can be had for money."

Mackie chuckled. "I have yet to meet a man who could not."

"Not so hasty, James. Our partner must not be tied to us. He must be a man who can keep a secret—and, on the chance he cannot, a man whose word could never stand against ours."

"There is Tobias Franck. He does a ripe business with the Desauniers sisters at Montreal, and the Caughnawagas visit him as freely as if he was hawking brandy in Canada. You may remember we set the justices on him, for trading with the enemy, and he paid a pretty price to stay out of jail. So it is known he has no reason to love us."

"Can we trust his discretion?"

"He'll not speak against us, not before witnesses. He can't very well take an oath on the Bible, can he? He is a man without a country, like all the Jews, dependent on the tolerance of his neighbors. He has borrowed deep. We can buy up his notes, and make it plain to him that the neighbor he needs to please is *you*."

Mackie took a swallow of whisky. "Of course, we could keep it nice and simple. The easy thing would be to just get this troublesome Indian drunk and hire some river rat to knock him on the head. It happens all the time. No questions asked. No explanations required."

"Brant seems to have given up drink."

"Good God." Mackie's mouth fell open in wonderment. "No wonder he's gone wrong in the head then." He finished his glass. "I see no real obstacle, though. Brant goes back to his old ways, weakened by abstinence. Can't hold his grog. Falls in the river."

Mackie's alternative had the appeal of simplicity, Livingston allowed. It left little to chance or betrayal. Yet, deep in the coils of the complicated plot he had hatched, Livingston was reluctant to let go of its further promise. To indict the French for killing a Mohawk who was no longer their enemy would be a masterstroke, equal to any of Joncaire's ruses. The possible role of Tobias Franck, the Jew from Amsterdam, opened further vistas. Livingston was not enamored of the idea of approaching Franck as a go-between, whether or not the man was able to testify against him on oath. But there might be a way of implicating Franck while keeping him in the dark—and of breaking a commercial competitor in the process.

"I will ask about the town," Mackie promised. "Joncaire always has eyes and ears at Albany, as in the Mohawk castles. It may be our man is waiting for us."

2.

Redhawk sat near the door of her lodge, in the Mohawk village at Two Rivers, her legs folded beside her. New Smile, her baby, watched from the safety of the cradleboard as her mother and sister stripped the husks from the newly gathered corn. Gripping an ear of corn in her left hand, Island Woman slipped the point of her husking pin inside the tip. Her wrist flicked sideways, her thumb closed quickly over the pin. As she pulled her arm down, toward her body, the husk tore loose from the corn. Soon she would have enough shelled ears to braid together and hang in bunches in the smoke of the firepit.

But Island Woman did not lay this ear beside the others. Her squeal of pleasure cut through the gossip of the other women. Redhawk and Moon Shadow came to see what she had found. On this ear, only two rows of kernels had filled out, leaving a bald strip in between.

"*Oate*. It's the Pathway," her mother conceded. Redhawk made a comical grimace, because the woman who finds *oate* is entitled to claim tribute—one ear of corn, ready for braiding—from each member of the husking bee.

Island Woman skipped around the circle, gathering her prizes.

With his back to the fire, in a ring of bright-eyed children, her father

sucked at his pipe and blew out the fragrant smoke of native tobacco
spiked with dried sumac. Vanishing Smoke was a favorite storyteller; his
lilting syllables captured and cradled his listeners. Now he was telling
the children why the ear of corn with only two rows of kernels was called
the Pathway. He lowered his voice when he spoke the name of Tsawiskaron, the Dark Twin, who whistles like the wind through the trees.

"Tsawiskaron loves to stir things up." Vanishing Smoke ruffled Talldeer's hair. His son scowled, not wishing—as a warrior fully ten years
old, with a gun as well as a bow—to be classified with the children. Yet
he, too, was captivated by the stories.

"The Dark Twin is always hungry," Vanishing Smoke went on.
"But he's greedy and he never waits to take his turn. You remember
how he pushed out of his mother's side instead of coming out the proper
way, just because he had to be first? Well, my grandmother told me
Tsawiskaron got very, very hungry waiting for the green corn to get ripe.
There was something in his belly that was biting him, and he had to
feed it right then. So he ran among the cornstalks, peeling back the
husks and licking strips off the green ears with his tongue. Island Woman
found the path he made."

Island Woman shivered, overhearing the last bit. Tsawiskaron was
tricky. You had to watch yourself when he was around. The winds
changed and set the ashes dancing. When the Trickster was around, all
you could count on was that nothing would go as you planned.

The story about Tsawiskaron's hunger made Talldeer's belly rumble. When the husking was done there would be cornbread, sweet with
berries, and corn cobs sooty from the fire. To lessen the pangs, he asked
for another story. He wanted the story of the vampire skeleton, but his
father said it would frighten the little ones.

"Then tell us the story of the Divided One." Talldeer had seen the
mask his father had made because of his dream, while rummaging inside
the sack where Vanishing Smoke hid his medicine things when the other
members of the family were out of the lodge. This had confirmed his
suspicion that his father was one of the men who ran through the village
like wind demons to scare away the spirits that brought disease. Talldeer
had wanted to try on the mask, but his boldness had failed him, because
of another story he had heard, about a man who had put on a mask he
had not earned. The mask had stuck to his face like resin. When others
pulled it away, his skin came off with it.

"That is not a story for tonight," Vanishing Smoke said curtly.
"There are stories that can only be told when the snow lies deep on the
ground. We must remember that the spirits are always listening. In midwinter, when everything is blanketed by snow, the ones who live in the
earth cannot hear us."

"*Skarratons!*" the younger children pressed. "Tell us a story."

There were many kinds of stories. There were stories that explained why things were the way they were, like the story of the Dark Twin licking the corn. There were stories that reminded people how they ought to behave. There were tales of heroes who walked where the earth was narrow. There were stories in which the listener could find himself: stories that enabled people to remember who they were and what they were meant to become.

Island Woman had finished collecting her trophies. She squatted next to her father and said, "Tell us the story of the first dreamer."

"This comes from a long time ago, from a time before the Peace-maker, when the Real People were not yet the Real People," Vanishing Smoke began. "People had fallen very low. They no longer remembered the Sky World from which our ancestors come. They no longer walked in the spirit worlds, because they had forgotten how to dream. They lived with snakes and woodchucks that live underwater and in holes in the ground. They thought that they *were* snakes and woodchucks. They had forgotten they were human.

"In these dark times, a man began to dream. He dreamed so strongly that he started whirling and whirling. He whirled up through the roof of his house and fell upward into the sky. He flew with the birds. They took him to the house of First Woman. He was bathed in a lake that shone like blue fire. When he was washed clean, the great ones changed his eyes and his hearing so he could understand what they wished to teach him. He journeyed through many levels of the Upper World, and discovered that he had relatives and teachers on all of these levels. They gave him songs of healing and songs of soul remembering.

"When the dreamer came back to this world, he was changed. He grieved for his people, because he saw how low they had fallen. One by one, as they slept, he called them to him in their dreambodies and taught them songs he had learned. When the sleepers' dreamsouls returned to their bodies, they reminded them who they were. They remembered they were not snakes and woodchucks, and began to live again as human beings.

"This is what *dreaming* means. If we cease to dream, how can the spirits talk to us? If we cease to dream, we will cease to be the Real People."

There was silence after this story.

Island Woman felt the weight of her father's sadness. She stroked the side of his face.

"The story is about *now*," Vanishing Smoke said quietly.

"Our people are still dreamers," Island Woman told him.

"But there are fewer and fewer of us who dream true. The newcomers have cluttered our minds and confused our senses. Never forget—" he spoke to the children with blazing passion "—that you are born to be *dreamers*. The dream world is the real world. It is your home. Your spirit came here from the dream world before you had a body, and it will return to the dream world when you leave your body behind."

Island Woman felt a chill, deeper than the river damp carried on the night wind.

"Father—"

"Time to tie up the bag," Vanishing Smoke smiled at the younger faces. "Maybe we'll have popcorn tonight."

This brought a bustle of excitement. Popcorn—*okarita*—was not an everyday treat.

Island Woman felt a shift in her energy field. She tried to *see* the source of the displacement, and the keener sense of unease that came with it. She closed her eyes, to read her father's second body. The gray haze that blurred the light over his abdomen had worried her since he came back from England, a source of sickness that would not be lifted. Yet it was no murkier than before. There was something else. She saw it as a shadow that fell over his head like a brown-black cowl. Something that threatened to swallow his light.

Talldeer, who had run off with the other boys at the end of the storytelling, came racing back with a message. There were men from Albany, with a message for her father. Island Woman saw them step through the gate in the palisades: an Indian she did not recognize, and a stubbled, thickset white man she had seen poling a bateau on the river above Schenectady. Her nose twitched. Even from this distance she could smell the liquor on the white man's breath. He stared hard at the native women, stripping them with his piggy eyes.

Vanishing Smoke walked over to talk with them.

Island Woman's unease deepened. There was something terribly wrong. The shadow over her father's head was deepening. He walked briskly back to the lodge. When she followed him in, he was gathering up his traveling pouch and the smaller of his medicine bundles.

"Father, who are those men?"

"One is called Snowsnake. He says he comes from Kahnawake. The name of the other is Bratt."

"You're not going with them." She beckoned to her mother, who left her cooking to join the exchange.

"I have to go."

"We don't know these people."

A flash of anger crossed Vanishing Smoke's face. He was not accustomed to discussing his travels with his daughter.

"It is about your brother," he told the women as he slung his firelock over his shoulder.

"Talldeer?" Redhawk exclaimed. "What's the boy done?" She had visions of Talldeer helping himself from a trader's tobacco jar, or running off with a farmer's pig.

"Not Talldeer. Cloud Singer. He is being held in Albany. The men say he will be held as a hostage, against the release of English prisoners in Canada."

They all knew this was a serious matter. Their people feared confinement far more than death; Indians died quickly—within weeks or even days—in white men's jails.

Island Woman felt for her brother, but the fear for her father remained.

"Don't go tonight," she urged him. "And don't go alone. We can all go together in the morning."

"The need is now. And I know my way to Albany."

"You don't know these men." She looked at the white man who slouched about the clearing. She knew his kind: the kind who thought the natives were less than human but would jump one of the girls without asking if he got the chance.

"They come from Tobias Franck." The name brought a nod from Redhawk, who had bartered furs at the trader's store. "Franck has never cheated us, or treated us as less than equals. He sends word that he may be able to have Cloud Singer released if I speak on his behalf. Perhaps going to London is worth something after all."

Island Woman walked with her father down to the boat the visitors had tied up at the landing. She tried to strike up a conversation with the Indian called Snowsnake, but he was taciturn and shifty, avoiding her questions about Cloud Singer and his family at the mission. Bratt leered at her openly, and offered her a drink when they got to the boat.

Island Woman shook her head.

"Pretty lady's welcome to ride with us." Bratt exhaled a cloud of cheap rum between his yellowed teeth.

"No," Vanishing Smoke said sharply.

When he embraced his daughter, she began to protest again. "I'm never far from you," he said tenderly. "Look for me in your dreams."

3.

At the desk by the window of his Albany townhouse, Tobias Franck squinted over the pages of Hayyim Vital's *Book of Transmigrations*. He was rereading a description of an exorcism performed by a circle of Cabalists in Safed a little over a century before. Tobias' grandfather had borne witness to the authenticity of the account. There was his signature, next to that of the author of the sabbath hymn, *Lekha dodi*, sung in temples all over the world every Friday night. How long since Tobias had heard it sung by a full congregation!

The woman of Safed who was said to be possessed was fumigated with smoke and burning sulfur. Tobias could picture her, choking as his own wife had been choking during her last, fatal bout with pneumonia.

How did the rabbis know the woman of Safed was possessed? Because she spoke in the voice of a moneychanger who died thirty-five years before. She knew the secret lives of his family, and could speak in tongues known to him—Turkish, Aramaic—that were foreign to her.

Why had the dead moneychanger jumped into her body? Seemingly because he believed that possessing a living person was his best way to avoid the awful suffering that awaited him in Gehenna, in punishment for his sins.

How greatly man's beliefs about the afterlife may shape his actions, even beyond physical death. Could it be that a normal man of business— a moneychanger in Syria—could be driven to such extremities by the fear of damnation?

The exorcism, Tobias noted, had not prospered. The rabbis had chased the possessing spirit away, with smoke and incantations and the scream of the shofar. But it had returned, to carry the poor woman's spirit away with it.

A grim theme for meditation, but powerful enough to divert the trader's mind from the business that awaited him. He had found himself much preoccupied with the afterlife since his wife's passing. He was nearing seventy, which was counted a grand old age on this rough frontier. He would have the opportunity to test the reality of the Otherword soon enough. Yet he craved knowledge *now*: a glimpse around the corner. He was wedded to books, yet it had become evident to him that what he craved to know was not in his books. Surely this knowledge could come only through personal experience of the most direct and immediate kind. His correspondent in Amsterdam insisted that what was required was prayer, and strict observance of ritual and the memorization and exact intonation of the holy names, the words that open and bind. These disciplines did not satisfy Tobias's thirst, but he would have welcomed the chance to discuss this with his friend in Holland. To whom would he dare entrust his deepest thoughts on these matters, here on the New York frontier? Certainly not to his fellow fur traders, whose sights were set on profit (no cause for criticism; money was his game too and he had often been reminded that survival for one of his own kind might require *portable* assets in significant quantity). Not to the Anglican minister, Mr. Barclay, who was more comfortable with spirits from a bottle than spirits of a different water.

It had occurred to Tobias that one man with whom he might be able to share his thoughts was a native. Brant Vanishing Smoke and the women of his family were fairly regular customers at the store. Tobias had heard—it was briefly the talk of the town—that Brant had undergone some kind of mental breakdown or religious conversion in London. This had led to a serious embarrassment for the governor in Peter Schuyler's own house, which was welcome news to Tobias Franck, since the Schuylers and, more particularly, Robert Livingston, had tried to cut him out of business more than once.

He was looking forward to seeing Brant Vanishing Smoke tonight. But the occasion made him edgy. Snowsnake, a Caughnawaga who had called at his store only once before, during Governor Hunter's conference, had come in with a Dutch river-jockey called Johannes Bratt in tow. Tobias had an instinctive aversion to both of them, though he had used Bratt as a subcontractor on the western routes, where furs could be had cheaper than the Albany cartel would allow, if a man was cheerful about breaking the law.

Tobias stacked his papers and bound the pile with a ribbon before locking it away in the drawer where he kept the ancient manuscripts bequeathed to him by his grandfather, the Cabalist of Safed. Perhaps his visitors would not come tonight after all. The hour was late; the street was quiet apart from the rattle of a cowbell and the guffaws of late topers at the King's tavern.

The venture that Bratt and the Caughnawaga had put before him promised a handy profit. Tobias was also flattered that he had been offered a chance to play a useful role in history, even if the bearers of this offer would not pass muster in polite company. The French Indian had told him in Canada pidgin that the Desauniers sisters had nominated Franck to be their principal broker at Albany. As a mark of their favor, he had brought Tobias some fine pieces of sterling silver, deeply discounted; the markings suggested they might have been taken from Deerfield, the village in Massachusetts sacked and burned by Mission Indians several winters before. Tobias respected the Desauniers women as shrewd merchants who understood the deficiencies of the law much as he did. Laws were made by showy monarchs to suit the whims of fine gentlemen. Law or no law, war or no war, business must go on.

Enterprising women, the Desauniers sisters. It seemed they had made themselves the channel for secret diplomacy, as well as contraband furs. They saw Brant Vanishing Smoke as a coming man among the Mohawks—rightly, in Tobias' view. They wished to arrange his visit to Montreal with a Mohawk delegation, just as Schuyler had fixed the visit of the Four Kings to London. Tobias was sure that the French agent Joncaire or his master Vaudreuil, the governor of New France, must be a moving spirit in these maneuvers. But his allegiance was not to flags and distant kings. There would be rich pickings in the shipments of contraband furs that would accompany the negotiations.

Tobias wound the clock. Where *were* they? His son, Simon, and Sarah, his black servant, were long abed. He would wait a half hour longer before following their example.

He was on his way to the kitchen to warm a pot of milk when he heard a light tap at the door.

He released the bolts, and Vanishing Smoke stepped into the parlor, followed by Bratt and Snowsnake.

"I am glad to be of service," the trader greeted him.

Vanishing Smoke scanned the room, looking for someone else.

"Where is Cloud Singer?" he asked in English.

Tobias looked to the others for guidance.

"We are expecting another envoy," Bratt informed the trader in Dutch. "It will not be a long delay."

"If you will just make yourself comfortable," Tobias told Vanishing Smoke. "I hope the wait will not be long."

Reluctantly, Vanishing Smoke folded his frame onto the bench below the window. He responded stiffly to Tobias' inquiries about the health of his family.

"*Snakira,*" Snowsnake proposed. "Let's have a drink."

"Of course." Tobias brought bottles and decanters. He rarely drank alcohol himself, but Indian trade was unthinkable without it.

Vanishing Smoke refused the first round. But as the wait grew longer, he succumbed to the continued pressure from Snowsnake and Bratt. *Just one drink. Surely it can do no harm.* There was a part of him that still needed it, a hollow his visions had not entirely filled. With his first swallow, the hollow deepened and widened.

Vanishing Smoke sensed there was something deeply wrong, something hidden from him. But its source was not the trader; he was sure of that. In Tobias Franck's house, he was on safe ground.

A sucking mouth had opened inside his belly. He watered it with another drink, and another. Bratt poured from the decanter, then from his own flask. Vanishing Smoke felt dizzy. He drank faster, hoping to regain his balance by calming the spirits that drank with him.

"I am giving you the good stuff," Bratt cried cheerily. "Not the stuff we keep for the Indians."

The scene disturbed Tobias. When the green snake got inside them, the natives were as volatile as a keg of black powder set too close to the fire.

He was relieved when a newcomer knocked at the door. But it was not the missing Caughnawaga envoy. It was a narrow-faced Indian he had never seen before, wearing a circlet of bones and a rattlesnake belt. He refused the offer of a drink.

He said to Vanishing Smoke, "I will take you where you need to go."

Vanishing Smoke was unsteady on his feet, his eyes unfocused. A heavy sweat beaded his brow.

"He is not himself," Tobias protested. "Let him sleep it off here."

"He'll be alright with us," Bratt grinned.

"But what of the arrangements we need to discuss?"

"Details. We'll be round tomorrow."

4.

Come to me, lost spirit. I am whistling to guide you.

Vanishing Smoke floated after these words, in his dreambody.

He had lost all sense of direction. He followed the dark wings of his guide, into deepening fog.

There was a black river below, and an island beyond it. He saw something familiar. It looked like his old hunting dog, snuffling and leaping after a woodchuck.

He called to the dog. It stiffened and cocked its ears, looking for the source of its master's voice.

Vanishing Smoke realized his dog could not see him. There was an invisible screen between them. It must film everything on this side from the sight of those on the island.

He pushed up against it, without meaning to. It yielded and stretched. He felt its suction, pulling him in and through.

This was not right. He was not meant to be here.

Where was the one who had whistled for him and guided him on its dark wings?

With a tremendous effort, he dragged himself out of the enveloping screen. It held onto him like resin, with a thousand streamers and suckers.

Where is my body?

He heard a shearing click, and felt something connected with him go slack. Evil laughter mocked at him, on a foul wind.

5.

In the morning, gathering firewood, Island Woman saw Canada geese flying overhead in tight formation. The birds made the pattern of a dead warrior, like those depicted on painted rocks along the river, or the death hammer her father had carried into battle with the Bark Eaters: arms and legs trailing from a headless, triangular torso.

The next instant, the stomach pains that had seized her during the night returned, and she sprawled full-length on the ground, retching on an empty stomach.

Her mother came looking for her.

"It is not my sickness," she told Redhawk, refusing her offer of medicine tea. "It is my father's sickness. It is passing, because my father is crossing over."

□

They found the body where it had been left to be found, on the bank of the Hudson, reeking of liquor.

The only hint that anything more than alcoholic excess might have been involved was the presence, near the corpse, of the body of a mourning dove with its heart torn out. This meant nothing to the white officials from whom the Mohawks demanded an investigation.

At the insistence of the clanmothers, Hendrick Forked Paths went to Colonel Schuyler to ask for a formal inquiry. Johannes Bratt was summoned, and swore in the presence of Secretary Livingston that he knew nothing of the manner of Vanishing Smoke's death.

"You know how it is with Indians, when the liquor is on them. He went off with French Indians against my protest, in no condition to defend himself from them or from himself."

Bratt disclaimed all knowledge of the whereabouts of the Caughnawaga who had accompanied him to and from the Mohawk castle.

"It's a bad business," Bratt told the commissioners when asked about the meeting at Tobias Franck's house. "Trading with the enemy in a time when honest men are dying for their country. I told them I would have nothing to do with their machinations. It would not surprise me if the French were at the back of this evil. I saw with my own eyes silver thieved from the families that was slaughtered at Deerfield in Mister Franck's house. Not that a Jew would mind picking the bones of our dead."

Livingston ordered a search of Franck's house. They found silver tankards, salt cellars and candlesticks engraved with the initials of the Williams family of Massachusetts. Threatened with arrest, Tobias agreed that he had information that French agents had conspired to murder the Four Kings, though he vigorously denied any personal involvement in their schemes. He was allowed to go free on payment of a stiff fine, and a private agreement with Livingston's factor. He agreed to deliver to James Mackie half the furs he received from Canada over the coming year.

Livingston advised Governor Hunter that there was now no impediment to the consummation of the Schoharie land deal. The thankful governor duly advised the Lords of Trade that the Mohawk Patent had been lawfully endorsed by the Mohawk Nation.

As word spread in Mohawk country that the French had poisoned Vanishing Smoke, the warriors rallied behind Hendrick Forked Paths, eager for revenge. "The eyes of our ancestors are upon us!" Hendrick roared in front of the war post, raising the hatchet. "We will go into battle with our hungry ghosts!"

None of this satisfied Vanishing Smoke's family, though Talldeer danced with the warriors.

Island Woman could not understand how her father had allowed himself to be made drunk by river scum like Johannes Bratt and the shifty Caughnawaga who would not look one in the eye.

"I hope you never know," Redhawk told her. "There is a demon who lives in the white man's bottle. Once he has made a space for himself inside you, he comes back again and again. Unless you fill that hole with something stronger than him."

"But my father was a dreamer," Island Woman protested. "Surely he had that strength. Surely he dreamed this before it happened."

"You speak of things that can only be known through *dreaming*. Remember what your father taught you."

Look for me in your dreams.

Island Woman remembered. She would ask her father to identify his killers, and would find the way to repay them. She would honor the light that had lived in him, even if that light had failed.

☐

"Now we fold you in the blanket of our mother Earth," the elder spoke over the grave. They had folded Vanishing Smoke's body like that of a fetus, ready to be reborn. His medicine bundle and his pipe lay with him, together with a small statuette. If his bones were disturbed, the part of his soul that would remain close to the earth could reside with this stone figurine.

The elder shook his rattle.

"I die this life," Redhawk announced, among the circle of her family and friends. Then she screamed the words so loudly they scared the crows out of the cornfield and the pigeons out of the sugar bush.

Redhawk flung herself on the ground, rolling her face deep into the muck. She grabbed at her hair and pulled out great tufts. She ripped at her clothes until they hung off her in shreds. She brought out her little treasures—silver brooches, pieces of cloth saved for a new skirt or leggings, looking glasses and jew's harps—and handed them out at random.

That night, the widow wandered the village like a ghost, white-faced with ashes from the fire she had extinguished when they brought back the body. She would eat only cold food, leave the lodge only after dark and dress without ornament, without sweetgrass or oil for her hair, for many days to come. She would continue in mourning for a full year, until the sun had journeyed to the south and returned.

6.

When Vanishing Smoke returned to his body, he saw that he had been shut out in the shadowlands for too long.

He would not walk in this sack of meat and bones again.

He felt immense relief, at laying down this burden.

It was exceeded by his longing to be with his loved ones and fulfill his promise to watch over them, and by the grief and guilt that flooded in when he remembered how he had allowed Bratt and Snowsnake to get him drunk.

But it was not the drink that killed my body. It was Two Hearts who shut me out and cut the cord. Where is he?

As clarity returned to him, in his dreambody, he was torn between the desire to pursue his killers and the love that drew him toward Two Rivers. He followed the deeper call of his heart, and was instantly back inside his lodge.

They were all gathered there: Redhawk, Island Woman, Talldeer and New Smile, who clapped her chubby hands and pouted her lips at him in a ploppy kiss.

Can you see me, little one? Maybe you can. Little ones live very close to the dreaming.

The love he felt for his wife and children—the love and anguish projected from them—moved through him like a bullet of light. Was it possible to endure such intensity of longing and pain?

In this moment, the light that exploded in his heart center moved toward a greater source. It made a bridge of light, shimmering like the Milky Way. It offered a passage beyond the surface world and the planes of confusion and appetency that form miasmal swamps around it.

Vanishing Smoke looked upward. So the stories of the old ones were true. The Path of Souls really looked like a bridge of stars. With the opening of the clear light, he felt himself rising, borne effortlessly aloft, toward a realm of impersonal, unconditional love. As he rose higher, some part of himself fell away. He looked down, and saw his dreambody drifting down, like an abandoned set of clothes.

This drew the attention of other beings. They came swimming on the astral tides. They had the unclean, ghostly pallor of possums scavenging by night.

Vanishing Smoke did not wish to leave his second body among these creatures. He turned his back on the clear light, and swooped down to reclaim his dreambody. As he did so, his pain and longing returned with doubled force, accompanied by a murderous hatred for the men who had cut his life cord before it was played out.

Out of the physical body, all the desires and emotions he had known in the flesh—love and hate, hunger and sexual craving, the warrior's blood frenzy—were vastly stronger and keener. He resolved that he would use this power to protect his loved ones. But first, he must destroy those who had wronged him.

I will drive their souls out of their bodies and hunt them through the Netherworld.

As the killing rage possessed him, the vampire spirits scattered, to observe him from a safer distance. As he set out to find the men he would punish, a flock of pale shadows flapped after him.

CHAPTER 8

CONRAD'S PROBLEM

1.

On the day Vanishing Smoke left his body behind him for good, a fleet carrying four hundred Royal Marines and fifteen hundred New England volunteers sailed through the narrows into the harbor of Port Royal, fighting a tide that rushed like a millstream.

Colonel Nicholson instructed his gunners to set up batteries on shore at once and commence a brisk cannonade of the small French garrison inside the fort, while sappers were put to work digging zigzag entrenchments that snaked toward the walls. He sent Iroquois rangers into the interior under Captain John Livingston—a relation of the powerful Robert Livingston of Livingston Manor—to prevent any interference by the fiercely independent Acadian settlers or by French Indians whipped up by their soldier-priest. The scouts were the gift of the Four Kings; Nicholson did not know that their number had been reduced to three.

The siege of Port Royal confirmed his belief that Canada was ripe for the plucking if he could only move the English government to act with some force and resolution. One week after Nicholson's troops disembarked, Commandant Subercase surrendered the town and, with it, the whole French province of Acadia—to the future delight of diners in Louisiana, who would inherit its Cajun cuisine.

On the English side, the casualties included a Wampanoag Indian from Martha's Vineyard named Nicodemus Skuhwattan. During the short campaign he became a good friend of Nicholas Etakoam, a Mahican who had once been called a King. The two Indians promised each other that if either was killed, the survivor would carry his army pay and his share of the spoils of war to his widow.

114

Colonel Nicholson's ambitious young Scots associate, Samuel Vetch, was appointed the first governor of what would now be styled the Province of Nova Scotia. In the incestuous society of colonial New York, this would bring a glow of family pride, and patriotic kudos, both to Robert Livingston, who was Vetch's father-in-law, and to Peter Schuyler, the uncle of the bride.

2.

Conrad Weiser stood in the clearing among the pines with his arms folded, his bare knees showing through the rents in his woolen breeches. James Mackie, sent by Livingston to silence the griping from the Palatines that was beginning to annoy Governor Hunter, contemplated Conrad with the deepest misgivings. The Weiser brat was only fourteen, according to the lists, but he was as tall as his father and almost as sturdy. Not an ounce of loose flesh on him. The skull showed under the skin. The jawline was strong and firm. There were deep hollows under the cheekbones. The boy was half-starved. All the Germans in the camps were in similar condition, though Livingston's man had trained himself not to see this. Conrad's head tilted down, displaying a buttress of bony forehead above the pale, deepset eyes that made Mackie think of a young bull getting ready to charge.

"Please to tell me, Mister Mackie," Conrad said in his fluent but stilted English. "Would you take this meat home with you to feed your wife and children?"

An open barrel of salt pork stood on the ground between them. The wooden barrel was unusually solid. Charging the governor for a few extra pounds of wood, in place of meat, was an easy way to increase profits. However it was not the weight of the rations the boy was complaining about.

Balancing on one foot, Conrad set the other on the rim of the barrel. He gave it a tentative push, and the barrel rocked back and forth. Livingston's man turned his head away from the stink of the mess of spoiled meat that slopped through a thick crust of salt and oozed down the side.

"The pork is not bad," Mackie pronounced, resisting the urge to cover his nose and mouth. "It may be a little overseasoned."

"We would not give it to our dogs."

"Be reasonable, lad. Beggars can't be choosers."

"We are not beggars. And you can take this shit to your own dinner table. We will not pay for it. Please to inform Mister Livingston."

"Pay for it?" Mackie cawed, half-admiring the boy's insolence. "Dammit, you lot don't have two pennies to rub together. It's all on the governor's account, and don't you forget it. You Palatines are a mannerless bunch. You should thank your betters you are fed at all."

"We pay with the sweat of our bodies," Conrad responded. His gesture embraced the settlers' log cabins, their little plots of wheat and potatoes, and the pine forests they had been ordered to rind and cut and burn to make tar for the Royal Navy. "We are set to work like animals, on land we do not own, so you and your master can grow even fatter. But we are not mules, or oxen. We are free men, and we will fight for the rights God gave us."

Mackie whistled. "You've become quite the poorhouse lawyer, young Master Weiser. But you can save your fine speeches. They ain't worth a twopenny damn up here. You are a bound servant, and if the fancy takes me I'll send you to Jersey to break rocks in a chain gang."

Conrad's lips disappeared. He shifted his ground a little, then put all his force behind a kick that hurled the barrel of slops toward Livingston's factor. With an ugly, sucking noise the contents erupted from the barrel and spattered over Mackie, coating him from head to foot in a fetid, yellow-pink slime.

"The devil take you, for you are his own spawn!" Mackie cursed, coughing and spitting. "Oh, sweet Jesus." The stench was worse than a cesspool. It made his head spin and his stomach churn. He gripped his cane by the shaft, lashing out at the source of his discomfort with the heavy silver knob.

The boy danced rings around him, fists clenched.

There were whoops of applause and encouragement from the Palatines who had gathered around. Buxom, ribald Magdalina Zeh laughed loudest. Though old enough to be Conrad's mother, Dina Zeh fancied the boy, and her bosom heaved with excitement as she watched him tormenting the factor.

"You'll pay for this!" Mackie yelled.

"Look out, Conrad!" Eva Feck screamed. "He's got a gun."

Mackie fumbled with the short fusee. He could hardly miss at this range. The gun was loaded with swanshot, likely to maim rather than kill, which was what he wanted. He would wipe the grins off those oafish faces.

As he squeezed the trigger, Dina Zeh landed a tremendous blow to the base of his spine with the handle of a chopping ax. Mackie howled and lost his aim, driving a squall of crows from the branches of a white pine.

Greta Weiser came rushing into the scrum, her yellow hair flying out from under her kerchief. She grabbed Conrad's arm. "Come away *now*, before the Englishman kills you."

Flushed with triumph and the spirit of rebellion that was stirring among the camp people—many of whom, following Dina Zeh's example, had picked up staves and axes—Conrad ignored his stepmother.

Mackie considered his odds and did not like them.

To cover his retreat, he spoke to the woman who was trying to pull the boy away. "By God, madam, if you are this man's mother, you will see he is beaten thoroughly before he is flogged by his betters."

Dina Zeh threw a clod of earth at him. Women and girls scooped up harder projectiles.

"White niggers," Mackie swore as he stomped away, followed by hoots and catcalls. These Palatines were a damned difficult, stiff-necked people. What had possessed Her Majesty to send them? The affair would have to be reported to Robert Livingston, and to Jean Cast, the half-Frenchman the governor employed to communicate with the Germans. The seeds of rebellion must be crushed before they took root. Nothing else would take root in this bitter season, with the ground already frozen hard.

3.

"I know how to feed a man." Dina Zeh winked at Conrad. "Come to my cabin when the children are asleep."

Conrad was tempted, but scared as well. Not of Dina's husband. Weakened by fever and the rigors of the voyage—and (some said) by his wife's drunken rages—he had succumbed to the first bitter cold and been buried before the earth froze. Nor of the other men he had seen slinking into Dina's cabin after dark; had he not proven he could hold his own with any man? Certainly he was not afraid of his father's judgment. For all his Bible reading and patriarchal pretences, Johann Weiser had forfeited any right to judge the morals of others—in Conrad's eyes—when he had taken Greta into his bed.

After all the nights of spying and wanting, was he simply scared of *doing it?* What if he couldn't get it up, when it came to the test? What if he just didn't *want* this big, meaty woman, as wide at the waist as he was at the hips, her hands roughened by work in the fields?

Yet, as he watched the color rise from her throat to her cheeks, he felt himself thicken, as if all his blood was rushing to one place, a place that was not ruled by his head and all its endless complications. *What are you saving yourself for?* an inner voice goaded him. *Why not now? Why not with her?*

"I'll come," he said thickly.

"That's good." Dina took his hand. She enclosed his thumb in her fist and gave it a quick pull, as if she were milking a cow. She chuckled deep down—a rich belly rumble—and strutted away, with a roll of her hips, to round up her children. She had at least six or seven, one only a year younger than Conrad.

Someone was watching him. He blushed when he saw it was Eva Feck. Her breasts had barely begun to bud. He marveled at the calm this girl seemed to inhabit. Sometimes he could almost see it about her body, a soft radiance, a gentle swirl of light that shifted from white to palest lavender. Could a girl like this ever understand the storm in his body?

Eva wanted to know if he would help her to gather firewood. Of course he would go. Later, when she asked him to read to her brothers and sisters—he was the best reader in the East Camp, next to his father—he agreed to this too. He had no wish to confront his family, and the reproaches of his stepmother, over the incident with Livingston's agent before he had called on Dina Zeh. And the activity would keep his mind off his coming performance, or lack of it.

☐

Conrad stepped in larger footprints, frozen into the ground. The night air pricked his exposed skin. It carried the smell of woodsmoke.

A dog barked as he neared the Zeh cabin, and he flattened himself against the tree. He knew the dog, and cooed to it, "Tristan, sshh. Be still."

Dina was at the door, beckoning him in, a blanket wrapped around her shift. As Conrad stepped through the doorway, she opened the blanket and drew him inside it, into an immensity of warmth and yearning. Her body molded itself to him like a pile of goosefeather pillows. He had not felt such springy softness since leaving the home his mother had made snug and safe in the Rhineland. It was intoxicating to be folded in all this warmth, to breathe a woman's skin, to feel her flow to welcome the force that was pulsing in him, pulsing and thrusting.

"Ssshhh!" Dina warned him, as he had warned the dog. "You'll wake the little ones."

She led him past their sleeping forms, to the space she had made private, with a curtain hung from ceiling hooks in the one-room cabin. The firelight caressed her white skin, making rose-dark shadows in the folds of her flesh. There was something in the scene that grieved him: a memory of the night he had seen his father plunging between Greta's thighs. He shivered and drew back, but Dina held him fast, feeling the ridge that had formed in his breeches.

"You're hungry," she murmured, approving. "Best take a sip of beer to set you at your ease."

The homemade beer was mealy, deeper and stronger than the poor excuse for ship's beer that Livingston supplied the camps as part of his contract with the governor. Conrad swallowed in fast gulps, wanting to blur the particulars of the scene, to shut out the glimpse of the rolls of fat around Dina's middle, the stretchmarks at the tops of her breasts.

"Come on, little bull," she goaded when the beerpot was empty. "Don't be a cockteaser."

She had it out. She was stroking and pulling. As her breasts tumbled free from her shift, he closed his eyes so as not to look at the taut red nipples, so as not to come before he had started. She squatted on top of him and drew him inside.

"That's it," she encouraged him. "Harder. Come on, fuck me *hard*. Suck my tits. Go on, that's the way."

He wished she would stop talking. The coarse words revolted him. She talked like a dockside whore.

"Don't stop!"

He gasped as his face was enveloped by her breasts. His eyes tight shut, he willed her to be all women. He thought of the slender native girl he had seen in the canoe on the river, of Greta, of a dark woman in an ancient land he had encountered only in dreams, who danced with a golden serpent.

His back arched. He was leaping beyond himself, beyond what was possible, as the salmon leaps at the waterfall.

"That's the way. Give it to me strong! Give me your juice!"

Not now. Not with her. But the part of him that said this was defeated. He gave himself over to the urgent rhythm, until he exploded inside her, leaping again and again and again.

He lay panting, his heart hammering at his ribs.

"Aaaah," Dina moaned. "Stay like that. Just for a bit."

She was doing something, probing with her curled fingers. He did not look, even when she moaned louder and sweat poured off her, drenching his face and chest.

The full weight of her body collapsed onto him, pressing the last air from his lungs. He saw himself lying under an immense cow. Then she rolled off him, and sadness came in with the bite of a cold draft through a chink in the log wall.

He could not hold it in. He sobbed and sniffed like a baby.

"It's alright, little cabbage." Dina hugged him. "Let it out. Don't be ashamed. It takes a strong man to cry."

She rocked him in her arms, humming an old song.

"It's your first time, isn't it?"

He clamped his jaws tight. He wasn't going to admit *that*. He was appalled by what he saw when he looked at her. Her skin was mottled and splotchy. Her swollen nipples were an indecent shade of scarlet.

"Is it all right if I go?"

"No." She laughed. "It is *not* all right. A young one like you has plenty to give, and tonight you're giving it to *me*. But first we will eat."

Supper was a warm stew, made with squirrel meat, he guessed, though it tasted passably like chicken, washed down with more of the malty homemade beer. With food in his belly he no longer felt faint, but the sense of disgust returned as the woman exposed her floppy backside, putting dishes away, and the smell of sweat and sexual emissions hung heavy in the air.

He let her play with him, and was startled when his cock hardened straight away and grew longer and thicker than before.

"The prince of sticks!" Dina whispered joyfully. "Now you're getting to know where to put it, you can take your time. Don't come until I say!"

She is all women, he reminded himself.

She did not finish with him until the gray hour before dawn, the twilight of the wolf, when she threw him out into the snow with a wet kiss and a gurgle of satisfaction. He staggered out to punch a hole in the ice and rinse himself off in the frigid water before he crept back to his family's cabin.

He was thankful that nobody stirred. The chorus of snores and steady breathing went on as he tiptoed to his straw mattress and curled up under the blanket.

Soon he was shivering again. It was almost as cold in the cabin as it was outside. There were only a few red sparks among the dying embers. He sat up, intending to put a few sticks on the fire, and took a few steps across the floor.

He stopped short, because someone was moving in the room. A woman. Was it Greta, going to tend the fire ahead of him?

No. This woman was smaller and slimmer than Greta, her long neck graceful as a swan's.

Goosebumps ran up his arms and across his shoulders.

It's my mother.

But this was not possible. It was the delusion of a gypsy fortuneteller in London, returning to him now through his fatigue and guilt.

The figure beckoned to him. He could see her features quite clearly. But all of her was pearly white, the white of the nightgown his mother had worn on her deathbed.

She beckoned again.

Something else was wrong. He could see through her, to the black silhouette of the tree beyond the oilpaper that filled the window frame. She had substance, but she was not made of ordinary stuff.

The cold moved into his marrow.

"It's not *you*," he told the shade. "You're not my mother. You're a shadow, a dream."

He backed away. He told himself that if he went back to bed, everything would be normal in the morning.

He turned to slide back under the blanket, then froze.

He saw himself lying in bed, turned on his right side, his knees drawn up like a baby's. He gaped at his body in horror. Had he died?

The thing that was and was not his mother was waiting for him.

There was neither love nor hate in the eyes, only cold appetency.

Had she been watching him with Dina? Had she come to punish him?

"Go away."

She waited, wordless, near the door.

"Go away. I'm not ready to go with you."

His little sister groaned and stirred. "Wake up, Sarah!" he urged her. There was no response. "Wake up, everybody!" Nobody seemed to hear him, except the ghost who watched without speaking.

Go back to your body. The command came as a thought that took on words. He felt sure it did not come from inside himself, but it had no outside origin he could identify. *Go back to your body,* the command was repeated.

"But how?"

You do it every night in your sleep, whether or not you remember. All you have to do is wish it.

Hovering between terror and bewilderment, Conrad tried to focus his attention on his physical body. He remembered how it had been used—stretching and spurting beyond what he had thought possible. He recalled the pleasurable soreness in his groin, the bruise on his upper thigh, the bite marks on his shoulders. The scene flickered. He had the sensation of falling, and landing with a bump.

A voice far away was calling his name.

"Conrad!" it called louder. Now he felt himself swimming up from a great depth. He tensed and relaxed his fingers. They moved. He opened his eyes, and immediately threw an arm across them to shut out the cruel white light, refracted from the snow outside the open door of the cabin.

"There's work to be done!" Greta informed him, her fists on her hips. "And we need to talk about where you were last night."

4.

Conrad promised himself he would not go back to widow Zeh's cabin, but when she gave him the eye he came running.

"Like a dog to its vomit," old Isaac Loucks, who did not miss much, chided him when the snow was deep on the ground, layered like wedding cake, fresh powder over ice and slush.

The old man surprised Conrad, bobbing up from behind the shed where the men of Weiser's section stored their tools.

"Are you spying on me?"

"What's to tell and who's to tell it to?" the old man responded evasively. "Just a word to the wise. A young man like you needs to keep his strength up. And it's a man's job to feed them that can't provide for themselves."

"I've been out hunting every day, with the dog." He was referring to Tristan, the shaggy mutt Dina had taken in, who now came running up to nuzzle Conrad's hand as that of an old friend.

"That dog's no good for hunting. Lover's name, lover's ways. No wonder you two get on so well."

"There's nothing to be had round here but squirrel and deermouse. I've not seen a deer all month."

"A nice leg of lamb never spoiled an appetite."

"What are you talking about?"

"Have you seen Livingston Manor?"

"I've seen the house from the river."

"You should take a closer look, from the land side. Mister Livingston may have married Dutch, but he is still a Scotsman in his taste for sheep."

"You mean he has sheep pens?"

"That dog could earn his keep for once," Loucks ruminated. "I'd say he has more than a pinch of sheepdog in him. He might cut you out a fat one, at that. Better be sharp about it, though. Robert Livingston won't hang you for shaming his hired man, not with the war on and our men needed by the English. But he'll flay you alive if you touch one hair of his sheep and he gets to hear of it."

□

Loucks had one more gift for him: a broken snowshoe, made by a River Indian. Conrad worked two nights trying to copy it. He used hickory splints for the frame, breaking several before Dina Zeh showed him how to make them pliable. With cross struts in place and the ends tied together, the shoes looked like flounders. Dina wove a web of deerstrings inside the frame, leaving a hole at the front for his toes. It took some experimentation before they worked out how to tie the snowshoes to the boy's feet. When they lashed the middle of his feet to the shoes with rawhide thongs, running a loop around the heels to give further support, Conrad found he could walk on the snow with remarkable ease. While his toes sank a little below the surface of the snow, his heels rose in the natural rhythm of his stride, while the snowshoes kept him from plunging down into the pack. But he could not walk like this in his creaking old boots. He decided he would go in two pairs of woolen hose, though Dina worried about frostbite.

Then Eva Feck brought him a present: a pair of deerskin moccasins, lined with fur, that must have taken her weeks to make.

"She's got a crush on you," Dina told him, when she saw the moccasins.

"Eva's just a girl," Conrad shrugged.

"Maybe that's not what *she* thinks. Don't mistake me, lovie. I'm not the jealous sort. You'll go to school with me until you've learned enough to school ladies your own age. Just remember that I am the one who will decide when your studies are finished."

"Dina—"

"Not a word. Get away with you and fetch me my dinner. I am sick to death of squirrel and salt pork."

"Can I take Tristan?"

"If you promise to bring him back." She gave him a squeeze, dropping her hand down to pinch his bottom. "And take care of your little ass. I've got more work for it."

□

Conrad went to bed after supper, and rose again soon after midnight to begin his walk to Livingston Manor. He looked up into a field of stars. Orion, the hunter, commanded the zenith. Though the moon had waned to a meager sliver, his snow-covered path was bright. Tristan came at his whistle, after only a single, exploratory bark.

"Good boy." Conrad scratched his chest, under the ruff of fur. "Just remember to do what you're told when we get to Livingston's."

There was only one scare during the walk. The sound of something heavy, crashing through the trees, propelled Tristan into the woods like a bullet from a gun, and Conrad lost nearly half an hour—as best he could judge—before the dog came back.

"Do that again," he promised, "and you'll spend all day tied to a tree."

His legs and ankles were aching by the time he came within sight of Livingston's barns and stone walls, and the proud manor house with its columns beyond, and the snowshoes—so light at the beginning—dragged like leaden weights. It was not yet dawn, and the lights in the Livingston house were out. The only man-made light Conrad could see was the dull red glow of a fire banked low, in a shelter behind a stone wall. The fire of a guard or a shepherd?

He had learned from old man Loucks—who had traded further information for a load of firewood and the promise of roast mutton—that the Livingston sheep were no ordinary livestock. They were prime breeders, handpicked in the Scottish highlands to survive the extremities of the climate in the colonies. They were the first sheep that had ever been seen in New York, maybe the first in North America. Livingston planned to crossbreed and grow a superior strain of wool that would command top prices and win him respect as a great man in the science of agriculture.

As he crept closer to the wall, and the sheep pens beyond it, Conrad observed that Livingston treated his four-legged friends rather better than his two-legged tenants. The sheep were protected from the elements inside a fine new barn, well-stocked with oats and hay. A lone ram raised its head from chewing on a sapling to contemplate Conrad over its black nose.

Tristan rumbled. "Hush," Conrad commanded.

He considered his options. Scottish shepherds (if Loucks was to be believed) lived close to their flocks, slept with them, smelled like them, came to look like them. There might be a man inside the barn. Almost certainly, there was someone dozing—or watching—near the fire in the shelter next to the barn. To cut a couple of sheep from the flock and herd them through the gate would involve covering a hundred yards without cover, even if Tristan did his stuff silently.

The dog was alert and eager, wagging his tail.

Maybe it was true that he was born to this work.

Could he send Tristan in by himself, trusting the sheepdog in him to drive the flock through the open gate?

How much noise would that make? Conrad had no idea how much of a racket a flock of frightened sheep might make. But it would surely be enough to rouse the drowsiest shepherd.

Maybe there was a back way into the barn. Skirting the wall, he ran at a half-crouch, the dog at his heels.

He was glad to see there was a back door, secured by a wooden bar. As he prised it loose, Tristan snarled and bared his teeth.

"Hush!"

The dog's hair bristled. Before Conrad could respond to the danger, a powerful arm was clamped around his windpipe. Several men massed around the boy. Their faces blackened by charcoal, their buckskins darked by grease and soot, they looked like moving bushes or tree stumps.

Tristan sprang at Conrad's captor, but was kicked aside. He was ready to try again, but paused when one of the attackers let out a strange, low, keening sound. Tristan cocked his head, whimpered, and lay down with his head between his paws.

Indians, Conrad realized with a mixture of relief and fear.

"You—" One of them poked his chest. "You are Livingston's man?"

No. He could not get the syllable out, but shook his head as hard as he could manage.

"What are you?"

The grip on his throat was loosened.

"I'm hungry."

They spoke to each other rapidly, in their own language, a series of clicks interrupting the quicksilver flow. It was like no language Conrad had heard in Europe. It contained the voices of birds, the grunt of wild animals, the sawing and cracking of trees in hard winter.

They had come to some decision. Conrad swallowed against the dryness in his mouth. He had heard that Indians killed without a second thought, sudden as rattlesnakes.

"Speak to your dog," ordered the one who spoke English.

"Here, boy." The dog ran to him. He cradled Tristan's head in his arms.

"Good. We do not like to kill dogs." He spoke to the others in his own tongue. Two of them fanned out to keep watch. Ignoring Conrad, the others slipped into the barn. The sheep bleated to their feet, banging against the wooden walls. Part of the flock spilled out the other side of the barn, into the snow-covered paddock. The Indians returned through the back door, hauling the carcasses of several sheep whose throats they had cut, making runnels of blood in the snow. They had hand sleds prepared. With a few twists of rawhide, they secured their prey to the barrows, and started dragging them in the direction of the frozen river.

The one who spoke English paused. He pointed at Conrad's snowshoes. "Where you learn that?"

"I copied a River Indian."

This drew a short, barking laugh. "That's good. Mahicans make the best. Moccasins not so bad." Nicholas Etakoam, who had once been called a King, tapped Conrad between the collarbones. "I remember you."

I'll remember you, too, Conrad told himself, noting the flight of thunderbirds tattooed on the right side of the Mahican's face and the serpent sideplate on the stock of his firelock.

As the Indians made off, he heard distant shouts. There were lights in the Livingston house. He had only an instant to decide whether to make off with his life—before armed men fell upon him—or take what he had come for.

He ran into the barn. There were a couple of stragglers left: wild, woolly-haired beasts, one oatmeal in color, the other soft gray. He quickened his stride, aiming to get between them and the door to the paddock, flailing his arms to drive them the way he had come.

Tristan was quicker. He bolted ahead, cut off the sheep's advance, yipping and snapping to turn them to his master's design. The sheep obeyed. Soon they were heaving through the snow, with Tristan at their heels.

Conrad looked back at the mess they were leaving in their wake and realized that Livingston's men could hardly fail to spot the tracks.

He needed to find a place—quickly!—where he could bury their trail, slaughter the sheep, and get them onto some kind of conveyance like the ones the Indians had used. He thought of the river, and of skating on the ice. There was surely no faster way to travel this country, in this season. But he couldn't skate in snowshoes, and he still needed a conveyance for the sheep. Maybe his best recourse would be to butcher the sheep, carry what he could manage on his back, and leave the rest of the carcasses somewhere they would not be found by other carnivores until he could come back. A messy business, but he was hungry enough for it.

There was a chaos of fallen trees over to the left, the effect of a blizzard or windstorm. If he could get the sheep through that, maybe he could mask their tracks and find a place of hiding.

Floundering and complaining in the snow, the sheep balked at fighting their way through the spiked wind drifts of spruce and pine. Only Tristan, snarling and biting, kept them moving, and Conrad had to drag them by main force over the larger obstacles.

Then he saw his stupidity. In place of footprints, he was now leaving tufts of wool, a trail any deskbound quill-driver could follow, let alone the hard bushlopers or native trackers Robert Livingston would certainly employ to hunt down the men who had taken his sheep.

There was nothing for it but to take what he could, on his own back, without losing more time. A red dawn was breaking, and the figures of a dozen or more men were clearly visible at the edge of the Livingston estate.

Though he had no particular sympathy for sheep, he avoided looking in their eyes as he cut their throats with the long hunting knife he had gotten for winning a footrace between the boys of the East and West Camps. He was appalled by the quantity of blood they gouted into the snow.

He tested the weight of the carcasses. Under the fluffy hair, they were not so big. He found he could sling one from his shoulders with little difficulty with the rawhide straps he had brought in his pouch. He tried adding the second sheep, but capsized under the burden, nearly breaking one of his snowshoes in the process. He resigned himself to hoisting the second carcass into the cleft of a tree. Maybe he would be able to come back to it. If not, perhaps someone with more deserving of it than Robert Livingston would find it. Any starving wolf had a better claim.

He set off with his kill in good spirits. But the weight grew heavier with every stride, threatening to tip him over. A new rush of energy came with the sound of a hunting horn, followed by shots and rough shouts, from somewhere behind him. But his spurt of speed brought on paralyzing cramps. He was forced to sit down and nurse his calf muscles.

He gnawed a little piece of dried meat that Dina had given him. The sun glared off the snow. It was painful to look back. When he did, he could see no pursuers. Perhaps Livingston's men had caught up with the Indians and were fully engaged with them. That would account for the shots.

"Out!" he commanded Tristan, who was licking the matted blood on the sheep's coat. He slipped his arms through the straps, vowing not to stop again until he was home. *Roast mutton for lunch. Very pink.* Dina probably wouldn't mind eating it raw.

He chuckled at the prospect of how Dina would reward him.

Tristan barked as a shadow fell over them.

"I reckon that would be Livingston's sheep."

The giant who loomed in front of him was as dark as the Indians who had blackened their skin for concealment, but his color was his own. He wore a floppy hat and a hunting coat with a flap over the shoulders that gave the effect of a short cape. He was trimming his nails with a knife that made Conrad's look like something that belonged on a butter dish.

"You steal that yourself?"

"I don't answer to you."

The black giant drove the point of his knife into the trunk of the tree behind Conrad's head, so forcefully a splinter drew blood from the boy's ear.

"I asked you polite," he said, withdrawing the blade.

"The dog helped."

Tristan bared his teeth. "Mighty fierce dog." A black dog, built to the same proportions as his master, materialized at his heels and claimed Tristan's full attention. He ran after her, sniffing and wagging his tail.

"Loose bitch." The black man grinned. "What's your name, boy?"

"Conrad. What's yours?"

"Listen to the mouth on you. *I* ask the questions, you got that? I guess you'd be one of them white niggers."

"*What did you call me?*"

"That's what they call you people up at Livingston Hall. You ought to know that, being as how you is so free with Mister Livingston's property and all."

Conrad waited, calculating his chances if he dropped the sheep and tried to fight it out with the giant. Or simply ran away. Something in him rebelled against the idea of giving up what he had worked so hard to get, even if the odds were horrendous.

"What do you mean to do?"

"I haven't got round to figuring it out yet."

"Are you one of Livingston's men?"

"You're on Livingston land. Everything here belongs to Livingston. Including your hide, I reckon."

"I won't be taken alive."

"That's fine by me. I figure he'll like you better in the same condition as that ewe you've got there. Except he'll want your balls separate. I guess you've got balls, running around with a Livingston sheep in all this white shit. Pity you don't have a brain to go with them. You stand around here shooting the breeze, they gonna get you for sure."

Conrad blinked.

"On your way, boy. You stupider than you look?"

"I thought you were Livingston's man."

"Oh, Mister Livingston *owns* me all right. That's on a piece of paper he got from Missus Kidd. But he don't own my opinions. And my opinion is that a boy that is called a nigger deserves a chance, even if he is the wrong color. All you gotta do is give me a little piece of that sheep."

"Of course. Just cut off as much as you want."

"Not for me, boy. I can't abide the taste of mutton. Just a few scraps to put off the dogs Livingston's trackers have got coming after you. In case a loose bitch ain't enough excitement for them."

"I don't know how to thank you." Conrad marveled at his luck.

"Can't think of a thing myself right now. Except the pleasure of seeing a white man in more trouble than me. About that name. They call me Cato, like I'm a dog, cause that's the way they is. If you get to see me again, you'll call me Fatumbi, cause that's who I am. Can you say that?"

"Fa-tum-bi."

"Not bad. You've got an ear on you. You speak Indian yet?"

"Not yet."

"I expect you will. You want to get along anywhere, you gotta drink the local firewater and know how to tell a man a joke in a language he can understand."

"Your English is very good, I mean—" Conrad stumbled, fearing he had caused offence.

"You mean for an African? Yours ain't bad either. For a white nigger."

CHAPTER 9

WAR MAGIC

1.

Fresh from the triumph of his expedition against French Acadia, Colonel Nicholson sailed back to England to present his trophies to the Queen and make sure the new government delivered on the promises she had made to him and the Four Kings. He carried home exotic souvenirs, including the beaded costume of an Indian princess, for Abigail Masham, the Queen's confidante, and Mrs. Masham again rewarded his attentions. She plucked her cocky but dissipated brother, John Hill, out of the gaming dens of London and persuaded Queen Anne to commission him a brigadier general, in command of the land forces that would sweep the French from North America. The last of the Stuart sovereigns was pleased by the addition of Nova Scotia to her dominions, and tickled by the notion that she would end her reign as Queen-Emperor, reigning over all the forests and rivers of America. She sent Francis Nicholson back across the ocean with three regiments and a battle fleet of fifteen ships of the line and forty support vessels, under the command of Admiral Sir Hoveden Walker, as dedicated a bottle man as ever walked a bridge.

Nicholson's strategy for the conquest of Canada was as simple as a pair of shears. The point of one blade was aimed at the rock fortress of Quebec. This was the target for Walker's fleet and General Hill's regulars. They would sail up the Saint Lawrence River, scale the mountain, and take Quebec by storm. The point of the other blade was aimed at Montreal. This was Nicholson's personal objective. He would lead an army of volunteers from New England and New York, with their allies of the Five Nations, through the forest to Lake Champlain, where they

would board a fleet of flatboats and canoes and take the French from
the rear.

The success of Nicholson's column would depend on the solidity of
the Iroquois alliance and the patriotic fervor of the colonists. Nicholson
counted on the fall of Acadia, and the personal influence of Peter Schuyler, Robert Livingston and the chiefs they had recruited to win the Five
Nations to his side. But Acadia was remote from the Real People. And
though the Mohawks had vowed revenge against the French they held
guilty for the death of Vanishing Smoke, the Five Nations heard many
voices, and swayed like high grass in the wind.

"We must show them the size of our fist," Schuyler counseled Nicholson when they met at New London.

They invited Mohawks, Oneidas and Onondagas to visit Boston.
The Indians inspected Walker's battle fleet, riding at anchor in the Nantasket Roads, and the army tents that studded the pastures of Noddle's
Island. They returned to their villages to report that, this time, the English fleet was no phantom, and that the British had fielded the largest
regular fighting force the Real People had ever seen.

Schuyler donated a two-year-old bull to the Mohawk castle for the
war feast. Hendrick butchered it with his own ax, and lapped the hot
blood. He invoked the memory of Vanishing Smoke, and of other Mohawks who had died at the hands of the French and their native allies.
As he led the Burned Knives in the war dance, the war frenzy built until
it seemed to possess the whole village. Even one of the *rotiyaner*—the
traditional chiefs—removed his antlered headdress and cut off his hair.
Talldeer came running with his father's death hammer to join the dance,
and stomped about smashing the skulls of unseen enemies until Redhawk rushed into the circle and dragged him away by the ear. The grown
men laughed, and the boy fought back tears of shame.

"I will avenge my father's death!" Talldeer promised his mother.

"You are too young for the warpath," Redhawk told him. "And this
is not the way your father chose. Besides, we do not know that the
French killed your father."

But he was lost to reason, driven by the fierce rhythms of the dance,
by the violence of stamping feet, by the dark ones who moved in the
smoke, drawn by blood and the fury that possessed Hendrick Forked
Paths. Hendrick threw back his head and howled. Talldeer bayed with
him.

Island Woman watched men and boys shapeshifting in their second
bodies, taking on the forms of warbirds and predatory animals. She
watched the hungry ghosts move from the smoke to dance with the
living and enter their bodies.

This was why a *royaner* was forbidden to wear the living bones—the
badge of his authority as a chief of the Confederacy—when he decided

to go on the warpath. When a chief became a warrior, he ceased to be a *royaner*, a "man of good mind," and became one again only when he had laid down the hatchet. A man who went to war was known to be half-crazy. He gave himself over to a raw and primal energy that was a stranger both to fear and love.

The killing frenzy spread to Onondaga, the capital of the Confederacy. Dekanisora argued the cause of peace, as he had done before, but the tide was running against him. Hendrick Forked Paths and Abraham Schuyler promised lavish gifts from the English: guns and powder for those who took the warpath, and a whole year's provisions for their families. The Indians who had gone to Boston described the strength of the English forces preparing the assult on Canada. Stronger than these tidings was the fact that, throughout the Five Nations, there was hardly a single family that did not have a blood debt to settle with the French. In every family, there were members eager to appease the spirits of their dead, and requicken their names in the person of live captives. Every village had Burned Knives eager to prove themselves in battle. Some believed that if they died in the fight, they would go to a better place than men who stayed home and expired on their sleeping mats, a paradise reserved for warriors.

When the war post was set up at Onondaga and the dance began, Dekanisora perceived that his people were no longer willing to listen to his talk of neutrality. And because a chief of the Real People was only the servant of opinion, in a society more democratic than Europeans had seen in two thousand years, Dekanisora shifted as his people shifted.

The Onondaga speaker told them: "I did not try to dissuade you out of fear of the French, but to honor the laws of the Peacemaker. Now I see you will go to war with the English whatever is said, I will place myself at your head, and be the first to lead you, even if the end of our path is slavery and destruction."

And he, too, joined the war dance.

2.

New Yorkers were not as keen as New Englanders to sign up for Queen Anne's war, perhaps because they had suffered less from French Indian raiding parties than their neighbors in recent years. And also because the traders and farmers on the New York frontier were keenly aware that their back door was wide open. If Colonel Nicholson failed to take Montreal, the French might very well have a go at Albany. Nobody had forgotten that they had burned Schenectady less than a generation before.

So enlistment for the invasion of Canada lagged in New York, except among Conrad Weiser's people in the camps on the Hudson.

Jean Cast called the List Masters together to hear the offer from Colonel Ingoldsby, the lieutenant governor.

The governor's deputy invoked hungry ghosts, no less than Hendrick, though he did not take off his buckled shoes and lead the Germans in a dance round a war post.

"We are all alive to the depth of your sufferings in the old country," Ingoldsby told them. "Homes gone, women defiled, children starved. We all remember who is responsible. Did not King Louis order his dragoons to lay waste to the Palatinate so thoroughly that a crow would starve to death before it found anything to eat in your valleys?"

The Palatine men stirred and grumbled their assent. Johann Weiser pictured his desolated vineyards, his wife Magda rolling in the hot fever that could not be broken, the sweet young girl from the apothecary's who had been raped until she ruptured and bled to death on the burned earth.

"Her Majesty gives you the chance to exact justice from the French for the crimes committed against you!" Ingoldsby shouted. "In joining our glorious cause against King Louis's minions in Canada, you will also avail yourself of the opportunity to repay the Queen for her favor and hospitality."

Johann Weiser asked to know the terms of enlistment.

"You will be paid provincial wages, with arms and provisions."

"We will march under our own captains."

"Under the command of regular officers, naturally. Your men must be trained and drilled."

"Many of us here were soldiers in our own country," Johann Weiser reminded the lieutenant governor. "There is little we have to learn about war, except the face of this country. And I doubt that we will learn much about that from English regulars."

Ingoldsby took a hard look at the speaker. A formidable man, physically powerful, exercising a natural command over the others, who seemed content to let him speak for all. A possible troublemaker. But Colonel Ingoldsby had seen enough of war to know that a man who is a troublemaker in peacetime may be invaluable under fire.

"We will of course be operating with native scouts and guides," Ingoldsby clarified. "None but a madman would try to cross the wilderness without them. You will serve under your own captains, subject to military approval."

"We must have guarantees for our families. That they will be protected, and well provided for."

"You live under Mister Livingston's protection. That is surely sufficient."

"And eat his slops!" Another voice, from a wild-eyed, angry man, with stringy hair that hung loose. The lieutenant governor leaned toward Jean Cast to get the name. Bertelsmann, Gunther Bertelsmann.

"I will take note of your complaint, Herr Bertelsmann. I am sure that Mister Livingston does the best that he can. I know that, if redress is needed, Governor Hunter holds your interests close to his heart."

"What about our land?" Gunther persisted. "We are not British bloodybacks, who serve for a wage and the threat of a flogging. If we take Canada for the Queen, we are entitled to the fulfillment of Her Majesty's promise to us."

The lieutenant governor was relieved to see that many of the Palatines seemed embarrassed by this outburst. The Germans—he had been informed—were an orderly people, willing to wait in line, preferring set rules.

"This matter goes beyond my purview," he told them. "But I believe I can say that if we succeed in this affair of Canada, there will be land aplenty for any man who is willing to farm it. The territory of New France is vast, and rich, and unimproved, through the sloth and vanity of its grand seigneurs. It awaits men of enterprise, with fire in their belly, to free it from the yoke of Paris and Rome."

The Palatines cheered. Even Gunther joined the applause.

Johann Weiser told his family afterwards, "Our fortunes are turning."

3.

The guns of Fort Orange saluted an Indian army big enough to make the ladies of Albany quiver, and the traders rush to open their stores in expectation of brisk business. There were a hundred and fifty-five Mohawks, led by Hendrick Forked Paths, and more than five hundred warriors from the rest of the Five Nations, including a few Shawnees who marched with the Senecas. There were a hundred and thirty-two Indians from other nations, including Nicholas Etakoam.

The provincials looked at the blaze of feathers and warpaint with mixed emotions. This was mostly a New England army, and plowboys and prentices from the New England frontier—reared on stories of Indian savagery and with fresh memories of Deerfield and other massacres—had a hard time telling one kind of Indian from another. They cursed and jeered and picked fights. A Westfield farmer complained that they were being sent into the woods with the same rattlesnakes that killed their kinsmen at Deerfield because New Yorkers were too lazy to fight their own battles.

The second half of this complaint gained strength from the character of the New York contingent. More than half of the six hundred New York volunteers were Palatine Germans from the camps, many of whom

did not speak English, though they could communicate well enough
with the Dutch.

Johann Weiser marched at the head of his own company, from the
Queensbury section. He felt a whole man again, with a musket in his
hands and a powder horn slung from his shoulder, leading his own people to a just war against the enemies who had destroyed their homeland.
Conrad had pleaded to be allowed to join the company, and had raged
at his father when he refused.

Johann had ordered his son to stay home with some reluctance, an-
ticipating the complaints he would hear from Greta on his return. Lord
knew what mischief the boy might accomplish, running about crazed as
a bull elk in rutting season. Johann was not overly exercised by his affair
with Dina Zeh, now an open scandal. That was just a young man sowing
his wild oats. Dina would do him no harm, whatever Greta said, though
she could hardly be counted on to improve the boy's morals. It was the
picture of Conrad running amok with the younger girls that troubled
Johann more. Put a bun in the wrong oven, and he could be saddled
with the wrong woman for life—or (perhaps worse) develop a habit for
ditching family obligations. Army discipline might have served to contain
some of Conrad's roiling energy; a taste of battle would surely have given
it a useful outlet. Yet a man was required to stand guard over Greta and
the children, and to provide for them on the chance that Johann Weiser
did not return. The lottery of birth made Conrad that man.

Johann had run into small parties of Indians on the river and on the
Queen's road. But this was the first time he had seen the natives in large
numbers and up close. He observed their feasting and dancing with keen
interest, wondering if the Mohawks and their allies deserved their rep-
utation as ruthlessly efficient killers, the masters of forest warfare. He
watched Hendrick kill a bull with his own hands and rip the beating
heart from its great chest. He was appalled—yet also thrilled—when the
huge Mohawk war chief stuffed the heart between his jaws and his
warriors came running to lap the hot blood. Even as a spectator, Johann
felt a surge of energy inside himself. A force had been released with the
savage slaughter of the bull.

"*Le sang c'est la vie,*" said a voice, close at hand, in passable French.
"Blood is life."

Weiser turned. The speaker was an ancient Indian with a storm of
white hair that blew halfway down his back. He leaned on a staff that
writhed like a serpent. He wore a simple deerskin tunic faded to the
color of bone. Johann thought he had a bird or animal on his shoulder,
something black and glossy that rippled in the firelight; he saw it was a
short robe. The old man's face was a maze of lines. The eyes shone like
mirrors.

"*C'est dégoutant, non?*" The old man gestured at the blood-drinkers. "Does it disgust you?"

"I have seen worse things in my own country." No Parisian would have admitted he could comprehend Johann's version of French, with its fallen nasals and alien, cloddish gutturals. But it was adequate for this exchange.

"Not so long ago, we ate human hearts." The old man cackled. "That's why they call us Mohawks. Man-Eaters. We ate the hearts of our enemies to capture their power and take their souls. And also because we liked the taste." He laughed harder, showing the gaps in his teeth, then stopped abruptly to register the impact on his audience.

Johann thought the old man was crazy but probably harmless. He put a plug of tobacco in his mouth and chomped on it stolidly.

"Men go to war for many reasons," the old man continued. "Some of our people go for guns and liquor. Some go to feed their hungry ghosts. A powerful killer like Hendrick Forked Paths goes for other reasons. He goes to hunt *power*. Why do *you* go to war?" He jabbed his bony forefinger toward Weiser's chest.

"To serve my sovereign and my country," Weiser said curtly.

"But this is not your country."

"I will dispute that with any man."

"Are your ancestors buried here? Do the spirits of lakes and mountains speak to you?"

"There are many ways of living on God's earth." Johann allowed himself to be drawn into the conversation, though he did not know why he needed to defend his actions—even his presence in America—before a deranged old Indian.

"You are Dutch?"

"Not Dutch. *Deutsch.* I come from a country of forests and rivers, like yours. The valley of the Rhine is beautiful, like the valley of the Hudson."

"Then why did you leave?"

"We were tired of killing and dying, tired of being under the heel of the French. Queen Anne promised us a new life."

"But here you are, killing and dying again." The old man cawed.

"Your people and my people fight together, in the same cause."

There was a great bellow from the circle of Indians gathered around the war post. Hendrick staggered among them, his face and body slick with blood and sweat. His muscles bulged as he held aloft the dripping head of the bull, by the horns.

"Our warriors are hunting power," the old man repeated. "What are you hunting?"

"We ask only what is ours by right."

"*Par droit?*" the old man echoed. "By right?" Their frontier French had failed. Or perhaps the failure was not in the mastery of vocabulary, but the gulf between the mental worlds of concepts and images that lay behind the words. "This day is a gift. The earth is borrowed. The moon is borrowed. The sun is borrowed. This life is a gift."

He was almost crooning, leaning his head on the knob of his staff.

There was no doubt of it, Johann thought. The old man was crazy as a loon, singing in bastard French under the sickle moon. Weiser's attention drifted back to the wild scene at the bull-feast. A suitable subject for Hieronymous Bosch.

"You." The old man poked him. It was not a physical touch, yet it commanded his full attention, as if something had reached inside and squeezed his heart. "What is your name?"

"Johann Conrad Weiser."

The old man experimented with it, frowning over the middle name. "You have a son?"

"I have several sons in this country."

"You have a son with the same name?"

"My eldest son is named Conrad."

The old man nodded. He said, "You will talk to my grandson. You may ask for Seth." He pointed to a tall young man who was dancing with the warriors. "But not tonight. Tonight he runs with the killer ghosts."

Johann was struck by the questions about his son. He wondered which of Conrad's deviltries might have brought him to the notice of the Indians. Had he been whoring after the Indian girls they sometimes saw on the river?

He was going to ask, but when he turned again, the old man had vanished. The suddenness of his coming and going was eerie. Dragging his worn bones on his stick, he could hardly have had time to lose himself among the press of Indians at the bull-feast, or to vanish into the water poplars beside the river. It was as if he had somehow materialized and then dematerialized.

Johann bit down hard on his chewing tobacco and spat out juice and saliva. He must not let himself slide into wild fancies, not on his first night camped next to the Indians. Who knew what the campaign would bring?

A pair of native boys jumped out from behind the trees and made fright faces at him as he walked back to his tent. They mocked him with whistling sounds he could not comprehend.

"*Shonnonkouiretsi!*" The syllables skipped and mocked. "*Shonn-on-kouir-etsi!*"

Johann did not know that they were jabbering that he had seen Longhair. Or that "Longhair" was the nickname for a famous shaman, whose true name was never spoken out loud for fear that he would fly at once to the person who dared to invoke it. Longhair did not show himself to many, not in his natural body. To see Longhair could be a high honor, a gateway to power or initiation. It could also be one's worst nightmare.

4.

After the feasting, Colonel Nicholson gave the order for the column to move out. The boatmen dumped their cargo below the upper falls of the Hudson, and refused to go further for any amount of money. Flanked by native scouts, the militiamen sweated their way through the deep woods along the snaking groove of an old trail, food for gnats, mosquitoes and woodlice. They were ordered to make camp in unhealthy swamp-land near the source of Wood Creek, which would be their passage to Lake Champlain and the great water route to Canada. Wood Creek was aptly named: there was so much fallen timber in its sluggish waters that it seemed the forest was growing sideways.

Nicholson set the Palatines to work sawing logs to build a stockade fort, and called for carpenters to built flatboats for the voyage down the lake. The Germans were inured to working timber by now, and obeyed without protest, though they would rather have been getting into the promised fight. The Indians stripped elm bark for their canoes, hunted deer and wild turkey, and shared their dreams.

Johann Weiser went over to the Mohawk camp before breakfast, looking for the man called Seth. He made himself intelligible to an Indian who spoke pidjin Dutch, and was guided to a group of natives squatting around a fire. He recognized one of them as the tall, hawk-nosed young warrior the old man had pointed out to him. As he watched, Seth picked up a stick and breathed on it with deliberation in the pauses in his recitation. Then he leaned forward and set fire to the end of the stick, puffing to make the flames stronger, until it was utterly consumed.

Seth looked up at the stocky German.

"*Hoo kop je an?*" he inquired in frontier Dutch.

"I am Johann Conrad. Your grandfather told me to ask for you."

Seth spoke to his companions in his own language, then rose to walk with Johann. He accepted the plug of tobacco Weiser offered. They walked toward the creek. On the rise, the union flag of England and Scotland fluttered above Colonel Nicholson's marquee. The general shared the risks of his men, but not their discomforts. He was eating his breakfast off bone china, and swallowing his morning grog from a chased silver goblet.

Johann was curious about the stick Seth had burned so ceremoni-ously.

"I had a bad dream," Seth said matter-of-factly. "I was burning what it left in my body."

"I have been told you are a people who believe in dreams."

"It is important to do something with a dream. Otherwise you will not dream well. What do *you* dream?"

"I dream of living close to the earth, in a place where my family may live at peace with their neighbors and with God."

"Is your Great Spirit the same as that of the blackrobes? Do you eat him in church?"

"That is a papist superstition!" Weiser bristled.

Seth did not understand what he meant by superstition. Only that Weiser's God was different from that of the French; that their spirits lived on different mountaintops.

"Today I go to hunt beaver." Seth held his left hand flat in front of his chest, then struck it sharply from below with the back of his right hand, miming the action of the beaver's tail beating water. "Do you know beaver?"

"I am a willing student."

"Then you will hunt with me."

Weiser leaped at the chance to make a friend and learn something of the native ways. He would ask Gunther to take charge of the construction team; nobody would miss him if he shirked one day of navvying. He sensed a deeper logic at work here than he could follow in his little everyday mind, and was willing to trust himself to that. The crazed old man had sent him to Seth for a reason.

Seth led him on a giddying course, a path that never ran straight, bending with every tree stump or boulder, making huge loops to an easier ford across a stream, or to skirt bogs and ridges. Johann was learning that there are no straight lines in the forest except those forced by woodcutters. They came to a clearer path: a logging trail down which beaver had dragged their timber, bitten off as neatly as if hewn by an ax.

The Mohawk showed Weiser how to set a deadfall trap near a beaver dam. "We must take the beaver when they are above the water. It is no good shooting them when they are swimming in the pond. They will sink to the bottom and their pelts will be lost."

Seth sniffed the air. He smelled game in the woods.

Johann tried to keep up as the Mohawk padded noiselessly through the underbrush. Seth paused to sniff the air again, then was off like a fox after a hare.

Johann lengthened his stride. Which way had the Mohawk turned between the big, blue-shadowed spruces?

He realized he had lost not only his guide, but his bearings. The sun was hidden behind a dense wall of cloud. Weiser had no idea which way might lead back to camp. He thrashed through the undergrowth, guessing at the direction Seth had taken.

The Mohawk jumped out and grabbed his arm, restraining his instinctive movement to bring up his firelock. Pointing at Johann's big feet, Seth shook his head violently. His meaning could not have been plainer: the white man made enough noise, blundering through brambles and dry twigs, to scare away anything on four legs.

Seth's keen eyes saw leaves that had been disturbed by another kind of animal. In pausing to rebuke the white man, he had forgotten his own woodcraft. He had let himself get downwind of something that might be hunting *him*.

Johann watched in horror as a mountain of flesh and fur reared from cover and caught the Mohawk up in its embrace. Raised on its hind legs, the bear looked human, or more than human: a giant from a race of titans that had owned the earth before men walked on two legs.

Seth sucked in his breath, but did not cry out, as the great claws pierced the flesh above his shoulder blades.

Johann watched in mute fascination as prehensile lips pulled back to release the long, deadly canines. The bear coughed deep in its chest and began to hum in a manner that was almost conversational.

Weiser shook himself from his daze and ceased to be a spectator. He cocked his musket, ran forward, and jammed the muzzle into the open jaws of the bear. They closed on the barrel with such force that he thought it must have been snapped off in the instant he pulled the trigger.

Then the thin light of the forest was swallowed, and Johann lay on his back in a dense, breathing darkness that pressed the air from his lungs. There was scalding pain in his left arm. He willed himself to ignore it, heaving and squirming ro recover the light.

The weight was too great for him. Consciousness ebbed away, before other hands pulled him out from under the bear.

□

The Mohawks feasted him with bear meat that night. Seth—who would wear the clawmarks on his back as a mark of pride—told Weiser, "We are now brothers, and will be so for life. Now I see why my grandfather sent you to me."

Seth asked many questions, about Johann's homeland and his family. He was astonished when Johann told him that he had fourteen surviving children by his first wife—though only eight had come to America—and one by his second.

No wonder the Germans went hungry in their own country!

"The earth groans, with so many mouths to feed."

"Is it so different with you, then?"

"In the old days, we had no more young children than the mother could carry, in her arms and on her back, when we needed to move camp or escape from an enemy. Now some have more, because the white death kills so many of my people."

"Your country is vast. I hear that the valleys of Mohawk country are fertile. To the eyes of an outsider, this land is almost empty. It could support many more people."

"You see with a newcomer's eyes, as you say. You do not see that we share this earth with many others, with the four-leggeds and the bird tribes. The earth supports all of us. It does not belong to any. If we drive the bear and the deer from our woods—as we have driven all but a few of the beaver—then we will also die. Our mother earth will shake us from her back."

"You speak very good Dutch. It is easy for me to understand you. I hope you can also follow my words."

Seth translated this into Mohawk for the benefit of his friends, who seemed to find it amusing.

"They say we cannot trust any white man. You close your mouths when you talk. Real People talk with their mouths open. Like this." A rapid rush of words issued in Mohawk. Seth never closed his mouth. Johann watched his tongue vibrate like the reed in a flute.

"What are you saying?"

"*Satonkariaks ken*," Seth repeated. "I asked if you are still hungry. It means, Is there something in your belly that is biting you?"

Weiser laughed at the brawny, muscular quality of the native metaphors. "I would like to learn your tongue. Though I am afraid I am no linguist. Your grandfather speaks better French than me. My son Conrad is the scholar in these things. He has an ear like a parrot."

"A what?"

"A parrot is a bird that can repeat whatever is said to him, just as it is pronounced. Conrad picked up English that way. It took him all of three weeks, when we were living rough in London."

"Then send him to us. We will teach him Mohawk."

It was an interesting proposal. Johann remembered the old man's particular interest in his eldest son. Perhaps the old man had already spoken to Seth about this matter. But why would he reach out in this way, even before the episode with the bear? And why had his choice fallen on Conrad, whom he had surely never seen?

"Your grandfather is an interesting man."

"Where did you meet him?"

"Here, in the camp. He approached me while you were dancing with King Hendrick in the war feast."

"This is not possible." Seth shook his head. "My grandfather was not here. He is opposed to this war, and he holds himself apart from us all."

"He was here the night of the feast. He was as close to me as you are. He told me to ask for you, and he asked me about my son Conrad."

"That was not my grandfather."

"He spoke to me in French. Does your grandfather speak French?"

"He speaks French," Seth confirmed. "He lived close to the black-robes for a time. But you did not speak to my grandfather."

"He wore an animal fur. It was black. Too small for a bearskin. Could it be a panther skin?"

"Maybe you dreamed this."

"It was not a dream. It was real."

Seth threw a bone to a mangy yellow dog that lay waiting beyond the circle of firelight. Then he let out a luxuriant belch and lowered himself onto his back, patting his belly.

Johann noticed his own stomach was uncomfortably tight. "Tell me about your village."

"You should ask my grandfather. He is the one who dreamed it."

"I do not understand."

"It is as I told you. My grandfather dreamed of a village on a violent river that would be a place of peace between the nations. He saw this village growing at the foot of Corn Mountain, in the valley of the Schoharie river."

Schoharie. The familiar word gave Johann shivers. Before he had crossed the ocean, this was the name he had given in his waking dreams to the promised land in America.

"The White Village grew from my grandfather's dream," Seth continued. "He planted a white pine in our clearing. He told us the roots of this Peace Tree would spread to the four quarters."

"I would like to see your White Village," Weiser said eagerly. "I come from a people who have also lost their homes. We do not wish to make our way by stealing the homes of others."

"This is good. I think you speak from the heart. But when the time comes, you will send us your son. We will learn from him whether your people and our people can live side by side."

"Conrad is a spirited boy." Johann tried to imagine what the Mohawks—and especially their women—would make of his son.

Seth turned from him to discuss something with his comrades. They all seemed highly pleased with the expression Johann had used to describe his son.

"*Rotkon!*" Seth exclaimed. "You say your son is a spirit man?"

"That was not quite what I intended. I meant to say he is high in energy." Like a horse that needs breaking, he added mentally.

"We will see what becomes of him, when he goes among the spirits of the Real People."

5.

On a miserable, drenching day that turned the cleared land around the stockade to gravy which stuck to Colonel Nicholson's boots—making him despair of the preservation of his fine silk hose—an express courier arrived from Albany on a dying horse.

"At last!" Nicholson shouted to Walter Butler, a bog soldier he had put on his staff. Lieutenant Butler was a square-built humorist, of the class that ranked in his native Ireland as half-mounted gentlemen, though he claimed a family connection with the great earls of Ormonde. He had endeared himself to the commander of the army by his capacity to hold his liquor and his fund of rhyming toasts, few of them suitable for a lady's ears.

"Walter," said Colonel Nicholson as he broke the seal and unfolded the letter. "Will you be so good as to fetch me a passable bottle of claret?"

The colonel was confident that this would be a moment for high celebration. The letter must bring the long-awaited news that Admiral Walker and Brigadier Hill had mounted their assault on Quebec, which would give the signal to loose his own forces against Montreal. The message had not come a moment too soon. Winter came early in these parts, and the provincials were already deserting in droves, to go home to their wives and harvests. The bloody flux and the yellow fever were rife among those who remained.

The letter to Colonel Nicholson was headed "from on board Her Majesty's Ship *Windsor*." The signature at the bottom, labored and over-sized as a schoolboy's, was that of Brigadier Hill. Nicholson read the following lines:

Sir, You must prepare your Self to hear a melancholly account of the disasters that have happend to us, after a tolerable good passage from Nanticket Bay to the mouth of the River St Laurence. A great fogg coming on obliged the Admirall to make the signall for lying bye till day light, by what accident, whethet Tide of Current, I cannot pretend to tell you, being no Seaman, wee fell in with the North Shore about half an hour after ten at night, and lost eight of our Transports, besides a Ship Laden wth provisions. The knowledge we have of those lost amounts to one thousand.

The Admirall and Captains of the Ships of Warr since this Misfortune were unanimously of opinion that the River is wholly Impracticable by reason of the Pylots which were given us at New England. We can con-

*sequently proceed no further on the Execution of her Majestys Commands
at Quebeck.*

*What method you will find for informing the Indians and keeping
them in the Queens interest I must leave intirely to Your Judgment and
Management.*

A drunken admiral had lost his fleet in a fog, and abandoned the
whole campaign against Canada without consulting the people who had
risked most to pursue it. How could this be explained to the Five
Nations? Or to the New Englanders? Or to the Palatines, who already
had little reason to be grateful to the Crown, given their treatment in
the camps?

After years of pleading and persuading—and of tickling the unlovely
Mrs. Masham—Francis Nicholson had materialized an English army of
invasion. And it had fled from a morning mist.

Lieutenant Butler returned with the claret to observe Colonel Nicholson engaged in a frenzied attempt to tear his powdered wig into two
pieces. The lining of the wig was too tough for Nicholson's fastidious
hands. He threw the object into the mud and danced a jig on it, yelling,
"Roguery! Treachery! Our forces are led by damned dancing masters!"

Walter Butler stole a look at the letter, and bit his lip when he came
to the bit about the Indians. His private ambitions were focused on
gaining a position that would give him access to the Indian trade and
the speculation in Indian land. He now saw the prospect of having to
fight New York Indians, instead of gently fleecing them.

□

The Palatines were marched back to their camps on the borders of Livingston Manor, without pay, to make tar. They found their families
nearly starving, abandoned by Commissary Livingston since their men
had gone soldiering. Men gathered at the Weiser cabin with blood in
their eye; there was talk of a rising against Crown authority, of burning
Livingston's grand pillared house.

"We will plan and act as an army, not a rabble," Johann said sharply.
They had kept their arms. They had seen for themselves—on the
wasted march to Wood Creek, and in the wasted drilling and building
that followed—that they were more willing soldiers and kept better order than other New York provincials, and that maybe they were the
match for British regulars. Weiser told his people they would wait their
time, because he had something better than the governor's promises.

He told Conrad in private about his conversations with Seth, the
Mohawk warrior from the Schoharie country, and his mysterious grandfather.

Conrad jumped at the chance to leave the camps and live with the Indians.

"Not so hasty," his father cautioned him. "We must get our bearings. And put some food on the table."

The Weiser family—and Dina Zeh's—had fared better than most, since Conrad had grown more proficient as a hunter. But there had been many days when they had been reduced to trying to convert Livingston's slops into something edible.

"But there will be no more sheep stealing," Johann said severely when he caught the glint in his son's eye. "They will hang you if they catch you at it."

"When do I go to Schoharie?"

"The Lord will show us the time."

He called the whole family together. They gave thanks, on their knees, that Johann had returned safe to them.

CHAPTER 10

GHOST WARRIOR

1.

Many people in the border country of New York and Canada welcomed the chance to get back to business as usual after the collapse of the Nicholson expedition. The war had brought windfall profits to smugglers who could get through the lines and commissaries who were actually paid, including such great men as Robert Livingston. But the Albany Dutch—who still remembered the time when New York was New Netherland—were no enthusiasts for Britain's adventures in empire building. French fur traders were eager to have access to English manufactures, which were cheaper and of better quality than their French counterparts.

The Five Nations had been sucked into Nicholson's grandiose plan for the conquest of Canada. Now that grand design had burst like a soap bubble, and the leaders of the Confederacy were leaning toward the traditional policy of neutrality. "We will bury the hatchet deep beneath the roots of the Peace Tree, where no man may find it," the Onondaga speaker promised new French envoys. Even among the Mohawks, the war faction led by Hendrick Forked Paths was rapidly losing support. In children's games and dream theatre—when the Real People play-acted their dreams—Hendrick was openly mocked. He was portrayed as a London fop, with a lisp and a feather in his hat, and as a Mohawk apple: red on the outside, white on the inside.

Peace was breaking out in New York, though the Peace of Utrecht (which would end the war that began with a dynastic wrangle over a vacant Spanish throne, and leave Nova Scotia, as well as Newfoundland and Hudson's Bay, in British hands) was still two years off. Peace was spreading in accordance with the utilitarian principles only recently formulated by Mr. Locke: "Things are good or evil only in relation to pleasure or pain. That we call 'good' which is apt to cause or increase pleasure, or diminish pain in us."

But Louis-Thomas de Joncaire, the most active French agent among the Indians, was not yet disposed to wage peace. The men responsible for bending the Five Nations to the English cause and threatening Canada must be punished. Joncaire favored a whirlwind attack on Albany. The French and the Mission Indians would seize the town and burn it to the ground. This would lead to the wholesale flight of white settlers from the New York frontier, divert the fur trade of the English colony to Montreal, and swing the Five Nations to the side of France. Listening to this strategy, Governor Vaudreuil leaned toward caution. He did not wish to overextend his forces and risk provoking a more resolute English attack on New France. Better to employ some of Joncaire's Indians for what they were best at, a game of hit and run: to sow just enough terror to induce the men of Albany to stay inside their walls and convince the Mohawks that the English were a broken reed. Joncaire knew the right men for the job.

He did not join Madeleine, his *canadienne* wife, that night. He gathered a band of hand-picked killers, some of them Caughnawagas from Sault Saint Louis, who knew the country they would be traveling. Two of these men had proved their value quite recently, in removing one of the Mohawks who had gone to London to sign up himself and his people as mercenaries for the English. However, they needed watching. Snowsnake was light-fingered and capable of selling to a higher bidder. And Two Hearts dabbled in things that would have earned him a burning at the stake in Joncaire's native France not so long ago, a fate Joncaire suspected the sorcerer might deserve even now.

Joncaire reminded himself that no sane man chooses killers for their morals. And that, in combat with Indians, one was required to fight the Indian way.

2.

David Ketelyn's house stood between the Saratoga road and the river, an hour's ride north of Albany. The soil was rich and loamy, but he had chosen the site with an eye to trade as much as farming. He was well-placed to intercept some of the contrabanders moving back and forth from the French trading posts around Montreal.

Ketelyn was uneasy, that night. Soldiers had come with a warning that French Indians had been seen near Saratoga. Some of his neighbors had fled to Albany, to seek safety under the guns of Fort Orange. But Ketelyn was reluctant to leave his new log house to be burned and his goods to be looted by Indians who had been his business partners yesterday and might very well be his partners again tomorrow. Besides, the sun was going down; there would be more danger on the road at night than behind stout log walls. And he had induced the three soldiers to stay with his family until morning.

With all of them crowded into the one big room, it was as merry as any Pinxterfest. Ketelyn's wife Hilletje, big with child, busied herself with her cooking pots over the open fireplace that blazed in the middle of the room, in the old Dutch way. There was a little genever left to share with the soldiers. His sister-in-law Alida played pat-a-cake with the children while he won a few coppers from the redcoats at cards.

It was past midnight, the women and children bundled together in the high, humped bed, the soldiers snoozing in front of the fire, when the rap came at the door.

"Who's there?" Ketelyn snatched up his firelock.

"*I-i,*" two Mohawk syllables wafted back. "It's me."

The soldiers bristled. Hans, Ketelyn's sixteen-year-old boy, had a fowling piece ready charged.

"Who?" Ketelyn peered through a loophole, trying to make out the features of the man outside.

The Indian knocked again. "It's me, Snowsnake," he called again. "I've got something you want. *Hanion oksa!* Hurry up! A man could die of thirst at your door."

"Do you know him?" the sergeant asked.

"Yes. He's Caughnawaga. Comes through here regular, war or no war. A sly son of a bitch, but I've never had trouble with him."

"It could be a trap." The sergeant replaced him at the loophole.

"I'll go to Franck's!" Snowsnake threatened.

Ketelyn was nettled by this reference to one of his Albany competitors.

"Don't go to Franck's!" he called back. "They'll stand on the weights and spit in your grog. Come back in the morning. I will attend to you then."

"I think my brother is no friend, to leave a traveler hungry on the road. I will go to Franck's."

"Wait!"

"David, what are you doing?" His wife's pale, scared face appeared from behind the curtain that screened the bed. "No honest man comes at this hour."

"You know *de wilden.* They are ruled by their appetites, like wild beasts."

"It's a trick!"

"It may very well be," Ketelyn conceded. "That's why Hans and our gallant friends here will stand ready to give the devils a warm reception, if it is needed."

"There's at least two more of the buggers," the sergeant reported.

"Tell your friends to stay back," Ketelyn called. "Put your gun on the ground where I can see it. You may come in alone and unarmed."

"He's doing it."

Ketelyn loosed the bolt, shielding his body behind the solid oak of the door as he swung it open a few inches.

Five or six muskets spoke at once. One of the balls drove an oak splinter into the Dutchman's ear. The one that killed him burst through the skull and settled at the base of his brain.

Hilletje heaved in wordless pain. Alida rocked her baby, pressing its face to her bosom to stifle the howls. The Ketelyn boy and the soldiers fired at shadows, trying to beat the attackers back. Choking back tears, Ketelyn's wife dragged her unwieldy body from one man to the next, reloading their muskets. At last they had the door secured; it was solid enough to withstand anything but a small cannon.

"Perhaps they will leave off," Alida said in a small voice.

Nobody responded. Hilletje ripped the top off a paper cartridge with her teeth. Hans was set to watch the back of the house, where the woods were thickest. He yelled when he saw bright points of light darting from the trees like fireflies.

The sergeant cursed when he saw what was happening. The walls of the log house might be impregnable, but the thatched roof was as inflammable as touchwood. Sweating heavily, the soldiers pitted their marksmanship against the Indians who were shooting fire arrows. But their smoothbores were erratic, and the archers were deft and quick. Within minutes, the roof was aflame. Black smoke swallowed the room; the beams groaned ominously.

"We'll have to chance it," Sergeant Gallup told them. "Shoot and shake a leg before them shitten elves can catch us."

"My mother is in no condition to run," Hans objected.

Sergeant Gallup chewed his lip. "They'll not touch a hair of her head," he promised. "It's a strange thing, but those devils respect the ladies."

"For the love of God!" Alida screamed as a beam came crashing down.

The sergeant cocked his musket. He was no coward, though he might promise what was not in his gift. He was first out the door, and first to die, as they stumbled from the burning house into the blackness beyond. One of his men managed to run the gauntlet of musket fire and took off into the woods, followed by the war whoops of his pursuers. The third soldier crouched in the doorway to shoot, and was felled by a flung tomahawk.

"Leave the gun, Hans," Hilletje appealed to her son. "It is the devil's drawing room out there."

The boy would not hear. His eyes were burning; he had his father to avenge.

He ran out shooting, aiming for the place where he had last seen the flash of a muzzle. He was felled by a crushing blow from a death hammer.

The women came out together. Hilletje prayed with her hands clasped over her belly. Alida crooned to the baby in her arms:

Trip a trap a troenje
de varken in de boenjen

She broke off with a shudder when a face out of nightmare pushed up in front of her own. She closed her eyes to that painted mask, and to much of what happened at the edge of the woods while the moon hid its face: to the killer who walked among the dead, tracing circles on their heads with the point of his knife before he ripped off the skin and hair with his teeth, to the exquisite death of the soldier who could no longer walk. When the raider started herding their captives north, Alida told herself not to think about the long miles of suffering that lay ahead, or what would face her beyond them. Her baby's heart beat against her own.

It is enough that my baby lives.

But the Indians ran like wolves. It was impossible for the women to keep up. Hilletje stumbled along for half a mile, puffing in hot spurts. Then she sat down at the foot of a tree, unable to go on.

The Indian who had laid claim to her yanked at the rawhide cord that bound her wrists to his waist.

"*Hagats!*" He tugged again, making his meaning unmistakable.

"I go no further." Hilletje pressed her palms to the sides of her swollen belly. She felt the baby kick hard. If it were born that night—

Snowsnake loped over. His eyes glinted inside the mask of blue-black paint. He spoke sharply to Hilletje's captor, who twisted his mouth in apparent disgust, but dropped the cord.

The baby kicked again. *I give thanks to God. They are going to let us go.*

Snowsnake leaned over her. He smiled when he touched her belly. *Even the devil respects new life.* She sighed with relief, for the baby, as she looked up at her husband's murderer.

Snowsnake's smile remained intact as he swung his hatchet. The razor-sharp edge bit through the base of Hilletje's neck, just above the collarbone. The blow was so powerful that it all but severed the head from the shoulders.

This is not real, Alida told herself, shaking violently.

Her baby was crying its lungs out. She rocked it in her arms, humming the old nursery song. *"Trip a trap a troenje."*

When Snowsnake turned on her and ripped the baby from her arms, Alida knew it was her own living heart that had been torn from her. She fought him with nails and teeth and elbows, and with all the wind in her lungs, but he kicked her away and others came to slip a choke collar around her neck. This may have been a mercy; she did not see Snowsnake take her baby by the heels and crack its skull, delicate as a duck's egg, against a rock. But she heard the laughter. It came from the blackest pit of hell.

□

They rested before dawn, above the upper falls, where the French Indians had cached their canoes.

But there was no rest for Snowsnake.

Something was stalking him through the woods. And something was walking through his mind. Where was Two Hearts, when he was needed? Two Hearts would know how to fight this thing. It came at him again, leaning into his mind.

There are things that are without forgiveness.

3.

Seth was hunting in these same northern woods. He was hunting visions. When Colonel Nicholson's army had folded its tents, Seth had returned to the White Village in the Schoharie valley. He had climbed the high limestone cliff to the cave where Longhair lived apart from his people, and reported his conversations with the German, John Conrad Weiser.

"It is as I have dreamed," the shaman told him. "Before the spring thaw, Weiser will send his son to us and we will make him one of the Real People."

Longhair had another dream.

"I have dreamed we must take our boys back to the forests and mountains where no newcomers have walked, to hunt *power*. Their fathers teach them only how to kill and how to mimic the newcomers. In the villages, their heads are fogged by white men's thoughts and the fumes of white men's liquor. We are losing our dreamers and our doctors of souls. We must take the boys before they are spoiled—when they have seen nine or ten winters. They will live apart from others, in the places of power where the gates between the worlds open most freely. Here they will find their guides and their animal guardians. They will hunt big dreams, the dreams that tell a person who he is. When they know who they are, they will know how they ought to behave, how they can best serve the people. When this knowledge has returned to them, we will bring the best of them to the White Village, so they will be a beacon for all our neighbors."

Seth carried the shaman's message to all the Mohawk villages. He was heard with respect, especially by the women. Fruitpicker, the Mother of the Wolf Clan at Two Rivers, called a meeting of the Women's Society and urged the mothers who were present to send sons who had not yet reached manhood to hunt visions in the places of power that would be shown to them. This would remove them from the influence of Hendrick Forked Paths and the Burned Knives.

Redhawk spoke to her son.

"This is a game for children!" Talldeer protested. He would soon be eleven. He respected Seth, and feared Longhair—as they all did. But his hero was Hendrick Forked Paths, the warrior with many notches on his death hammer who dressed as grandly as any English lord and had awed the English Queen. Talldeer resented the fact that he had not been permitted to join the warriors who had gone with the Nicholson expedition, though his resentment had ebbed since the warriors had come home without scalps or victories.

"You will do this for your father," Redhawk told her son sternly. "Never forget what he taught you. If we lose the dreaming, we will no longer be the Real People. We will be walking dead."

So Talldeer had gone, with a dozen boys about his own age, to camp out in the woods with Seth, hunting visions. He had led them to a mountain of white quartz, on the edge of the Berkshires, where they chanted and drummed together, and into the deep forest around Saranac Lake, where Longhair was waiting for the party.

The shaman told the boys to separate and walk through the woods until they found a tree with which each of them felt a special connection.

Talldeer was drawn to an ancient yellow maple.

"That is where you will make your nest," Seth informed him.

"Nesting is for birds."

"Who says you are not a bird?" Longhair cackled.

□

The wind swayed the branches. Trees sawed and creaked and dropped dead limbs to the forest floor. On his heap of leaves and soft grasses, Talldeer rolled between sleep and waking.

There was something wrong with this place.

He tried to shut out images born in the shadows around the firepit, when the old ones told stories when snow was deep on the ground. Stories of flying heads, carried by the winds. Of wild spirits who preyed on people who were out alone in the woods at night. Stories to frighten children.

He raised up so suddenly he lost his perch and had to save himself from falling by grabbing a branch of the maple with both hands. When he pulled himself back to a safe position, the flying head was there, right in front of him, hovering at eye level.

If this was a dream, it was entirely real. Just as his father had told him.

He began to lose his fear of the apparition because, though horrifying, it was familiar. Red and black. The distended lips, the staring eyes, the hair that swung like horse's tails. It was the Face of the Divided One. A face from his father's dreaming.

It revolved in front of him, still hovering in midair, inviting him to share its vision.

Talldeer looked through its eyes.

He felt himself propelled out of himself with tremendous force. It was like flying into a wind funnel, into the core of a twister. He hurtled into a different scene, a place of slaughter. He saw a settler's cabin burning like a pine torch. He saw men felled like pigeons. He saw a pregnant woman butchered, a baby's skull smashed like an egg.

He was revolted. Was this what it meant to be a warrior?

No. This is what a warrior must avenge. Talldeer thrilled with the recognition that his father's thoughts were walking through his mind.

He saw a man crazed with blood dancing among his victims, knotting the scalps he had plundered to his belt. A man he knew, despite the mask of black paint, to be one of his father's killers.

He willed himself to be fully present, to use the power that had been given to him to strike *now*. He felt himself shifting form. His nails were lengthening into claws. His jaws pushed forward, making a long V, spiked with teeth that could shear and tear.

Not yet. He sensed his father's caution. *Mark the place where you will find him. Tell Seth and the others. When you come again, come fully armed.*

□

Talldeer crashed through the woods, in the twilight of the wolf, looking for Seth and Longhair.

Seth stepped from behind a tree and caught him by his ponytail.

"If I were an enemy," Seth told him, "you would be a dead man. We dream in order to *live*, not to die like woodchucks. What scared you so much you forgot the skills of survival?"

"I saw my father's killer," Talldeer panted.

Three men heard him tell the story: Seth, Longhair, and Bloodroot, a River Indian from the White Village, only a few years older than Talldeer, who had been brought to help watch over the boys while they pursued their solitary quests.

They made Talldeer go over the details of his vision until they were sure they could identify both the place of the massacre and the location of Snowsnake's camp.

"This business with the Dutch people is shameful." Seth assumed his authority as a chief. "But it is not our affair. Their ghosts do not speak to us. They go to a different place from where the Real People go."

Longhair listened without speaking.

"My father showed me this thing," Talldeer insisted. "I saw through his eyes. He showed me his killer so I can avenge his murder. We must go now, before Snowsnake gets away."

"It is not possible," Seth judged. "Even if we get there in time, the odds are too great."

"We outnumber them," Talldeer protested. He held up both hands, then his right hand alone, to show the number of the Mohawks who were camped in the woods. He had counted no more than ten of the French Indians.

"Boys!" Bloodroot exclaimed. "You are not ready to take on men who have killed again and again."

"I will go alone, if I must." Talldeer spoke with quiet determination. "You brought me here to find a dream guide, and I found one. My father came to me, and showed me what I must do. I must honor this dream."

"Talldeer dreams true." Longhair spoke at last. His white hair brushed his sunken chest, falling as low as the spot, just below the ribcage, where a hard knob projected under the skin. *The shaman's bone*, the old ones called it. "Talldeer must honor his dream, as he says. But he will not go alone."

"You would risk the boys?" Seth was aghast at the prospect of sending the children who had been picked as *dreamers* and possible healers to face fire-hardened warriors, some of whom used human skulls as their drinking cups.

"The boys will stay in the woods," Longhair ruled. "Bloodroot will go with Talldeer to guide him and watch his back."

"It is too dangerous." Seth was already trying to picture how he would face Redhawk if he failed to bring Talldeer home to her. A handsome woman, too soon a widow. He had asked himself whether he might be able to persuade her to move her sleeping mat to his own lodge at the White Village, when they returned from the dreamquest.

"The spirits will decide," Longhair reminded Seth. "The spirits have called Talldeer and they will walk with him." He dug a stick into the fire, scattering a trail of burning coals. A spark flew from one to another and expired with a puff of blue smoke. "I think that tonight our spirits are stronger."

4.

What have I done?

Pain and grief ripped through Vanishing Smoke. He was torn apart, like the False Face he had used to communicate with his son. He had now exposed Talldeer to danger from an enemy who was utterly without mercy, and who was defended not only by a band of powerful killers but by the warrior spirits who walked with them.

He had vowed to watch over his family. Instead, he had drawn his son into danger because of his craving for blood vengeance.

I am becoming like them, he thought ruefully, glancing back at the flock of hungry ghosts, his white shadows.

What could he do now, to save his son?

What waited for him, when the killing was over?

Would the bridge of light open to him again, or was it lost to him for all eternity?

He floated low above the tips of the pines, monitoring the passage of Talldeer and Bloodroot. They were moving as fast as couriers on the hard earth of the Iroquois Trail. Looking ahead, Vanishing Smoke saw that Snowsnake's camp was not yet astir. There was a chance that Talldeer and his escort would reach the French Indians before they broke camp. And what then?

Vanishing Smoke realized he was not alone. An eagle sailed beside him on flat wings. Its intent yellow eye dissolved space. It spoke to him in the voice of his teacher: *Snowsnake cannot be killed by ordinary means. You must go inside.*

The memory of the earlier battle returned to Vanishing Smoke. "It cannot be done," he signaled. "Snowsnake's magic is too strong." The answer came:

> *It will not protect him here. I will take care of that. You must catch him while his dreamsoul is traveling. You must go inside and take control. You will not be able to possess him for long. But you will be able to determine what becomes of his body. You can do this only if you do not allow yourself to sink into his identity. Control your passions. Remember who you are.*

At the French Indian camp, Snowsnake was slipping deeper into sleep. From their height, Vanishing Smoke and his guide watched the warrior's dreambody lift from his ordinary body and speed toward the Dutch woman who lay spreadeagled on the ground, tied by her wrists and ankles to stakes rooted in the earth. In his dreambody, Snowsnake looked just the same as in his physical body, except that he was completely naked and his erect penis jutted to an impossible size, like the instrument from which he had borrowed his name.

Your moment is now, Vanishing Smoke's teacher signaled. *When a man lets his fish think for him, there are many things that escape his attention.*

Vanishing Smoke hesitated for an instant, then shot straight down, a tiny point of light that shimmered like a minuscule firefly. He entered Snowsnake through his open mouth.

His consciousness swirled. He was falling into red darkness, tumbling and spinning. The primal force of the juices sloshing around him made him faint and queasy, yet in the next moment ravenously hungry. He felt unaccustomed body sensations, both intimate and alien: the ache of an old wound, over the kidneys; the corded strength of biceps and calf muscles; the throb of a jutting penis.

Aaaah!

Something collided with him. He thrust against it, closing the entry to it.

He clamped the jaws shut, noting the missing teeth at the front, the abscess behind the gums. He sat up and blinked. The salmon sky fractured into a myriad shards, like a broken mirror. Then the whole scene turned upside down. He stared at trees that were rooted high above him, at a man who walked on his head.

The scene righted itself. He looked at a big man he did not know, a warrior who had shaved his head to a tuft of fierce bristles above the fontanel.

"*Hagats,*" the stranger said. "We must hurry."

Vanishing Smoke picked through a raft of memories that did not belong to him. "Black Fox," he greeted the stranger, deciding this was his name.

"Black Fox is with the canoes," the stranger responded.

Two Dogs Fucking. Could this be right? The memory came to him, from the mind he had occupied. This one's mother had seen two dogs fucking, just after she gave birth. It wasn't polite to say the whole thing. Two Dogs was his name.

He stood up. He tested the weight of Snowsnake's death hammer. As he swung it, he saw the faces of dead and dying people. These brought no sense of pity. His blood rushed stronger. He remembered how he loved the hot spurt of an enemy's blood, how he had drunk the life force of the strongest and enslaved their souls.

Remember who you are, his teacher's thought moved through his mind.

Something slapped his temple. He brushed it away, remembering.

You are gone, Snowsnake. You are a dead man.

Where was his son?

He thought he saw a stirring among the leaves.

"We go now," he told Two Dogs. "You go on. I'll bring the woman."

He cut the Dutch woman free.

She spat in his face. "Kill me now," she said hoarsely. "You have taken everything I loved."

He hesitated. The rest of the raiding party had gone down to the river. He was poised between them and his son, who still imagined he was invisible, with this woman. He looked at her, and the hunger came on: to rend, to tear, to consume. The hunger came not only from Snowsnake, but from the things that lived in his energy field, darting and undulating tongues of appetency.

Remember who you are.

He threw down the knife. "You go."

The woman froze for a moment. She stared at the knife until her resolve was shaped to its point. Then she scooped it up and rushed at the man who had killed her baby.

He raised the death hammer. It was easy work, to drop this desperate woman. One of his women in Canada would braid and sew her flaxen hair into something pretty.

Remember.

Vanishing Smoke forced down the strong arm that was ready to release the death hammer. The body obeyed him reluctantly. Moving it to his purpose was like trying to walk thigh-deep in wet sand. And something flapped at his face, beating at his eyes, at his mouth. It murmured, *Let me in.* The words rattled against his teeth. *Let me in, let me in.*

He shut it out, closing his eyes, clamping his mouth, exposing his throat to the blade.

Let me in. Or I'll take the boy.

His intention wavered. He veered away from the plunging woman, so the knife merely grazed his shoulder. The delicious smell of the hot blood flowing from the wound made him avid to drink.

You're losing him, his teacher's thought contended with other voices, other yearnings.

Through a red fog, he saw an enemy at the edge of the clearing. A stripling. He could take him with a toss of his throwing hatchet.

He grinned as he pulled it from his belt.

The boy cocked his gun and misfired. Better still. He would take this enemy at his leisure, and drink in the energy of his dying breath.

A tremendous blow to the back of his skull recalled him to his identity. For a moment, he was viewing the whole scene from a different level, outside the body. He saw that the Dutch woman had picked up the war club he must have dropped. The body he had occupied was on its knees, fountaining blood. A batlike thing winged toward it, trying to reclaim it.

No, Vanishing Smoke told his enemy. *You are a dead man.*

Snowsnake fought with him. As they skirmished in their second bodies, Vanishing Smoke saw he had allies. The swarm of enslaved souls that had traveled with Snowsnake were escaping from him, now that his body was dying. They came beating toward him, intent on revenge.

Snowsnake screamed and fled from them. Vanishing Smoke flew after them, toward the Land that is lost to the light.

CHAPTER 11

CAVE OF THE MOTHER

1.

"Tell the dream."

The clanmother's fingers fluttered against Island Woman's wrist. Fruitpicker squatted on the girl's right. Redhawk sat across the fire; she must not bring her own pain, or the rattle of her own thoughts, into her daughter's telling. The other women sat with their eyes closed, following the flow of their breathing: ready to enter the dream.

Island Woman shuddered, not wanting to go back inside the evil dream. "You are not alone," the clanmother reminded her. "You are within the light, and surrounded by the light. You are loved and protected on all sides."

Island Woman's shoulders rose, her upper arms quivered as she let the blue heron—her bird ally—carry her back into the dream. A tunnel opened, and she flew into it, gaining speed until she was *there*.

"Many people are gathered on the far shore of a swampy river," she reported. "I know some of them. I see people from our village who have passed over, warriors killed in battle, women taken by the sickness of spitting sores. They are smiling and waving. I am glad to know they are alive. I am hoping to find my father. I am going to cross to the other side to look for him. I know he does not belong here. I have to rescue him."

"Why do you have to rescue him?" Fruitpicker asked softly.

"Because this is the wrong place. From a distance, everything looks normal, but it is all wrong. There is evil here."

"But you are going to cross the river anyway."

"Yes. I must find my father."

"How do you cross?"

"I have a canoe. I am pushing out from the bank. There is someone with me. I do not see the face. This one is powerful."

Island Woman squirmed. "I begin to see how people are living on the other side. Some of them are possessed by their sexual appetites. There is a woman who takes partner after partner, men and women both. Her head and bottom seem to be back to front. She rolls with many people, in a thrashing heap.

"The people on the other side are no longer themselves. They are mindless vehicles for lust and appetite. Their spirits have left them. They are easily seized and occupied by alien entities."

"Do you see these entities?"

"I see them as whirring things, like tiny wasps."

Fruitpicker nodded. "Are you still in the canoe?"

"I am nearing the shore. Now I can see clearly that the people on the other side are not really alive, not people. Their flesh is rotting. Their mask of welcome falls away as their hunger takes over. They are surging forward, trying to grab me. It's horrible! *Everything* on their side of the river is coming against me—animals, insects, bushes and trees. The earth itself is moved by this terrible hunger. *Keep away!*"

The girl flailed her arms, pushing the evil dead away as she relived the dream.

"I am fighting them. It is hard. I must avoid being touched by these creatures, even when they resemble loved ones. My companion is helping me. He shoots darts at them.

"*I can see my father.*" The girl's body vibrated so strongly she seemed to be lifting off the ground. "He spreads his arms to embrace me. I want to hug him, to give him my love. Aaaargh! He is not my father. There are worms in the sockets of his eyes. I have to get away—get away—"

"You are safe," Fruitpicker reassured her, tightening her pressure on the girl's wrist.

"I am running and falling."

"Where is your boat?"

"I don't know. I must have left it when I saw my father. I have to get away!"

"Call on your helper."

"Someone is coming to help me. I am not sure whether it is a man or a woman. He brings three little boxes, with openings like trapdoors. He releases the trapdoors, and whirring things come out and explode like firebombs. I am released from this place, but I am not yet safe.

"I am racing down an incline. I slide faster and faster over snow and ice. I find myself in a vast cavern, a place of blood offerings. Worshipers writhe in front of war posts and fetish stones. War priests move among them, wielding choppers with huge blades. Blood spatters everywhere.

"I leave this place of blood. Meeting strangers, I make a sign at the level of my heart, to show I am not one of the mindless dead who have lost their spirits.

"My helper asks if I am ready to go. He wraps me inside his feathered robe and carries me back to the canoe. When I recross the river, my blue heron is waiting. I fly home on her wings."

Island Woman slumped on the earth, exhausted.

"How do you feel now?"

"As though I could sleep for a week. I have been drained like a gourd."

"Rest for a little."

"Grandmother, what does it mean?"

"It means you have been called." Fruitpicker looked at the others. All of them were mature women, women who had borne children or were beyond the age of childbearing. Many belonged to the inner circle of the Women's Society, entitled to call themselves by its secret name. "You have been to the Land, and returned to tell the living. Our need took you there. Your love, and the guidance of the spirits who watch over you, brought you back to us."

"There is so much I do not understand." Island Woman could not hold back the tears, remembering her encounter with the ravening horror that had worn the semblance of her father. "Why did my father attack me?"

"*That was not your father,*" Fruitpicker counseled her. "You knew this, inside the dream. You saw something your father has discarded. The bright souls do not go to the Land. Those who choose to live there are souls who are lost to the light or who have stolen the souls of others. The rest are shells. We call these the husk people. They are not what they seem. Yet they often disturb the living and draw us far from our paths."

"Why was I shown these things?"

"It is a big dream." Fruitpicker paused, silently seeking consensus from the women. "A big dream must be honored." The clanmother searched the women's minds, finding hesitancy in some, not only because of Island Woman's youth. The story of firing darts and releasing whirring things from a box disturbed them. It hinted at the powers of a witching shaman, of a *rataenneras*, one who shoots arrows from afar. Island Woman could go that way, Fruitpicker recognized, if she lacked the wisdom and protection of the Burden Straps, the women who had dedicated their lives to healing bodies and souls. *Orenda*—the life force that moves all things—can be used for light or dark. Island Woman had already been straying toward the dark side, in her fierce determination to avenge her father's murder. Perhaps this was why the dream had come to her: to show her it was time to abandon this path and move on.

Perhaps it contained a darker and more urgent message: that Vanishing Smoke was in desperate need of help, to move on into the Light.

Fruitpicker's eyes rested on Redhawk's handsome but careworn face. Redhawk had aged so much since Vanishing Smoke's death. There was a streak of gray around the parting in her glossy black hair, a rarity in a Mohawk woman of her age. The clanmother felt Redhawk's withholding; she was afraid that her daughter would be exposed to terrible trials too early, blown apart by a flow of energy greater than body and mind could bear. To work this power was to couple oneself to the lightning. Without proper grounding, it was fearfully dangerous, not only to one person but to all around her.

Yet the power already moved strongly in Island Woman. Safety lay in the grounding that could only come through initiation into the inner circle. Fruitpicker tried to convey all of this to Redhawk, from her heart center, and felt an answering glow.

"Island Woman is young," Fruitpicker ruled. "But her body is already a woman's. And we knew when she came to us that she is an old soul, for whom the gates between the worlds are open. She will be cleansed with fire and water. She will descend into the body of the Mother, to a place where no man but the twice-born may go."

2.

Island Woman was smudged from head to heel with the smoke of sage and white cedar, and bathed in a fast-flowing stream. Under a crescent moon, she was escorted by two of the Burden Straps to the first of her tests. On a high ledge, above a limestone gorge, she was sent to walk naked between the violent rush of a waterfall and the cliff face behind it. She slipped on the shelf of rock. Between the hard spray and the rock face, she could not breathe. She felt as though her lungs would burst. She was tempted to stick her head out through the spray, though she knew the force of the cascade would thrust her down, into the green-black river at the foot of the gorge. She found a pocket of air and gratefully drank from it. She felt her breath move beyond her lungs, down through her belly, filling and renewing her. It felt like being reborn. For a moment she thought she saw the face of her birth mother, fatigued but triumphant, as she clutched her newborn to her heart.

The Burden Straps wrapped her in a clean shift, blindfolded her, and made her run with them along looping trails until she lost all sense of direction.

When she was unwrapped, she found herself standing at the edge of a hole in the ground, a passage of unknown depth only a few inches wider than the span of her shoulders.

"The way up is the way down." She no longer recognized the

woman who spoke. The Burden Strap wore a mask unlike the False Faces of the men. The eyepieces were huge and yellow, the nose curved like the beak of an owl. A shower of white feathers flew over her shoulders.

Island Woman tried to master her fear. *Nothing that faces me can be as terrible as the village of the evil dead where I journeyed in my dream.*

The woman with the face of a snowy owl handed her small corn cakes that smelled of honey.

"For the guardians of the threshhold."

Island Woman accepted the offerings, unsure what she was supposed to do with them.

Ssss-sha-sha-sha-ssssh.

The girl jumped at the first stir of the rattle. One of the Burden Straps was shaking a small turtle rattle. Noting Island Woman's moment of fear, she twisted her body into a sinuous snake-dance.

"It is not too late to turn back," she hissed. "But once you enter the tunnel, you cannot return by the way you entered. You must face and endure everything that confronts you. Or your body will rest forever in the womb of the Mother."

"I am ready," Island Woman made the promise to herself, more than her wards.

As she lowered herself into the hole, her heels found shallow steps. She began to gain confidence. Then her heels slithered off smooth, damp walls and she went falling and spinning into the void. She landed with a thump that rattled her bones, in a breathing dark.

She could not see her hand in front of her face, when she tried to check it for injuries. The silver light of the moon was gone; she could no longer find sky above her.

She *felt* she was not alone. Her fall had stirred something in the black depths of the tunnel, something that moved in its coils to seek the intruder.

She longed for her cat's eyes, for the eyes of the panther who had come to her in childhood. When she found them, she saw in her own light what was searching for her. Its scales rippled over a body thicker than her legs.

She threw the sweet cakes to it.

"I am here by right," she asserted. With her panther eyes, she found an escape. A low passage, no higher or wider than a woodchuck's hole, opened at the base of the tunnel.

When she tried to squeeze through it, her shoulders jammed.

When she withdrew, she saw the coiled danger rising to attack her. *You cannot return by the way you entered.*

She reversed direction, forcing the passage feetfirst. It yielded to her a little, like a living membrane. But her shoulders snagged again.

Your body will rest in the womb of the Mother.

A tremendous force seized her by the ankles and dragged her back and down. She was flying backward. Something clapped her forehead with the force of a bear's paw, and she dropped her body.

She flowed toward the Mother. She saw her as vast and beautiful and fertile, with the face of all women and the colors of all races. She opened to Island Woman, and the girl flew through the dream gate without hesitation, without reflection.

She flew through the womb of the Mother, into other worlds.

She walked on the face of the moon, and spoke with the spirits who live there, those who help the living and those who interfere with them.

She flew beyond the stars. Beyond the Wolf Star, she found a place of light that was inconceivably small and unimaginably dense and powerful. The stars and the planets, everything that composed the universe, seemed to emanate from it, rippling from this single source. She saw it as a seed, then as an egg.

She was told by a voice as deep as a mountain:

You are born of earth and sky, but your spirit comes from this star.

In your spirit, you are neither man nor woman. But in your body, you are woman, and you must teach and practice what belongs to women. Women are the life givers. Women are the healers. Women do not need to shed blood to gain power, as men do, in their darkness. Women return their blood to the Mother with the moonflux. This is part of your power. It is why you are feared by men, who place walls and taboos around you, and kill in the effort to steal the power that is yours alone. You will remember this, and live it. You will be an arendiwanen, *a woman of power. You will use this power to heal, to release and rescue souls, and to remind your people of who they are.*

☐

"Tell the dream," the woman in the mask of the she-wolf commanded. Island Woman knew this was Fruitpicker only because she held the wampum belt that confirmed her rank as Mother of the Wolf: the belt that depicted Ohwako, the she-wolf, suckling a boy and a girl.

Island Woman spoke haltingly. She felt drugged. She did not remember how she had returned from the cave, or how she had come to this larger cavern, where words ricocheted among the ancient paintings on the rock walls, above the deeper rhythms of the underground river.

"She has *seen*," Fruitpicker confirmed when Island Woman had shared as much as she could. "The Mother has confirmed her calling. She will be our sister. She will wear the burden strap."

They draped it around her forehead: a simple carry-strap, made different from what any woman would wear to support a child in the cradleboard or carry a basket of corn or firewood only by the delicately worked beading and the moosehair designs. The masked women wore similar straps, draped like sashes over their shoulders since they had put on the faces of their bird and animal allies.

It was not the way of the women to give themselves grand titles or fancy emblems in this society of healers. They called themselves Burden Straps and chose as their insignia the simple tool of a woman's work, because their mission was to carry the load of their people, both the living and the dead.

They no longer called Island Woman daughter or granddaughter. They called her sister. "You are not what you were," Fruitpicker confirmed. "You are the Burden Strap."

They rubbed her skin with sweet-smelling herbs, and oiled and scented her hair.

Then Fruitpicker said, "Island Woman was called to join our circle in this hard moon for a reason. She has come to help us stop the killing. She has reminded us where the killing fever comes from. It comes from our hungry dead, who try to feed on the life force of the living. It comes from men who are possessed by them. It comes from the greed and jealousy of men, who try to take what belongs to women by shedding blood, because they are incomplete."

Snowy Owl reached for the talking stick, and Fruitpicker yielded it to her. "This sickness comes from Hendrick Forked Paths," she observed with the night hunter's discernment for the pattern of things. "It will not stop until Forked Paths is pulled down."

"I know this thing," Fruitpicker agreed. "I am Wolf, and he is Wolf. Ohwako lives in both of us. But this is not a matter we can resolve tonight. We do not take from the tree until the fruit is ready to fall. What we can do, and must do, is to join the energy and healing that flows within the circle to the work Island Woman has been called to do *now*."

The clanmother offered the talking stick to Island Woman.

The daughter who was now a Sister took it reluctantly. She said, "I have been called to release my father's bright soul."

No one envies such a calling. No one in their right mind asks for it. But everyone in the circle of women understood the wisdom and the urgency of the dream.

"We will all stand guard over your body," Fruitpicker promised her. "The Earthkeepers we honor and invoke will watch over you at the gates between the worlds. You must call your own guide, the one who protects you and counsels you in your dreams."

Island Woman brightened. She could sense his coming. Sensuous and strong when he came, as now, in his panther's skin.

3.

Longhair watched over Island Woman, as she journeyed the roads of the dead. He was moved by the depths of the girl's love for her father, but even more by the courage that allowed her to go where few mortals chose to go.

Remember it is not enough to brave up. You must know when to hide your light.

In place of the feathered robe in which he had folded her, Longhair watched Island Woman create her own shield of concealment, surrounding herself with an egg-shaped field of indigo blue.

She was learning fast. Or rather, she was *remembering* in a hurry. After all, she had done this work during and in between plenty of other life experiences.

As Longhair had hoped, the force of a daughter's love was pulling Vanishing Smoke up from the hellhole he had dug for himself. She was guiding him upward, showing him the bridge of light he had seen and rejected before. He was rising quickly beyond many dimensions of the Otherworld that no longer had interest or relevance to him. He did not even notice many of the collective belief territories in which different religious groups tried to hold together their conventional versions of what the afterlife was supposed to contain. These looked to Longhair like stage sets where the props were in need of constant repair.

Vanishing Smoke was ascending toward his own image of paradise, which bore some resemblance to the stereotypical happy hunting ground. He would outgrow it, after a while; for one thing, he would get bored with stalking animals that can always be caught.

Watching Island Woman, Longhair was struck (as he had often been in the past) by the vital importance the *living* may assume in the guidance of spirits who have crossed to the other side.

The bright soul of Vanishing Smoke was home where it belonged, until it was ready to move on. Had Island Woman seen the need to put the dreambody—and the soul-stuff that still powered it—somewhere safe? Maybe not. In any case, it was time for Longhair to take over.

Vanishing Smoke had dreamed of a second death, a second burial, which is something all of us need. The blackrobe missionaries gaped at the ritual of the second burial conducted by the Hurons, Island Woman's birth people. But the priests saw only the movement of bones to a new grave. They did not see what was released, and what was laid to rest with the bones.

To listen to the priests, you would think that man has only two vehicles, a body and a soul. But spirit has many vehicles. At death, the body releases several souls, or vehicles of spirit, and they go to different places. It is quite important to know this, especially if you are required to deal with lost souls.

When his bright soul ascended with Island Woman, Vanishing Smoke finally took leave of his dreambody: his second self. This was not yet an empty husk. It was still fueled by a lot of vital energy.

Longhair scared off the nasty characters who were taking an unwholesome interest in this relic of Vanishing Smoke and its energy.

You cannot destroy energy. You can release it, transform it and relocate it.

The shaman captured what remained of the dreamsoul in his soulcatcher, a perfect prism of quartz crystal. He flew with it to a green hollow where bears were mating. He blew it into the mother bear's womb. A part of Vanishing Smoke would live with the bear, in a land that had never dreamed of a bear garden.

4.

Longhair shifted his attention from the relocation of souls to the relocation of bodies.

It would no longer be safe for Island Woman and her family at Two Rivers. They were threatened from two sides: by Hendrick Forked Paths and his warmongers, and by Two Hearts, the sorcerer, who followed the light like a moth that was sometimes powerful enough to bat it out.

Seth needed a new wife, and Redhawk was drawn to him. They would marry after a suitable interval. There would be no obstruction from the spirit world, now that Vanishing Smoke had been released. Already Redhawk's health was improving, her energy rising.

Island Woman would be safe at the White Village. *And closer to me.* Who heals the healer? Longhair would have need of her skill with medicine plants and her vibrant energy in winters ahead.

The shaman had dreamed of others who would come to the valley where he had planted the White Village with its Tree of Peace. He glided low over the woods where they were skinning and bleeding the pines, then soared aloft to get above the clutter and confusion of the newcomers' thoughts.

CHAPTER 12

REVOLT IN THE PINES

1.

The Palatines at the East Camp had celebrated the promise of the previous spring with a sugaring and a taffy-pull at the maple bush beyond the Fecks' cabin. When Conrad had gone over, he had found Eva tending the fire under a big black iron kettle filled with maple sap, gurgling and hissing as it boiled. When she saw Conrad, she dipped a spoon in the pot and poured some of the sap over a cake of ice, which she offered to him as it cooled. The homemade candy was quite delicious.

However, the Palatines and Governor Hunter had both learned that there was more to making tar than to boiling up maple sugar. For the governor this lesson was proving to be damnably expensive. Livingston had produced a local farmer, Richard Sackett, who claimed some knowledge of tar making. It turned out that Sackett had never actually made tar himself but knew someone who knew someone in the Carolinas who had. Despite his evident lack of qualifications, Sackett had a stolid, confident manner, and might be the closest thing to an expert Governor Hunter was likely to find. Bridger—the Queen's Superintendant of Woods—had decamped back to New England after cautioning the governor that it would take two years to produce his first shipment of tar for the Navy. Two years of paying Livingston's commissary bills before the Palatines would start earning their keep! Make that two and a half; they had come too late to make any progress in their first year.

Sackett advised that the Palatines should strip the bark from the north side of the pines, in order to concentrate the resin, while the coopers made barrels. As the sap rose in the pines, in sugaring time, it was noticed that there was a flaw in Sackett's method. The pines the Palatines had skinned were languishing. Some were clearly dying. He had ordered them cut them the wrong way. The job would have to be started over.

The governor fell into black melancholia. *This province will break me and spit me out.*

Conrad's people were unbroken, but their patience had run out. As the sap rose, the unicorn showed its horn.

The revolt began in the West Camp, in the wild country across the river. During the winter the Palatines around Sawyer's Creek had been reduced to grubbing for ground acorns and stripping the inner bark from the trees to boil up a meager vegetable stew in their out-door bake ovens. When the ice on the river broke up, they were in no mood to peel more pine trees. They wanted decent land where they could plant crops and raise livestock.

They harassed Jean Cast with demands for hoes and grubbing hooks and seeds. They raged over the quality of the hardscrabble they had been permitted to till for their family needs. God fearing but deeply superstitious, they murmured that a curse had been laid on them, and grew desperate.

One of their List Masters—the headmen recognized by the gover-nor—grew a monstrous kidney stone that would not pass. He reached the point where he could no longer make water, even when his sons helped him to stand on his head. He died in twisting agony, bloated by his own urine. Jean Cast picked Johann Christian Gerlach to re-place him as List Master. Gerlach was not a popular choice. He bore an evil mark on his back: a huge mole, fat and round as a cherry, with thick hairs sprouting out of it.

He is not one of God's people, said the older women. *The eternal Ad-versary has marked him as his own.*

Some of the men from the West Camp crossed the Hudson in home-made boats to discuss their complaints with the leaders of the East Camp. They met by a campfire in the Queensbury section, where Johann Weiser was List Master. He posted Conrad and several other young men to keep idlers and possible informers away.

Every man at that meeting had a fresh tale of hardship and injus-tice to report: a son or daughter carried off to Long Island or Jersey as a bound servant; a loved one lost to cold and sickness without proper food or doctoring.

"The Queen promised us our farms and our freedom," Gunther Bertelsmann said angrily. "How long before we take what is ours?"

"We eat the Queen's bread," Christoph Zeller reminded them. "We owe her our labor."

"We eat Livingston's slops!" Gunther jeered at him.

"Our grievances have been made known," Heinrich Rauch spoke up. "We will have redress, so long as we are known to be Her Majesty's loyal subjects. How many of us have volunteered to fight the French?"

Many of the men present indicated—by nods or grunts—that they had offered to go as soldiers.

"When Canada falls to the English," Rauch pursued, "we will have our reward. What is required of us is loyalty and patience."

"Loyalty and patience!" Gunther railed at him. "Always the good German! What did those virtues bring us in Germany? What have they brought us here? We are used like slaves, and fed less well."

"Nonetheless," Zeller repeated stolidly, "we eat the Queen's bread and we owe her our service."

"We came to America to do more than earn our bread," Johann Weiser intervened. "We came here to secure lands where our children will be able to support themselves and live in freedom after we have gone."

"That can't be done in the camps," Gunther protested. "So what is to be done?"

"Patience," Rauch counseled again. "We have been in America less than a year."

"Patience is for mules," Gunther complained. "It will break a man's back."

Johann Weiser took charge. "We have not survived all that God has given us to endure in order to throw away the prize when it is within our grasp. I understand Gunther's anger. My own boy Freddie was sent to Long Island as a bound servant. I have watched my family go hungry. But I did not come to America to make war on the English."

"They call us white niggers!" Gunther objected. "Livingston's factor said it to your own son."

"Hear me!" Weiser boomed. "One ignorant man, be he English or German, does not speak for a people. We will have justice. But not if we act and reason like a mob. The Queen is our friend. I believe Governor Hunter is not our enemy, even if he is deceived by grasping men like Livingston. We must remember what we have learned from He who brings the kings and the nations to dust. Did Moses fight Pharaoh? Did he lead the Children of God against Pharaoh's soldiers? No. He waited for the time when the Lord of Israel compelled Pharaoh to let his people go. And he brought them safe into the Promised Land."

"Is it Moses you would have us call you now?" Bertelsmann mocked him.

"I am no more than any man here. But I know in my heart we will have our Promised Land, and if you wish any to lead you, I will be that man."

"When?"

"We will be shown the time. We must be ready to meet it. Those of us who have been soldiers must train others, so we can defend ourselves whatever comes. We must send scouts ahead, to be pathfinders for us in Indian country."

"To reason with the wild men? That is not how Moses dealt with the Canaanites."

Gunther was proving himself a relentless troublemaker, but Johann Weiser knew the depths of his grievance. Gunther had lost his eldest son this past winter, and two fingers of his right hand to a slip of the ax while barking pines. Bertelsmann was not a man to turn from a fight, and men like this would be needed for what lay ahead.

"The Indians have been robbed and abused, as we have," Weiser said patiently. "I believe we can make them our friends. To do this, we must know their minds and share their lives."

Gunther was skeptical, and someone muttered that the natives were "devil's spawn."

"I have taken this task upon myself," Weiser said firmly. "I will risk my own son to make a path for our people. Can any man offer more?"

"What about the tar?" Gunther held up his mutilated hand. "I will cut no more pines until we are given the lands we were promised."

"There won't be any tar," old man Loucks commented. "Wrong trees, wrong method. They *might* get a little tar from the pine knots. I've seen children make tar from pine knots up north, in Sweden."

"I didn't know we had an expert. You have waited a time to tell us."

"No point in inventing new chores."

Weiser decided they would put some of the children to work, gathering and burning pine knots according to this Swedish method. If they produced any tar at all, that would surely put the governor in an accommodating mood. And the new activity might divert the governor's men from what Johann had set in train.

A runner had come from Seth at the White Village. He had given Weiser a knotted deerhide cord. Each knot marked a day. In so many days, Seth or his envoy would come to bring Conrad into Mohawk country.

Conrad's father stared across the river to the blue ridge of the Catskills. In his inner vision he saw beyond the mountains, to a golden valley and a comfortable farmhouse flanked by tall red barns, wheatfields as neat as pressed handkerchiefs, and a flourishing vineyard like the one he had planted in the Rhineland.

2.

The anger to which Gunther had given voice was not easily contained. Some men and boys in the West Camp chased a party of surveyors out of the woods. Then they marched to one of Livingston's warehouses, tied up the storekeeper, and carried off whatever food and provisions they fancied. They left the salt pork. With the milder weather, the meat had come alive; it looked ready to walk across the floor.

Jean Cast had spared Governor Hunter no detail of the deteriorating situation in the camps. He had faithfully reported the quantity of salt in Livingston's barrels, the talk of mutiny, the dimensions of the mole on List Master Gerlach's back. Now he wrote to the governor to advise that the Palatines had thrown their riders.

The Palatine rising not only threatened to sink Governor Hunter's personal fortunes; it posed an immediate threat to the security of the Province of New York. The Germans on the Hudson River outnumbered the whole population of Albany. They represented more than a tenth of the white population of the entire province. In a time of war, the dis-affection of the Palatines could affect the balance of power across the entire continent. The Palatines would surely never defect to the French; every family harbored bitter memories of French invaders in the Rhine-land. They had suffered a full year under the heel of Marshal Villars, who had ordered his dragoons to leave no village unburned and no woman undefiled. But though the Palatines would not go over to the French, a full-blown mutiny would open a second front, deep inside English lines.

Robert Hunter had been a soldier as well as a courtier; now he acted like one. He took sixty men from the Albany garrison, crowded them into boats, and set off downriver for the Palatine camps, leaving orders for more soldiers to follow.

The governor stormed through the West Camp, confiscating fire-locks.

"Your arms are the gift of Her Majesty," he reminded the Germans. "Since you do not fulfill your obligations to the Crown, they revert to her possession."

There was no open resistance in the mean villages along Sawyer's Creek, with their cabins made of logs laid horizontally and glued with clay, roofed with bark or (like Weiser's across the river) with cedar shakes, laboriously split in the late fall. Even Gunther Bertelsmann beat a tactical retreat when the governor ordered an assembly of the Germans in the West Camp. Flanked by fusiliers with fixed bayonets, he had Jean

Cast remind the Palatines of their terms of service—that they would
work for an indefinite period, until their debts were discharged—in the
German language, punctuated by drumrolls.

The governor called a private meeting of the leading men. Since
Jean Cast reported that Johann Conrad Weiser had influence with all
factions, the Weiser house was chosen as the venue for this gathering.
Robert Hunter was pleased that Weiser's wife, at least, seemed anxious
to please, offering little cakes from her stone oven.

The governor posted a heavy guard of fusiliers around the house.
The Palatine men crammed into the Weisers' single room, whose sole
luxuries were a few hanging pots and a Bible print of Moses crossing
the Red Sea. The governor spoke with his hat on his head and his left
hand on the hilt of his sword, pausing from time to time to allow Cast
to translate.

"Gentlemen, I am come to remind you of your most solemn covenant, which requires you to work at Her Majesty's pleasure in the business of Navy stores, until you have repaid the monstrous high costs that
the Queen, in her generosity, has seen fit to incur by shipping and sub-
sisting you."

When the Palatines were asked for their views, their complaints centered on Robert Livingston and the quality of the food he delivered.

"I will hear nothing against Mister Livingston," said the governor,
defending his adviser. "He has shown considerable restraint in the face
of dreadful impositions. His stores and even his prize breeding stock
have been thieved, and his agents insulted. I am sure that, in the matter
of food, Mister Livingston does the best that can be done on Her Majesty's allowance."

Johann Weiser's patience had reached its limit. He knew his son was
in the yard, trying to eavesdrop on the pretence of stacking firewood.
"Conrad!" he called out. "Bring the governor some of Livingston's dinner."

"There is no need for this charade," snapped Hunter.

Conrad dashed behind the bake oven and returned with a tin plate
that his father submitted for the Governor's inspection.

Robert Hunter's fine, discriminating nose twitched uncontrollably.
He threw up his hands. "*Take that away,*" he gasped, coughing into his
handkerchief.

The gray meat on the dish was animated by numberless worms. The
governor felt his stomach rise and fall with their motions.

"This matter of food will be looked into," Hunter promised. He
meant it. He had promised himself that he would break any German
who stood against him. Now he saw that a prime cause for the Palatine
unrest was the man he had trusted as his chief adviser. Commissaries

were expected to cheat a little, but Livingston was cheating beyond prudence as well as honor. *He is not only stealing from the Palatines. He is stealing from me.*

Johann Weiser shocked the governor by saying, "We do not need food from you. We are the best farmers in Europe. We will make the best farms in America, as soon as we are given the Mohawk lands the Queen promised us."

The hard memory of the failed meeting with the Mohawks in Peter Schuyler's parlor returned to the governor.

"Mohawk country is unsafe for you, so long as the French are in Canada," Hunter informed the Palatines. "You cannot farm with a plow in one hand and a sword in the other. When the war is done, and you have discharged the terms of your covenant, you shall have what was promised."

"Why not let some of us go to Schoharie now?" Weiser pressed him. "We are used to fighting the French. Those who go to the Mohawk Patent will defend the borders and grow food fit for humans, while the rest of us fulfill our contract by making tar. This will be fair to all."

The governor stamped his foot. "I am not here to argue with you people, but to remind you of the terms of Her Majesty's charity. Here is your land. *Here* is where you live or die!"

"Not me," Gunther announced.

There was a stir outside. Conrad, who had loitered within hearing of the conversation inside the house, ran off in the direction of Dina Zeh's cabin.

"You, man." Hunter spoke to Bertelsmann. "Yes, you. Do you presume to tell me you would break your covenant with the Queen?"

"It seems to me it is the Queen's servants who have broken her covenant."

"This is intolerable! I will have that man arrested! And any that speaks similar treason."

"My friend is intemperate," Johann Weiser said clearly. "But he speaks what is in many minds. We have no quarrel with you, sir. But we are free men and we will have what is ours by right."

"Free men? You are bound to serve at Her Majesty's pleasure! And do not imagine that I will hesitate to put any man in irons who forgets it!"

The captain of the guard put his head through the door.

"Captain Rutland—" Hunter seized this opportunity "—I want *that man* placed under arrest." He pointed at Bertelsmann.

"If I might just have a moment of your time, sir."

"What is it, man?"

"I think you'd better see for yourself, sir."

Governor Hunter joined him at the door. Across the brow of the hill, with Conrad Weiser in the van, a column of Palatines with firelocks over their shoulders marched with military precision. They were followed by a crowd of women and children led by Dina Zeh. Many of the women were armed with broomsticks, spades and chopping knives.

"What is the meaning of this?" Hunter thundered at Johann Weiser.

"When the call came for volunteers to fight the French in Canada," Weiser reminded him, "half the men in the camps signed up. There is the living proof we are ready to serve Her Majesty."

And to fight me, Hunter thought.

"Two hundred with firelocks, sir," Captain Rutland whispered. "If there's one of them. And if it came to something, I believe they would have us enfiladed."

"Her Majesty will be gratified by this show of loyalty," the governor told Weiser, his mouth tight. Clearly, it was not the day for arraigning rebels. He could return with more soldiers and try to take the Palatines piecemeal, disarming them village by village. But this would be the height and depth of folly, with the prospect that the French were preparing new acts of revenge for the botched attempt on Canada.

"I have been gentle with you this far," the governor cautioned the Germans. "But I warn you that if you persist in defiance you will feel the edge of my blade. This is my province, under God and Her Majesty, and I will supply a rope for any rebel."

3.

Conrad watched a woodpecker with yellow tailfeathers drilling through the bark of a dead elm to get at the insects inside the wood. How did the bird know that its food was there? Surely not by smell.

The woodpecker is a powerful ally. He takes his food from the unseen.

Conrad shivered. Where had this thought sprung from?

Shift to the second attention.

He had no idea what this meant. He experienced a jerk of pain, on the right front side of his head. As if the woodpecker were poking its bill inside his skull.

He sat down under the dead elm, wiping ice and snow from among the roots and pulling his matchcoat down under his bottom so his breeches would not get soaked through.

Shift to the second attention. Let yourself flow.

The glare of the sunlight reflected from the ice was fierce. He closed his eyes against it. Behind closed eyelids, he saw only a granular dark. Then something began to open, like a trapdoor. It was indistinct at first. Then he had the clear impression of a doorway opening wide. He felt himself moving through it, gathering speed. Scenes of the woods flashed by. White cliffs. A high shelf of rock. A cave. He was scared to look inside, scared of the old man with panther eyes who was waiting for him.

Look for me and you'll find me. Don't look for me and I'll find you.

Conrad shuddered and opened his eyes.

Seth stepped between the trees.

"My grandfather says it is time for you to come to the Real World."

PART TWO

SHAMAN'S
APPRENTICE

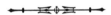

1712–1729

The Iroquois have, properly speaking, only a single Divinity—the dream. To it they render their submission, and follow all its orders with the utmost exactness.
　　　　　　　　—Letter of Father Jacques Fremin, S.J. in
　　　　　　　　　　*Relation de ce qui s'est passé en la Nouvelle France,
　　　　　　　　　　les années 1669 & 1670*

There is no birth of consciousness without pain.
　　　　　　　　—C. G. Jung

Raise yourself up, when you have left your old self behind, like an eagle.
　　　　　　　　—The Teachings of Silvanus *in* The Nag Hammadi Library

CHAPTER 13

LONGHAIR'S COUNTRY

1.

Longhair was one of the twice-born. Among the Real People, it was recognized that a shaman must die and come back from the land of the dead. He must walk the roads on the other side and learn the cost of entry at each of the gates. He must know how to pacify or outsmart each of the gatekeepers. He must know when to hide his light and when to let it shine. How else can he guide souls on the paths to the Otherworld?

Longhair had not asked for this calling. As a young man, he had run away from it repeatedly. He had tried to shut out the guide who came to him in dreams. Until the lightning had claimed him.

The storm had broken while he was dozing under a great white oak. A lightning bolt had ripped him from his body with claws of fire and hurled him beyond the moon, into the Upper World. He had flown over a country as fresh as the first day. He had walked with a teacher who showed himself as a radiant being of light. His teacher recalled him to knowledge that had belonged to him before he was born among the Real People:

I am with you always. Your mind on my purpose, my purpose on your mind. This is how you will always find me.

You were an interpreter before your world was born. You chose to come back in a savage time, among a warrior people, because of your love for humans and your deep nostalgia for a time when humans lived close to the earth and traveled between the worlds in dreaming. You championed the earth peoples even before the Link was formed, when others believed that an experiment with such a primitive species, so grossly enmeshed in physical reality, could not prosper. You chose to return among a people held to be primitive even by other humans because you saw that they kept the dream gates open and, because of this, were closer to the source of higher consciousness.

You returned to defend this people, and make bridges of understanding between them and the peoples with whom they are warring. You believed you could repeat the feat they attribute to you in their stories, of calling their dreamsouls to you in order to remind them that their spirits are starborn.

You fell into the confusion and amnesia that are characteristic of the earth plane. In place of your dream people, you found a people caught up in a toxic transition, divided within themselves and among themselves. You saw the dream gates closing, which is soul-death to humans. You struggled bravely, for a time, to hold the dream gates open. You reached out to Vanishing Smoke, as you reached to the little nun in Canada who was called to the New World by her dreams of you.

But, little by little, you too fell into the fog of forgetting. The miasma of the thoughts and appetites that surrounded you began to envelop you like swamp gas.

It was necessary to make you forget a great deal, when you came down the birth canal. This was essential to your survival. You remember this clearly now. How could you have survived childhood, remembering all you have lived as man and woman, and beyond the human condition? You would have been consumed by guilt or by pride, which might have been worse. You would have kicked and fought against the restrictions imposed on any child. It would have been very difficult for you to veil or contain your natural ability to influence events by pure thought. Among the people you chose as your own for this life experiment, this would have marked you as a powerful witch. It could easily have cut your life cord.

As you grew in age and in strength, I returned to you in dreaming to return to you, little by little, the soul knowledge that belonged to you before you were born among the indigenous population of the North American continent. There was a time when you performed the same service for me. We have reversed roles frequently. You remember this now, but you will not recall it fully when you go back. There is a limit to what the human equipment can bear.

As you grew the pride and the musculature of an Indian warrior, it became harder and harder to communicate with you. Soon you would hear me only when I assumed the form of a native god. Then you shut out even the voice of the Peacemaker. The spirits of war took possession of you, aided by distilled spirits. You could drink alcohol without serious damage in other lives—though it cost you your clarity and once your virginity, when you inhabited a woman's body. But as an Indian, it was dangerous for you to drink at all. Your native body could not metabolize alcohol, just as it cannot metabolize cow's milk.

You got sick in body and soul. In this condition, your spirit was often out of your body, but it was still impossible for me to communicate with you. Out of the body, you continued to blunder about in the same fog of blood lust and addiction.

You were saved by lightning. Now lightning is your ally, as your native friends would say. You had better say a special word to the Thunderers when you join in their prayers.

Longhair had not wanted to go back, to that world of pain and confusion. The Indians of his village had not expected him to come back. When he descended into his body, he found it folded in a shallow grave. Worms slithered over it. Maggots were already beginning to nest under his skin. They had pushed his knees up to his chin, the position of a fetus ready for rebirth. However, they had not pictured the grave as his womb in a literal sense.

When he pushed up through the thin layer of earth, his wife screamed her lungs out. She had blackened her face and ripped her clothes for the ritual period of mourning. When he reached out to her, pleading for her love and recognition, she had fled from him. When he followed her to the village, his people did not know him. Or worse, they raised hex signs against him, fearing him as the living dead, a vampire corpse. They had chased him from the village with stones.

When he saw his own face in the river, he understood. He had aged twenty years in appearance. His legs were withered. His hair, once black as the raven's wing, had turned completely white.

He saw that his people were right: what he had been was dead and buried.

When he remembered who he was, his people no longer knew him. He laughed at the bitter irony, and hardly recognized the noise that issued from his vocal chords. The harsh cackle drew an energetic response from a great black crow that was nesting in the lightning-struck oak.

Then the pain had flooded in, not only the pain of losing his identity and his loved ones, but the full torment of the flesh. He buckled under it. He felt as if red-hot needles were being driven through his veins. Huge areas of his skin shrieked like an open wound. He wanted to rip his skin off. He hurled himself into the river, hoping that the cool water would bring relief. It doubled his pain, making him howl so wildly that children at the village screamed and buried themselves in their mother's laps.

With practice, he learned to ignore physical pain. He did this by shifting consciousness. He learned that his body could not tell the difference between a thought or an emotion and a physical happening, so long as he empowered that thought or feeling with his focused intention. He could now do tricks, like walking on live coals or blowing fire from his mouth. There was no sleight of hand, but they were merely conjuror's tricks, all the same. He used them sparingly, and only for demonstrational purposes for the benefit of people who only trusted the evidence of the senses, and saw only with ordinary eyes.

By this time, he no longer lived with his birth-people in the north. He ranged far and wide, in his physical body and in his dreambody, over the Turtle Island the newcomers called North America. He explored the country of the Mound Builders. He wintered with a people who lived close to the arctic icecap and subsisted on a sickening diet of whale blubber and sealfat, but remembered how to dream. Shapeshifting into the form of the panther—a power animal they recognized and honored—he studied the ways of a lineage of shaman-priests on a mountain south of Mexico, a people who raised their apprentice shamans in total darkness and near-total isolation for the first fourteen years of their lives so they would never make the mistake of confusing the daylight world with the Real World. He sought among the newcomers for dreamers for whom the gates between the worlds were still open, or might be reopened. His best student was the little nun from Anjou that Canadians called *Marie des Anges*, Mary of the Angels.

It was not so easy for him to get about now, on an old man's brittle bones and arthritic joints. He had rested for a time with the Mohawks who lived at the French mission at Kahnawake. The children nicknamed him Shonnonkouiretsi, the One with Very Long Hair, and now he was content to be known by his nickname. Life at the mission was easier than in the Valley, as the life of a dog on a leash is easier than that of a wolf who runs free. But Longhair wearied of the constant meddling and suspicion of the blackrobes, who were terrified of *dreaming*, and of endlessly being challenged to psychic battle by killer shamans and power-crazed sorcerers. He saw how the decay of a spiritual tradition— the loss of the Link with higher consciousness—breeds power maniacs and black magicians. The tools of Power are mistaken for its purpose.

He dreamed of a place of peace, where people of all races might join together under the shelter of the Great Law of the Peacemaker, the message of redemption that spoke directly to the hearts and minds of the Real People. This was the birth of the White Village. The community born of Longhair's dream in the Schoharie valley had never been free of its own troubles. It stood athwart great crossroads, leading north and south, east and west. From all directions, people were drawn by its beacon. But they came hauling all their psychic litter, all their old vendettas and new appetites, with them.

So Longhair lived alone at the top of his high mountain wall, on the edge of the Helderbergs. He rarely showed himself in his physical body. But his bird and animal allies stood watch over the Valley. And the shaman made many visits in his dreambody. Some of those he visited in this way found the experience so real that they swore, like Conrad's father, that he brought his physical body with him.

2.

On the trail across the mountains, southwest of Albany, Conrad heard the trees snapping like musketry as the sap froze hard. The boughs of the hardwoods were bare, except for the brown, crimped leaves of the oaks. Oaks hang on.

The Mohawks set a cruel pace. Seth, his father's friend, ran in front. Talldeer, a boy his own age or a little younger, came on behind. At dusk on the second day Conrad twisted his ankle, scrambling out of an icy stream. Talldeer passed him and jogged ahead, without looking back, leaving Conrad to hobble after as best he could manage, or spend the night alone with the wolves and bears.

At last they stood on a hill above the Schoharie valley, and Conrad's heart leaped, because he saw that his father's dream had a counterpart in the natural world: in this broad, fertile floodplain, surely created for farmers.

The Mohawks showed him the place, above the White Village, that gave the valley its Indian name. The river in flood had uprooted whole stands of trees and swept them up into a huge natural bridge, taller than a house, rising to a point like a pyramid. This bridge of floodwood spanned the Schoharie just below the place where it was joined by the waters of a lesser creek.

At the village below Corn Mountain, on a hook of land formed by a bend in the river, Conrad was taken to live with Seth and his new wife, Redhawk, in a drafty bark lodge where the smoke was so acrid and the lice so persistent that he often crawled out at night to sleep in the fresh air under the stars.

At least, he told himself these were the reasons. There was another that was stronger than discomforts shared by natives and newcomers alike: the disturbing beauty of Redhawk's daughter, Island Woman. She was slim and supple, with swimming brown eyes. Fire glowed under her skin. It was painful watching her shaking out her hair and brushing it before she wound it into plaits, more painful still to see her dressing and disrobing—as all the family did—without concern for the presence of others. Though when she caught him spying on her, she would turn her back and cover herself modestly enough.

Conrad did not know enough of anything to be able to guess whether

Island Woman was taunting him or leading him on. Or simply impervious to what he believed to be his obvious endowments. Hadn't Dina Zeh assured him he would never have trouble getting into a girl's skirts?

He had no idea how to approach this one. Either she knew no English or pretended this was so, in order to avoid conversation. This at least was a goad to him to get on with his study of the Mohawk language.

Wherever he went, he would point at things and wait for one of the Indians to give him a native word for it.

The first words of Mohawk he learned, as a matter of formal instruction, were given to him during his first dinner with Seth and his family. They broiled a haunch of venison over the fire.

"*Owaron,*" Seth pronounced the syllables distinctly.

"O-wa-ron," Conrad parroted. This proved to be a generic term for meat.

"*Iawehkon.*" Seth smacked his lips.

When he put the words together, Conrad had constructed his first sentence in the Mohawk language. "*Owaron iahwekon.* Meat tastes good."

It was no easy task, to master a language whose grammar and logic were utterly alien to Europeans. The words piled on syllables like swarming bees. The business of pointing and asking for Mohawk names was often embarrassing. Miss an inflection or a glottal stop, and you might be mouthing an obscenity.

One evening Island Woman brought a friend to dinner, a bold, brassy young woman who was introduced as Moon Shadow. Conrad admired the way Moon Shadow consciously used her body as a weapon aimed at him. This was how he chose to interpret the way she rolled her hips and shook the hair back from her face. Moon Shadow smelled sweet, but different from Island Woman, who carried the scent of pine trees and wildflowers. Was the new girl wearing cologne?

She seemed to enjoy participating in his student game of point and name.

"*Satien,*" he practised on her, assuming the rights of a co-host for the evening.

"*Satien,*" she agreed, squatting down on the mat by the firepit that he had indicated. "*Satien onitskwaron.*" She began to expand his vocabulary. She translated, "Sit down and spread your meat," and burst into hoots of laughter.

□

On the surface, Conrad was excluded from little. He was not admitted to religious ceremonies in the Longhouse, and could only speculate on what went on there. But he was welcomed at the social dances, and that was where his troubles began again.

□

The deep rhythms of the waterdrums set the pulse of the village. Island Woman and Moon Shadow were among the first of the young women to arrive. They both loved to dance. The difference was that Island Woman confined her party games to the dance floor. She did not go off with the young bloods, like Moon Shadow, to drink trader's rotgut and couple in the woods or among the corn rows.

Island Woman was pleased that her mother's husband was lead singer tonight. Seth had a deep, compelling voice, and he kept the dance step good and fast. He shuffled around the earthen floor, bringing his bare feet down hard.

When the music changed to the duck dance, Island Woman was annoyed because the newcomer jumped the line to get in front of her. He might be handsome, as newcomers went, but he did not appeal to her. With his jutting brow and light stubble, he reminded her of one of the newcomers' goats, getting ready to butt. He smelled goatish, too. He was hot to get his hands on a woman. She could smell it.

And he thought he was such a gift to women, strutting around with his chest puffed out, when he could not even dance.

Conrad was out of step with the rest of the dancers, raising his arms when the other men were swooping down like drakes, rocking forward when they were rolling back. At sea with all this, Conrad tried to show off in his own way, stomping and leaping, vibrating his pelvis.

He was so busy doing this he all but missed his moment when the women bounced forward and the men's clasped hands came down, enclosing them. Conrad grabbed for Island Woman, squeezing too tight. His whiskers chafed her skin. He smelled of blind, impersonal sex, not that of animals, who knew their seasons, but that of the white men who lusted and lurched in all seasons without spirit or shame. She felt him harden against her. He glared into her eyes with wild triumph. He was actually proud to be rubbing himself against her.

Cloud Singer pushed Conrad away, rescuing his sister. Cloud Singer seemed to be contemplating stronger action against Conrad, so Island Woman murmured, "White men can't dance."

This relieved the moment of tension in the lodge, but did nothing for the tension that was roiling in Conrad.

When the dance was over, he saw Island Woman going off into the woods alone. He shadowed her, not an easy affair, since his big feet were forever snapping twigs. He saw her enter a shelter, no more than a lean-to under a tree. Was she meeting her lover? He lay in watch for a while, but no one came. He was tempted to seize this rare moment of privacy. There was little of that in Seth's lodge. He could not recall an occasion when he and Island Woman had been alone together for more than a few minutes. And that had been when she was doing something secret with dried roots and a medicine bundle, and had made it very plain his presence was unwelcome. Why not try his luck here and now? From what he had observed, the unmarried girls of the village were completely uninhibited from puberty to their wedding day. He had spied on their couplings in the fields. None of them, as yet, had given him a straight invitation, though he was sure Moon Shadow was willing. But Island Woman was the one he wanted. Her resistance added a little savor to the chase.

All the same, there was reason for caution. He was here as a guest, in the house of the girl's mother. Back in the camps, many people depended on the success of this mission. It would not do to offer Island Woman an insult that might lead to a rift. Was he really sure she was only teasing him? It seemed to him that when he had pressed himself against her, she had not pulled away. Until her big brother intervened.

He would wait for a clearer moment.

As he wandered back toward Seth's lodge, he heard gusts of laughter nearby, and changed his course. Bloodroot and some of the young bucks were drinking. There were girls there, too. He recognized Moon Shadow's throaty laughter.

"*Kats kanaka!*" Moon Shadow called when he showed himself. "Come here!" She patted the ground beside her, tilting her bosom.

Conrad's thwarted lust began to turn toward her. Bloodroot, an ugly, well-muscled brute, left no doubt he was not enthralled by the newcomer's presence. Conrad was no great drinker, but he calculated he could probably take on the whole bunch in a drinking bout and leave them stretched under the trees. Indians, notoriously, had no head for liquor.

This was a miscalculation. An hour later, after constant infusions of rum, Conrad was too woozy to notice Bloodroot reaching for his war club when he presumed to give Moon Shadow's thigh a friendly squeeze. The Mohawk came at him with an explosion of sound that left Conrad too dazed to get altogether out of the way. The fall of the death hammer almost dislocated his left shoulder. He balled his right fist and answered it with a killing punch to the heart that would have dropped any man he knew.

Not this one. They all came at him. When his survival instinct took over and he ran like a hare for the safety of Redhawk's lodge, he heard them screech, "*Sakoryas!* Killer!"

3.

That night, Conrad tossed in and out of sleep, fogged by rum, tormented by the throbbing pain in his upper arm and the deeper throb at his loins, bedeviled by monstrous things that violated the borders between sleeping and waking. Things that wriggled and squirmed. Things on many legs that swelled to the size of sheep or wolves. The phantom of his mother, who drifted coldly by, indifferent to his troubles.

Finally sleep took him and he fell into the dream:

I am back at the social dance, but everything is different. I am striding into a circle of naked women of all shapes and ages. They are avid for me. I pleasure them, one by one. My sexual power is immense and inexhaustible.

But this is only preparation for the one to whom I will be mated, the one who is She. She is young and tall and proud. She walks like a goddess. She embraces the serpent power that rises stronger than ever from my loins, and we shoot beyond the stars.

He woke with an erection so immense and so urgent that he felt he was going to burst his skin. He grabbed up a hunting coat and set out like a sleepwalker, back to Island Woman's shelter in the woods.

It is the dream, he told himself. He had listened, understanding a few words here and there, when Seth and his family shared dreams each morning and decided how to act on their guidance. He had formed the impression that the Mohawks regarded dreams as a final authority, that must be honored at any cost. The Indians believed that dreams revealed the wishes of the soul. Could Island Woman refuse him the fulfillment of his dream?

He felt a renewed surge of energy, rising from the root of his penis, as he barreled through the low opening of Island Woman's lean-to. The girl sat up, quick as a cat, and looked at him.

She smelled the fumes of liquor and sweat and raw sex.

"Go away," she told him distinctly, in English. "It is dangerous for you to be here."

"Dangerous for me?" He snorted. "That's a good one!"

He groped for her. He got a feel of her firm, high breasts before she slid away from him.

He stumbled after her.

She was outside the shelter now, naked in the cool moonlight.

"Go away," she repeated. "I do not wish to harm you."

"Come on, girl! I know you want it!" He grabbed with both arms. They closed on empty air. Where had the vixen gone?

He lurched around. She was returning to him through the shadows.

"I knew you wanted it," he panted.

He grappled with her. And recoiled from a force inconceivably stronger than his own.

Fuddled, disbelieving, he gaped up into the great dish face of what was surely the mother or father of all bears.

Okwari drew Conrad toward his terrible embrace.

Okwari considered the force with which he caressed Conrad's flesh. He touched the young man lightly, only enough to open the shoulder that was already bruised to the bone.

4.

When he came round in the morning, to find himself back on his sleeping mat in Redhawk's lodge, Conrad would have dismissed the whole affair as a nightmare or a drunken hallucination, except that he was groggy from loss of blood. And when he removed the poultice on his wounded shoulder, he saw five red gouge-marks that had just begun to mend.

Island Woman came with a fresh poultice, smelling of mint. She applied it with brisk and wordless practicality, as if this was part of their regular morning ablutions.

"Tewatokwas," he addressed her in Mohawk.

"*Serihokten*. Stop the words."

"I have to know—"

He stopped, because as she raised her chin, the skin drew tight against the skin and she no longer appeared as a handsome girl about his own age. She seemed quite ancient, a priestess from before the Flood.

"I will say this only once," she told him in English. "And we will never speak of it again. You will never again approach a woman in her time of power."

She said the rest with her mind, though she doubted the newcomer could receive it clearly. *You will be careful of the spirits of the Real People, when you rouse the anger of the Bear.*

5.

Island Woman did not speak of what had happened to the people of her village. But Cloud Singer and Bloodroot were determined, for their own reasons, to drive Conrad out.

Conrad's Mohawk was good enough for him to comprehend their words, as well as their intentions, when the thaw came and the river ice started to break up. Young people from the White Village had gathered to spear bass and sturgeon in the gaps above the floodwood bridge. And Cloud Singer announced curtly to Conrad, "You will run with us today."

Conrad walked with him down toward the river where Bloodroot was waiting, stripped to his breechclout despite the cold. Conrad supposed the slick of bear grease blunted the Indian's sensitivity to the temperature; he could still not abide the smell.

"What is the course?" Conrad shouted.

Bloodroot pointed to the mountain of dead timber that spanned the river. "Over and back!"

Conrad did not much care for this course. The heaped logs were coated with ice. Every step would bring the risk of toppling down into the angry river below, whose current, swelled by newly melted ice and snow, was treacherous and strong.

But, from the corner of his eye, he saw Island Woman and Moon Shadow watching. In their presence, he would not refuse a dare.

"Over and back?" Conrad repeated. "What is the prize?" He had observed that the Mohawks loved to gamble. A man might wager everything he owned on a throw of the bones—rounds sliced from deer antlers, blackened on one side—or the peachstones.

Bloodroot grinned and pointed at Moon Shadow.

She laughed, enjoying the spectacle of young men fighting over her. But she cried out, "Woman decides! *I* choose my man!"

This earned Moon Shadow an approving nod from Island Woman.

Bloodroot was no longer smiling. Mohawk women were strong—stronger, maybe, than the warriors they sent into battle. He should not have jested that a woman was the prize, even if Moon Shadow was tickled by his gallantry. Island Woman was watching, and she was a woman of power, one whose thoughts could kill—as well as heal—from afar. He resolved not to let his doubts impede his performance against the newcomer. The newcomers had no respect for women. Surely Island Woman, as well as Moon Shadow, would honor him for his victory, even if he had stated his intentions in a foolish way.

"When I win," Bloodroot announced, "I will take that."

He indicated the firelock Conrad had slung from his shoulder: the gun his father had brought back from the campaign against Canada. The gun that had saved Seth's life, when he was caught by the bear, and had won Weiser's people an invitation to this country.

"What will you give when *I* win?" Conrad countered.

"You can have this—" Bloodroot unslung his musket. "And this," he said as he dropped his death hammer. "But it will not happen."

□

Walking the floodwood bridge was like climbing tilted panes of glass. Conrad curled his feet inside his thin moccasins, willing them to be grappling-hooks, as he slithered and slipped on the ice-slicked logs.

Soon he was down on all fours, hugging the trunk of an uprooted pine. It made a crazy spire, pointing toward the sunset. Somehow, he clambered and wrested his way to the top of the heap of dead timber. Far below, on the east bank of the river, he saw Indians who seemed to be splitting their sides laughing as they monitored his slow torment, while Bloodroot skipped lightly and surely toward the far shore. How did the Mohawk manage it? Had he borrowed Mercury's winged sandals?

Conrad tried to draw energy from the prospect that Moon Shadow would welcome him into her bed if he won this contest. He could see her full body arch, feel her thrum against him as he entered. *Aaah!* He sprang unright, full of fight. He took a bold leap forward—and skated over the edge.

He saw the violent river, seething under the ice. Falling toward it, he managed to break his fall by grabbing hold of a protruding branch. It creaked, but bore his weight for long enough for Conrad to find a foothold and start clambering painfully back toward the top.

He no longer thought of Moon Shadow, and whether she would have the winner. He was sickened at the thought of losing his father's gun.

Clearly, the race was lost. Bloodroot had already made it over to the far side and was on his way back, chanting some song of battle.

The unevenness of this contest made Conrad boiling mad, beyond any sense of decency or honor. As Bloodroot approached, he threw out his arm and caught the Mohawk by the ankle.

Missing his step, Bloodroot lost his balance and plummeted down into the river. Conrad did not watch what ensued down there. Slowly, methodically, he crawled to the far side of the Schoharie. Then he crawled his way back, getting back on his feet only when he could see solid ground below him.

He expected to be greeted with blows and bitter jibes. But little about these Mohawks conformed to what he had previously learned of human nature.

The Mohawks seemed to think what had happened was a great joke.

"You won!" Moon Shadow applauded him.

"*Sakoryas!*" someone yelled. Others took up the chorus. "Killer! Killer!"

Conrad's amazement deepened when Bloodroot appeared to accept the judgment, offering his gun and his death hammer—which Conrad had the sense to refuse.

□

That night, Seth told a story for children, about how the turtle outsmarted the fox in a race across the ice, by having his identical cousin push his head up through a hole near the far side, so everyone was tricked into thinking he had made it across first. Conrad was learning that the Real People respected cunning as much as courage.

6.

He went looking for Moon Shadow with a bottle, bartered from one of the Dutch traders who haunted the valley for a pair of fox furs and a batch of coonskins he had taken with his own gun.

The long nights of solitary yearning made him urgent, when they lay naked together on a bed of soft grass. He tried to remember the tricks Dina had told him, the arts that pleasure a woman.

They were difficult to apply, because Moon Shadow boxed him in her own way, holding him prisoner until she was ready to bring on a caged explosion.

As he vented his seed, she gave him a new Mohawk phrase.

"*Khenoronhkwa.* I want your soul."

CHAPTER 14

SWEAT

1.

Moon Shadow had a cabin of her own, near the Schenectady road. It seemed to be a place of considerable traffic. Conrad noticed mementos of various nations: a Seneca moose-bone comb, a soapstone pipe from the West country, a Mission Indian cross, Delaware beaded leggings. Then there was all the white man's stuff: jewelry, whole bolts of satin and calico, pots and kettles. There never seemed to be any shortage of alcohol, even though Moon Shadow was as lusty a drinker as any man Conrad had come across.

"Where does all this stuff come from?" he asked her.

"I have a head for trade."

The item among Moon Shadow's possessions that intrigued Conrad most was a collection of locks of men's hair of varying colors and fineness.

"What are these? Your scalp locks?"

"You are right!" Moon Shadow screamed with laughter, showing the root of her tongue. "These are the scalps I have taken!"

She let out such a realistic impression of a Mohawk scalp-yell that Conrad was temporarily immobilized.

He had just learned the Mohawk word for scalp. *Onononra*. He did not yet know its etymology. *Onononra* literally means "spirit head." Mohawks said that when a warrior lifts a scalp, he captures a part of his adversary's soul.

Conrad was not jealous of Moon Shadow's other lovers. He was content to enjoy her body, whenever and wherever she was willing to have him, without plying her with questions. But he was obliged to ask him-

self, after a time, what was in it for her. She was beautiful, but wooden
in bed. Sometimes he felt as though he was having sex with a puppet.
He tried to interest her in some of the tricks he had learned from Dina
Zeh, but Moon Shadow's preference was to lie almost perfectly still, with
her legs clamped around his back, until she vibrated inside and made
him shoot off. He did not notice many signs of animal pleasure on her
side, although occasionally she mewled like a cat in heat.

They did not speak of love. Moon Shadow was actively hostile to
the concept of romantic love. She claimed there was no equivalent for
the word "love" in the Mohawk language, something Conrad later found
to be untrue.

Did she merely want to add another scalp to her collection?

He avoided her, laughing, the first time she tried to cut a piece of
his straw-colored hair.

"I will stalk you," she promised. "Like a warrior woman. I'll get
your scalp when your back is turned."

□

Moon Shadow had suitors who were less tolerant about competition than
her latest lover.

Indian men who had slept with her, or wanted to, laid in wait for
Conrad, challenging him to single combat. Sometimes they ganged up
on him and made him fight off a whole pack.

They needed no more pretext than the nickname that had been
hung on him at the White Village. *Sakoryas*—Killer—was in itself an
invitation to a fight. Conrad was now obliged to live up to it.

White men also gave him trouble. He got a black eye at Schenectady
from one rough Dutchman who called Moon Shadow a "trade squaw"
and "prime meat," implying he knew what he was talking about.

□

Conrad was puzzled by the fact that Moon Shadow and Island Woman
were friends. They were utterly unlike, in the way they lived and the
things they lived for. Perhaps this was the secret of their friendship, that
they complemented each other as do light and dark.

Conrad was not present the night Island Woman told Moon Shadow
they could no longer be friends.

"I *see* you," Island Woman warned Moon Shadow. "I know what you
do. You must turn back while you can. There are things without forgiveness."

Moon Shadow laughed like a screech owl.

"I am warning you," Island Woman repeated. "*Do not harm him.*"

"What is it to you? Why should you care anyway? *You* are the one
he tried to rape, in your time of power."

"How do you know that?" Island Woman was both furious and alarmed. She had ordered Conrad to keep secret the incident in the shelter where she stayed during her moonflux.

"I see things too." Moon Shadow laughed.

"You will not *see* me any more. I will not let you."

2.

Moon Shadow called Conrad to her bed in *her* time of power. Being a stupid white man, he would probably not even notice the difference.

Conrad *did* notice the altered sensations, and stared at the slime of blood and mucus when he withdrew his penis.

It made him uneasy. "I thought this was forbidden," he told Moon Shadow.

"All that nonsense our grannies taught us? I am a modern woman. I do as I please."

He accepted this. He did not see Moon Shadow carefully extract the pad of dry moss, on which she had caught his seed, from her vagina and tuck it away in a special pouch.

The liquor flowed faster and harder than ever in Moon Shadow's cabin that night.

"Trade must be good," Conrad observed.

"Drink it down! Less talking, more drinking! *Snekira!*"

Conrad did not see that, for once, Moon Shadow was drinking only water. His masculinity under threat, he kept up with her glass after glass, until he was heaving up on the grass outside the cabin.

He fell into a violent, roiling fever.

That was when Two Hearts, the bodythief, came after him.

Two Hearts had paid Moon Shadow well for this opportunity. The sorcerer was aging, and fatigued easily in his sack of meat and bones. In addition to his withered arm, he now dragged along on a crippled leg, the effect of injuries sustained in the fighting around Ketelyn's house, on the Saratoga road, when he had been preoccupied with shielding himself against being observed and attacked by Longhair, the shaman. It was time to take a new body. Why not the body of a young, vigorous newcomer with a good stiff cock and possible access to wealth and possibilities beyond the scope of the Real People?

Come to me, lost soul. I am whistling to guide you.

Outside his body, Conrad blundered about in a blanketing fog. There was a voice in the distance, calling to him.

It took on form. He saw his mother, opening her arms to receive him in her embrace. In the midst of the fog, he felt an answering surge of love, and shot toward her.

This is not my mother. It cannot be my mother.

He recoiled in fear and disgust from the evil phantom that revealed itself. It kept the form of his mother, but the light was gone from it. Nothing of the bright soul remained. It reached for him, as it had reached for him after his first night of sweaty sex with Dina Zeh, with impersonal, devouring appetency.

He fled from it blindly. The fog deepened.

Where am I? Where is my body?

A rush of wind sent him reeling. The winds swirled and reformed and resolved into visual forms. He saw two great war birds beating their wings, flying at each other, ripping with beaks and claws. One was a carrion bird, bigger and darker than any vulture Conrad had seen. The other was a shining golden eagle.

The eagle was stronger. As the tide of the conflict turned, it pursued its attack relentlessly. It seemed to be trying to capture the carrion bird in its talons. When it tightened its grip, the carrion bird shapeshifted into a serpent that slithered from the eagle's talons and fell away. The eagle swooped after it.

Mesmerized by this struggle, Conrad had all but forgotten his plight until a commanding intelligence reached into his mind.

Go back to your body.

He saw a path open to him and began to follow it. But something immense and evil rose up to block his way. It reminded him at the same time of a sticky, insect-eating plant and a woman's vulva. He was not going to go in *there*.

He tried to get round it, but was rebuffed by a living wall of blackness that pushed back at him.

Go back to your body. Do it now.

But how? Where? He stumbled around, lost and terrified. Then he noticed the smallest speck of light, high above his head. He started moving toward it. The speck of light became a round opening like a skylight. As he passed through it, he heard a bell-like sound and felt lighter, as if some burden he was carrying had dropped away.

He was rising toward an immensely greater source of light.

A figure took form. It looked like his mother. He hesitated, terrified of a further deception. He saw the soul-light shining in her eyes, and surged toward her. He was safe at last.

Go back to your body. You are not ready to pass over.

He wavered again, caught between the radiant vision of his mother and this insistent, compelling pressure on his mind. As he hesitated between the worlds, a great bird pounced on him in a rush of wings and caught him up in its claws. He watched from outside this other self. He saw it carried down, a lifeless corpse, in the talons of a storm eagle whose wings shadowed mountains.

3.

Conrad rolled onto his left side, but found no relief and returned to lying on his aching back, trying to breathe. His world was now reduced to the struggle for air. His gums were sore, his palate chapped and dry, from days and nights of breathing through his mouth. He focused his will on clearing his nasal passages, though this was quite painful. In—hold it—out—hold it. He noticed his belly swell as he sucked the air deep down into himself. He felt his ribcage lift, his chest contract as he breathed out. For a time he held the sensations of pain and conflict at bay, mindful of nothing except the rhythms of his breath.

He had no clear recollection of how long he had been lying here, back in the lodge of Island Woman's family. He had some memory of the pungent cloud of wood smoke that rose from Moon Shadow's cabin when Seth's people burned it down. Had he dreamed or witnessed the weird hunt among the high grass, first for a snake, later for a woodchuck that had been trapped and also burned? Who was the ancient man with the storm of white hair who had walked through the fire, jabbing with his stick?

I am your interpreter.

The words were not spoken aloud, but Conrad heard them distinctly, as he had heard them when he was trapped outside his body. This time the sender presented himself in what seemed to be fully corporeal form. He was standing by the firepit with Seth and Island Woman, leaning on his stick. An ancient white-haired man with shining eyes.

Longhair said, "You need to be cleansed."

□

They stripped Conrad naked and pushed him under a low tent of skins. They carried hot stones from the fire in cleft sticks and placed them in the middle of the enclosure. They sprinkled water mixed with herbs on the hot stones and the smoke hissed and curled.

The heat rose until Conrad felt as though he was going to burst through his skin, in every part of his body. He was still not sweating, though he remembered sweaty moments. Climbing a steep hill. Mucking out a pigpen. Running in the woods in blackfly season. Coupling with Dina Zeh. The dry heat in his body continued to mount. It was insufferable.

He felt as though he was going to explode like an overinflated bladder. He had to get out.

When he began to crawl toward the entrance, a firm hand restrained him.

He was panting in short, violent spurts. His belly sucked in and pumped out as if it had its own life.

Then the fever broke, and sweat gushed from every pore.

He saw himself as a corpse buried in the earth. He saw his body deliquescing, turning to jelly and liquid. He was sloughing off everything that had perished, releasing all the poisons he had ingested. He knew that when this process was complete, his bones would be picked from the earth, rinsed clean, and reassembled.

□

They carried Conrad, still weak from the long fever, to the cold stream and lowered him into the water.

Longhair told Seth, "Now his path is opening. When he can walk, you will send him to me."

CHAPTER 15

DREAMING TRUE

1.

"How can I repay you?" Conrad asked Longhair.

The shaman shrugged. "You can get me some firewood. It's hard for me to get around on these old bones."

Conrad spent a day hauling fallen timber to the shelf of rock outside Longhair's cave. Then he began the work of chopping and splitting. On the second day he was diverted by the spitting growl of a big cat—could it be a mountain lion? He slipped and gashed the calf of his left leg, quite deeply, with the ax.

Longhair ambled out of the cave, drawn by Conrad's moans and curses. He proceeded, at a leisurely pace, to bind Conrad's leg with a strip of cloth that he tore from the boy's shirt. He brought Conrad inside the cave and made him lie down while he brewed up some dried herbs in a pot. He rubbed the salve into the wound and pressed together the strips of skin and flesh that were hanging loose.

"You wouldn't need all this doctoring if you dreamed better," the shaman said.

"What do you mean?"

"You wouldn't have cut yourself with that ax if you paid attention to your dreams."

"I didn't dream this!" Conrad protested. "Don't you think I would remember if I dreamed I all but chopped my leg off?"

Longhair shook his head. "You newcomers are all the same. Like drunks on a bender. You go out at night and you don't have any idea where you were or what you did. No wonder you get in trouble all the time."

"Are you telling me I dreamed this was going to happen, even though I don't remember?"

"Nothing happens before it is dreamed. The dream world is the Real World, and everything that happens in the Shadow World begins there. That's why dreaming is important. If you can see what is coming, you might be able to change it. You might not have to go on chopping your leg off."

Longhair cackled so raucously that Conrad might have taken offence if his attention had not been diverted by the state of his wound. Whatever the shaman had put in the salve was amazingly potent. The bleeding had stopped. As he watched, he saw his torn flesh stitching itself back together.

"Look at me." Longhair reclaimed him. "How old do you think I am?"

He could be a hundred, Conrad thought. He had never seen anyone who looked this old. But he had also never encountered anyone in whom the life force blazed stronger. Longhair managed to light up everything around him. You could see the man's power, burning in his eyes. He walked the skies, yet he was fully present.

"Pretty old," Conrad said.

"I wouldn't be here, except for dreaming. When I was a young man, walking the warrior path, I dreamed where my enemies were lying in wait for me in ambush, so they got a surprise instead of me. When I was a hunter, I dreamed where a buck was feeding off the evergreens in the starving time. He had a mark on his chest, the size and shape of a child's hand. I shot him with an arrow in that spot, in the dream, to make sure he belonged to me. When I caught up to him the next day, I shot him again, in the same place."

Conrad listened, nursing his wound, not sure how much to believe. The old fellow certainly knew how to tell a story.

"It was always this way," Longhair continued. "Before *your* people had guns, before they even had knives or spears, dreaming was what kept them alive. That was the time of Stone Giants, and four-leggeds taller than pine trees. By dreaming the dangers they would have to face, people were able to survive. They might get a message from a dream visitor. Or they might go scouting ahead, in their dreambodies, to get a look at what was round the corner."

"If dreaming is so important," Conrad interjected, "why is it that I forget most of my dreams?"

"Most likely you're scared."

Conrad bristled.

"It's all right to be scared. Fear makes you sharp. Facing your fear is what makes you strong. But if you keep losing your dreams, you are probably running away from something they are showing you. Maybe it's something about yourself you don't want to look at, because you think it is shameful or because you see weakness there. Maybe it's something else. What are you afraid of, in your dreams?"

"I—" Conrad gagged on the bland phrase with which he had intended to turn the question aside, because the image of his fear returned to him. He saw his mother, not alive and not dead, as she had come to him the night he had slept with Dina Zeh.

"I'm afraid of my mother," he confessed. "I don't know who or what she is."

"Don't tell me. Show me." The shaman took his wrist, holding it lightly as if feeling for the pulse. "Go back into the dream."

"*I can't.*" Conrad started shaking uncontrollably.

"You must face your fear," Longhair reminded him. "You must finish the dream instead of running away from it. Remember you are not alone and it is acceptable to ask for help."

Still trembling, Conrad allowed himself to slide back into the dream. He felt himself moving at increasing speed. The vibrations became jolts of energy that surged from the soles of his feet to the crown of his head. He felt inclined to follow a point of light that appeared high above his head, above and behind his ordinary line of vision. Then he was shooting through it, moving at incredible speed through a round opening that became a tunnel.

He found himself in a darkened cabin. Was he really back in the East Camp? He looked for the sleeping forms of his family, but found only the thing that was and was not his mother. Her form was a dull bluish-white, diaphanous. As she reached out to him, he saw sticky threads hanging off her, drifting toward him. He did not want to be caught in these sticky, toffee-like filaments.

He remembered his intention. "Are you my mother?" he demanded.

There was no response, no sense of another intelligence at work. Only a blind desire to envelop and entangle.

Shield yourself, an inner voice instructed. *Surround yourself with the light.* Conrad could not tell whether his guidance came from Longhair or a part of himself more knowing than his everyday mind.

He pictured himself surrounded by a shining aura, and it instantly appeared. The ghostly figure retreated from the light.

"Where is my mother?" Conrad demanded.

Your mother has gone on, the same inner voice told him. *You will see her again, but only when you are ready to go higher.*

"Then what is *this?*" He looked with disgust at the husk-thing, whose tendrils were drifting toward him again.

It is something your mother discarded. You must dispose of it properly.

"How do I do that?"

No answer came. Conrad realized he was being required to improvise, in territory that was utterly foreign to him. The thing that resembled his mother looked more and more like an abandoned garment. He imagined rolling it up in a tight bundle and sealing it up in a chest, like the metal strongbox his father had brought home from the wars. To his surprise and satisfaction, he saw these things done.

Had he done the right thing? Had he really succeeded in confining whatever had been preying on his mind?

The harsh chatter of the shaman's rattle pulled him out of the waking dream, with these questions still on his mind. Longhair passed the rattle over his head and shoulders, then rubbed vigorously at the base of his neck. Conrad felt something hard being held firmly against this area. When the pressure was relieved, he saw Longhair drop what looked like a dried peachstone into a little deerskin pouch. The shaman pulled the drawstrings tight and handed the bag to Conrad.

"You should bury this out in the woods."

"I don't understand."

Longhair gave his irritating, familiar shrug, suggesting that this was of no consequence to him. "You can't destroy energy," he remarked offhandedly. "All you can do is move it around and change how it's used. Things that cling to the earth sometimes need a safe place to go."

Longhair busied himself with the fire, indicating that he was not minded to explain anything more for now.

"Can I ask you about the dream?"

"So many questions, rattling around in your head. If you stopped the noise, you might be able to *see* for yourself."

"But that's just it. I did see. I mean, I felt I was really back inside the dream."

"You were there. You were dreaming."

"And the thing that I saw—"

"That was not your mother. Trust what you learned. That was something your mother discarded. You can put it out of your mind now, and start dreaming better."

"Will you teach me?"

"Why should I bother with you? You'll never make a *dreamer*."

"Why not?" Conrad was deeply disappointed. He had believed that, in going back inside the nightmare, he had passed some sort of a test.

"It is like this. A real *dreamer* is always hunting his power. He goes out every night, like a hunter with a net, to stalk and catch dreams. The more dreams he catches and brings home alive, the more powerful he becomes. And *you* think because you brave up enough to face one unfinished dream, you're some kind of a *dreamer!*" Longhair hooted, then rinsed his mouth with tobacco water.

"If I bring you dreams, will you teach me?"

"Better you bring me some of that good German bread."

The mention of homemade bread—wheat and rye, inside a good thick crust, instead of the native cornbread, always greasy and sooty from the fire—made Conrad's stomach rumble. It reminded him how much he missed his countrymen, and their simple pleasures.

"You will bring both of us some of that German bread soon," Longhair told him. "Your dreams will show you when and how, when you learn to dream true."

2.

Longhair taught Conrad that there are big dreams and little dreams, and one of the ways you know the difference is through your feelings.

"Always trust your feelings," the shaman counseled him. "When you are dreaming true, you will know it because you feel you are *there:* all your senses awake, the colors are all alive. When you find your guide, you will know if it's a true guide by your feelings of *awe.* A big dream makes you shiver a little bit everywhere inside."

"I had that feeling you were talking about," Conrad told him a few days later. "I dreamed I was flying high up in the sky. I could see for miles and miles, all the way to the sea. I wondered how I could be so far up. Then I realized an enormous bird, maybe an eagle, was carrying me in his talons. The moment I saw this, he dropped me. I was falling and spinning. I was scared I was going to be killed. I wanted to get out of the dream, to get back to my body. But I stayed with it, like you taught me. When I stayed with the dream, I found I didn't have to go on falling, because I could fly by myself. Perhaps that was the eagle's lesson for me."

Longhair was not impressed. He contemplated his student with the expression of a boy who has just torn a wing off a captive fly, to see how it works.

"That was you, wasn't it?" Conrad challenged him. "The eagle who dropped me. *Was* it you?"

"*Serihokten.* Stop the words. You are too busy talking to *see.* Look at this." He showed Conrad a broad, fleshy leaf. "You go in the woods and get me more like this."

Conrad took the leaf. He was not confident about his assignment. At first glance, the leaf seemed indistinguishable from those of dozens of other plants he had seen in the woods. He examined it more closely, noting the slightly serrated edges, the furry underside. Well, he would do his best. He stood up.

"Where are you going?"

"To the woods, like you told me."

Longhair laughed. "You think you can just go in the woods and find this medicine? This *ononkhwa* likes to hide. You have to dream it. If it is in your dreaming, it will give itself to you. Then you can ask the *ononkhwa* spirit how you should use it."

Seeing Conrad's bewilderment, Longhair ordered him to sit down. The shaman got out his drum and tested the tightness of the skin.

"You keep forgetting you don't need to take your body with you when you travel. And you don't need to go to sleep in order to dream. To dream true, you need to *wake up*."

Longhair banged on the drum without warning, so violently that Conrad thought he was being shaken out of his skin.

"Good," Longhair cackled. "You are starting to wake up. Now, the best way to find *ononkhwa* is to ask the Bear to guide you. But I don't know whether the Bear is going to dance with you today. I don't think you are that powerful yet. So what you are going to do is this. You are going to get out of your body and ask the medicine spirits to help you. The spirits will always help if your purpose is good. They are with us now. They came as soon as they heard the drum. This drum is alive."

The shaman tapped lightly on his drum, laying down a steady, monotonous rhythm. "The drum will give you power and remind you of your purpose, which is to find this medicine. Close your eyes, so you can start to *see*. Follow your breathing."

Conrad began to relax into the flow of his breath.

"Now you can start to see another *you*. He's sitting just in front of you. He looks just like you. Look at him until he becomes completely real."

Conrad looked. He had no trouble visualizing this second self. It was astonishingly real. He noticed a mole at the back of the neck he had not realized he had.

"Now you are shifting consciousness," the shaman instructed. "You are moving into your second self. Take a moment. Feel yourself flowing into your dreambody. Look around from inside it. Now start walking around the cave. Look for something you didn't notice before."

Conrad found himself ranging the darkest recesses of the shaman's cave. There was something hanging from a spike of rock, inside a woven bag. He had not noticed it before. It seemed to be a mask, turned to face the wall. He wanted to go inside the bag, but Longhair recalled him to his purpose.

"Now you are ready to go out of the cave and look for the medicine. Ask the *ononkhwa* spirit to guide you. Ride on the drum. When the drum calls you back—" the shaman sounded four harsh, peremptory beats "—you must come even if you have not succeeded. Remember your purpose. Focus on the leaf from the medicine plant. You are moving into the woods. You are looking for its counterpart."

Conrad was outside the cave. He looked back, at the pattern of sun and shade on the limestone ledge. He felt a tug, something that pulled him back toward his physical body. He resisted it.

He was in the deep woods, traveling in dappled light. He was drawn to a cool stream. Day lilies were in bloom along its banks. A lime-green snake flashed out from under a rotting log. There was a sweet fresh smell in the air, the smell of ripening berries. Native women moved near the water, gathering cranberries in their baskets.

Island Woman was with them. Her coppery limbs swung free from a short deerskin tunic-dress. She popped a berry in her mouth. The juice moistened her lips like a kiss.

Island Woman turned her head and looked at him. The directness of her gaze startled Conrad.

He wondered if she could see him.

Island Woman set down her basket and waded through the bushes to the edge of the stream. She squatted down with a kind of reverence, as if she were praying. She patted the earth at the foot of a plant that came up to her shoulder.

Conrad recognized the fleshy leaves. This was the medicine plant he had come to find. Island Woman knew how it was used. The clue was in the appearance of the leaves. They looked like animal tongues— like the tongue of a doe, licking its newborn clean. This plant was used in cleansing, not only the skin but the blood and all the fluids of the body. There was more. It came too fast to separate out into a list of particulars. But he felt that at the right time he would be able to unroll all this information.

Was it coming from Island Woman, or from the medicine plant itself?

He wanted to touch Island Woman. She was even more beautiful than he had recognized. But what moved him was not sexual gravitation—or rather, it was something that remembered sexual desire but went deeper.

She pushed the hair back from the side of her face, where Conrad brushed her with his lips.

Could she feel him?

Something was pulsing louder and harsher. As the noise gripped him, the scene near the cranberry bog began to blur. He was being pulled away. He was hurtling back to the shaman's cave.

He landed with a bump. Something was misaligned. He twisted his shoulders, putting things back together.

He opened his eyes.

"Tell the dream," Longhair instructed.

Conrad rubbed his eyes, and pushed back the loose strands of hair that had escaped his queue.

"I seemed to be really there." He described the scene at the cranberry bog. It was a place he knew; he was sure he could find it again.

When he had finished, Longhair grunted. "You have dreamed true." It was the first compliment he had paid Conrad. The shaman brought out a couple of tiny tobacco ties. "When you go to gather the medicine, you will ask the leader of the plants for permission. You will return thanks with tobacco. We take nothing from the earth without returning thanks. You must bring the root as well as the leaves."

"How will I know the leader of the plants?"

"Don't ask what you already know. Island Woman has shown you."

"Island Woman appeared to me in my dream as a guide. Was that really her?"

"Island Woman knows the medicine spirits. Few men know them as she does, and only those who walk with the Bear. Island Woman can also teach you, if you stop looking at her as a man looks at a woman. She is not for you. She is an *arendiwanen*, a woman of power. That's something you don't mess with."

3.

Conrad found the plant, at the place he had dreamed, and embarked on further expeditions in his dreambody. He found that it was not hard to shift consciousness and leave the physical body, even without the aid of the drum. Longhair told him this was partly because his illness had loosened the connection between his physical body and his dreambody.

All he needed to do was relax, close his eyes, and picture where he wanted to go or whom he wanted to visit. His sexual appetites, never dormant for long, sometimes blew him off course. But he discovered that his sexual drive could also help to power his journeys. One night he started remembering his lusty nights with Dina Zeh. The memories gave him a throbbing hard-on. Instead of rubbing himself to orgasm, he let the vibrations roll through his whole body. The next instant, he was shooting off over the darkened Valley. He flew right into Dina's cabin, where he found her heaving and grunting in bed with a new lover. The scene was less than appetizing.

He left Dina's cabin and floated around the East Camp, noticing things that had changed. His father had built a new bakehouse and enlarged the vegetable plot. Johann Conrad had worked himself to the edge of exhaustion, providing for the family, defending the Palatines against Livingston's depredations, waiting for the signal to lead his people out of bondage into the Promised Land. Conrad felt his father's pain and fatigue, and the depth of his love for those who depended on him.

He felt an answering love in himself, and was anguished that he had found it so hard to express this.

How could he have allowed his hostility to Greta to come between them? *It is not good for man to live alone.* He now knew that his father had been justified in quoting that.

I love you, Dad.

He hugged his father, in his waking dream, releasing all the emotion he had kept bottled up. He was deeply moved by the family reunion that ensued. There was practical talk, of continued problems in making tar—they had been given the wrong instructions, and barked the trees the wrong way—and the possibility that Governor Hunter would abandon the project for good. People Conrad knew only slightly, or did not know at all, kept joining the conversation. There was urgent concern about raising money to buy land from the Indians directly, and about which of the roads to Schoharie would be safest for women and children if soldiers were sent in pursuit.

Conrad forgot he was dreaming, caught up in the intricacies of these discussions. New characters came and went. The Amsterdam jeweler to whom his father had sold his mother's brooch. A huge black man. He got into bed with Conrad and gave him a warm embrace, which seemed perfectly natural inside the dream—though it confused and disgusted the boy when he tried to sort out his memories later.

At some point after the black man got into bed with him, there was an abrupt change of scene, and the dream changed dramatically in its quality. While everything up till now had been happening in a murky half-light, the colors came vividly alive, and all of Conrad's senses were vibrantly awakened:

> *I am with Freddie, my younger brother, who was taken to Long Island as a bound servant. I am happy to see him. We walk among immense numbers of peach trees, groaning with fruit. The air smells of ripe peaches and salt water. We are near the ocean. There are oysters here as big as my foot.*
>
> *There are Indians here too. They are warning me about spirit bears, creatures set to stand guard over a sacred place.*
>
> *I see the bears. They are huge, as tall as high cliffs facing a rough sea. These cliffs are wildly beautiful. They are ablaze with colors—red and yellow, black and white. The ocean below them is also an unusual color. It is stained deep red, the red of fresh blood.*
>
> *I am not afraid of the spirit bears. I am going through a secret opening in the cliffs. I am scared of what lies beyond it. An immensely powerful being dwells in this place. It comes from beyond this world.*
>
> *My passage is blocked. I am sinking into something soft and rubbery that molds itself to my body. I am terrified it will swallow me like quicksand. When I fight its hold, its pull becomes stronger. I cannot breathe.*

But someone comes to guide me. I have to calm myself and move my arms and legs in a series of ritual postures. When I do this, the passage is open to me.

I am inside the sea cave. There is gold in the cave, bags and chests of it, spilling over.

The gold is of no consequence compared to the being that lives in this place. I do not know whether I can see this being in his true form and live. He makes me understand I may take some of the gold, no more than is needed.

Conrad woke from this dream charged with excitement, full of juice. There was a sweet, spermy smell of whale oil. He recounted his dream, in considerable detail, to the group of men who had gathered at his father's cabin.

Then he remembered he was dreaming. He woke up, a second time, among the familiar smells of rawhide and charred corn in Seth's lodge.

□

"You are learning that there are many levels of dreaming," Longhair instructed him when he had reported this dream. "To get to some places in dreaming, you must go through many doorways. You travel from one dream into another. On the way back, you wake up many times, into many dreams, until you are back in the dream of this Shadow World."

"It seemed so *real.*"

Longhair sighed. How many times would he have to remind the newcomer that the dream world is the real world?

"I found gold in that sea cave."

"This is a white man's dream."

"But do you think that cave really exists?"

"You went there. You should know."

But Longhair was also remembering a place on the coast he had seen in his youth, in the days when the Flint People still visited the Dawn People to trade for quahog and conch shells. A place where power had rested.

"You were given this dream for a reason," the shaman observed.

"What should I do with it?"

"You must begin by making sure that you understand everything you saw. You spoke with your father. I think it will soon be time for you to visit him. But there are things that are less clear. Who is this Amsterdam jeweler?"

"I saw him one day of my life. He is the man who bought my mother's jewelry."

"One of two things is possible. Either you will meet him again. Or you will meet someone who resembles him. When you dream about people you have not yet met, you often confuse them with people you already know. Now tell me about the black man."

"It's nonsense." Conrad was embarrassed, all the more so because he had omitted the scene of getting into bed with the black man in recounting his dream. The shaman had simply reached into his mind and plucked it out. Was it possible to have secrets from Longhair?

"Yes," the shaman answered his unspoken question. "But only when you truly dream strong. Are you friends with a black man?"

"No." But Conrad wavered, remembering the slave on the Livingston estate who had helped him when he was making off with one of the proprietor's prize sheep. A black man who had insisted on being addressed by his African name. "Well, there is a black man I knew slightly, when I was living with my family."

"Then he is part of your future too. And your brother?"

"Taken as a white slave when we came to the colony," Conrad recalled bitterly. "He is living with his master on the east end of Long Island."

"Then you will go to him. He, too, stands on your path."

"But the cliffs of many colors? The sea cave with the hidden treasure?" Conrad pursued eagerly.

"For this, you will need help of a different kind. I will dream on it."

CHAPTER 16

CAPTAIN KIDD'S LEGACY

1.

Robert Livingston had a recurring nightmare he shared with no one. In the dream, he was back in Wapping, a suburb of London he had once known quite well. It was a mild afternoon, and a good-sized crowd was gathering for the public entertainment at the execution dock, coming by coach and litter and Shanks' pony. There was raucous laughter because the pirate who was the center of attention was roaring drunk, bawling obscenities to the chaplain who was trying to extract a statement of contrition, giving the finger to the hangman who waited at the ladder.

Livingston was pushing his way through the mob, anxious that he was going to miss his last chance to speak with the condemned man. He saw the pirate mounting the ladder. He wobbled, but with people pushing below and pulling above, they got him to the top. The hangman kicked the ladder away and he swung. His cheeks plumped out, the tip of his tongue showed bluish between his distended lips. An obscene erection strained the coarse fabric of his seaman's breeches.

Livingston was sickened. It was too late.

But the crowd gasped as the rope strained and gave way under the pirate's weight. He fell to the ground, half-strangled. The chaplain swooped over him like a crow, hungry for words of repentance. Livingston bulled his way to the condemned man's side and peered into the empurpled, embattled face.

"Do you know me, Kidd? Can you forgive me?"

Captain Kidd opened his eyes.

The pirate hissed, "I'm taking all of it with me."

□

Kidd had done it, too: that is to say, taken all the pirate gold that counted
to Livingston, which was his own rightful share of the rich cargo of the
Quetta Merchant. This was the East Indian treasure ship seized by Kidd
on the Malabar Coast, the act of piracy for which his neck had been
wrung at Wapping and his body hung in chains at Tilbury Point for the
crows to pick, a festering caution to all sea rovers.

Livingston remembered the origins of his partnership with the pirate, Kidd. He had been doing profitable business with French buccaneers on the island of Hispaniola. Trading with the enemy in the West
Indies brought even richer rewards than trading with the enemy at Montreal, though the risks were not for the faint of heart. Livingston sent
Captain Cornelius Jacobs on the sloop *Orange* to sell the hungry French
a cargo of flour and butter, bread and pork. Captain Jacobs made the
return voyage safely. But there was a problem at New York. The customs
collector had been tipped off about the itinerary of Livingston's ship.
The captain told a good story, of how he had been driven into the
French port by foul weather, and relieved of his cargo by rogues who
had given him only a fraction of its value in exchange. The customs
collector had the gall to insist on inspecting the hold. He found bags of
pieces of eight and Spanish doubloons, and a quantity of linen and lace
worth several times the value of the outgoing cargo.

Livingston was brought to trial in New York on the charge of trading
with the enemy. The evidence against him was overwhelming. It threatened total ruin. But Livingston had one thing in his favor: the foreman
of the jury that heard the case was one William Kidd, a man who knew
that a favor owed can be better than money in the bank. Livingston was
found not guilty, and Kidd found a way to claim his favor.

Kidd hit on a sure-fire scheme to make his fortune. He promised
Livingston, whom he tapped as his promoter and prime investor, that it
would make him richer than he would ever need to be. Though Livingston considered that such a promise could never be fulfilled—how
could he ever be richer than he *needed* to be?—he was tempted by Kidd's
plan. Kidd would apply to the British government for a charter as a
privateer, a license to prey on enemy shipping. The government did not
issue such licenses willingly; the men who sailed under them had a habit
of overstepping the line between privateering and piracy, and they diverted seamen from the underpaid, undermanned Royal Navy. Kidd
would base his public appeal on the idea that he would be the scourge
of pirates, hunting down sea rovers from Madagascar to Snake Island in
an overpowering ship of war. His private appeal—the one that mat-
tered—would be based on recruiting several influential English noble-

men as silent partners in his project. This was work for Robert Livingston.

During a visit to London, Livingston enlisted the support of Richard Coote, the Earl of Bellomont, an impecunious Irish peer who was soon to become governor of both New York and Massachusetts. Bellomont nobbled a few of his powerful Whig friends, and Kidd's "war against the pirates" was born. There was an important catch. Not everyone was convinced that this hard-drinking, two-fisted sea dog would remember the terms of his charter once he was out on the high seas. The government, and the English investors, required guarantees. So Livingston put up the money to purchase a 10,000 pound bond for Kidd's good behaviour, in addition to providing part of the cash required for the purchase of the *Adventure*, a warship equipped with oars as well as sails, and thus a formidable fighting machine in all weather. Rarely had a juror been better rewarded for his vote.

What ensued was one of the most notorious scandals of the day. Every Fleet Street hack and popular romancer worth his salt, from Daniel Defoe down, had improvised on the theme. It continued—and would continue long after all the principals were buried—to excite the dreams of fortune hunters all over the world.

Kidd collected a motley crew from the London docks, and a second crew at New York. The seamen were engaged on the standard plan: "no prize, no pay." They would each get a share of the treasure they expected to seize from the pirates Kidd was expected to rout from their lairs. No booty, no wages.

Kidd sailed for the red island of Madagascar, a famous haven for pirates. He found no pirate ships worth plucking. He sailed on up the Malabar Coast and into the Red Sea. Still no pirate treasure worth fighting over. But there were fat, full-laden vessels out of Aden and Bombay, carrying silks and spices and slaves and the treasures of the Great Mughal himself. The fact that they sailed under the protection of the East India Company seemed a trifling detail, out here. Kidd could always say he thought they were French, or were flying the skull-and-crossbones. Or that his men were like starving dogs he could not hold back, which was true enough; he beat out the brains of one mutineer with a wooden barrel, hooped with iron.

So Livingston's partner, advertised as the scourge of pirates, turned pirate with a vengeance. He converted the grandest of the Great Mughal's treasure ships, the *Quetta Merchant*, into his flagship and sailed it back across the Atlantic. There was need for caution now. There was probably a warrant out on him; the East India Company, for certain, would want his head. He counted on his partners, Livingston and Bellomont, to protect him. But they might need to be reminded of the reasons. He could not go sailing into Boston or New York harbor until he had spied out the lie of the land. And it would be useful to convert his bulkier cargo into portable wealth: gold and gold dust and bills of exchange, for preference. He went island-hopping in the buccaneer waters of the Caribbean, dodging the Royal Navy, blurring his trail. He tied up his ship in the mouth of the Higuey River in Hispaniola, familiar territory to the Livingston clan, and opened a market. He watched silks and cinnamon turn into gold, neatly stashed in bags and coffers. By the time he was ready to sail north, in a smaller, faster ship, he had 500,000 pounds in highly convertible assets in his possession.

He was on his way to Boston, where both Robert Livingston and Governor Bellomont were waiting for him. But he was not going in blind. He had hired a lawyer to explain to the governor that his actions had been misunderstood, that any piracy committeed was the work of mutineers who had briefly seized control of his warship. He sent presents ahead—a fabulous diamond brooch for Lady Bellomont, a somewhat chaster diamond bracelet for Alida van Rensselaer Livingston—as a taste of what his partners might expect if they stood by him. He received reassuring messages in return, including a letter from the governor at Boston that he took to be a safe-conduct:

> *You may safely come hither and be equipped to go and fetch the other ship; and I make no manner of doubt but to obtain the King's pardon for you.*

Safety, Kidd perceived, lay concealed in that phrase: "to go and fetch the other ship." He must take only enough of his treasure with him to hone Bellomont's appetites. If he could hide enough of the gold in places where the governor and his partners could never find it without his help, they would surely never touch a hair on his head.

"Five hundred thousand pounds?" Robert Livingston echoed the number Kidd had just mentioned, when they met in Livingston's rented lodgings in Boston. "For half a million pounds, you can buy King William and all his ministers and still have change to buy every governor in the colonies."

"My feelings exactly."

"It's hard to imagine such a quantity of ready money. How much do you suppose it weighs?"

Kidd shook his head.

"How much did you bring with you?"

"I have brought you a small dividend on our investment." Kidd passed some bills of exchange across the table. Livingston inspected these with satisfaction; they were as good as cash, and lighter to carry. But his imagination was inflamed by visions of pirate gold.

"But the *gold*, man?"

"I have a forty-pound bag where I can put my hand on it quick enough."

Livingston licked his lips. A forty-pound bag of gold would be a sight indeed. Still, it represented only a fraction of the claimed half-million.

"You must be direct with me, William. We have known each other a long time. You would never have put to sea, but for me. You have sailed too close to the wind, and we could swing for it together. Forty shares in the prize are mine by right of our agreement. Now you will tell me, and tell me clear—*Where have you hidden the gold?*"

"I will not put you in danger, Robert. A man should not know more than he needs to know."

"You'll not outfox me so easily, Mister Kidd. And I warn you that if you speak to the governor in this way, he will show you the inside of the stone jailhouse before they ship you home to a gibbet."

"We'll talk some more on it, when I have seen Bellomont."

Livingston was frustrated with this interview, and filled with gloomy misgivings. Kidd was so damn cocksure that his buried gold would buy him out of anything. He did not know that Governor Bellomont's back was up against the wall. The panjundrums of the East India Company were howling for Kidd's blood, and they would soon be howling for the governor's dismissal if he failed to deliver up the pirate he had publicly endorsed. Livingston was not present for the discussion between Governor Bellomont and the pirate, but it ended as he had feared. Kidd was clapped in irons and put in Boston's stone jail.

This might not be the end of the road, Livingston calculated. The Boston jail had a way of losing its inmates. Within the past year, another notorious pirate had made his escape after a warder left the door open for him. At the very least, he might be able to dangle the prospect of escape in front of Kidd in a way that would convince him to say something useful about where he had cached his spoils.

They would not let him talk to Kidd alone, though Livingston greased several palms. A very bad sign.

"If you don't get me out of here," Kidd vowed, "it will all go down with me."

Livingston confronted the governor. "We are risking a fortune."

"I risk more than that, if we do not do this straight."

"Let me have another talk with Kidd. I'll work him around."

"You'll not jiggle with me, Mister Livingston."

Livingston spoke to James Mackie, his confidential man. Kidd's last ship, the *Saint Antonio*, had been seized by the customs men. Whatever was on it was already lost to Kidd's investors. But it was possible that, by retracing the exact route the *Saint Antonio* had followed, from the mouth of the Higuey River to Boston harbor, they could locate the places where Kidd had concealed his cargo.

"Find any man that served on the *Saint Antonio* with Kidd," Livingston instructed his agent. "There must be some that are still in the town. You'll know how to make them talk."

"That I will, sir." Mackie grinned, cracking his knuckles.

From drunken sailors in low taverns and knocking shops around the docks, Mackie began to construct the log of the *Saint Antonio*. Some of this, of course, was already in the hands of Bellomont and the customs men: the visits to Gardiner's Island (where gold was later found concealed in the eponymous Gardiner's mattress), to Block Island and other small ports of call off the mainland. There was a detail that caught Livingston's attention. At some of these stops, Kidd had gone off in a rowboat, or on foot along the shore, escorted only by slaves who did not speak English.

"Find me one of these slaves."

Mackie brought him in. He had stayed on at Kidd's lodgings after the pirate's arrest. Mrs. Kidd—who had hurried from New York to try to intercede for her husband—had been glad to sign over his papers, for a fair sum. His physical size and strength were unsettling, and he seemed to communicate in no known language.

"Angola? Congo? Madagascar?" Livingston probed. These words brought no show of recognition.

"Slave Coast, most likely," Mackie suggested. "Though Kidd will have taken him off one of the Moors he fleeced on the other side of Africa."

"Here." Livingston produced a gold sovereign. "You've seen plenty of these, have you not? You were burying gold with Captain Kidd. I want you to show us where you went."

They had a map of the eastern seaboard on the table. When they set it in front of the African, he scrutinized it with keen interest. He held the sheet up, looked at it from different angles, then spread it out on the table. With great solemnity, he pointed to a place with his forefinger. Livingston leaned across to see. The map was upside down, and the slave was pointing to a place in Newfoundland.

"The man is an idiot," he snapped.

"Or pretending to be one."

"You may be right, Mister Mackie." He watched the black man from the corner of his eye. There was something there that the African concealed when you looked at him head on.

"We will take him back to the Manor," Livingston ruled. He was already in the habit of referring to his Hudson estate in this way. "We will learn him some English and question him further."

Livingston decided to call the slave Cato. He did not ponder classical allusions. Slaves and dogs all had names like that.

When he could communicate in English—or simply decided to give up the pretense that he could not—the African told Livingston nothing about Kidd's last voyage that he had not already heard from others or that was not palpable fiction. Like the story of a giant squid Livingston once overheard him telling the servants' children. If the African who would one day introduce himself to a sheep-stealing German boy by his true name shared any part of Kidd's secret, he was saving it for himself.

I'm taking all of it with me, the condemned man vowed to Livingston in the recurring dream. Livingston always woke up in terror at this point. Sleeping or waking, there was nothing that gave the Scotsman the cold sweats as readily as the prospect of losing money.

2.

Longhair's people believed that there are dreams that require the participation of the whole community. An extraordinary council was called together at Seth's village, under the brow of Corn Mountain, because of Conrad's dream about the sea cave.

Not the least extraordinary feature of this gathering was that Longhair—who had long avoided showing himself in public—not only called it but attended in person. Children shadowed him as he walked to the council house, twisting their faces into caricatures of False Faces, whistling and blowing air like wild spirits of the forest. Their parents and grandparents, taking their places on opposite sides of the council fire, found the shaman's presence both thrilling and unsettling. Though Longhair was a "white" shaman, who used his powers to heal and protect, the Trickster energy was always with him. You never knew what was going to happen when he was around, except that you had better expect the unexpected.

Another unusual feature of the gathering at the White Village was that Island Woman, a girl still in her teens, was permitted to sit with her mother among the mature women on their side of the council lodge. This reflected the community's respect for Island Woman's precocious gifts as a dreamer and a medicine woman, and for her special relationship with Fruitpicker, the Mother of the Wolf Clan. Though the clanmother stayed at Two Rivers, Island Woman—believed by many to be Fruitpicker's chosen heir—would represent her in spirit.

Seth did much of the talking. The German boy they had nicknamed Sakoryas—Killer—had proved himself as a hunter, a dreamer, and a friend of the Real People. It was time to offer him a real name, and formal adoption into the Real People. This was approved without dissent.

"I know his father and his father's people," Seth pursued. "As do many of our warriors. We camped together on the Bulging Lake and shared many hardships. Those who have visited the Germans in their camps say they are hard-working farmers, who live close to the earth and respect the Mother. They make crops grow where none would grow before. They have been used as beasts of burden by greedy men, as our brothers have been used in New England. Yet they are brave and honorable warriors who stand by their promises.

"Now we have one who can interpret between us and them. I say it is time to invite the Germans to come and live beside us."

There was a stir of protest. Cloud Singer gave it a voice. "Redhawk's former husband gave his life to prevent these lands being taken from us and given to the newcomers. Are we to give the same lands away without recompense to this hungry swarm who will leave the deer no place to graze?"

"All of us here are newcomers," Seth countered. "My brother Cloud Singer lived beside the French until he came to us. Many of us under this roof were born among peoples far to the north or the east who speak in tongues the Real People do not understand. My grandfather dreamed that the White Village would be a place of light, a sanctuary for all who come in peace. Here we follow the teaching of the Peacemaker. We extend the rafters of our lodge in all directions."

"What will they pay?" Cloud Singer persisted.

"They may give us a share of their harvest. They will share their tools and their ways of farming. And their knowledge of books and of the science and medicine of the newcomers, because we must learn these too."

Cloud Singer grunted, unimpressed.

"Better than a few kegs of rum, gone by morning, along with our minds," one of the women observed.

"There may be more," Seth added carefully. "Sakoryas has dreamed of gold."

"All white men dream of gold," Nicholas Etakoam spoke up. "It seems the boy has not lived with us long enough to dream better."

Longhair tapped his staff on the beaten earth.

They all fell silent.

"I have dreamed with Sakoryas," the shaman told them. "He is young in years, like Island Woman. But like her, he dreams true." He described the dream of the sea cave, with its brilliantly colored cliffs. "I believe I know this place," Longhair continued. "It is the place of a powerful spirit. This dream must be honored, not because of the gold, but because one of the great ones has spoken. Etakoam and I will speak of this together."

□

Nicholas Etakoam, who had gone to London as one of the Four Kings, had risen and fallen, fallen and risen, as frequently and dramatically as any of his comrades. He had lived a wandering life, much confused by the bottle, before Seth invited him to join the community at the White Village. In the fall after his return from London, he had sailed to Port Royal with a band of Mahicans and New England Indians and taken part in the battle for Acadia. He had fought shoulder-to-shoulder with a Wampanoag Indian, Nicodemus Skuhwattan, who was killed by a French sharpshooter. After Skuhwattan's death, Nicholas had kept his promise to take his friend's widow his army pay and his share of the booty of war. He had made a long journey by land and water to the home of the Wampanoag's widow, Bethiah, on a remote neck of land on the west side of the island of Martha's Vineyard, off Cape Cod. These were the lands of the Dawn People, distant cousins of Nicholas' own people, the Mahicans.

Longhair asked Etakoam to walk him back to his cave, and told Seth to summon Conrad to join them there.

When Conrad arrived, he stared at the Mahican's close-set eyes and the flight of four tattooed thunderbirds that covered the right side of his face, from temple to chin.

"We have met before."

"I know you," Nicholas agreed, remembering the youthful sheep-stealer he had surprised at Livingston Manor. He glanced at Conrad's footwear. "You have better moccasins."

"We need your help," Longhair told Nicholas. "Conrad has dreamed of Moshup."

The River Indian's expression changed. His black eyes glinted like obsidian. Moshup was a powerful spirit. It was said he came from the sea, but there were old ones who whispered he came from the stars. The Dawn People said Moshup was a giant who rose from the sea and gave them the whales they killed for food and oil and covering. They whispered that this spirit now lived deep in the earth, in the hollow hills behind the sea cliffs that were dyed red with the blood of the whales.

Longhair instructed Conrad to tell the dream again.

When he had finished, Nicholas questioned him about the shape and color of the cliffs he had seen. Conrad let his consciousness flow back into the dreamscape. He saw black cormorants perched like sentinels on rocks that rose above the tide, on either side of the cliffs. He revisited the entrance to the inner passage that led to the sea cave. He looked down into a well of swirling energies; it was like looking into a whirlwind. He sensed again the immense power of the entity that lived beyond it, something more ancient than the human species. The sweet smell came back, a smell like a spermaceti candle.

"It could be Moshup's beach," Nicholas told Longhair, when Conrad had answered all his questions. The cliffs were on a remote neck of land on the island the English called Martha's Vineyard. The Wampanoag still lived there, sheltered by the sea from the despoliation their kinsmen had suffered on the mainland, under the ambiguous protection of missionaries supported by the Society for the Propagation of the Gospel in London. Wampanoag accused of stealing or sacrilege had been sold as indentured servants by their supposed protectors. Nicholas had been disgusted by the discovery that the son of his friend Skuhwattan had been bound over to a settler on Long Island for a term of thirty years.

"They have treated our people the same," Conrad told him, as these details emerged. "My younger brother Freddie is also a bound servant on Long Island, one of the first that was stolen from his family when we came to this colony."

Listening to this, Nicholas began to see the wisdom of Longhair's design of bringing the Palatine Germans to live beside the community at the White Village. Though they were newcomers, they had suffered at the hands of white men with rank and wealth in the same way as the Real People.

Longhair said, "I think Conrad must go to Moshup's beach, because of this dream. You know the Dawn People, and can make yourself understood in their language. Will you go with him?"

"I will go with him," Nicholas agreed, though he was not sure that this expedition was part of his own dreaming.

He wondered if the new events could be related to a dream that had haunted him for several months. In this dream, he saw Hendrick Forked Paths, wearing the antlered crown of a *royaner*. When someone pointed out that this did not belong to him, Hendrick flew into a killing frenzy, lashing out at his own people with his death hammer. In his dream, Nicholas was divided, unsure whether to side with his old friend or the people he was attacking. Then he realized that a man who was sleeping near to him was waking. The man was Vanishing Smoke. As Vanishing Smoke stirred, Nicholas understood that he must dehorn Hendrick. He ripped off the antlers and handed them to a woman.

Now he remembered the scene in Schuyler's house in Albany, when Vanishing Smoke had refused to sign the deed to the Schoharie lands, in defiance of both Hendrick Forked Paths and the Royal Governor. If Conrad's people came to the Schoharie country now, through a direct arrangement with Seth and the council at White Village, it would be a direct—possibly fatal—blow to Hendrick's authority. *I have dreamed this too*, Nicholas the Mahican decided, as he packed dried cornmeal for the journey.

3.

Conrad and the Mahican followed mountain trails back to the Palatine camp, to avoid the traders' towns and their questions. Conrad's father and siblings were overjoyed to see him. Even Greta seemed pleased and relieved. For the first time, Conrad found he could return his stepmother's embrace without the intrusion of anger or sexual guilt.

"Look at Conrad!" His sister Catrina skipped around him, delighted with the beaded Mohawk bracelet he had brought her. "He's nearly as big as Papa!"

"Nonsense," Greta judged. "He's nothing but skin and bones. Did you forget how to eat among the Indians, Conrad? Sit down, sit down. We have turkey, and dumplings and strudel. We'll soon put some meat on you."

After the meal, when Conrad was deliciously stuffed, Johann Weiser sent Catrina and Jacob to fetch the men he most trusted, to hear Conrad's account of life on the Schoharie. They liked the sound of the White Village, and the vision of harmony that inspired it. They liked even more Conrad's detailed description of the rich loamy bottomlands along the river.

"You say the Indians will sell to us direct?" Joachim Feck wanted this clear.

"That is what Seth told me."

The Palatine men talked this over. Their savings were modest. Their women had earned a little money over the past year, weaving and spinning and selling baked goods, but barely enough to furnish their kitchens and replace worn-out clothes.

"They will take payment in kind," Conrad reassured his elders. "Cash money has little meaning for them."

But what the Indians wanted most—metal tools and weapons, woolens and linens from English mills, not to mention liquor—were not in the possession of the Palatines. They would need things to barter for them, even if the Indians were willing to be patient and accept a share of future harvests as part of the purchase price.

"It will never work." Gunther shook his head. "Even if we find a way to pay them, and the Indians leave us in peace, the governor's men will come after us. There is no way the governor will recognize any sale to us by the Indians."

"One step at a time," Johann Weiser said firmly. "Possession is nine parts of the law. Let us establish ourselves on the Schoharie land, and then see whether Governor Hunter or a whole regiment of redcoats can winkle us out."

This was received with general approval. But some of those at the meeting had a further concern, given voice by Peter Helm. "What of our children that were bound out as white slaves? If we go among the Mohawks, will we ever see them again?"

"The Governor took my own son, Georg Friedrich," Johann reminded Helm. "If we are to get our children back, it will not be by dumb submission, but by demonstrating that we are a power to contend with. If we do this, the Queen will give us justice."

There were doubters at the end of the evening, but the dominant mood was of hope and defiance. The men squeezed Conrad's hand and shoulder, patted his back, soft-pummeled his chest. They all wanted to touch the young man who had been to the Promised Land.

□

"I'm going to see Freddie," Conrad announced to his father when they had a moment alone.

Johann was excited; it was many months since they had had any word of the son who had been taken to Long Island. But Weiser was concerned for Conrad's safety. According to the law, he could be held as a runaway servant who had violated his bond.

"I will go by a clever way," Conrad assured his father. "I will travel with a River Indian who knows the back routes."

He had decided not to share the dream he had told to Longhair and Nicholas with his father. He was not sure his father believed in dreams. On the other hand, if Johann interpreted this dream as literally as the Indians, it might encourage false hopes.

But Conrad did need to enlist his father's help in fulfilling one element in the dream, the part that embarrassed and confused him. He had dreamed of getting into bed with a black man. Longhair had insisted that he must find this black man.

"You must omit none of the steps that led you to the cave of treasures," Longhair had told him. "You must find the black man who is on your path. This is vital to manifesting the power of your dream in the daylight world."

Conrad described the black slave on the Livingston estate who had helped him when he was fleeing from Livingston's men with a stolen sheep.

"Livingston owns many slaves," Johann mused. "Robert Livingston owns too much of *everything*. But I will ask after the one called Cato. Why do you wish to talk to him?"

"It is a personal matter. I owe him a favor."

Johann Weiser did not challenge this. A boy who had wintered with the Mohawks must be counted a man, with a man's power of decision.

□

Eva Feck came with the news that one of her brothers had met Cato, and was going to look for him. She brought Conrad a keepsake: an intricate paper cutting. She must have spent many hours on this *scherenschnitte*, folding and refolding the paper as she snipped away at the elaborate continuous design. The white on black scissor cutting depicted a sturdy oak tree whose branches were full of hearts and calling birds.

"I made it for Saint Valentine's day," Eva told him. "Since you were not with us, I saved it for you. I heard you are going away on a long journey. Perhaps this will keep you safe."

"It's beautiful."

He bent to kiss her on the cheek, like a sister. She pressed her face up to his, offering her mouth. When he hesitated, she blushed and ran off.

He turned to see blowsy Dina Zeh wagging a finger at him. "I told you you'd be turning all the girls' heads when you graduated from *my* school, Conrad Weiser!"

It was Conrad's turn to blush.

4.

"So the white nigger came back." Cato Fatumbi accepted a plug of chewing tobacco, one of Conrad's offerings. "I figured they'd have measured you for a rope or sewn you up in a sheepskin by now. Did you ever see that happen to a man? They roll him in the hide when it's wet. When the sheepskin dries, it tightens and he's slowly squeezed to death. I saw James Mackie do that to a hungry man who stole a sheep."

"James Mackie should be shot. He is lower than any dog."

"Can't disagree with you there, boy. Given all the joys of life under Livingston's shadow, what brings you back?"

"I had a dream."

"Get out, white men don't dream."

"Maybe white niggers do. I dreamed you and I were in bed together."

"Get off!" Cato spluttered. "You ain't my type." But he was paying close attention.

"I'm not sure what it means. If two people are in bed together, it means they are close, doesn't it?"

"I guess. Though I've had to sleep in irons next to men who would have cut my throat rather than spit."

"I think it's about being close to each other—helping each other—in relation to something important." He told the rest of the dream just as it had come to him, without commentary, without efforts to interpret.

When he came to the part about the multi-colored cliffs and the sea cave, Cato grew very still.

Then he reached out and stabbed his forefinger and middle finger into the flesh of Conrad's neck, on either side of the windpipe, pushing with such force that he immediately cut off the air.

"Who told you about that?" Cato bellowed. "Talk to me fast, boy. James Mackie ain't the only one who knows how to finish a sheep-shagger."

He released his grip. Conrad's breath rasped in his throat. He nursed his Adam's apple as he tried to convince the African that he had truly dreamed what he had reported. Through his pain and fear, confronted with the rage of this man-mountain, Conrad was excited that his dream had awakened exact recognition in the black man.

Longhair was right. He had dreamed true, and this black man was one of the keys to the fulfillment of his dream.

They talked, and argued, and Cato started to reveal something and then cut himself off and brought out some rum. They drank a little, took a walk in the woods, drank a little more. Then Cato said, "How you figure on getting there?"

Conrad explained about Nicholas.

"Who else knows about this?"

"An old medicine man who lives among the Mohawks. He is the one who said I needed to walk this dream."

"Seems to me like you let too many people in on the deal already. But I might as well tell you. What I know ain't going to do me no good while I'm tied up here. And I won't get far with what I know without getting in bed with somebody else. In a manner of speaking."

It came spilling out, like a boys' adventure yarn. Cato's story began with his capture by a Moorish slaver, his sale and resale, his second capture by the notorious pirate Captain Kidd, and his role in Kidd's final voyage on the *Saint Antonio*, from Hispaniola by a serpentine course to Boston.

"Kidd had a shipload of gold and he was mad to hide it away where no one could find it. He picked slaves like me—men who could speak no English or affected not to—to do his digging work. Our last stop was at an island below a cape. I don't know the names. But I'll never forget the cliffs on that island. Soft clay. You fall in, you feel you're going to be buried alive. And the colors! I've never seen colors like them. Blood red, black as the pit, yellow as egg yolk."

Captain Kidd had chosen a natural marker to help him find the place where Cato and a second slave had buried a portion of his treasure below the spongy cliffs: a red stone shaped like the head and body of a whale.

"You'll have your share if I find it," Conrad promised.

"My share is my freedom. I bind you only to that. You find the gold, you buy me from Livingston, or get somebody else to buy me, and give me a paper that says I'm a free man. A paper nobody can quarrel with."

"You have my word."

"I know you'll keep it. Else I'll be looking for you with a wet sheepskin."

CHAPTER 17

MOSHUP'S BEACH

1.

Conrad and Nicholas Etakoam journeyed east into Massachusetts, instead of south along the river. Nicholas had family at Stockbridge from whom he believed he could borrow horses. And though a voyage down the Hudson by homemade canoe or on one of the broad-bottomed Dutch river sloops might be faster than the overland trek on which they were now embarked, it would heighten the risk of attracting unwanted attention, and leave the problem of finding a way to travel eastward.

They passed a ragged band of Indians—women, children and old men—moving in the opposite direction, their meager possessions bundled on their backs. Nicholas spoke with them, using hand signals more than words, and reported that they had been driven off their lands in the Connecticut valley by disease and the steady encroachments of European settlers. An elderly woman whose face was as deeply wrinkled as a dried-up apple offered Conrad a basket. Though Conrad had no use for the basket, he bought it from her with some of the money his father had loaned him for the journey to the coast. He felt a stab of sympathy for these migrant paupers; they reminded him of the grim exodus of his own people from the Rhineland.

"You got any use for that?" Nicholas challenged him. The Mahican inspected the basket and found a hole in the bottom. "It won't even hold corn."

"I felt sorry for them," Conrad responded gruffly. "That's all."

"You're not like the other newcomers."

"How do you mean?"

"You don't see the color of a man's skin. You don't step on people when they're down. And you dream the way we do. Or at least, the way we used to do, before our minds got confused by the clutter of white men's thoughts. How'd you get to be this way?"

"Longhair's a pretty good teacher."

"Before that."

"I don't understand."

"It must have started a long time before you came here. Maybe before you were born. Or else Longhair would not bother with you. Are there any others in your family like you?"

"Some people said my grandmother was a wise woman. But I hardly knew her."

"You dream about her too?"

"I don't remember."

"The gift runs in families. Sometimes it jumps a generation."

"Is it like that in your family?"

"It was once." The Mahican's face tightened. Conrad sensed something close down, like a vizor. Nicholas turned the flawed basket in his hands. "My mother sold baskets from village to village, to buy rum. Until they found her dead from the cold in a ditch." He balled his fist and drove it through the bottom of the basket. Then he flicked his wrist and sent it skimming away above the canopy of the forest.

□

The horses Nicholas borrowed at Stockbridge were not young, and the Connecticut roads were rougher than the average deer trail, but the weather was obliging and the travelers made good time on the journey to the coast. The sight of sandy pine barrens, followed by a glimpse of the blue waters of Long Island sound, made Conrad's heart leap.

His father had advanced him enough money to hire a fishing boat to ferry them across the sound. At the landing, Indians were roasting oysters and clams in the ashes of their fire. The oysters were huge. Conrad measured the size of one of them against his foot; they were very nearly a match. In the distance were scores of peach trees, a natural orchard.

If this expedition was madness, he told himself, it was a driven madness, goaded and supported at every turning by his dream of the sea cave.

He watched Nicholas trying to make himself understood by the Long Island Indians, some of whom were almost as dark as Cato the African. Even with the aid of sign language, it was evident they were having a hard time understanding each other.

"I wonder—" Conrad spoke fairly loudly, to everyone and no one in particular among the group about the landing "—if anyone can direct me to the residence of Mister Joseph Smith."

"I'm on my way there now," said a red-haired wagoner, who had
been haggling over the price of clams. "Come on, I'll give you a ride.
I'll be glad of the company."

When Nicholas walked over, the wagoner changed his tone. "I don't
know about *him*. Mister Smith don't care for Indians."

"You should be careful of your manners. This is King Nicholas, who
went to London as a guest of Her Majesty."

The story of the Four Kings had evidently reached as far as this
harbor. The wagoner all but tugged his forelock as he helped them climb
up.

□

They rode among flatlands where there was scarcely a bump in the
horizon, natural country for potato growers. The wagoner pointed to a
pretty shingled house with a widow's walk on the roof overlooking the
sea.

"That will be Smith's. I'd keep the Indian out of sight even if he
is a King. Mister Smith has an evil temper."

Nicholas slipped away while Conrad walked boldly up to the front
door. His knock was answered by a middled-aged woman with a handsome but careworn face. The smells of baking wafted through from the
kitchen. Mrs. Smith's hands were dusted with flour; she wiped them on
her apron as Conrad explained that he had come in search of his brother.

"Freddie is like family to us." She smiled. "Why don't you make
yourself comfortable on the porch while I fetch you some nice peach
cobbler? A young man your age must be hungry. I would ask you in, but
I'm afraid Mister Smith doesn't hold with visitors in the house when
he's away."

"I don't want to be any trouble. If you could just let me see Freddie—"

A shadow passed across the woman's face. "Oh, dear. I hope you
haven't come to take him away from us."

"If there is money owed, we will pay it." This was a half-truth;
Conrad could offer only the *promise* to pay.

"Oh, we would never hold Freddie against his will. It's just that—
since my own son died—he's been like my own boy." This brought
tears and a copious handkerchief. Mrs. Smith recovered herself. "Well,
of course you must see him and talk."

The fact that Mr. Smith was away in the city was another specimen
of the rare luck that had attended Conrad since he had shared his dream
with Longhair. He tried to remember the exact words the shaman had
used to describe this effect. *Dreaming, you can reach into the well of possibilities from which events in the daylight world are drawn.*

Dreaming, you can choose between the events that will be manifested in your waking life. When you make these choices in your dreams, you draw different people and circumstances toward yourself. Things come together in a different way, in the manner of dreams. The extraordinary becomes ordinary. You can remake your world.

Mrs. Smith had clearly lavished the best of her baking skills on Freddie. Conrad's brother was pink and plump as a roasting pig. He was wearing a well-scrubbed Osnaburg shirt and buckled leather shoes that looked new.

"You're turning into a country squire," Conrad teased his brother.

"And you're turning into an Indian," Freddie rejoined, inspecting Conrad's weathered skin, buckskin leggings and beaded pouch.

They strolled toward the dunes. Freddie was hungry for news of the family, as well as Conrad's stories of life among the Indians, but there were few indications that he had been pining away. His employers had required only light work around the garden and the house and down at the dock where Mr. Smith kept his pleasure boat.

They sat together, watching the swell of the incoming tide. Conrad's gaze drifted eastward, to the imagined profile of the bright cliffs of his dream. Was he supposed to involve his brother in this adventure? Freddie seemed an unlikely candidate, though he might be useful if he knew his way around seagoing boats.

Conrad was still wondering how much—or how little—to tell Freddie about his plans when Nicholas materialized from nowhere.

Freddie jumped up with a yelp at the sight of the heavily armed Indian with the tattoos on his face.

"Calm down, Freddie. Nicholas is a friend. He's the one who got me here."

Freddie shook hands gingerly, offering only the tips of his fingers.

"Are you sure you have the same mother?" Nicholas asked Conrad in Mohawk.

"Freddie's all right. He just hasn't lived very much yet."

"I found him." The Mahican switched back to English. He distended his lips, indicating the direction of the barns.

"Who?"

"Nicodemus Skuhwattan's son. The one the missionaries sent here as a bound servant."

"You must be talking about Boaz," Freddie contributed, now he had got his heartbeat down.

"Boaz?" Conrad echoed, struck by the succession of improbably Biblical names.

"Missionaries," Nicholas grunted. He made the gesture of turning a page, and running his finger down it. "They take everything from their book."

2.

The Wampanoag boy, unlike Freddie, had not enjoyed his stay at the Smith estate. Boaz had been forced to do manual labor and muck out stables and chicken coops. He had run off several times, and been flogged when he was caught. He regarded his service as a monstrous injustice. He had been charged with petty theft by one of the Mayhews, the principal landowners on Martha's Vineyard; a charge he vehemently denied. He claimed that his real offense, in the eyes of the missionaries, was that he had tried to keep alive certain ancient rites of passage they considered heathen abominations.

He was eager to return to his own people, and leaped at the chance Conrad offered him.

When he got wind of what was in train, Freddie declared, "I'm coming too."

"Are you sure about this? You seem to be some kind of favorite of Missus Smith."

"She's all right. But she's not *family*. And I'm sick of talking in someone else's language."

"There will be danger."

"I'm not scared."

"No?" Conrad tested Freddie's guts—and his reflexes—by throwing a sudden punch. To his approval and mild surprise, his brother side-stepped the punch and got in a quick jab that glanced off Conrad's ribs.

"You're in," Conrad agreed.

But how were they going to make the crossing? Boaz was in favor of taking Smith's boat. Freddie objected that this was unthinkable, in view of the kindness Mrs. Smith had shown to him, and Conrad himself had qualms about returning the favor of Mrs. Smith's friendly reception by stealing her husband's boat. Conrad doubted he had enough of his father's money left to hire another fishing ketch. Maybe they could "borrow" someone else's boat. They would have to hope that Boaz and Freddie possessed (or could instantly develop) the skills to handle it in open seas and to outstrip any pursuers. This was not a satisfactory plan, and Conrad worried about it all the way down to the landing.

He noticed that the boat that had carried them over from the Connecticut side was still tied up. A fresh plan began to hatch.

"We'll wait this out for a bit," Conrad announced.

An hour later, he recognized the captain who had ferried him across the sound, rolling back from a visit to one of his lady friends. He turned a bleary eye on the young Palatine who accosted him.

"Captain Slaughter? You brought me over from Mystic with my Indian friend."

"Never saw you before in my life." Slaughter huffed out a fog of raw liquor.

"I'd like to hire you for a longer voyage."

Slaughter squinted at Conrad, trying to reduce the blur in front of his eyes to a sharper image.

"Let's see the color of your money."

The captain guffawed when he felt the weight of Conrad's slim purse. "Not big enough to spit in."

He resumed his lurching, bow-legged walk toward his boat.

"There's more." Conrad clutched at his sleeve, as the inspiration came to him. "We left two good horses stabled at the port. You saw them yourself."

"Those broken-down nags?" But Slaughter's interest had been pricked. He slowed his stride.

"They are yours if you get us to Martha's Vineyard." Conrad did not dare to scan Nicholas's face for the Mahican's reaction. The horses were the property of his Stockbridge relations.

After further negotiation, well watered by rum and ale in the nearest tavern, Captain Slaughter agreed to accept a note of hand from Conrad, countersigned by Nicholas's Turtle Clan emblem, as surety that he would receive the horses as payment for carrying unspecified passengers to the Vineyard.

When they had weighed anchor, Nicholas traced a circle in Conrad's hair, above the fontanel. "You don't pay my kinsmen back for the horses, they're going to lift a piece just this big."

"Trust me," Conrad said. "Haven't I brought us luck this far?"

"I said you were different," the Mahican grumbled, "because my English is bad. What you are is crazy."

□

Off Gay Head, Conrad saw the cliffs from his dream. The colors were almost impossibly brilliant for earth hues. The waves at the edge of the beach were a deep blood red. On the south side of the cliffs, a natural formation in the clay reared up in the shape of a gigantic bear.

Boaz was staring as hard as Conrad. Then he bowed his head and made a series of rapid gestures, thrusting his arms out wide, raising them like antlers, crossing them over his chest, as he chanted singsong words in his own language.

"What is he saying?" Conrad asked Nicholas.

"He is thanking the spirits for his return to his own country," the Mahican said with respect. "He is asking Moshup to grant us a safe landing."

It seemed this stretch of water was notorious for shipwrecks. There were treacherous rocks off Gay Head, and though Moshup's beach was in plain view, the captain refused to go in close enough for them to wade or even swim ashore. He carried them round to East Tisbury, a small port on the other side of the island. There was a long walk ahead, to the place of Conrad's dream. Boaz, who seemed to gain energy and even physical size from the moment he set foot on his native island, wanted to start out at once. But Freddie pleaded exhaustion and hunger. Boaz had a keen nose for a clambake. He led them to a spot by the water where some of his people were baking quahogs. They ate clams and native cornbread until they were ready to lie down under the stars.

Drifting between waking and sleep, Conrad reflected on the unlikely succession of events that had brought him to the short, dark-skinned Wampanoag with the Biblical name who was proving to be central to everything. *My dream led me to Freddie who led me to Boaz.* Once again, waking events were following the logic of dreams, which was quite different from the logic of Aristotle. In part of himself, Conrad bucked and shied away from this heady play of coincidence and chance encounters. In the part of himself that Longhair had recognized and helped him to open wide, he recognized that coincidences, like the dreams they mirror, were homing beacons. He resolved to sail by their light as far as they would take him.

□

Boaz helped them to run the gauntlet from the port to the neck of land, called Gay Head by seamen, where the Wampanoag had managed to maintain relative isolation from the newcomers, at a significant price. The Dawn People had kept out the settlers who had spread over the rest of the Vineyard by giving Protestant missionaries a free rein.

One of the principal promoters of the Christianization of the Dawn People was Samuel Sewall, a witchfinder who was one of the judges at Salem. Judge Sewall had the sinister distinction of having voted in the space of a single year—1692—to sentence nineteen alleged witches, mostly young girls, to death by hanging. There were some who believed that Sewall's interest in the Wampanoag was a means of appeasing a guilty conscience in his advancing years. However, the Judge's tolerance for native folkways was no greater than for Anglo-Saxon girls accused of flying on broomsticks. Whatever his motives, Judge Sewall, in alliance with the Mayhews and other missionaries, had inspired the Society for the Propagation of the Gospel to take the extraordinary step of purchasing the whole of Gay Head Neck from Lord Limerick, with the design of turning it into a vineyard for the Lord.

Conrad had no interest in abstract theology. He already knew— though it would be years before he could articulate this clearly to other

white men—that true spiritual authority is the authority of experience:
of personal visions of things unseen. Yet he also knew, from the torment
in Europe from which his people had fled, that men kill each other in
the name of religious ideas more readily than for any other reason. He
doubted that this killing, and those who promoted it, had anything to
do with the teachings of those who inspired the religions in whose names
such crimes were committed. *His* Christ was a teacher who overturned
the orthodoxies of the pious and respectable, who healed in the way of
a shaman, by casting out evil spirits and through the direct transmission
of energy, and whose coming was announced in dreams and confirmed
by visions. At its beating core, was there really so great a difference
between the practice of Christ and the practice of Longhair?

He noticed that, after many years of contending with Europeans and
their religions, the Indians took sides in these matters according to calculations of survival. Mohawks went to live at the blackrobe mission at
Kahnawake in the hope the Jesuits would preserve them from war and
depredation. Wampanoag welcomed Protestant missionaries to keep out
settlers. The compromises rankled with some, like Boaz. It could never
be easy, living in two worlds. Conrad felt that division in his own being.

Boaz led them along a rough road, over several fords. He made complicated turns to avoid the house of the local sheriff, who had arrested
him when he was charged with theft. They crossed a narrow strip of
land, no wider than a causeway. Boaz was home. He leaped up the
hillside, flung himself full-length on the ground, and kissed the earth.

□

The indispensable Boaz was part of the solution, but also part of the
problem. He had gone along with everything willingly so far, seizing at
the chance to go home. Among his own people, he asked some searching
questions which revealed to Conrad that whatever Nicholas had told (or
not told) the Wampanoag was not sufficient for their purpose.

Boaz's mother, Bethiah, was a pleasant, flat-faced woman who welcomed her son's deliverers as members of her own family. In her *weeto*,
she served Conrad an excellent chowder in a bowl carved from an elm
burl.

But after the food and the family greetings, Boaz turned to Nicholas
and said sternly, "Why does the newcomer wish to go to Moshup's
beach?"

"Tell him I dreamed this," Conrad replied, when this was translated.
"Tell him a holy man told me I must make this journey because of my
dream."

This was not greeted with the same enthusiasm that Conrad had
encountered among Mohawks. Maybe Boaz believed—as many of the
natives seemed to do—that white men do not dream, or dream only of

making themselves rich. His eyes fell on the Bible that Boaz's mother had left on a shelf, next to an old powder horn carved with a scene of whale fishing. The sweet smell of whale oil wafted from the homemade candle set in a tin cup on the shelf above.

Nicholas frowned. "It's not so good," he reported. "Boaz says you are not permitted to go to Moshup's beach. This is a sacred place."

"Good God!" Conrad erupted. "We gave him his freedom and brought him back here, and this is how he repays us?"

"It is a serious matter," Nicholas said. "These people have lost many things."

Boaz spoke rapidly, with considerable force. "He says the power that lives in this place must not be disturbed. If the power leaves this place, the Dawn People will no longer exist."

Conrad was tempted to leave the debate. Surely there would be a chance to slip down to the cliffs with his companions and find the marker that Cato had described to him. On the other hand, it might be hard to find anything, thrashing about in the dark. And given Boaz's mood, it was easy to picture him rounding up some of his gang to drive them out—or worse, to confiscate anything they found.

Tell the dream. That was what Longhair would counsel.

It was hard going. Conrad had to pause often to allow time for the translation. He cast again and again to find synonyms for words that did not convert readily into the stew of Mahican and Wampanoag that the Indians were using.

As he stumbled on, Conrad sensed Boaz's hostility deepening. But he persevered. He tried to describe how he had gone back inside his dream and seen himself molding his body into several formal postures, to match the shape he saw inside the tunnel.

When Conrad mimicked these gestures, spreading his arms wide, then crossing them across his chest, Boaz leaped up and barked like an angry seal.

"He says you are copying him," Nicholas interpreted.

"How is that possible?"

"He says you saw him make these signs on the boat, when we were approaching Moshup's cliffs."

Conrad remembered. Yes, there *had* been a resemblance between the Wampanoag's curious hand signals and the motions he had made in the dream. But something different as well. He tried the motions again, this time holding one arm out flat from the shoulder while he raised the other in a vertical line above his head.

Boaz gaped.

He touched his eyelids with his fingertips. Then he touched his tongue. Conrad had no idea what was happening now. He looked to

Nicholas for guidance, but the Mahican shook his head, equally mystified.

Boaz crossed his hands over his heart. Then he reached out and placed his left palm over Conrad's heart.

"He says you speak truth," Nicholas translated. "Before sunrise, he will take you to the place you have dreamed."

3.

The cormorants perched on the guardian rocks, out in the surf, on either side of Moshup's cliffs. Conrad walked in his bare feet, following Boaz over a path of smooth, slippery stones into clays that slipped and yielded, remolding their surface as he passed. Though the sun was breaking, on this side of the cliffs it was still dark. In shadow, the form of the giant bear was even more striking; it seemed to be a living thing.

They waded around the point, where the waves washed against the cliffs. And walked into a blaze of multicolored light, like sunfire bursting through crystal. Half-blinded, Conrad was also exhilarated, drunk on all this light energy. He danced through the waves and threw his arms wide and high to greet the sun.

Boaz stepped over the narrow, pebbly beach and knelt in white clay, chanting to his spirits.

The cliffs reared above him, showing a thousand shapes and faces, shapes remolded by every rain and windstorm, every snowfall, every high tide. A place of savage beauty and infinite transformation, where forms were never constant. Even the stones where the cormorants perched were being resculpted every day, by the tides.

Conrad sought for words to offer his own prayer, in this place of power. As his eyes dropped to the ground, he saw the swell of a dark red rock that was almost at his feet, alternately revealed and concealed by the seawater lapping over it. Its shape, for now, was clearly defined. He saw the head of a whale, with its jaws slightly open.

He looked up at the cliff face above. There were several holes, or deep indentations, starting twenty feet or more above his head. How far would Kidd and Cato have gone? Surely no farther than necessary. Especially not if they were working at night, with the prospect of being discovered by Indians like Boaz.

"I think I've found it," he called to Nicholas and Freddie.

Boaz walked toward him, with his jaw set hard. Was he having second thoughts? Boaz took a pendant from his own neck and handed it to Conrad. It was something Conrad had not seen until now, a whalebone disk carved with a scrimshaw of designs that were unknown to him.

"He says you must go as one invited," Nicholas translated. "He gives you this so you may prove you have permission to enter."

"Thank you," Conrad nodded to the Wampanoag. He repeated it in Mohawk. "*Niawen.*"

He stripped to his breeches. Then, on reflection, he removed these too and stood naked apart from the whalebone medallion and his knife. This was going to be messy work. He noticed Boaz's quick smile of approval.

"He says this is how a warrior goes to meet the spirits of this place," Nicholas spoke for the Wampanoag.

Conrad asked Nicholas and Freddie to form a human platform, giving him a lift above the lowest, spongiest levels of the clay. To climb higher he had to dig in deep with hands and feet, and move on fast, because each handhold or foothold he established soon started to crumble. He was almost at the first hole when he lost his purchase and slid off the cliff face, landing in a heap of bones.

Freddie laughed. "You look like you've been mud wrestling a pig."

"You'll be the pig if you don't get me back up there fast," Conrad told him. He realized that he was slathered in clay from head to foot. The colors formed impromptu patterns, red on gray, black on yellow. He told himself he looked like an ancient warrior, not a pig wrestler.

On the second try, he made it up to the first hole. But this proved a false opening. It was either just a transient sinkhole, or it had been blocked solid by an earthslide inside the passage. Remembering the blocked opening in his dream, he tried to muscle his way through, but it soon became clear that there would be no passage without a major excavation, for which there was neither time nor equipment.

Wiping mud and clay from his eyes, he hauled himself up to the second hole. This seemed more promising. Down on all fours, he could wriggle along it at an angle that slanted gently down from the horizontal. When the clay was not sucking him in, though, it was devilishly slippery. He went skating on hands and knees into a grainy dark, at a steeper angle. He circled his fingers, trying to slow his downward slide, but succeeded only in breaking two nails while gaining more speed.

He was whirling downward, in a near-vertical descent. His head was pounding. He was terrified this place was going to swallow him up, without hope of rescue. He landed face downward, with a bone-shaking thump, in a deep bed of clay that instantly molded itself to his form.

And he knew that the dream had truly driven him to madness. There could be no way out of here. And he had risked everything for nothing. The idea that Kidd would send anyone slithering about in here—or risk treasure to such a sucking hellhole—was preposterous.

He moved his arms and legs, trying to free himself from the clay, hoping against hope that some way out of this trap would reveal itself. Unthinkingly, he windmilled his arms in the postures of the dream.

As he completed the series, he felt—or perhaps only imagined—something yield. Yes, there was definite movement in the tunnel. A slow earthslide, a deepening of the constant eroding and rearranging of the cliffs.

He was falling again, through the blockage. This time his fall was different. He fell on a moving bed of clay that supported him like a giant's palm. He fell through depths of color—surely invisible in the dark, yet fully alive to the other senses—to a place of green-blue lights, of light filtered through seawater.

He lay on his back in the sea cave, deep inside the dream.

There was a presence in this place, a power that overwhelmed him. It inspired both terror and reverence. It communicated with him by thoughts that escaped linear translation, and through images that he could not convert into stable, recognizable forms. Like the cliffs, it was ever-changing. This entity lived vastly longer than any humans, but was not immortal. It could manifest itself in many life-forms. It came from beyond the known world, yet functioned like a force of nature.

Are you Moshup?

Conrad's question was answered with an impression of wry amusement, the tickle of the softest downy feather.

You show yourself as people are able to receive you. Is that right?

Again, the sense of wry amusement, this time melded with approval.

And you like to listen to people's stories about you.

Quickening amusement. Conrad found himself laughing in sympathy with it.

Many more things came to him, things transferred in a moment-point of time that might take years—a whole lifetime—to unfurl. At some moment, lost to any conception of time, Conrad remembered that he had come in search of pirate treasure.

That's not why you came. Was this his memory of Longhair, or the entity itself? *You came because you were called.*

Still, there was Kidd's treasure to be hunted. If the rest of his dream had been fulfilled, why not this? And it was what people expected.

He began to explore the sea cave. He saw now that there was a small opening, barely big enough for one person, under the surface of the waves. He would be able to swim out, though this would clearly limit what he could take with him. Unless he could lead the others back, under the water.

He knew instantly that this calculation was wrong. *He* was the one who had been summoned.

What he was seeking was in plain view, though camouflaged by

encrustations of barnacles and molluscs. He brushed some of the ropes
of seaweed off the top of the chest. It was not locked, but the hasp was
deeply rusted, and he had to use a rock to tear it from its rivets so he
could get the chest open.

Gold and jewels blazed inside the box, a storybook treasure, beyond
even his dream.

He considered the possibilities. The rubies and diamonds must be
the most valuable items, as well as the easiest to carry, but it might be
hard to find a discreet fence for them. Maybe not so hard, he corrected
himself, remembering the Amsterdam jeweler in his dream, whom Longhair had forced him to think about. He would compromise. He emptied
one of the bags of gold coins and refilled it with jewels and small pouches
of gold dust. He tested its weight against a heavier bag of sovereigns
and doubloons. Surely he could manage forty or fifty pounds and still
swim underwater.

Longhair had warned him to take only what he needed.

But who could say, exactly, what was needed? There were many
people to provide for, and the Schoharie Indians to be paid, and the
expenses of the homeward journey, and Boaz's silence to be bought,
and . . .

These calculations left him struggling with a savage undertow,
among sharp rocks that bruised ribs, weighed down by the twin sacks,
without a free hand to help him beat his way off the rocks and strike
back toward his companions on the beach. He had to choose. He chose
the lighter bag, filled with brilliants and the dust of the sun.

CHAPTER 18

THE FALL OF KING HENDRICK

1.

The leaves were turning when Conrad and Nicholas landed at Woods Hole, on a packet that plied regularly between the Cape and the island, and began their homeward journey. They had money for horses to speed their way through the red and yellow fires of the maple woods—and replace the two horses Nicholas had traded for passage to the Vineyard—though they had to take great care not to display their wealth in the sight of strangers. It was dangerous enough, weighing and bartering a few grains of gold dust with a merchant at the port.

In the Palatine camps, Conrad's father read the signs of a long cruel winter drawing near. He suggested to the other List Masters that they should confront Governor Hunter and demand a guarantee that their families would have edible rations to enable them to survive the starving time.

"We'll never get food fit for a pig from Livingston," Gunther pointed out.

"We will demand an honest commissary," Johann Weiser told the German men, though he doubted this demand would be met. Though stories were rife of a falling-out between the governor and Mr. Livingston, Governor Hunter was known to be deeply in debt; he was unlikely to risk a definitive rupture with a major creditor.

The governor's troubles were deeper than the Palatines knew, and Robert Hunter was determined they would not go unshared by others. When Johann Weiser went downriver, with three other deputies, to confront the governor at Fort George, Hunter received them wearing his sword.

"You men should count yourself fortunate I do not place you in irons, after the hospitality you accorded me in the camps. However, I wish to be fair and open with you people, so I will say my piece. Since you came to this colony, I have attended to your care and feeding at my own charge, and Her Majesty's Treasury has not deigned to recompense me for my expense. There seems to be no prospect of making tar in the quantities we hoped for—"

"Wrong trees, wrong place," Weiser observed.

"Wrong instructions," Joachim Feck added.

"Enough!" Governor Hunter pressed his fist to his temple. "I will brook no interruptions! This whole affair of tar-making gives me headaches. I will be brief. I can no longer pay for your maintenance. You must provide for yourselves until such time as your services may be required by Her Majesty again."

"How do you expect us to survive?" Johann challenged Hunter.

"That is no longer my concern. You are able-bodied men. You may hire yourself out to such Yorkers as need laborers."

"We did not come here to be servants. Is it not enough for you that you took our children?"

"Silence! Weiser, I warn you lest you forget yourself once too often. I remind you that you remain bound by Her Majesty's covenant until all your debts are discharged. You will stand ready to serve when you are summoned again.

"There is one thing more. It is reported that some of you people have been tampering with the Indians in the Schoharie country. This land is spoken for. If you presume to remove yourselves there and disturb our borders, you will be treated as rebels."

Johann Weiser knew better than to push this exchange to open confrontation under the guns of the soldiers of Fort George. He returned to the East Camp with the grim message that a Royal Governor had decided to treat free men worse than slaves. What kind of plantation owner turned his slaves out into the wilds to starve and then rounded them up when he wanted them to work again?

In the camps, the Palatines tallied all the abuses they had suffered. The cautious decided they might manage to eke out a living on the paltry plots they had been allotted on the lands the governor had purchased from Livingston. Some of the bolder chose to try their luck in Pennsylvania, where other Germans, led by Pietist and Lutheran ministers, were known to have settled. The boldest rallied with fiercer determination to Weiser's vision of the Promised Land of Schoharie. A hundred and fifty families, including the Fecks and the Zehs, declared they would go over the mountains with him. Some were eager to leave before winter closed in. But Johann—fearing the rigors of the starving time ahead and missing the son who would be their interpreter—decided to wait out the winter months at Schenectady, on the Mohawk River. So many of his people went with him that the price of bread in the town doubled, eating into meager savings.

2.

On the long ride to Stockbridge, among lengthing shadows, Conrad thought often about his dream of Moshup's cave, wondering over the exactness with which it had been fulfilled once he had allowed himself to trust Longhair's advice to look for a literal counterpart for every element within it. Yet there were still elements that had not found a place in the pattern of waking events. The Amsterdam jeweler was the one that was most on his mind. They would need a man who knew gems, was not over-scrupulous about their source, and could yet be trusted to deliver a fair price and keep his mouth shut.

He was elated by the value of the gift he would bring his father, and their friends who had suffered so much in the camps. At the same time, he found himself deeply reluctant to face the demand for explanations that must follow when he revealed his find to his family. He could hear Greta nagging and accusing. *Conrad must have stolen this hoard. You know he is a wild animal, capable of anything. He will bring bloodhounds down on our necks.* And he could hear her whining and calculating, in the next breath, *This belongs to us, to our family. Divide it, and it is only a pittance.* Was he being unfair? He had found it no hardship to be civil to his stepmother, when he last saw her. Yet he remembered how she had cheerfully waved goodbye to Freddie when the governor's men placed him in bondage, and had urged his father to let them take him as well. *One less mouth to feed.*

So he was not disappointed when he arrived at the East Camp to find that his family had already moved on, having sold their log cabin to Widow Gerhardt, one of the few Palatines who had any ready money. He concluded it would be no disloyalty to send Freddie on to Schenectady while he returned across the Catskills to Seth's village, back to the people who had trusted his dream.

□

Longhair displayed no more surprise or excitement when Conrad showed him the contents of the sack than he might have done had he been looking into a bag of parched cornmeal.

"Tell me what is in your heart."

"I want you to take whatever you need. But for you, I would never have had the courage to find what was waiting for me."

"My needs are small. A pinch of tobacco, a little English tea, cornmeal for the winter. My old sack of meat and bones hardly remembers what it is to be a man. What do *you* want?"

"I want this to be a gift for all. My father's people need land to farm. Your people should be paid an honest price for it."

"This is a matter for the women," Longhair judged. "The women are the owners of our fields, so far as the body of the Mother can ever be owned, though there are men of the Real People who have forgotten this. And our women know how to deal with the traders. Our men cannot do this. They drink from the trader's bottle, and then the bottle drinks them. I will search the minds of our women. But first you will tell me what you found at Moshup's beach. *Not like that*," the shaman cut Conrad off, as he opened his mouth to speak. "Have you forgotten so soon?"

They lay together, shoulder to shoulder, hip to hip, on the floor of the cave, and Longhair entered Conrad's vision inside the sea cave. When the shaman came back he sighed deeply and, for the first time, Conrad saw tears in the old man's eyes.

"The spirits have called you," Longhair said with deep certainty. "Now you will be joined for this life to the spirits of the Real People."

□

Redhawk decided they would go to Tobias Franck. Vanishing Smoke had trusted the Jewish merchant, and his trust had been confirmed when Tobias had come to her—at the risk of his life—to tell her what he knew of the events that had led to her husband's death. Franck had always struck a fair bargain with Redhawk and Island Woman for the furs and craft goods they brought him. And Redhawk had once seen him use a jeweler's eyeglass to appraise a necklace brought back from a Mohawk raid on a French village. A final mark in Tobias's favor was that he was known to be a bitter enemy of Robert Livingston, who had tried more than once to destroy him, and would certainly have no objections if the consequence of this trade upset Livingston's plans.

3.

Seth and several of his warriors accompanied Conrad, Redhawk and Island Woman on the northward trek to Albany. Other Mohawks were gathering in the little city on the Hudson at the same time. Queen Anne had delivered on her promise to send a missionary among the Mohawks, and Hendrick Forked Paths traveled to Albany at the head of a reception committee.

Hendrick was not overly impressed by the Reverend William Andrews, the young Anglican minister who had been chosen by the Society for the Propagation of the Gospel to take up residence in the little stone chapel that had been raised inside the stout wooden walls of the new fort the English had built near Two Rivers and named in honor of the governor. Only recently ordained, Andrews seemed utterly inexperienced in the ways of the world, and plainly ill at ease in the presence of warriors sporting tattoos, nosebobs and skulls shaven to a ridge of fierce bristles. Still, Hendrick calculated that the new minister would be pliable, more so than Godfrey Dellius, the Dutch minister Forked Paths had once known well, who had conjured a modest land deed into a crooked patent for fifty square miles and sired several bastard children by his French Indian interpreter. And the mere presence of William Andrews at Fort Hunter, like the presence of the redcoat garrison commanded by Captain Scott (a soldier's soldier who was generous with a bottle) would be tangible proof of the power and determination of Hendrick's English allies.

Forked Paths was keenly aware that not all of his people saw things this way. Young Mohawks—some of them Burned Knives who had once marched to his drum—had assaulted the Dutch carpenters while they were building the fort. There were those who said the English had brought soldiers into the Valley in readiness to drive the Flint People from their lands. There would be those who would say that the young minister with the eager, unlined face had come to steal souls.

Alone among the Four Kings, Hendrick had created and maintained a real power base and cleaved to the military alliance with the English. Vanishing Smoke was dead, a defector before he was killed. John Laughing was a slavering, full-time drunk. Nicholas Etakoam was playing games of his own, with the community at White Village that insisted that Hendrick had never spoken for *them*. Hendrick knew he was walking a razor-edge. There were many who were eager to pull him down, and his wife's pretensions did not help. Showing off in ballgowns and riding in a carriage like a grand English lady were not ways to endear yourself to your neighbors, especially when they whispered that these luxuries were bought with bribes your husband accepted for sending other men to die and for selling land that was not his to sell.

Hendrick garnered two pieces of ominous news at Albany that deepened his sense of threat. The first was that, far across the ocean, the sovereigns of England and France were putting out peace feelers to each other. If peace broke out—especially if it brought no specific gains to the Five Nations—Hendrick would lose much of his value, both to his English supporters and his own people. He was respected as a powerful killer, even by his worst enemies, but such men are often broken and discarded when the need for them is gone.

The other news came from James Mackie, who invited him to share a bottle at the house of young Robert Livingston, the son of the master of Livingston Manor.

"I do not care for all this fiddling and flirtation between the Palatines

and the Schoharie Indians," Mackie announced. "I have heard that a
German youth—a rogue called Conrad Weiser—has been living at Seth's
village and imbibing their ways."

"I heard he ran away from them last winter and was sick unto
death."

"He recovered, more's the pity. The worst of it is, he may be an
advance scout for a whole parcel of these people who are planning to
move into the Schoharie country. This, of course, would contravene the
law. But they are a stiff-necked people. I very much fear that if they
persist in their ways, they may be a blight on both our interests and
yours."

Hendrick was alive to the danger, though he had not yet decided
on how to deal with it. The Schoharie Indians were not easily ruled, and
the opposition to his own authority had grown in their territory since
Vanishing Smoke's widow had married Seth.

He agreed with Mackie that they would both watch the movements
of the Palatines, and discuss appropriate counter-measures.

4.

Tobias Franck had dealt his share of jewelry and family heirlooms,
looted by Mohawks from the *habitants* of New France, or by Praying
Indians from the border settlements of New England, or sold off grudg-
ingly by Albany Dutch patricians who had fallen upon hard times. But
never, even in Amsterdam, had he seen treasures comparable to those
the people from the White Village brought to his store. The rubies were
worthy of a maharaja.

Tobias thought of his cousin, Benjamin Franks, who had accepted
a different rendering of his surname by a colonial recorder. Ben Franks,
also a jeweler by trade, had moved his business to Jamaica, where he
made and lost several fortunes before giving up. Ben had never lost his
love for sparklers; he was already an old man when he had signed on
with Captain Kidd in hopes of getting his hands on diamonds of the first
water again. He would have given his right arm for any one of these
necklaces!

Tobias looked speculatively at the odd delegation that had brought
him these riches. Redhawk and her daughter were old business partners,
but he had never looked to them for more than a few winter furs and
some Indian souvenirs for the cabinets of curiosities of fine gentlemen
in England. The German youth was an original. He spoke Mohawk like
a native, and English like an Oxford scholar. He had gravitas beyond his
years and a further, unsettling quality. He seemed to look right inside a
man, while at the same time he seemed to be searching for something
beyond. Conrad Weiser did not look much like a thief, but Tobias had

no doubt thievery was at the root of this business. You did not find baubles like these under your grandmother's mattress.

"A remarkable collection," Tobias pronounced. "Would I be correct in assuming this is part of Captain Kidd's treasure?"

"What if it were?" Conrad snapped back.

The trader was astonished by the boy's fierceness. He had dropped the remark about Kidd as an innocent jest, inspired by his thoughts of his cousin Ben. He considered it the height of bad manners to ask about the source of property that was offered for sale in this way. Was it remotely possible that the German youth and his Indian friends had stumbled on part of Kidd's storied treasure?

"Well—ah—that would be unfortunate," Tobias picked his words carefully. "Kidd's treasure was condemned by the Admiralty, as you are surely aware. If this is part of Kidd's hoard—" his gesture embraced the jewelry and cut gemstones he had sorted and neatly arranged on a velvet cloth "—I am afraid it would be deemed to be Her Majesty's property, liable to confiscation by the authorities."

His visitors gave him hard looks. He cleared his throat and added hastily, "Of course, it is not my custom to make a tedious issue out of the provenance of a gentleman's, or a lady's, property."

He explained it would require time to get exact valuations and to lay off the haul among dealers in far-flung places. He might wish to ship some of stones back to Europe for direct sale there if he could find trustworthy couriers. It would be prudent to break up the settings, even if this meant losing part of the value. One never knew who might recognize one of these pieces.

Franck jotted some figures on a piece of paper. "This is what I can do for you." He pushed the paper across the table, tapping with his forefinger to indicate the size of the store credit he was willing to give them, and the amount that would be conveyed in bills of exchange, or in gold coin if they were willing to wait a few days.

His visitors conferred among themselves in Mohawk. Their expressions indicated they were not impressed by Franck's offer.

"You will give us half what you receive from others," Redhawk spoke for all. "And an exact accounting."

The trader laughed out loud. *Half* the proceeds? For stolen goods? This was absurd.

"You have heard our offer," Redhawk pursued. "There are other traders."

Tobias was not altogether sure she was bluffing. He resolved to use finesse instead of mounting a direct challenge. There was no way that the Indians, or a German tar-maker, could know the market value of these gems. Whatever share of future proceeds he agreed to give them could be adjusted later, without risk of discovery.

"I will give you the store credit and an advance in cash money, against a quarter share of my profits," Franck told them. "You will not do better than that anywhere in the colonies."

After further conferral, these terms were accepted.

Tobias decided he would be fair with them. He felt a degree of personal responsibility toward Redhawk and her family since he had been used as a pawn in her husband's murder. And who knew what more they might bring in? He might give them ten percent.

"There is one thing more," Conrad spoke up. "Robert Livingston owns a slave called Cato. You will arrange to buy him from Livingston and give him his papers as a free man."

"You wish me to arrange manumission for one of Livingston's slaves? This is a rather singular request, Master Weiser."

"You will do this or there will be no sale."

"What if Mister Livingston refuses to sell?"

"Livingston puts a price on everything. He will not refuse if the price is right. You will pay him whatever is required."

The trader had to agree that Conrad seemed to understand Livingston quite well. Though puzzled by this complication, he was cheered by the thought that, in some obscure way, he might be helping to even an account with the master of Livingston Manor.

□

Hendrick Forked Paths was sleeping off a drunken night at Mackie's house when his brother Abraham called for him.

As Abraham crossed the threshold, Hendrick snatched up his war club, believing that an enemy was about to attack. He saw this enemy as a nightmare figure whose face was streaked black and red.

James Mackie grabbed the warchief's arm to restrain him. This was as easy as wrestling an ox.

"It's only your brother, man. Leave off!"

The fog in Hendrick's head cleared a little.

His hand shook violently, releasing the death hammer.

He slapped his cheeks and rubbed his knuckles into his eyes to cast out the evil dream that had bled through into waking life. In his confusion, he had been about to do battle with a ghost warrior. The figure he had seen in the doorway was Vanishing Smoke.

Abraham brought information that was scarcely less troubling than Hendrick's hallucination.

He reported that Redhawk, Vanishing Smoke's widow, had been observed entering the house of Tobias Franck with people from the White Village and the young German who had been living in the Floodwood Valley. They had spent hours closeted with the trader. When they departed, Franck had ushered them out like visiting royalty.

"I told you this flirtation between Seth's people and the white niggers would come to a bad end." Mackie's voice was thick with drink. "If we don't put a stop to it soon, we will all be fucked."

5.

Conrad carried the good news to his family at the lodgings Johann had taken in Schenectady, together with part of the money Franck had advanced. "It is the Lord's gift," Johann pronounced, marveling at their windfall.

Seth's people hauled their share of the advance—tools and trinkets, hatchets and blankets—back to the White Village, and Conrad traveled with them. He could not envision spending the winter in the cramped, smoky confines of his family's rented quarters. He could easily afford to rent his own room, but he felt like a stranger in this rough river port. Besides, at an age when the sons of the gentry might be sent to college, he had been fortunate to find a private tutor, and he was eager to return to his studies.

During the winter, while his father pored over maps and builders' plans, Conrad chopped firewood for Longhair and speared fish for the shaman's supper through the holes he broke in the ice on the creek.

In sugaring time, his father led the rest of the Weiser family south, dragging their belongings and the smaller children on sleds over snow that still lay three feet deep on the ground.

The Palatines fanned out to found several settlements along the Schoharie, on lands the women of Seth's village had assigned to them. By the time the ice-jams on the river broke up, more than thirty log houses were standing on a dirt road winding east to west, across the river from the White Village. Johann Weiser, in his patriarchal mode, named his settlement Weisersdorf.

The snow was replaced by an immense carpet of white flowers as the sweet clover came out. The Palatines banded together to break the sod, sharing horses and plows. They sawed rustic chairs and tables from logs, and built communal bakehouses where the women gathered to gossip and make bread and cakes. The boys raced Mohawk youths from Seth's village, and learned to play lacrosse and fish with spears and nets. Later, the Mohawk women taught the Palatine girls new survival skills: how to identify medicine plants, how to cook skunk cabbage and burdock, where to find wild potatoes and ground beans in the hungry times.

On Sundays, Johann Weiser read aloud from his black-bound Bible and thanked his God for preserving his Chosen people. He gave thanks, in particular, for the tolerance of *die Wilden* and the windfall his son Conrad had brought to both natives and newcomers in this valley.

Greta fretted that their sudden wealth would bring the law down on their necks.

"The law will come after us in any event, if the governor keeps his promise," Johann reminded his wife.

Conrad's father was right.

□

Governor Hunter did not show the edge of his sword immediately. He began softly, sending an agent called Bayard who told the Palatines he was authorized to issue a proper deed to every landholder who would show him the exact boundaries of his property. Hans Schmidt, a trusting soul who could not read in any language, agreed to sign.

Johann Weiser smelled a rat. He stormed over to Schmidt's cabin, followed by an angry crowd. He yelled to the governor's agent, "Show us your deed! Before any man signs, we will have an exact translation so we can know what is in it."

"You are interfering with Crown business!" Bayard rejoined. "Mister Schmidt is entitled to decide for himself."

"Show the deed!" Several voices took up the cry.

"Don't sign, Hans!"

Gunther and Dina Zeh had blood in their eye. They roared for Bayard to come out and prove his honesty. When he barricaded himself inside Schmidt's house, they armed themselves with firelocks and fired through the straw roof, forcing its owner to hide under his bed, while the agent returned fire with a brace of pistols.

Hunter's man fled to Schenectady under cover of dark, never showing a specimen of his deed, without collecting a single signature. Though the Palatines could not yet prove it, their suspicions were right. The paper the Governor had wanted them to sign was not a title of freehold, but a lease agreement, binding them to pay rent to Hunter's nominees after a fixed period. If they had signed the document, they would have added another form of bondage to the one that had burdened them since they signed the covenant in London.

Thwarted in one line of attack, Governor Hunter was willing to endorse more direct means. He sat with Robert Livingston, a man he had learned to distrust but still valued for cold-blooded ruthlessness, and heard an interesting proposal.

"We will set the Indians on them," Livingston promised.

"But the Palatines have good relations with the Schoharie Indians. They even claim to have come by invitation."

"There is Indians and Indians."

"I seem to have heard this before."

"Trust me. I know the men for the job."

Governor Hunter waited to hear the price.

"You must make a public grant of the Schoharie lands to reliable men, men whose names command respect, so there will be no more disputes about ownership. We will resell at a profit to smallholders who know their way around a gun. There will be no difficulty in finding such men to take over the lands the Palatines have improved. If Germans remain who have not run away from the Indians, they will run away from armed white men, with legal title, backed by the full severity of the law."

"Naturally, you will wish me to make you a prime beneficiary of this grant," the governor observed drily.

"I am not one to make a display of myself," Livingston said coyly. "Robert Junior's name will fit the bill just as well. You might give a taste to James Mackie, an excellent man in this kind of work. Of course, your interest will be fully protected."

6.

In the gathering dusk, Eva Feck watched her father leading the gray horse they shared with the Weisers away from the sunset. Darkness pooled in the fresh furrow. When he turned horse and plow to start over, she waved to him. "Supper is ready!" Joachim Feck flapped his arm, long and lean as a scarecrow's. He would work until the last light was gone, and then maybe some more. There was no stopping him, now that he farmed his own land, with his family all together in the house they had built with the help of their neighbors. Later, after eating a supper gone cold, he would smoke a pipe until he fell asleep in his chair. And Eva or her mother would keep watch in case the pipe dropped from his hand and scattered sparks on the floor.

She turned to gaze across the Schoharie creek. The fertile floodplain was surely the dream of all farmers, but the violence of the river in the spring thaw had scared her, and forced some of the Palatines who had built too close to the bank to build again at a safer remove. Eva could see the twinkling fires of the Indian village at the foot of Corn Mountain. The White Village was no more than two miles away, as the crow flies, but what a world of distance lay in that gap!

Conrad still chose to live there, among the Indians instead of his own people. For as long as she could remember, she had known him. It seemed to her she had loved him even longer. She had tried to understand why he had grown apart from her, as his body hardened into that of a man's. She had tried not to blame him for going with older women, even Dina Zeh, whose mouth and morals were as rough as any sailor's. And she believed she did not hold these dalliances against him. Perhaps it was true that men's needs were different. But now the hot springs of desire were rising in her own body, and it hurt her that Conrad did not notice. He did not see her. Once it was because he did not see her as a woman, now it was different. Conrad was different, more than half Indian. She had seen him stalking in the woods half-naked, slathered in bear grease, like the natives, to keep off the flies. He followed dreams, instead of Bible lessons. The Indians made her nervous, though she had known kindness from some of them, especially the one called Island Woman, who might be Conrad's age.

I would follow you even to a bark lodge. But she had not been invited.

"Still mooning?" her mother called to her. "Come inside and eat. Someone should eat while the food is hot."

Her mother did not approve of Conrad, even though his defiance of the governor and his extraordinary success in wooing the support of the Indians had made him a hero to many. Eva's heart was not ruled by her mother's opinions. She had decided even before they came to this New World that Conrad would be her husband, and she was deaf to her mother's speculations about other possible candidates for marriage.

"He's got a native woman, you can count on it," her mother said, testing her resolve at the dinner table. "He'd never speak their language so good without a squaw to teach him."

"You must *not* call them squaws!" This was one of the few things Conrad had taught her about the Indians. She tried not to let her mother pull her into the coils of jealousy. But she *was* jealous, of that tall, handsome Island Woman who ran like a deer and knew the ways of plants and herbs.

"You're not eating," her mother accused.

It doesn't matter how many women he goes with, she told herself. *He is the only one for me. One day, he will* see *me.*

□

Eva was roused in the hollow of the night by a sharp whinny from the gray horse her father had tethered behind the house. She rushed to the window. Behind the oilcloth, shadows leaped and reared.

Then the violence of men and horses claimed the night.

Eva screamed for her father, who rolled heavily from the bed, groping for his firelock.

She rushed to the door. The gray horse was down on its side, hooves flailing at the air. A black giant with something like a lightning bolt across his face and a fierce crest of bristling hair was hacking at the horse's withers. As the horse's writhing subsided, the giant grabbed her tongue. He hacked it off close to the root and hurled it toward the door of the house with an evil, ululating cry that dragged the whole village out of sleep and into nightmare.

As the Palatines spilled out of their houses, fire-arrows set their thatched roofs aflame.

Joachim Feck raced after the giant who had butchered the horse without pausing to load his gun, swinging it like a club.

"Father! No!"

The giant swiveled and coolly measured the arc of the blow from his death hammer that laid Eva's father on his back, streaming blood. It was a mere feint, a shadow play, by Hendrick's standards, aimed to stun, not kill.

Hendrick Forked Paths would mark no notches on his warclub that night. He had given his warriors strict orders that the Germans were not to be killed, simply scared out of their wits. Their livestock, their houses and crops, however, were fair game.

The Indians were gone before Johann Weiser had time to get the men into fighting formation. They left scorched earth behind them, where there had been ripening grain. Ferrying water from the river in leather and wooden pails, the Palatines were able to save all but four of the houses. But their cows and pigs were run off or slaughtered, like the gray horse.

"You promised we could trust the Indians!" Gunther's wife screamed in Johann Weiser's face. She had just lost her home and her pet goat. "What do you have to say now?"

Johann had nothing to say. He stared across the river, toward Seth's village.

"You have brought us here to be murdered!" the woman squalled.

7.

Conrad came across the river before dawn, with Seth and Nicholas Eta-koam and a large party of Indians from the White Village. They helped to stamp out the last smoldering fires.

"This is not our doing," Seth told the Palatines.

"Nice of you to warn us then," Gunther said with heavy sarcasm.

"We will find out who did this and make them answer to us," Seth promised. "An attack on you is an attack on us."

Conrad comforted his little sister Catrina, who had lost her favorite rag doll in the hubbub. "It's Eva you ought to comfort," Catrina pouted. "She *luuhvs* you."

"Don't be silly."

All the same, Conrad soon walked over to the Fecks' house. He was horrified by the deliberate sadism that had accompanied the slaughter of the gray horse.

"Why did he cut out the tongue?" Eva was beyond tears. "Was it to warn us not to talk, not to hit back?"

Eva wanted to talk. She described the black-daubed giant with the lightning flash on his face. Conrad called Seth and Nicholas Etakoam over and made her repeat the description.

They spoke among themselves.

They told the Germans only, "We will attend to this in our own way."

☐

"Women must decide. Women are the lifegivers." The Mother of the Wolf Clan spoke over the great wampum belt that demonstrated the authority that flowed to her from all those who had gone before. All the clanmothers had come to Two Rivers for this council, but the one who had pride of place was Fruitpicker, because the man who faced their judgment belonged to the Wolf Clan.

The traditional chiefs and the elders were also assembled in the council house, but on this day they came to witness, not to rule. Redhawk and Island Woman had formally requested this gathering, in a secret meeting of the Women's Society, when they had presented their evidence that Hendrick had led a terror attack on the Germans in the Schoharie Valley.

Hendrick had come in some of his London finery—ruffled shirt, a sky-blue coat trimmed with silver, and a tricorne hat, gussied up with lace and silver braid. This was his way of asserting his rank in the presence of the silent *rotiyaner*, who alone were entitled to wear the deer horns of the Confederacy. However, Hendrick's usual poise was lacking. He moved like a man who was half-asleep. He had been up drinking very late with James Mackie and Captain Scott, the commandant at Fort Hunter, and had not yet shaken himself clear of the fog.

The meeting had been sprung on him by surprise, though he had long expected some attempt of this kind. He was confident, despite his wicked hangover, that he would survive it. The old women—he included the traditional chiefs in this definition—would retreat before his power. Behind him were the guns of the English soldiers at the fort and the God of the awkward young Anglican minister, and the passions and thirst of the Burned Knives who would join him in any enterprise that promised blood or liquor. Beyond these, though he was a modern man, who had learned the tricks of the newcomers, he commanded old-fashioned terrors that everyone in this council house would remember and respect. He patted the medicine bundle that consorted oddly with his courtier's clothes, the bag that contained the power to kill from afar and enslave souls.

I am walking through your soul, he spoke to Fruitpicker with his mind. *You are weak and old. You cannot touch me. Your soul is becoming blue.*

Hendrick gasped as something invisible to the outer senses whirred at him. It slapped his head, again and again, leaving him giddy.

Addled and nauseated, he stood speechless and mindless while Fruitpicker recited the list of indictments.

"You have sold lands that were never yours to sell."

"You have sent our young men to die in wars against their brothers that are no concern of the Real People."

"You have set yourself up above others, forgetting that a chief of men must be a walking stick to their people, that they may lean on."

Hendrick Forked Paths tried to swim back to this place, to prepare a bold speech that would silence his adversaries. *To walk through your soul and take your heart in your hand. Do you feel my fist on your heart, squeezing it tighter and tighter?*

Some force of the unseen rushed at Hendrick like a stone fist. It slammed into his forehead, throwing his head back so violently that he fell backward, driving a cloud of dust from the earthen floor of the council lodge. In that stunning moment, he had the awful impression that a host of dark things where whirling to attack him, like monstrous birds.

"You join with newcomers who are no friends of the Real People against those who are proven friends," Fruitpicker continued her indictment.

Hendrick lost much of it. Someone gave him a sip of water, and he recovered himself enough to recognize a man he knew well rising to speak at the clanmother's invitation. It was Nicholas Etakoam. Hendrick had no idea what Nicholas was about to say, but the Mahican's presence gave him a very bad feeling.

"Etakoam is not entitled to speak beside this fire," Hendrick protested. "He is not one of the Flint People."

"Etakoam is what you were before we accepted you as one of our own," Fruitpicker observed. "And he is something you are not. He is one who dreams true, and honors his dream. Tell the dream," she instructed Nicholas.

The massing in the air swirled so strongly about Hendrick's ears that he caught only gusts of the Mahican's speech, but what he heard filled him with gathering horror.

"I saw Forked Paths wearing something that does not belong to him. It was the feathered crown of a *royaner*, with the living bones . . . I had to take this from him and give it to a woman."

"Dreams must be honored," Fruitpicker told Nicholas, when he had finished telling the dream.

When she pointed her lips at Hendrick, the Mahican did not hesitate. He swept the cocked hat off Hendrick's head and laid it at the clanmother's feet.

"Women decide," Fruitpicker repeated. "When our chiefs lead the people astray, we bring them down very close to the Mother, so they may recover her wisdom."

CHAPTER 19

SHAPE-SHIFTERS

1.

Conrad returned to his studies with Longhair, and discovered new ways to fold space and time. In brilliant sunlight, he looked down on a finger of rock, pointing straight up at him from the ledge above the gorge. He hovered above it, noticing things that had escaped his attention from the ground. There were fragments of bone on the tip of the rock; hawks or eagles must have used it as a mortar, to get to the marrow of their larger prey. He revolved slowly over the scene, delighting in his freedom and power of vision. No movement escaped him. He saw the ripple of a snake in the long grass, the shimmer of fish in the brown-green river.

The part of him that remained detached, monitoring his thoughts and actions even as he monitored the scene below, floated an interesting question: *How am I able to see in this way?*

He looked down at his feet.

They were not human feet. They were scaly red claws.

I'm dreaming, he told himself.

With that awakening, he found himself falling like a bird with broken wings toward the rocks. The sensations were intensely real. Panic gripped him. He started to will himself out of the dream, back to his ordinary body.

He checked himself. *I am dreaming and my dream is completely real. I can fly because I am a hawk as well as a man.*

He beat his pinions, regaining height. He caught an updraft and sailed high above the Valley, reveling in his newfound power.

He could do it. He could shapeshift.

He flew over Seth's village. A white dog barked at him. He flew downriver to the Mohawk castle. They had hung fresh-butchered meat out to dry. The sight made him hungry.

He remembered that Cloud Singer—Island Woman's older brother, now a good friend—had gone with Talldeer to a hunting camp somewhere far to the west.

He thought it would be fun to show Island Woman's brothers what he had learned.

But how could he find his friend? He had never set eyes on the Ohio country, hundreds of miles away. But in his new dreambody, he seemed to possess new tools of navigation. As soon as he pictured his friend's face, he found himself speeding westward, over beautiful, narrow lakes in Seneca country that looked from above like the spread fingers of a hand. He saw a vast body of water to the north, spreading like an inland sea. Then he was kiting over a sea of grass.

He hovered over a herd of buffalo, rolling toward their wallows along the Ohio river. The moving mountains of meat sent up tantalizing smells, rank and greasy. But Conrad remembered his target: Cloud Singer's camp.

He found it where a fast-running river made a furious entry into the Ohio, hurling foam and driftwood to the far shore. Conrad followed the twist of smoke from a campfire. From a great distance, his keen eyes spotted the glint of white ribs in the carcass of a young buffalo bull. Crows were gathered. They croaked and flapped as the hawk began its dive, warning the poacher away.

The squall of the crows diverted Cloud Singer's attention from the piece of liver he had jammed on a forked stick, to broil over the fire. Cloud Singer shouted and stamped, snatching up stones to drive the birds away. He paused to look up at the silver-white belly of the big red-tailed hawk that had excited the crows.

Conrad laughed. He made a giddy swoop, brushing Cloud Singer's hair.

It's me! Can't you see it's me?

Cloud Singer hopped about, patting his head for signs of damage, half-puzzled, half-angry. Hawks were messengers; all the old ones said that. But what was this hawk trying to tell him? Cloud Singer cupped his hands to his mouth and gave his impression of a red-tail's slurring cry.

Conrad's hunger was urgent. He gathered height for his dive, then pounced on Cloud Singer's dinner. He shot off with the liver in his talons until he found a safe eyrie where he could consume it at his leisure. The rush of the juices made him blood-drunk and dozy. It dulled his senses.

He did not know he was in danger until a larger bird dropped on him in a blur of feathers and he felt a stab of pain as its talons dug into his shoulder.

The eagle released its grip, spreading its wings in a high, heraldic arc that exaggerated its size.

When Conrad looked again, the eagle was a man.

"Did you forget who you are?" Longhair spoke to him, with his mind. "Do you think this world is your meat locker?"

Embarrassed, Conrad started falling out of the dream. The landscape went fuzzy. He thought of his body, and immediately felt its pull, as if someone had tugged on a rope to which he was tied.

"*Stop.*" The shaman's shining eyes held him back from his sleeping body. He hovered between dimensions. His dreambody floated like a hammock between the bed and the ceiling.

"The gifts of power are given for a reason," Longhair told him. "Maybe your friend needs your help. You must look for him again."

Conrad felt the shaman's touch on his shoulder, this time a gentler pressure, guiding him upward, helping him to achieve lift-off. He flew back up the Valley, back across the sea of grass, his journey slowed by headwinds. He found Cloud Singer's camp. The Mohawks were asleep. They did not seem to have posted a guard.

"What is it you want me to do?" he called to Longhair, hoping the shaman was somewhere nearby. Conrad had lost track of him during the flight. Eagles fly high!

"The hawk sees far. Almost as far as the eagle." The thoughts Conrad received seemed disembodied, unless they were coming from that dancing point of light, too high up to be a firefly, too mobile for a star. "Read the land."

Conrad circled lower. He saw more buffalo, and a lone wolf stalking the herd. He saw a raccoon, driving a snake away from her sleeping kits. He watched the ebb and flow of the waves of grass. And noticed a pattern that was too regular.

They had made themselves headdresses of grass and leaves. The gloss of their skin was dulled by ash. When they crouched down, motionless, they were invisible against their backdrop. They were armed with bows and spears as well as firelocks. Were they stalking buffalo, like the wolf?

No. They were moving parallel to the river, in the direction of the Mohawk hunters' camp. One of them darted from cover to examine tracks in the damp earth close to the water. He threw back his head and released a howl of invitation: a single, sustained note that rose quickly and ebbed slowly away to a soft tremolo. From the far side of the camp came a she-wolf's answering call. But Conrad could see what moved with it. A second file of warriors, painted for killing.

He flew over them. He was sure they were enemies, maybe Flat-heads from the south, or one of the local tribes that disputed the Mo-hawks' right to hunt on Ohio lands. The warriors of this band were not grass-runners. They were buffalo dancers. Their leader wore the horns. He danced heavily, in odd footgear, with two of his braves, while the rest of his warriors beat a clear trail through the grass.

Conrad followed them, not understanding. The buffalo-men pushed their trail to a gap in the bluffs above the rapid river. Bunching together, they moved through the gap to a muddy beach at the bulge where the river slackened its frenzied course toward the Ohio. It was a likely place for a buffalo wallow. Conrad watched the warriors dance hoofprints into the mud, and grasped their purpose before they scaled the bluffs, con-cealing themselves among rocks and trees. They were laying a trap for the Mohawks. When Talldeer and his companions saw the flattened grass and the buffalo prints, they would follow the false trail into an ambush. Those who escaped would be taken by the second band of enemies, the grass-runners who had already done their vanishing act on the other side of the camp.

Conrad must warn his Mohawk friends at once.

He flew to the hunting camp. He saw the buffalo skull the Mohawks had set up on a boulder to greet the rising sun, the slabs of meat hung on frames to dry near the fire, so they would weigh less when the hunters paddled their canoes upriver. A possum was raking through a meager pile of refuse. When he flapped at it, the possum curled up and mim-icked death.

Conrad felt awkward and vulnerable on the ground.

Several Mohawks were sleeping by the fire, or under a crude shelter cobbled together from skins and fallen branches. Conrad was astonished that there was no sentry on guard, so far from the lands of the Five Nations, with enemy war parties on the prowl. Where was Cloud Singer?

Sleeping under his canoe. Conrad knew him by the beaded wrist-band, displayed on the arm he had thrust out in his sleep.

"Cloud Singer!" Conrad called to his friend, with his mind.

No response. The Mohawk slept like a dead man. Like someone whose soul is far away.

Conrad poked at him.

The response was a snarl, from somewhere close by, followed by a short, muffled bark. Conrad whirled round. A huge gray timber wolf confronted him, its hackles raised.

Conrad forgot his message in that moment of raw terror. All he could think about was getting away. Getting out of the dream.

Longhair stepped through his mind: *Remember you are not confined to one form.*

The thought steadied him. He told the wolf, "This is a dream. You

can't hurt me"—though part of him wanted to add, "Can you?" He
returned the wolf's stare, and copied its rolling gait as it moved around
him. He felt his proportions change. He was becoming the wolf. The
timber wolf sniffed him and ambled off to mark a tree, asserting its
territory without menace.

He found that in his new shape, his hunger was ravening. He longed
to sink his teeth into the bloody meat hanging from the racks. Even the
scent of Cloud Singer's sweaty moccasins brought saliva sloshing through
his jaws. His sense of purpose wobbled again.

"Cloud Singer!" he called again.

The timber wolf ran back, head cocked, and stared into his eyes.

"Can *you* speak to him?" Conrad wondered.

They ran together, fleeting as shadow, fluid as running water. Conrad
led the timber wolf to the ambush that been set by the river, and then
to the hiding places of the grass-runners.

When it had seen all that needed to be seen, the timber wolf shot
back to the camp like an arrow. Conrad watched it fly straight toward
Cloud Singer's sleeping place, and vanish under the canoe.

Time passed. Then Cloud Singer sat upright, lifting the light canoe
from his head with his fists. He let out a short *peeeet*, like a waterbird
starting from cover, that roused the other Mohawks instantly.

Cloud Singer told them, "I have dreamed we must leave this place
at once."

2.

"What did you learn?" Longhair quizzed his student.

"I learned that I can go places in my dreambody that I cannot reach
in my physical body, and get there much faster. I learned that my dreambody is not confined to one form. That I can shapeshift into the form of
a bird and an animal. Does this mean I can shapeshift into completely
different forms?"

"I am asking the questions," the shaman reminded him. "What have
you *not* learned?"

"To control my appetites."

"Ah. You finally noticed this."

"I couldn't believe how *voracious* I became, when I shapeshifted. I
lusted for blood, for the joy of tearing and killing. It was almost a sexual
thing. It all but possessed me. I kept forgetting my mission. I nearly
forgot that my friend's life was in danger. Assuming that what I saw was
real."

"The ambush was real," Longhair confirmed. "Death was hunting
Cloud Singer, while he slept. You dreamed true."

"Then if I had failed to get the message through to him, he would have died?" Conrad was appalled by the weight of the responsibility that had fallen on him.

"Perhaps. Don't forget others were watching."

"You. And the timber wolf. I thought they were crazy, sleeping without a sentry. But they had one, didn't they? The timber wolf watched over them. He was Cloud Singer, wasn't he?" It made sense. Cloud Singer was Wolf Clan. The spirit of the wolf had lived in him from birth. It was part of what he was.

"Think about it," the shaman cautioned Conrad, leaving the boy to go through the steps by himself.

"I could not communicate with Cloud Singer by thought. He seemed to be far away. I could not wake him. I *could* communicate with the timber wolf, but not by speech, or by thoughts that can be translated into words. It took place on a more primal level. The sense of smell was more important than the other senses. Behind it, there was a direct way of knowing that did not require speech. An animal way of knowing."

"Wolf to wolf," Longhair laughed at him.

"But I was *pretending* to be a wolf. My mind was still my own."

"Even when you smelled fresh kill?"

"I got sucked into the part," Conrad conceded. "But the timber wolf was different. He wasn't human at all. He was all wolf. I thought he was real when he crept up behind me."

"He *is* real. He could take a bite out of you right now, if he were with us."

Conrad frowned. In Longhair's world, the boundaries between different orders of reality always seemed to be shifting. "Are you telling me the timber wolf could have killed that possum I saw in the camp, instead of just frightening it? Could it have killed one of the hostile Indians?"

"Certainly. The timber wolf is real," Longhair insisted.

"But he's also Cloud Singer, isn't that so? I saw him spring into Cloud Singer's body, when he was still sleeping. At least, that is what I *believe* I saw. The wolf dissolved into him. Then Cloud Singer woke up with the information he had received in his wolf form. I met Cloud Singer in his dreambody, after he shapeshifted. In this condition, Cloud Singer had forgotten who he was. He was more mixed up than me."

"He did not fall into a feeding frenzy."

"I saw him lift his leg against a tree."

"He was guarding the camp, marking his territory. That was his job."

"There is something I need you to explain."

Longhair made an elaborate ritual out of stuffing his pipe and lighting it with a glowing splint from the fire. Real teachers don't give you answers you can figure out for yourself.

"I shapeshifted from hawk to wolf and back to human. Each time, the experience seemed utterly real, and brought new appetites and sensations. Yet it was also like putting on and taking off different sets of clothes. The timber wolf seemed different. It was all wolf. It was solid."

"That is because the timber wolf is a double."

"You mean it is a dreambody, the form taken by Cloud Singer's dreambody."

"Certainly not. The dreambody and the double are different entities. Until you know the difference, you will not dream well."

"Then teach me."

Longhair sighed. Though Conrad was unlike other newcomers in many ways, he belonged to them in his endless hurry. Tell me now. Give it to me now. He wanted the knowledge that came to a *dreamer* only through many hard winters of journeying between the worlds—of patient stalking and of braving up to meet the spirits and the tests they set—and he wanted it skinned and gutted and cooked to a turn. Yet Longhair would feed the boy a little more, because the Real People had need of him and because, despite his youth, he dreamed true.

"If you had met Cloud Singer in his dreambody," Longhair explained, "you could have talked to him as easily as you are talking to me. When you went to his camp, Cloud Singer was making a far journey. He had left the timber wolf to guard his body against possible enemies on either side of the dream gate. If the hostile Indians had moved against the camp, the timber wolf would have wakened him. If an enemy sorcerer had tried to attack him while his spirit was far away, the timber wolf would have defended him."

"Does everyone have a double?" Conrad struggled to understand.

"Not everyone. Doubles can be created. This is accomplished by the deliberate transfer of energy to the chosen form. All strong dreamers have a double. There are some that have many. But this can be a risky business because any harm that is done to the double—and any harm that it causes to others—will rebound on the dreamer. This can cause sickness, even death."

"What is the use of the double?"

"What is the use of a friend, or a trusted dog? The double can be a protector, as the timber wolf is for Cloud Singer. It can run errands for you. It can carry messages, or scout for you in one direction while you put your primary attention somewhere else. It is sometimes useful to have the ability to be in two places at the same time. *If* you can control your appetites."

Longhair broke off, because he saw a visitor climbing the hill—a welcome interruption, since he had spoken more directly than he intended. Conrad's openness and eagerness for knowledge had a way of tricking him into giving more words than was customary among the Real People. Longhair recognized that this weakness for explaining was connected not only to his pupil's constant invitations but to a counterpart self that loved to talk about the most complex and subtle matters. He had encountered this counterpart self in journeys to a time and place very different from the one he inhabited as a Mohawk *ratetshents*. It had taught him that, while a dreamer may invent a double, he is born with counterparts in other times and other worlds whose life experiences condition his own.

Conrad watched Longhair deal with his guest, a tall, handsome young man as light-skinned as himself, who turned his "R"s into "L"s in the manner of the Oneidas.

The Oneida had brought gifts of food and tobacco, no doubt in hopes of a consultation or a healing ritual. When Longhair went into the depths of the cave to fetch tools of his trade, the visitor strolled over to Conrad. He was surprised by the young man's fluency in Mohawk.

"You are his son?" the Oneida asked, wondering if Conrad had been adopted.

"I call him Grandfather. I am learning how to dream better."

"*Io-ionnere*," the visitor said with respect. "This is good for everyone." He offered Conrad a twist of beef jerky. "I am called Swatana."

"You are on a journey?"

"I was up north," the Oneida said vaguely. "Now I go south. It is always good to ask for protection when you go among strangers. I think I am in luck. I did not expect to find Longhair here. I thought they were tricking me at Two Rivers when they told me he was at home. I even took bets that he wouldn't be here."

"Why were you so sure he would be away?" Conrad was puzzled. Longhair had stayed close to these limestone cliffs all the time he had been living among the Mohawks, though he only allowed himself to be found when he wished to be found.

"I saw him up north, the morning I left, seven night's walk from here. Everyone was talking about how he fixed the witch. He is an old man who walks with a stick. I never thought he would make it back here ahead of me. I guess an old head remembers some good shortcuts."

"He can be tricky," Conrad said casually.

Longhair made it clear, by his body language, that Conrad was not invited to sit in on the consultation. He went down to the creek to check the traps he had set. He freed a muskrat and brought back a brace of rabbits a couple of hours later, when the Caughnawaga was leaving.

"Now you can make me some tea," Longhair told him, when they were alone. The shaman preferred English tea to the kind he brewed up from herbs and roots for his doctoring.

Conrad commented on the fact that the visitor had imagined he had seen Longhair "up north" a week before.

"He did see me," the shaman said casually.

"But you were here. We were together. I brought you the deer I stalked. Surely you haven't forgotten."

"I was also up north. At Kahnawake. They needed help against a soultaker."

"Are you telling me you were in two places at the same time?"

Longhair snatched up his rattle and shook it arrhythmically. The sound was painful and jarring. "The thoughts in your head go banging around like that," the shaman told Conrad derisively. "They drive whatever you've learned right out of your head."

"I'm just trying to understand."

"You will never understand these things by talking about them. You can only do this by dreaming and remembering. You are becoming a dreamer but you keep on forgetting. One day you will forget *me*."

"Never."

"Oh, yes. It is the way of all men. Remembering and forgetting. You could even forget who you are."

The shaman folded himself on a pile of skins and pulled his blanket up to his eyes, shutting out Conrad's questions.

CHAPTER 20

THE PEACEMAKER

1.

Conrad went fishing and brought back some fat trout for Longhair's supper. The old man ate voraciously, mopping the grease from his lips and chin with a chunk of cornbread before he tore into that too. Then he pummeled his heap of furs into a comfortable backrest and lounged at his ease. When he had huffed fire into his pipe, Conrad asked him about his Oneida visitor.

"Swatana came to the Oneidas from another people, as you came to the Mohawks," Longhair told him. "The difference is that he belongs only to the Real People, while you must walk in two worlds. Swatana is a warrior, like Hendrick Forked Paths. But though young, Swatana knows better than Forked Paths that the greatest warriors know how to win their battles without fighting. I wish I had possessed his understanding when I was his age. He travels for the Confederacy. Now he is going south into the country of the Lenape and the Shawnees, to carry our law to them. Some of your people live in this country too."

"Yes." Conrad had heard that several more Palatine families had decided to make the long trek south into Pennsylvania.

"I think you met Swatana for a reason. I think you are going his way."

"I have found the place where I belong."

Longhair shook his head. "You are a man, and must live us a man. You will marry and raise children and be a defender for your birth people, and a bridge-builder between the Real People and them."

"I have no thought of marrying."

"But you think of women all the time." Longhair chuckled. "I have watched you, stamping and flaring like a bugling elk in his season."

Conrad blushed to his ears, which brought hoots of laughter from the shaman.

"If I were to think of marrying," Conrad defended himself, "I would look for a partner like Island Woman."

"You can put that right out of your head. She is not for you. Is there something wrong with white girls?"

"It's not that. It's—"

Conrad faltered, aware of how hard the old man was staring at him. Under that gaze, he no longer felt entirely at home in his Mohawk leggings and ribboned shirt.

"You are not Swatana," Longhair repeated. "You are required to walk a different way. When you know us more deeply, you will see why this must be."

"I don't understand." Conrad felt rejected, and resented this bitterly. Surely he had passed all the tests Longhair had set for him. Why was the old man pushing him away, back toward the confinement and hidebound ways of his father's people?

Longhair closed his eyes. When he spoke, in a singsong cadence, he seemed to have drifted far away from the issue at hand.

"Each day, the wound between earth and sky grows deeper. Once our dreamers could travel the sky world in their bodies of meat and bones. Now we fly only in our dreambodies.

"As the rift between earth and sky widens, the Real World dies a little each day. I have folded time and visited the grandchildren of our grandchildren, and the generations that will follow them. I have seen the Real People vanishing like snow in the sun. I have watched the elms die, and the maples. I have seen shoals of dead fish floating belly-up on the streams and oceans, killed by the poisons excreted by men. I have seen cities taller than mountains, inhabited by hungry ghosts, men who have lost their souls. I have seen a world in which humans no longer know who they are, or what our Creator wishes them to become. A world where men have forgotten that in our bodies we are earth and water, and that our spirits are sparks from the Tree of Fire in the sky world. Not knowing who they are, ignorant that everything is related in the circle of life, they are capable of any evil. They plunder and poison the earth and the seas that sustain them until the Mother stirs in pain and fury to shake them from her back."

Longhair paused. "You can truly know only what you see and experience for yourself. I tell you where I have been and what I have seen to prepare you for the journey you must now make alone."

Conrad trembled. Beyond the force of the shaman's words and the shining intensity of his gaze, he felt a rush of energy inside the cave, beating the air like enormous wings.

"You came among us as a sexual animal, crazed as a bull elk in the fall. You walked on the dark side, and the dark ones flocked around you. And you fed them. Yet you never forgot entirely who you are, because you listened to your dreams. You have the gift of tongues, like a mockingbird or a parrot in a white man's cage. But the gift of tongues does not make you an interpreter. A true interpreter is a messenger between the worlds."

Conrad tried to sit still, but his legs were shaking. His whole body seemed to expand and contract. He was in a place without boundaries. His senses were muddled. He *tasted* the shaman's words, bitter as salt, sweet as crushed strawberries. He saw things that were not spoken.

"Use your fear," Longhair told him. "Turn it into good. Use it to power your journey. Energy is energy. Once released, it cannot be suppressed, only transformed. Whatever its source—even if it is hate or fear—energy can be *used*. How it will be used is your choice.

"There is a teacher you must visit, in the Upper World. This teacher is the one who made us the Real People. He came among us when we had fallen lower than the things that crawl and slither on the earth, when we fed on each other's flesh. He led us out of the Dark Times. In the Dark Times that are returning, he will lead us again. He taught us that his truth is not only for one people, but for all the races of humankind. He will speak to all who dream true. It may be he will speak to you."

Longhair put sage and tobacco into the fire, and thick curls of smoke rose to the ceiling of the cave.

The shaman reached into his medicine bundle and brought out a rock half as big as his head. It was unlike any rock that Conrad had seen. The rough core was surrounded by walls of translucent crystal. The angles and facets of the crystal blazed diamond-bright in the dancing firelight.

"I give you a place to *see*," the shaman told Conrad, offering the stone.

Conrad received it in his cupped palms. He was staggered by its weight. It fell through his hands. He nicked himself on a razor-sharp edge, trying to hold on to it.

Longhair watched. Where power rests, he reflected, you can feel its weight.

"Tell me what you see."

Conrad stared at the rock.

"I see a mountain."

"It comes from a sacred mountain." As the Peacemaker did. "Look closer."

Conrad half-closed his eyes, letting his sight go out of focus.

"I see a doorway."

"That is the way you will go."

"I see a boat. Maybe it's a canoe. It is at the heart of the crystal. There is also a tree. A tree whose leaves are sparks of fire. There is a figure—perhaps a man—who is with the tree. No. It is shifting. The man is in the boat."

Yes.

"Is that right?" Conrad looked across the fire. "Is that what I am supposed to see?"

"You will see what you are ready to see."

Longhair took up his beater and began to pound monotonously, hypnotically, on the waterdrum.

2.

When Longhair called Conrad back from his trance journey, his skin had a drowned man's pallor. He had been lying for a long time on the cold floor of the cave, his chest hardly stirred by his breathing.

Longhair decided he had been out of his body long enough, and abandoned the steady tapping on the waterdrum he had used to power Conrad's journey and keep him focused on his purpose. He brought the beater down hard on the deerskin, whacking it several times to give the recall signal. The boy was still out. Longhair banged away in a ragged, jarring rhythm.

Still gone.

During the drumming, the shaman had shifted back and forth between glimpses of Conrad's dream journey, memories of his own visions of the Peacemaker and his grandmother's stories, and regular scans of the environment, both outer and inner. An important part of his job was to stand watch over the dreamer, to make sure his body was safe and that his dreamsoul was not attacked by any malicious spirit on the sublunary planes.

Conrad had journeyed far and high, skirting or overcoming many adversaries, pushing through the cloudlike membranes that divided the many levels of the Upper World. Longhair was satisfied with his apprentice. But now it was time to get him back.

The shaman whistled, then tweaked the boy's toe. Still no response. He felt for a pulse and could not find one.

Longhair was uneasy. Had he pushed Conrad too far? He was a natural for this. *As all our ancestors were.* But a limit must be set. He did not want to risk soul-loss, or damage to the physical vehicle, which could be drained of energy by a protracted journey.

Longhair put down his drum and became the eagle.

Conrad opened his eyes and squinted at the striations in the cave ceiling, trying to get his bearings. When he sat up, he felt light-headed. There was no strength in his legs.

He urgently wanted to talk, to tell everything before any of it slipped away. His voice came as a hollow croak. When Longhair gave him a sip of water, the words poured out in a rush.

"*Serihokten*," the shaman commanded. "Stop the words. You eat, you walk, you get right back inside your body. Later, we talk."

Longhair fed him a tasteless bowl of corn mush, possibly the blandest food on the planet, without even a pinch of seasoning or a few berries to give it flavor. Yet Conrad wolfed it down like a starving man. Then Longhair pushed and pulled him through a ragged circle dance, shaking his rattle.

"Tell the dream," Longhair instructed, when they were both near exhaustion.

"I did not want to come back." Longhair nodded.

"I saw myself carried down, a lifeless body in the claws of a tremendous eagle. His wings shadowed mountains."

"And before?"

"I went through the doorway in the stone. I rode in the canoe. It took me upward. I saw many things, on many levels. I saw a tree that contained all the fruits of the earth and shone in its own light. I saw a woman who gives birth endlessly and consumes her young. I came to a point where I could go no further in human form. I became a fireball, shot out among the stars. I flew with winged beings. I saw—" He paused from the cascade of words and images. "He Who Raises The House. Is that *his* name?"

This was a name the Real People never spoke out loud, except during the secret ceremonies of the Longhouse, when the journey of the Peacemaker who had chosen Hiawatha as his interpreter was relived.

"It is one of his names," Longhair confirmed.

"He looked like—" Conrad faltered again.

"Go on."

"He looked like Jesus."

Longhair said nothing.

"That is, he looked like Jesus to begin with. Like the Jesus of an Italian painting, with a glowing nimbus all around him. Then he changed form. Not once, but again and again. He appeared as an Indian. He took on the features of men of all ages and all races. He changed sex and showed himself, again and again, as a woman. And none of this seemed like a deception. I tried to understand what I was seeing. I was shown something I cannot describe. Behind him, at the source of his being, was an immense light. To look at it was like trying to look into the darkness at the heart of the sun."

Conrad's tears streamed down his face. He felt as though his heart would burst with the joy that flowed through him. His chest heaved.

He gasped, "Oh, God, I'm sorry. I can't go on."

"Power never gives you more than you can handle."

"But this pain in my heart!"

"This is the way we know what is true."

"I feel like I'm going to burst into flame!"

Longhair could see this too. The boy's energy field had changed. The light around him flamed like a candle, high above his head, piercing the roof of the cave.

Now he has the shaman fire. I was right to choose him.

Patiently, in gentle phases, Longhair helped him to unbundle all he had seen and experienced. He had followed the Peacemaker through all the stations of his ordeals. But there was something in his account that differed from both the inner and the outer tellings of the native story. Conrad did not speak of Hiawatha as a character in a story. He spoke as if he were seeing things through Hiawatha's eyes.

The tears came back when Conrad reported, "He asked me to be his interpreter."

"Now we tie up the bag," Longhair said matter-of-factly, packing his drum and rattles away in their containers. "You can go home, now you know how to live. Without a big dream, it is impossible to know this."

Conrad's confusion returned. Longhair picked up his shoulder-pouch and tossed it across the cave.

"Go on. I have nothing more to teach you."

Conrad was close to tears.

"Go away!" the shaman said harshly. "You don't even know how to cook fish right."

Conrad felt vertigo, at this hurried descent from the transcendent heights of his trance journey to this brutal farewell.

Longhair watched him walk, slump-shouldered, down the broken trail from the limestone cliff. A good teacher knew when to send his student on alone.

Yet something in Longhair softened. Or perhaps it was a foreboding about what lay in the future that led him to call out, "Come back!" Hope lightened Conrad's expression, but the shaman's tone was gruff when he added, "You forgot something that belongs to you. I don't want your things cluttering up my home."

Longhair held out the massive, multi-faceted quartz, with its ballast of rock and clay. *A place to see.* When Conrad banged his head against the surface world, and forgot what he had seen and lived in the Real World, perhaps the stone would give him back his vision.

CHAPTER 21

DREAM LOVER

1.

After his dream of the Peacemaker, Conrad crossed the river to live among his own people at Weisersdorf. To family and neighbors who clustered around him, eager to share his experiences of Indian life, he spoke of simple things, of things that could be seen and touched with the ordinary senses. He spoke to the boys of running with the deer, and to the young women of how the natives gathered plants according to dreams and the phases of the moon.

Eva Feck brought him wild mint and asked him if the Indians used it for healing. Conrad carefully inspected the drumstick-shaped leaves and small blue petals. He chewed one of the leaves. It had a fine, sweet taste.

"I don't know what it heals," he told her. "But I bet it's good for cleaning teeth."

Her white teeth flashed. He noticed how Eva's eyes held the pattern of stars, the delicate tracery of silver rays against the deep sky blue.

"Will you teach me, Conrad?"

He rolled a mint leaf into a tight ball and sniffed. Clean and fresh, like Eva. Yet it seemed she had grown into a woman all at once, like a flower that opens in sunlight. How had he failed to notice until now? The subtle curves of her long body, inside the modest blouse and skirt, the way she returned his gaze boldly and held their eyes locked.

I will make him see me.

They strolled together, up the high beak of land overlooking the valley and Seth's village, at the far edge of the floodplain.

"What would you have me teach you?" He trod lightly around her question, which opened on chasms of possibility. It was the same question he had asked Longhair.

"What it is to be free?"

To look into her eyes now was to plunge into a deep blue lake. There were depths here that he had not expected.

"What makes you think I am free? I spent most of today digging in my father's fields."

"I think you would be a free man even in prison, Conrad. You belong to yourself. You live as if you have wings."

For a moment, Conrad saw them soaring together, high above the river, on silverbright wings.

"How do you know me so well?"

She gathered up her skirts and perched on a grassy knoll, patting the place beside her. When he sat down, he could feel the warmth of her thigh against his own. He did not shift away.

Eva said, "I have been dreaming of you all my life."

"Do you know what the Indians say? They say white people don't dream."

Eva recognized this for what it was—a stone skimmed across the water to test the surface—and let it pass.

"Do you remember when we were in Bible class together? You were seven. There was a Sunday when you pretended to be sick so you could go fishing with Klaus Mohr."

"There were plenty of those."

"I am talking about the Sunday you went fishing alone. You fell in the river and got stuck in something under the water. A tree limb, the wreck of a barge. Something that snagged your leg. You were drowning. Your whole life flashed in front of you. When you got free, you had lost your pants." She smiled over the last detail.

"How do you know about that?" Conrad frowned at her, as the memories flooded back. He was sure he had told no one about this episode.

"I dreamed you were drowning. In my dream, I tried to help you. I swam underwater and pulled you to safety."

Conrad had seen many wonders, but nothing that had stunned him more than the revelation that the girl next door had been *dreaming*—as he and Longhair dreamed—all these years.

"What else do you dream about me?"

"I dream of us." The color rose from the neck of her blouse, no adolescent blush but the life-force of a woman whose body was ready for love.

They kissed for the first time. As their bodies flowed together, Conrad found himself back inside another dream, a dream from his first nights in Indian country.

I am naked, moving into the midst of a circle of naked women. They are grinding their bodies to a primal pulse, the heartbeat of the drum. They are offering me their bodies. My sexual force is immense and insatiable. I couple with them one after another, women of all shapes and all ages. The serpent power that moves at my loins is inexhaustible.

At last the circle reforms. I am bathed clean. My skin and hair are scented with sweet-smelling oils. All that has passed was preparation, in-itiation and healing. I am now to be mated with the one who is She. She walks straight and proud. She takes me as her lover and her soldier and we fly beyond the stars.

He had woken throbbing with desire, mad to find the girl of his dream and to couple with her. The dream had driven him to risk trying to force himself on Island Woman, and, when he was rebuffed, to lying with Moon Shadow, a woman whose voracity matched his own.

Now, on this hill above the German farms, as his body leaped to fill Eva's hollows, he knew that he had mistaken the woman in his dream. She had been waiting for him all along, among his own people.

"Not now, Conrad," Eva warned him as he pushed deeper. "Not here."

Living the dream, he had been ready to penetrate her here, on this open hilltop, where anyone might see. He stammered apologies, as he realized how close he had brought them to disgrace. And something he had not paused to consider, as he moved with the hot tides of his passion: that for all her poise and boldness, Eva had never lain with a man.

"I'm going to marry you," Conrad announced to her.

"Of course you are."

2.

In the months that followed, Conrad adjusted to the rhythms of a farmer's life. He plowed and seeded and threshed and carried stones for the new gristmill, all in due season. He chopped firewood and hauled sacks of grain for his own family and Eva's on alternate days and ate meals with them in strict rotation.

Frau Beate Feck left him in no doubt that he was expected to pass muster, and that this would not be yielded overnight. She tried to ar-range things so there was no corner of privacy in which he could be alone with Eva for long enough to steal a furtive kiss, warning her daughter that Conrad was a "sex maniac." This was a deformation of character she suspected in many men, being frigid herself and thankful that her husband's appetites had waned. It was compounded in Conrad—in Beate Feck's estimation—by the fact that young Weiser had run wild among the Indians and no doubt been possessed by their *wegweisende Tiere*, their guiding animals.

Eva's father liked Conrad and valued his strong back in the fields, but was a man of few words who was rarely inclined to express views that ran contrary to his wife's.

On the other hand, Johann Weiser was delighted with the match. The Fecks were solid neighbors, and Eva a fine, modest girl—though a little on the skinny side—who would bear his son fine children. Johann's one concern was whether there would be a church wedding. The Palatines had no minister of their own, so this would involve either a long trek to Pennsylvania, where there were German preachers of both the conventional and the apocalyptic kind, or recourse to one of the Anglican priests in the vicinity: Mr. Andrews at Fort Hunter or Mr. Barclay at Albany. Nobody favored a long journey to the Pennsylvania settlements. The governor and the Livingston gang had left the Schoharie settlers in peace in the two years since the fall of King Hendrick, but no one supposed that this state of affairs would last indefinitely. Pharaoh would smite the Chosen People again, Johann Weiser believed. Every able-bodied man would be needed, Conrad more than most, because of his ability to talk to the Indians and solicit their help and intelligence of possible enemy movements.

Johann did not care for the idea of sending his son to be wed under the guns of the redcoats at Fort Hunter; it was possible that Governor Hunter would seize this occasion to execute his promise to punish the Germans as rebels. But it was soon learned that Thomas Barclay, the minister at Albany, was unavailable. Mr. Barclay had fallen into a puzzling dementia, running through his house, scattering live coals from his hearth, setting fire to carpets and drapes. His friends had been obliged to confine him to a darkened room to prevent him from doing serious damage to himself and his property. It was variously rumored that Mr. Barclay's derangement had resulted from his dealings with Indians or with the bottle. Whatever the truth, the man to marry Conrad and Eva— it was agreed—was William Andrews.

A date was tentatively set for the fall. There was one unexpected catch. William Andrews' mission was struggling. His Mohawk congregation had fallen off sharply since Hendrick and his family—prime supporters—had decamped for the Upper Castle at Canajoharie. He had tried to carry his missionary work into Oneida country, but had been chased away, with raised hatchets, after an outbreak of smallpox the Oneidas attributed to his coming. There were Sundays when his congregation at the Queen Anne chapel consisted of a few traders' wives, a couple of soldiers from the garrison snoring off a drunk, and a handful of native children who came mostly for the beads and trinkets he handed out after the service. Each day brought Andrews fresh evidence of the survival of pagan superstitions. Each night he was tormented by the pulse of drums from the Mohawk village and the rippling laughter and tinkling deerhoof rattles of the native girls.

Mr. Andrews was resolved that the least he could do was insist on evidence of true religion among the whites who sought his services. He had heard that the young German who wished to be wed had lived among pagan savages and danced in their rituals. He would search Conrad closely for signs of heresy, or something worse.

□

William Andrews' sense of duty surprised Conrad. From what little he had observed of Anglicans, he had received the impression that they would tolerate almost anything except bad manners.

Talldeer and Bloodroot, long since returned from their hunt in Ohio country, had come across the Schoharie with a gift of venison and decided to accompany Conrad to Fort Hunter. The chaplain contemplated Conrad's native escort without enthusiasm.

"It appears your friends are not among the baptised. Might I ask whether you are in a similar condition?"

"I was baptised in my own country." *In truth, I have been baptised by fire and water.* What would this soft priest make of the ritual in the Longhouse in which Longhair had placed a glowing coal over his heart, and requickened the spirit of a great one in his mortal body?

"It is my firm conviction that the rites of the Established Church should be extended only to those who share its doctrines and submit to its obligations. Are you familiar with the Nicene Creed?"

Conrad glanced over the page the minister held open in the Book of Common Prayer.

"It is similar to what we Germans subscribe to."

"Can you repeat it in good faith?"

I believe in the communion of saints. Oh, yes. I have seen them.

I believe in the resurrection of the body. Surely not in coming back in the same sack of meat and bones. But in the possibility of rising in a spiritual body, or of returning to earth in another body?

"Certainly."

"Do you believe in our Lord Jesus Christ as the only Savior?"

"Christ is my teacher." *I had forgotten that until I went among a people who do not invoke him by that name.* "I believe in Christ as the saving power of love in this world."

Mr. Andrews frowned. There was some evasion here, and certainly a strangeness that hinted at murky depths.

"I wish us to speak plainly, Mister Weiser."

"It is my habit."

"You are quite young."

Not much younger than you, though something in you has already gone stale. I can smell it.

"It is my understanding that you lived alone among the Indians and learned their customs."

"This is true."

"In what way did this experience alter your religious views?"

"It brought me back to God."

"That is of course commendable. But I would like you to be more specific."

"The Indians taught me to dream."

"Ah, yes. But surely the addiction to dreams is the worst of their superstitions."

"I mean no disrespect, sir."

"Go on, go on, sir. Speak your mind." Andrews quivered, scenting a possibly damning confession.

"Our book is the Bible. The book of the Indians is their dreams. But surely our book also exhorts us to dream. Pharaoh released Joseph from slavery, because Joseph was able to go inside Pharaoh's dream and tell him what it meant. The angel of the Lord spoke to the other Joseph in a dream and told him of the coming of the holy child. The lives of the holy family were saved by the dream of the wise men that warned them against Herod."

"I see you know something of Scripture." Andrews resigned his attack. "Very well, I will marry you in the fall of the leaf."

3.

While Conrad explored theology with William Andrews, Dinah Zeh took charge of a part of Eva's education that her mother had left sorely untended.

"You'll be wanting to please your husband," Dina told the girl. "And that's right and good. But don't forget to please yourself. The greatest secret men hide from women—and misguided mothers hide from daughters, God love them—is that sex is fun. If you do it right and do it often, you may find it is even more fun for you than your husband, especially as the years go by. Even if a man is cock of the walk, he has his limits. A woman has no limits except those she straps on herself. You can take your pleasure as many times as you wish. Make him do it slow, that's one secret. Another is, don't be shy of *tickling*."

Eva blushed scarlet, forgetting her resolve to show herself always now as a mature woman, ripe for the marriage bed, as Dina proceeded to explain in substantive detail what *tickling* might involve.

□

The winter wheat and barley had brought a rich harvest, and the fall harvest of corn and peas promised to be even better. The air about Weisersdorf was malty with beer and yeasty with the fresh breads baked in the outdoor ovens. Life was good.

But there was a shadow over the Valley, one never wholly forgotten. It took on solid form when a Dutchman called Adam Vrooman arrived with a party of builders and surveyors and started raising a stone house as sturdy as a fort in full view of the Germans at Weisersdorf, on land they had purchased from the Indians at Seth's village.

Vrooman was building on land that had been assigned to Widow Zeller. His surveyors were drawing lines across flats that Gunther and Fritz Hauptmann had planned on plowing the following year. Gunther had acquired a formidable blunderbuss from a Delaware Indian and was eager to put it to use at once.

Johann Weiser urged caution.

"We will talk to the Dutchman politely, and explain how things stand."

"We must give no sign of weakness," Gunther insisted.

"We will be as strong as we need to be," Weiser agreed.

Johann was as sensitive as any man at the meeting to the fact that if they allowed one intruder to establish himself on the lands they had purchased from the Schoharie Indians, a host would follow like vultures.

The Dutchman and his party were heavily armed, and confident in their rights. Vrooman displayed a land deed duly signed and sealed at Albany. He was the first beneficiary of Governor Hunter's new arrangement with Robert Livingston who had dared to present himself in the Schoharie Valley. Johann Weiser felt a degree of sympathy with him. The Dutchman looked to be sixty, a grand old age by the standards of the colony. His huge hands were calloused by hard labor. He had come to farm, on lands he had bought and paid for. He was cut from a different cloth than the smooth connivers who had engineered his coming.

Yet Vrooman could not be allowed to stay.

If the Palatines made that concession, they would soon be besieged by invaders. The situation was already worse than it looked; Vrooman's patent encompassed no less than a thousand acres of Schoharie land, land already apportioned to half the families at Weisersdorf.

"There will be no killing," Weiser prescribed. "We must consult with the fox as well as the wild boar."

"That's his Indian son talking," Widow Zeller observed.

"We will wait till their guard is down. We must wait until the Dutchman's seed is in the ground, and the house is all but done, and there is no possibility of starting over before winter freezes hard. That is the way to discourage them."

☐

When Weiser determined the time was right, the Palatines drove their horses and oxen over the Dutchman's freshly seeded fields, trampling them into muck.

When the stone house was almost complete, they drove the builders away with musket fire and war-whoops; Conrad's impression of a Mohawk battle cry was so convincing that one of the carpenters ran straight for the river and hurled himself from the bank, fearing an imminent scalping.

Then they pulled down the house, stone by stone, scattering the pieces, and burned the timbers.

☐

"The white niggers have played into our hands," James Mackie announced with satisfaction to Robert Livingston. "When the governor hangs the most insolent of the buggers, the rest will yield ready enough. Germans love to take orders. I watched them in the camps, taking abuse no black nigger would abide."

"Do not be overly confident," the master of Livingston Manor cautioned. "A man who is defending land he believes his own may have more fight in him than others."

Livingston fingered the warrant Governor Hunter had issued for the arrest of Johann Weiser and his son Conrad. The language of the warrant made it clear that the Weisers faced an execution party, if taken, and that the governor would be equally gratified if they were taken dead or alive.

"Do you think our friend Sheriff Adams has the backbone to execute this warrant?"

"Adams will do what he is told," Mackie said smugly. "He is bought and paid for. But I am thinking the sheriff will need stout men at his back."

"None stouter than you, James."

"It will be my pleasure, sir." Mackie smirked at the prospect of settling accounts with the Weiser brat who had drenched him in rancid fat in the East Camp.

4.

There would be no wedding at Fort Hunter that fall. Though he had not yet heard about the warrant, Johann Weiser knew he must now be an outlaw, and that his son must stand in equal peril. All the men of

Weisersdorf must stand guard over their homes and fields. Sentinels were posted on high ground, to watch for intruders. Johann sent Conrad to Seth's village to ask his Indian friends to perform the same service. If any hostile force were approaching, the Indians would be the first to know.

"We see many looks away," Seth agreed. "We are sorry for your trouble. We see the hand of Hendrick Forked Paths in this, as well as the devils of Albany. Our promise remains true. We will watch for you as for ourselves. We are one heart, one mind."

Island Woman was waiting for Conrad. "Is it true you are going to marry Star Woman?"

"Star Woman. What a lovely name." It fitted Eva well, he realized, thinking about the silver star patterns in her eyes. "Yes, it's true. Though I'm not sure when we will have the wedding, since we are now at war with the governor."

"I saw this before you did," Island Woman told him.

"It might be so. I was blind for a long time. That night in the lodge—"

"*Wa'katerientare.*" Island Woman stopped him from recalling the night he had tried to use her body against her will. "I know this matter. You are not the same person. You died and came back. You are not responsible for the one who died."

A look of puzzlement came over her face. "Why do you have to wait to be married? Is it because you are guarding your power for this war you will fight?"

It was Conrad's turn to be confused. He knew exactly what she was talking about, yet since he had returned to living among his own people he had slipped back into many of their customs and ideas. Mohawk warriors abstained from sex for long periods, when they were preparing to take the warpath, or to seek a vision, or simply to play a game of lacrosse. This was a way that had been wholy alien to Conrad, when he came among them, and even now seemed unnatural to him. Sexual abstinence gave him headaches. He had had plenty, yearning to press himself between Eva's thighs while confined to staid sessions at the family dinner table.

"It's not the war itself," he tried to explain. "It is the necessity of doing it proper. Our families expect a church wedding. I suppose Eva expects it."

"Have you asked her?"

Conrad stared. He had never been backward with any halfway attractive woman except the one he was determined to marry. Out here, under the stars, where Eva was called Star Woman, the convention of a church wedding seemed preposterous. Among the Real People, the whole earth was a church. Marriage was a sacred rite, no less solemn and spiritual for being extremely simple. There was no need of a priest; the compact was with the Mother herself. Lakes and mountains, woods and rivers, stood witness to its truth.

"You are right," he told Island Woman. There was no need for more words between them. He *saw*, as Island Woman saw, what he must do.

□

Eva trembled as Island Woman helped her to free herself from ribbons and buttons. She blushed furiously when the Mohawk girl pointed her lips, indicating she was required to take off *everything*.

"You don't have anything I have not seen before." Island Woman laughed at her.

It was hard to drop her knickers while she was trying to conceal her breasts with her arms. Island Woman turned away, not to spare her embarrassment, but to stir the mixture of sage and sweetgrass she had set burning in a bowl of charcoal.

Island Woman brought up a spray of white feathers and started to smudge Eva, brushing the sweet-scented smoke over every part of her body. She made Eva lift her feet so she could push smoke under them, too. As the Mohawk woman fanned the smoke, she crooned what sounded to Eva like an endless lullaby, wave upon wave of sound.

The sound received her and gentled her until she forgot her modesty and hesitation and stood as nature made her to stand, tall and straight and free.

The bite of the cold, fast-running water brought out goosebumps when Island Woman led her by the hand into the creek, adding the blessing of water to the blessings of wind and fire.

Then they stood together on the generous earth, and Island Woman burned tobacco and sent the curling smoke to the four quarters and the above and below.

We return thanks to the Mother, for her bounty.
We commune with the spirits of earth and air, fire and water.
We give thanks to the animal helpers and to the bird tribes.
We give thanks to the Thunderers.
We give thanks to our Grandmother Moon and to our Elder Brother
Sun who brings light and life into our world.
We give thanks to the invisible powers of the Creator.
We give thanks for the love of our Creator, that brings our world into
being and maintains it daily.
We commune with the Power that is in everything and beyond everything.
We join in the Power of All That Is.

Though the words were foreign to Eva, the music and the power of their intention claimed her. It seized her with joy. An immense energy rolled through her, an energy born of life itself, clamoring for renewed and expanded life.

We give thanks to our guides and teachers
We give thanks to our helpers and protectors
We give thanks to the friendly spirits who watch over us
Continue to watch over us and those we love
Guide us and protect us, shield us from all harm
Lead us in the ways of Light
Join us in the song of Making

Eva felt and saw light burst from inside her heart and her belly, a double starburst of white-gold energy radiating out to the extremities of her skin and beyond it, to form a shimmering nimbus. She saw Island Woman standing in this same extraordinary light, except that in the case of the young *arendiwanen*—the woman of power—the light flamed high above her head, forming a pillar of white fire taller than the trees.

"Now you are ready for the dance of Making," Island Woman told her gently, leading her to the shelter they had made together, out here in the virgin woods, far from the squabbles of settlers and governors. Her bed was a springy bank of dried moss. Her roof was constructed from spruce boughs, laid one across another tightly enough to protect them if the rain came, loose-meshed enough to let in the light of the moon and a glimpse of the evening star.

Where were her second thoughts now? Where was the crushing spasm of panic that had made her tell Conrad she *had* to turn back when they were only halfway across the ford?

I would have asked him if he had delayed much longer, she reminded herself. *I would have asked him sooner had I known it would be like this.*

She sat alone for a time, tracking her thoughts through the changing shapes of the fire Island Woman had laid with sticks of cedar and juniper in front of the shelter. It was deliciously warm under the sleak beaver robe Island Woman had given her.

She heard the murmur of voices.

Island Woman crawled into the shelter, bearing gifts: a loaf of bread, a haunch of smoked meat, a beautiful beaded pouch with the design of a spreading tree. It reminded her of the scissor-cutting she had given Conrad to carry on his journey to the coast.

"He asks if his gifts are pleasing to you," Island Woman said formally.

"They are." With equal formality, she broke open the loaf and swallowed a small morsel of bread, then bit into the dried venison. Among the Real People, a husband-to-be must show he can provide. His intended bride shows her acceptance by receiving his gifts and using them.

Woman decides.

Island Woman withdrew.

He came to her then, with the strength and passion of her dream lover. The pain of his entry shocked her. But slowly, as they rocked gently together, she found a shared rhythm and followed it. He was tender, murmuring words from the heart, loving and reverencing every part of her body. *Make him do it slow*, Dina had warned her. He was gentle, but perhaps he could never have been slow enough, that first time. The birth of new life—of new ways of being human—always involves pain.

Later, when they flowed together, the starburst rose from her deepest core, until it exploded into the spiral whorl of an expanding galaxy.

CHAPTER 22

A STIFF-NECKED PEOPLE

1.

The nights were getting longer. Cutting winds tore the red and yellow leaves from the maples. Island Woman fetched the newlyweds to stay in Redhawk's lodge in the White Village.

From here, at the base of Corn Mountain, they could watch the Palatines across the river preparing their barns and freestone silos for the winter. On the near side, there was activity among the ruins of Vrooman's house. Surely not an attempt at new construction so late in the season, with the German settlers on guard.

"No," Seth reassured them. "Some of your own people are marking this place for their own." Stone by stone, they watched the cairn mounting, another flung gauntlet in the faces of the governor and the Livingston ring.

To the south, the roads to the headwaters of the Delaware and the Susquehanna rivers, to the busy Mohawk trading village of Oquago and the German pioneer settlements of Pennsylvania lay open. Germans who had gone on ahead sent word back that the masters of the Quaker colony were hospitable to new pioneers, that the natives were friendly, and that Philadelphia was a beautiful and civilized city where a family could find mental furniture that was mostly lacking in the back settlements of New York: bookshops and music lessons and dancing classes and talk of the new principles of philosophy and science.

Conrad felt the tug of a new frontier. It was not yet the kind of undertow that bowls a man over and sweeps him away with it, but it was there, a small hand plucking lightly at his sleeve.

□

It is the pull of his unborn children, Longhair recognized, as he kept watch from his eyrie on the high limestone cliff. The shaman put the matter into the fire. He cast dried herbs and native tobacco onto the glowing coals and followed the shapes that moved in the thickening smoke. He saw a leavetaking, a journey, a new path of trials on which Conrad would be required to separate himself from everything that was safe and familiar. He saw a figure in the smoke that struggled under the weight of a corpse on his back.

He will die and come back again. He will struggle under the burden of his former self. It will weigh on him like a vampire skeleton, feeding on the energy of those who will not let him change. He will fall down many times and get up again, until he has buried this old self. Then he will rise like an eagle.

Longhair poked the ashes to disperse the patterns of smoke. Conrad would move on, and many of his people would move southward with him, though few of them knew this yet. Men tried to lay straight paths, to eliminate surprises, to tame the future. But the future cannot be tamed. Tsawiskaron, the Dark Twin, will make sure of that. As soon as you think you've got everything figured out, the Trickster will pull the ground from under you. This is essential to life. If everything was predictable, people would die of boredom. For his own part, Longhair was quite certain he did not want to see everything that was going to happen to *him*, though he made many forays into the future for the benefit of others. For example, he had no inclination to visit the moment of his physical death. When he needed to know this, it would be shown to him, through the spontaneous wisdom of the Dreamgiver.

It is not possible or desirable to tame the future.

But in the Real World, where there is only *now*, you are not the captive of time. You can enter the future and change it if you don't like what you see. While men try to convince themselves that their lives are set in fixed patterns, that they are slaves of custom and circumstance, the shaman knew that there are only two things in a person's life that can never be changed: his character and his allotment of time and energy in the body his spirit possesses. However, some events carry a greater fatality than others.

Longhair, the timefolder, lay down on his mat and closed his eyes. There was something else he had glimpsed in the smoke. He needed to dream on it now, because it was something growing close at hand, and it is the future that is closest to you that is hardest to change.

□

Conrad sat up on his sleeping mat. Something had entered the space he shared with Eva beside Redhawk's fire, behind the moosehide curtain

Island Woman's mother had hung up out of respect for the German girl's shyness or the passion of new lovers.

It moved again, almost a physical thing.

The brush of sleek fur against his skin. The softest pressure of retracted claws. The impression of shining eyes, very close to his own.

He closed his eyes, in order to *see*.

Shift into the second attention, Longhair's thoughts moved in his mind.

Conrad let himself flow gently upward, till he was floating just a few feet above his physical body.

Longhair's panther had come to show him something he needed to see. He shaped himself to its intent. He felt a surge of power as his dreambody molded itself into the racing beauty of the great black cat.

I know the place we are entering. The stockade, the houses on Myndert Street. My father wintered very close to here before he moved down to Weiserdorf.

Men are gathering, with horses. They are heavily armed. Coarse, brutal faces. One of them is generous with his flask, and with a show of gold coin. It is James Mackie. He is going to kill my father. He will attack the village from two directions. He has hired native killers. They will come by stealth, while Mackie and his bought sheriff make a show of enforcing the law.

Conrad was seized by the urgent need to warn his father. Mackie's hired killers were preparing to move out. They would be counting on taking Weisersdorf by surprise, before sunup.

Conrad thought of his body, and shot back to its sleeping place as if pulled by a string. He reentered too fast, landing with a bump that left him feeling bruised all over.

He kissed the corner of Eva's mouth. She smelled warm and yeasty, like bread rising in the oven. She smiled and rolled toward him, reaching for his penis. Conrad had been very pleasantly surprised by how bold and venturesome his virginal bride had proved to be in their lovemaking. She had shown *him* things he had never imagined.

"I must return to Weisersdorf."

Now she sat up, worry clouding her eyes. Both of them had known, from the moment they eloped, that they were going back. In the face of common danger, the settlers must stand together. But they had counted on a longer honeymoon before facing their parents' recriminations.

"There is trouble. I must warn my father."

She did not question this. She started pulling on her clothes.

"Stay here," he told her. "You'll be safe."

"I don't want to be safe without you."

2.

James Mackie wiped his mouth with the back of his hand. It was thirsty work, hunting farmers. Cottonmouth, one of his mixed-blood trackers, had taken out the dozing sentry the Palatines had posted to watch the Schenectady road. The operation was already a success. Mackie had beaten from the boy, with the knob of his blackthorn stick, the interesting information that he was one of Johann Weiser's sons. He had Freddie Weiser trussed and bound, with a balled rag in his mouth, so he looked exactly like a roasting pig slung over the bouncing rear end of Mackie's horse.

The bloodred sunrise threw long spikes of shadows across the valley from the white pines that crowned the foothills.

"Red in the morning, a shepherd's warning." Mackie grinned at Bratt. "We will teach these sheep-shaggers to remember that line."

The posse rode past the first of the Palatine settlements. Farm boys rushed into the road to goggle at the hard, whiskery men with the long guns.

"Stay in your homes if you wish to avoid trouble!" Sheriff Adams called to them. The men on his list were all at Weiserdorf. Johann Weiser. Conrad Weiser. Gunther Bertelsmann. Hans Stahl. Enough to make an example. The governor's orders were to ship them to New York for a quick trial and a public execution. James Mackie would urge that they should be hanged at Albany, in sight of their own kind. A man thinks twice about asserting his rights when he has seen a neighbor's eyes plucked by crows for doing the same.

The sheriff wore a gorget and a silver medal, and had put on his finest broadcloth and silk hose. He understood his role perfectly: he was to represent the might and respectability of the law, against a band of turbulent, scruffy peasants. *Peasants with guns as well as pitchforks*, he remembered uneasily. Armed peasants were still no match for the law, when enforced by killers as sanguine as the gang Mackie had hired. If there were any real justice in the world—which Sheriff Adams doubted, as one in the know—Johannes Bratt would have been measured for a rope long before this. That river rat enjoyed killing and maiming almost as much as he enjoyed violating defenseless women. *Must keep him off the frauleins. That could be a nasty business.*

Weisersdorf was in sight. The village was still asleep, which seemed a little odd to the sheriff, since farmers are generally up long before dawn. He jumped at a crash of timber, then relaxed when he saw it was only a party of Palatines felling trees half a mile to the east. The sight of men about their business suppressed the caution he had been about to offer to Mackie.

James Mackie dropped Freddie from the back of his horse like an old blanket roll, and stood in his stirrups. He raised his right arm aloft, gripping the bullwhip he had used on the slaves at Livingston Manor.

"At—the—*gallop!*" he called.

Mackie leaned into his roan stallion's neck, digging his spurs into its flanks. The ground melted away before him. His men whooped and roared. No need for silence and secrecy now. Bratt got ahead of him, showing off. *Or slavering after German quim. If it's a race he wants, I'll give him one.*

He flogged the horse on without mercy. Its hot lather frothed into his eyes. Which house was Weiser's? *That one.* He saw the rebel's wife at the door. *Good knockers on that one. Wouldn't mind a go myself.*

Then everything stopped as suddenly, as violently, as if he had slammed into an invisible wall. The horse screamed and reared, hurling him from the saddle. Mackie fell like a coalsack, with a dull thud punctuated by the crack of breaking bones. He felt his chest imploding as his ribs snapped.

The horse stamped and shook like a drunk in a delirium, losing its legs. Conrad Weiser ran out from behind the house, ducking to escape the wire he had strung between the cornice and the barn. He was sorry for the horse's pain. The wire had cut to the bone. It would not walk again.

Conrad crouched next to the great shaking head. Everything was sharply defined, with the clarity of October light. He saw the pink spot on the stallion's nose that must have caused him sunburn in high summer. He saw the beauty and terror of the huge dark eyes. He murmured, "I ask permission to free you from this life," before he cocked the gun and pulled the trigger.

This would feed on his conscience, though it was a fair return for the slaughter of the old gray mare the Weisers and the Fecks had shared.

While Conrad put Mackie's horse out of its misery, a battle was raging around him. The odds were not what Mackie had fancied. The Palatines not only greatly outnumbered his bully boys; thanks to Conrad's warning, they had claimed the advantage of surprise that Livingston's agent had thought belonged to him. Among the houses, the horsemen could not maneuver freely. Farm boys came batting at their horses' fetlocks, dragging the riders out of their stirrups.

As Conrad ran to his brother, Bratt swung round. He took aim over his pommel at the young man who was cutting the hostage's bonds.

"Conrad!" Dina Zeh came panting between the houses.

The shout allowed Conrad time to throw himself to one side, so Bratt's bullet whistled harmlessly past his ear. Half a dozen farmers ran toward Bratt with guns and axes. Bratt did not like his chances. He wheeled his mount and kicked the exhausted beast back toward Schenectady. Most of his companions followed after him, many on foot since the Germans had claimed possession of their horses. These foot-sloggers were pursued by the Palatine women, wielding corn pounders and broomsticks. Many would find it painful to sit down for a week.

Cottonmouth and his half-Delaware killers, outcasts from both the Five Nations and their tribal enemies, had sat apart from the battle. They had come for a share of the spoils. As soon as it was clear there were none to be taken, they lost their motive for fighting. Now they chased after a couple of horses that were running loose and drove them southward, toward Delaware country.

No killing. Johann Weiser's fiat had been honored. Their attackers had suffered only broken bones.

The Palatines held two men captive—James Mackie and Sheriff Adams—when they had driven the others off their land. Mackie was bleating about his wounds, but had thus far suffered only a couple of broken ribs and bruises to body and pride. When Sheriff Adams began to prate about his warrant, Gunther seized it from his hand and tore it to shreds. While others held the sheriff down, Gunther proceeded to push the warrant down his throat in generous portions.

"These two need *tickling!*" Dina Zeh announced, winking at Eva. She soon made it plain that in Dina's vocabulary, *tickling* could mean many things.

Her powers of improvisation were considerable. Perhaps inspired by the Indians across the river, she got the women and children to form lines and made Mackie and Adams stagger between them, while they whacked away with any utensil that came to hand. Then she suggested they should haul the two men through the churned mud and steaming piles of cow dung in the barnyards. The women ripped off their clothes. They squawked at the pendulous belly that slopped down from under the sheriff's corset. Dina hooted at the narrow pizzle, shrunken by cold and fear, that showed itself briefly between Mackie's legs.

"How do you find it in the hair?"

Eva shocked her mother again by taking to this game with a passion. As she helped to pull Mackie through the barnyard muck in a leather harness, she asked, "Does this remind you of the slops you used to serve us in the camps?"

Tarring them would have been a good preliminary to the next entertainment, with poetry in its echo of the Palatines' ordeals in the camps. But tar was in short supply at Weisersdorf, worth saving for purposes more important than redecorating this scum.

"Ride them on a rail!" Dina bellowed.

The cry was taken up by a chorus of voices.

"Ride them on a rail!"

The fence rails came down, and Sheriff Adams and James Mackie were given their new mounts. They squealed and clutched at their inner thighs and their privates as they were bounced and jounced along over hills and furrows, the sharp edges of the wood cutting deep into the skin and threatening the loss of manhood.

"Ride!"

From Weiserdorf to Hartmansdorf and down to the river and up the slope of Weiser's Nose. The sheriff's eyes bulged from their sockets. Mackie's head twitched and jerked as if he had been bitten by a rattler.

"Oh, for the love of God! My cock!"

"You won't miss what you never could find." As *belle dame sans merci,* Dina achieved her moment of epiphany.

She rode them for seven miles, as a crow might fly on a day of fat pickings.

When Mackie was at last released, torn and bleeding, to groan in a ditch, Dina served him her coup de grâce.

His eyes glued shut by mud and blood and cowshit, Mackie lay on his back gasping for a drink.

"Just a wee drop. I am begging you, missus."

Dina squatted over him and peed in his open mouth.

Hunting farmers is thirsty work.

CHAPTER 23

TOBIAS'S LADDER

1.

Tobias Franck looked through the open leaf of his Dutch doors at the rain pounding down on Handlaers Street. The water running off the spout that projected straight out into the street from his gutters made a miniature cascade as it fell to the cobbles. The rain shone on the leaves of the high elm at Wendell's door and pooled in inky bottle-green shadows. Something in the shining carried him back to Amsterdam. He saw a bridge over water, a woman's face among willows behind the barred gate of a cloistered courtyard, a winding stair that spiraled tighter and tighter. For a moment, he was *there*, back in the city of moon and sea, capital of transitions and illusions borne on the astral tides.

If the play of light and water could carry him so vividly, in all his sensorium, to another place, might it not be possible to make the transit in a similar way to the Otherworld? The question had plagued Tobias since he had found leisure to return to his studies, as it had plagued the scholars and Cabalists of past generations of his family, wandering under many names and disguises from Safed to Salamanca, from Bohemia to Brazil.

There were those within his own family who maintained that the Jewish religion did not require belief in an afterlife, and contained no clear teaching about the destiny of the soul after death. Tobias had combed the Tanach, the Hebrew Bible, for references to this subject, and what he had found was scant and distressing. There were passages that implied that the shades of all men—both saints and sinners—were consigned at death to Sheol, a miserable place under the earth. Yet there was another tradition, preserved through whispered transmission from master to pupil and in writings passed down from hand to hand. It was founded on the visionary experiences of men who had actually gone to the Otherworld, escorted by angelic guides.

One of these great travelers was Enoch, remembered in Genesis as "one who walked with God." Tobias had brought with him from Amsterdam, in a sealed box, a precious manuscript in the Hebrew language that contained a vivid account of this man who had gone to heaven without dying. Enoch had been visited in his sleep by an angel who had led him through the many palaces, shining like crystal and like fire. He had been shown the condition of those who were being punished or rewarded on the many levels of the Otherworld. In the seventh heaven, he visited the court of the God beyond gods, and had been transformed into an angel with a body of fire.

Could such stories be true?

Was it possible for an ordinary man, a man of flesh and bone, to cross to the Otherworld and return from it, short of physical death?

There were rabbis who said that it was, though they were frowned on by respectable congregations. One of them was Tobias Franck's maternal grandfather, one of the celebrated Cabalists of Safed, who had bequeathed the book in the sealed box, together with a set of mystical dialogues that contained a passage that both fascinated and frustrated him:

> *What does it mean, to master the secret of ascending to heaven and returning to the body? It is like having a ladder in one's house and being able to go up and down it at one's will.*

As the years shortened his breath and made his bones brittle, Tobias Franck found it of pressing concern to master this art of going beyond the gates of death before dying. Thanks in no small part to the windfall Conrad Weiser and the Indians had brought him, he had more money than he would ever spend. He had discharged all of the debts he acknowledged, including the purchase and manumission of Livingston's African—the strange giant who insisted on being called Fatumbi—that Conrad had insisted upon. He had provided for his children. He had paid to help fellow Jews escape from the toils of the Holy Inquisition in Spain.

Now he needed to know about things that endured. He had passed long nights in watching and fasting, his head bent between his knees as he recited the holy names of God, and the secret names of the guardians of the portals of the Otherworld. He had tried to visualize the heavenly palaces described by Enoch and make the images real, to enter them with all his senses. He had glimpsed strange and wonderful things: a throne of fire, a moon chariot drawn by bulls. Yet he distrusted these images, borrowed from books. They were not his own property. All his austerities, all his learning, had not brought him the sense of *being there* that had come spontaneously when the play of light and water on an Albany street whisked him back to the city of his youth and the vision of a woman in a cloistered courtyard, seen once and loved for a lifetime.

He saw a familiar figure loping along Handlaers Street, holding a flap of his matchcoat over his straw-colored hair against the rain. It was the German boy, Conrad Weiser.

Tobias beckoned to him. "Come inside, quickly!"

Conrad swung through the Dutch door and shook himself dry on the parlor rug like a shaggy dog.

"What are you thinking about?" Tobias rebuked him. "Don't you know the danger you are running? You and your father are wanted men."

He had kept a copy of the wanted poster, announcing a reward for the capture of:

> *one John Conrade Wiser and son Conrad, Covenanted Servants of his Majesty, who have been Guilty of Several Mutinous Riotous and other disobedient & illegal practices, now skulking in this County to avoid punishment for their Crimes.*

He found the document among the heap of papers on his desk, and offered it to Conrad.

"They have to catch me first." Conrad grinned.

Tobias bolted the door and surveyed the street from behind the curtain of the leaded window, to see if the boy had been followed. A farmer's cart rattled along, spattering water and mud.

"Nobody saw me come. I've learned a thing or two about skulking from the Indians. Though I confess I am less at home in the city than the woods. Too many people. Too many eyes."

"Why have you come?"

"We need salt. Even me. One thing the Indians never managed to teach me was how to eat food without it. And we are short of all metals— tools, pins and needles, nails and latches."

"We will make a list. I will arrange for everything you need to be delivered to your people in the Valley. You must not be seen abroad, Conrad. Your life is at risk."

"There is something else I require. Silk for a wedding dress."

"So you are to be married! Well, well, that is splendid!"

"I am already wed. I am afraid Governor Hunter and Mister Livingston have delayed the formalities."

We were joined in the presence of earth and wind, fire and water. And in the presence of the unseen.

Tobias studied Conrad, as his housekeeper fetched the tea-things. Young people grew up fast in the colonies, faster than aspens after a forest fire. Yet the growth in Conrad was not merely of height and muscle and brain, or the ability to fulfill the duties of a husband. Tobias could see the change in the blazing intensity of the eyes, and in the way the young man inhabited his body. Conrad moved with spontaneous, animal grace. The eyes missed nothing, and reached behind the surface of things.

"There is something I would like to ask you. I have dealt with the Indians for many years, but I have never lived with them, as you have, or mastered their tongue. What have you learned from them?"

"To survive," Conrad replied without hesitation. "To find food where there is nothing a white man would recognize as food. To read the tracks of a muskrat, or a deer, and to run it down. To find voices in trees and stones, and know that everything is related, everything is alive."

"So they have turned you into a mystic."

"If a mystic can be a practical man. The Indians live very close to the earth, and every day of their lives is a battle for survival."

"Yet they have time to dream."

"Dreaming is a very practical business. It brought you your share of Captain Kidd's treasure."

"Do you dream many things before they happen?"

"I have come to believe what the native dreamers say. That we dream *everything* before it happens. Naturally, it is possible to remember only a small portion of what is dreamed. But as we develop the gift of remembering, and the ability to enter dreams at our choosing, we learn that in dreaming we are not confined to place and time."

"Are we confined to this world?"

Conrad was struck by the depth of this question, and the intensity with which it was stated. He had not expected an Albany trader to broach these matters. But he had seen enough, in his years, to know that each man is many men, and few can be reduced to the masks they show those around them.

"You have touched on the heart of the Indian way of dreaming," Conrad told him. "The Indians do not dream only to put food in their cooking pots. In dreaming, they go to the Otherworld and talk to the spirits."

Tobias could not hold his teacup steady. It rattled loudly against the saucer when he set it down.

"Have you done this yourself?"

I have journeyed beyond sun and moon. I have looked into the darkness at the heart of light.

"I have done this."

"So you believe it is possible for a white man to dream as Indians dream. To know the destination of the soul."

"I *know* it is possible. I speak only of things I have seen and experienced for myself."

"It is like this." Tobias struggled to contain his emotions. He felt close to tears. "As you see, I am not a young man, and my wife is long gone. I have had cause to reflect often, in recent years, about what may await me on the other side of death. And what may be expected of me. I have studied these things in the holy books of my people, but their promises are confusing and contradictory. Forgive me. It must seem strange to you, an old man rattling on about death."

I died and came back. All that is strange to me is that so many white men tell themselves that death is just a black hole of oblivion, and live without wings.

"To speak of these things is natural. I learned from my native teacher that the only thing of value in a man is the soul."

"But how can I *know* for certain?"

You will know soon enough, old man, when your spirit drops its body.

"This side of death, you can know only through dreaming."

"But I don't remember my dreams!"

"You will remember when you are ready to face your deepest fears and to master them."

And when you stop trying so hard. Your big self is trying to speak to you every night, in your dreams. All you need do is listen.

"The Indians begin each day by sharing their dreams. You might experiment in the same way. Tell yourself tonight that you wish to remember your dreams. Give yourself time in the morning to lie abed, and let the memory of your dreams float back to you."

"What if I still do not remember?"

"Do not fret yourself. Be quiet, be gentle. Roll your body softly in your bed, as you moved during the night. As your body resumes the postures of the night, it may coax your dreams back to you. If you still have no dreams, consult your feelings. Your feelings will be a clue to what happened during the night. Even when we do not remember dreams, we feel their shadow, in our moods and our bodily sensations."

"I must write this down." Tobias rushed to his writing desk and snatched up a quill.

Longhair says white men are forever writing things down because they have lost the ability to remember.

Tobias will find what he is seeking if he can only silence the chatter of the bookish pedant who lives in his head.

*His wife is reaching out to him, from the other side. She wishes to
prepare him for the great journey that lies before him. I can feel her.*

2.

Johannes Bratt visited Franck's truck house, with a bundle of furs he
had bartered from an Abenaki with a keg of rum generously watered
with his own product. He overheard one of the clerks discussing the
quality of the watered silk that Conrad Weiser had ordered for his bride's
wedding dress.

He shared this information with Sheriff Adams, who had lost the use
of his right eye, as well as his left testicle, riding the rail through the
Palatine settlements.

When Conrad returned to Albany to collect the fabric for Eva's bridal
gown, the sheriff's men were waiting. Adams made sure he landed a
memorable kick to Conrad's privates before throwing him into the
lockup.

□

Conrad's father had left Weisersdorf. He was riding to Boston with Wil-
helm Scheff and Johann Walrath—sober, steady men who could be
trusted to put their case without insult or unnecessary emotion. A new
sovereign sat on the throne of England. King George was a German,
who spoke the language of the Palatines and had been reared as a Lutheran. Johann Weiser believed his people must receive justice from a
German king, not comprehending that the interests of monarchs rarely
coincided with those of their subjects, and that their patriotism was of a
different kind.

In the absence of the elder Weiser, there was no clear leadership
among the Palatines of the Schoharie valley. Vrooman was building
again, with an armed bodyguard that kept watch day and night. Conrad
was not the only prisoner in the Albany jail. Other Palatines who had
gone to Albany for salt and staples, including Dina Zeh, were also taken.

Gunther Bertelsmann favored a night raid to free them. This plan
drew little support. The spirit of defiance was waning in the valley, after
a poor harvest. Some of the settlers had moved south into Pennsylvania,
or west to the edge of Mohawk country, farther from the reach of Governor Hunter and the Albany bosses.

Eva went across the river, to the people who had arranged her wedding night under the stars.

Island Woman and her family listened closely. They could not understand how a man could be hanged for a crime they did not recognize: for defending his people and the land they shared.

Island Woman said, "We will dream on this."

3.

If you had remembered your dream, you would have avoided this trap.

The thought that came to Conrad in the night, as he lay on the hard, clammy floor, was cold comfort.

His jailers had offered him a chance of release. If the Palatine prisoners agreed to sign leasehold agreements, acknowledging that the lands they had paid for were the property of Robert Livingston's son and his friends, they would be allowed to go free.

What kind of freedom was this?

"I piss on your lease, shitface!" he had heard Dina bawling from another cell. He wondered whether she had had the gall to do it in front of their faces.

It occurred to him that signing the lease would be no real betrayal. His father's land was not his to sign away. On the other hand, Hendrick and the other Mohawks who had deeded it to the governor's gang had even less right to it, and their agreement was held to be binding.

Clear your mind. Shift to the second attention.

He tried to set aside the confusion of his little self and the deep body-aches bequeathed by a series of beatings. He shifted consciousness, and moved through the dream gate that opened to him, folding time.

The cell door swings open. No one prevents me from walking out of the jail as a free man. But there is danger in the street. I cannot see its source.

I don't want to look any more. But I must look. I must see all of it.

I am on my back, looking up at the night sky. Rough faces leer down at me, only for a moment. Now I am looking down at them, at their floppy hats. I am rising on a cloud. I have dropped my body like a worn-out set of clothes.

Conrad struggled to master the terror that came with this waking dream. *I have seen my death.*

He reminded himself of Longhair's teaching: if you can see the future, you can also change it.

He had not seen—or anyway, had not remembered—his capture. But he had seen this ambush, and what flowed from it.

He must go back inside the dream, to understand how it could be changed.

This time he could identify his attackers. The man who wielded the

knife was Bratt, one of the riders who had attacked Weisersdorf. Eva
was there too. Bratt was molesting her, after stabbing Conrad.

Why was Eva in this scene?

He pictured money changing hands, money advanced by Tobias
Franck. He saw a jailer pocketing his bribe.

Eva, you must not do this! You must not come!

Surely he could reach her, traveling on the cord of love that joined
their hearts. He found her sleeping, not in the cabin he had built for
her, but in a bark lodge. She must have gone to Seth's village, searching
for help.

She was beautiful. He noticed how her body was ripening. Was she
carrying their first child?

Eva!

He saw her dreambody sit up, lifting partway out of the sleeping
body on the bed. He tried to communicate what he had seen.

*Don't go to Albany. Don't try to bribe the jailers. They will lay a trap for
us both.*

Eva sat up in her body of flesh and blood. He saw the worry and
pain in her face. She was rousing Island Woman.

Good. She had received his message.

The image flickered. He tried to hold it steady, to be sure.

He was appalled by what he found. Eva was telling Island Woman
she must go to Albany, because of her dream.

That's not right! Listen to me!

But already Eva was gathering her clothes.

4.

Conrad yelled at the door, for the jailer.

"Tell the sheriff I will sign the paper if he releases me tonight."

"The sheriff's abed," the jailer grumbled. "Like any respectable
man would be at this hour."

"Then rouse him. You'll not be sorry."

The jailer's dull eye brightened, at the hint of a bribe.

The sheriff came down to the jail, curious to know what had broken
the German boy's will. Perhaps it was the last beating, or the jailhouse
slops. Nothing like a diet of swill to change a man's mind.

Conrad expressed contrition, and respect for the might of the law.

"That's all well and good," Adams told him. "But I am not releasing
you tonight, whatever you sign."

He had a strict agreement with James Mackie that if the Weiser boy
broke, he was not to be let out of jail until Mr. Mackie was given due
warning. Mackie had an account of his own to settle.

Conrad surprised him by saying, "If you release me tonight, I will persuade others to sign."

This was an interesting proposition. Some of the Palatines might have been pliable enough, but Dina Zeh had whipped them up to a spit of defiance. Mackie's employer would certainly be gratified if the sheriff could serve him a whole plate of signatures, and his purse was a sight deeper than his agent's.

"Frau Zeh can bend others, if I persuade her. Give me some moments alone with her."

Conrad's request to be left alone with Dina was the occasion for much low ribaldry among the sheriff's men.

"Better you than me, lad. The fat tart will bite it off when you tell her you've lost your balls."

Dina's initial reaction was not all that far removed from this prediction. She calmed down as Conrad explained his thinking, quickly and quietly, without invoking its dream source.

"What we sign in here will be patently the product of coercion," Conrad told her. "It will be rescinded in any honest court of law."

"I've yet to come across one of those," Dina interjected.

"My father is on his way to London to claim justice from our German king."

"Kings never did anything for *me*, whatever language they speak."

"The nub of it is this," Conrad lowered his voice. "We will sign the *wrong names*."

"Do you think they are blind?"

"They believe we are all unlettered."

"Well, half of us are."

"But we are all capable of writing our names."

This, at least, was agreed.

"Well, jumble them up. Have the men write illegibly, so their names cannot be made out plain. It will serve. They will accept what we give them. They take pictures of animals from the natives."

It worked.

They spilled out into the night air of Albany, scented with cow dung, just in time to be noticed by Johannes Bratt, who was rolling toward the whorehouse after a serious session at the King's Tavern.

Bratt swore thickly at the sight of Conrad at the head of the party, flanked by women.

"Hey, you!" he bawled at Conrad. "You have more quim than you can serve. Do a real man a favor and share it around."

His rank laughter puddled into more foul words as it dawned on him that these were some of the Palatine rebels he had fled from in the valley. Turning to identify the source of the obscenities, Conrad saw the floppy hat from his dream. As if back in the dream, he saw, in slow motion, Bratt reaching for his blade.

The correspondence paralyzed him for a long, dangerous moment.

Had he succeeded only in bringing the fulfilment of his waking dream?

Dina Zeh charged Bratt like a maddened cow. She swung her balled fist at his throat, and he went down spitting blood. She stomped on his chest until she heard the ribs crack. The other women joined in the party, paying special attention to Bratt's erogenous zone. By the time they were finished, it seemed doubtful that Johannes Bratt would have any use for the whorehouse.

It was not the dream, he reflected. Eva had not come. Because he had seen saw the future, he had been able to change it.

CHAPTER 24

THE RELOCATION OF
SOULS

1.

Conrad and Eva were married in the eyes of the church by a Reformed
preacher, Johann Friedrich Heger, who came to minister to the Palatines
in the Schoharie valley. The wedding took place in Johann Weiser's
house, but Conrad's father was not present.

The elder Weiser's path of trials had grown even more arduous since
he boarded his ship for England. On the outward journey, as if Captain
Kidd had risen from his grave, Johann's ship was seized by pirates, and
he and his fellow envoys were stripped of all their possessions. In London, while languid courtiers kept him waiting for an audience with any
man of power, he was thrown into a debtor's prison. The Palatine em-
issaries found that George, though German-born, had no time for Germans from his American plantations. By the time the King's officials
deigned to give them a hearing, Governor Hunter had been recalled from
New York and made a personal appearance before the tribunal where
he systematically wrecked their case. It was cold comfort for Johann
Weiser that he was soon able to exact partial revenge on this enemy. He
refused to sign a certificate attesting that Hunter had provided food and
supplies to the Palatine emigrants "pursuant to the Queen's orders." On
the strength of this, the British government declined to reimburse Governor Hunter for the huge personal debts he had incurred through his
disastrous tar-making project.

Conrad and Eva's first child was born two summers after the official
wedding, and they had him baptised Philip. For more than a decade,
since Longhair had sent him back to his father's people, Conrad applied
himself to building a normal family life and championing the cause of

the Palatine settlers. The sheriff did not come after him again, and Governor Hunter, despite his threats, did not send redcoat soldiers along the Schoharie Creek. The lords of New York, impressed by the stiff price of facing the Palatines head-on, had resolved to wear them down. They issued more deeds to tough Dutch farmers like Adam Vrooman, who built their stone houses, loopholed for musketry, next door to the Palatine settlements and steadily encroached into their lands. It was never possible for the families at Weisersdorf to lower their guard. They felt grinding, unending pressure. When Eva's mother found her kitchen garden plowed under overnight, she persuaded her husband to follow the settlers who had moved on to Pennsylvania.

"You should make the Weisers come with us," she told Eva.

Johann Weiser, home empty-handed from London, was not willing to give up his Promised Land. And Conrad found that he shared his father's reluctance, though in his dreams he kept returning to scenes of departure and migration; he saw himself in the midst of his siblings, struggling to drag an overloaded handcart along the weary roads from his native village to the Dutch coast. But Eva was pregnant again, and he told himself this was not the time to contemplate a journey of hundreds of miles through the American wilderness. He found the dream gates were often closed to him, even when he sat staring into the crystal rock. His children needed religious education, and his family needed respectability, so he sat in the airless meeting house, trying to subsist on the thin diet of the Reformed minister's sermons and scripture readings. Yet he was far from eager to leave the landscape where he had discovered gateways to other worlds.

Then he dreamed that a noose was being tightened around his neck and woke feeling half-strangled, clutching at his throat.

Eva lit a candle and flustered over him. "What is it? Are you unwell?"

"It is only a dream."

Eva frowned. She would have accepted this dismissive remark from any of their German neighbors, but not from Conrad. "Do not push me away. Tell me the dream."

"I believe your parents were right. We must prepare to go into Pennsylvania. We are finished with New York. There is no room here for us to breathe."

He did not tell her about the rope. She might take this quite literally, and might even be right to do so. There were men in Albany and at Livingston Manor who would still welcome the chance to measure his neck for a noose.

He made a journey of reconnaissance, traveling westward by woodland trail and bark canoes to Otseningo, where he traded furs with the Indians and asked after Swatana. The Oneidas and Cayugas at the village

on the Susquehanna told him that Swatana was at a trading post downriver, and that was where Conrad found him.

"Longhair's student," the Oneida chief greeted him. "I have been
expecting you."

2.

Before Conrad returned to Weisersdorf, Longhair had decided that his
remaining student, Island Woman, had completed her training, and that
she would be his last apprentice, at least while he owned his present
body. The shaman was ready to pass over. This, too, would be a teaching
experience.

"The path of the soul after death," he instructed Island Woman, "is
the same as the path of the soul in dreams, except that after death you
cannot return to the physical body you previously possessed. This is why
running away from dreams is so foolish. Where are you going to run
when you no longer have a physical body to run home to?"

The shaman cackled, but Island Woman frowned, sensing the thin-
ness of the old man's blood, the pain in his joints.

"We are about to receive a visitor," Longhair announced. "Tell me
who it is."

Island Woman closed her eyes and saw Conrad, a stronger, sterner
man than the panting youth who had come to live at the White Village.

"It is Skycatcher."

"You see true. He has not walked this path for many winters. He
has come to tell me he is leaving us. But he will never be a stranger to
us, because one of our spirits lives in him."

They remembered the ritual of requickening, when Longhair had
laid a glowing coal over Conrad's heart and called the spirit of the great
one into his body. The ritual in which Conrad received his new and
shining name: Skycatcher.

The requickening had nothing in common with the black arts of
sorcerers like Two Hearts, which Longhair abominated as exercises in
vampirism and bodysnatching.

While Two Hearts had attempted forcible entry into another person's body, Conrad had willingly opened himself to fusion with a radiant
being that he perceived as part of a universal energy.

Longhair found it impossible—and unnecessary—to set the images
that flowed through his mind into linear sequence. He saw scenes from
his final battle with Two Hearts, the bodythief, who had tried to possess
Conrad. Longhair believed that he had acted in the right spirit, though
the combat with Two Hearts had brought out his killer instincts. There
had been need for a warrior shaman, and this was what Longhair had

always been, however hard he had sought to gentle the force and retract his claws.

He had played the same trick on Two Hearts the sorcerer liked to play on others. He smiled at the memory:

I shut him out of his body. He got into the body of a snake. We hunted the snake and killed it. But Two Hearts was slippery. He got into the body of a woodchuck. The Master of Air, the great taker of souls, reduced to a chubby rodent, his proper proportions.

We pursued the woodchuck to its hole and burned it.

Then the real chase began. I hunted him between the worlds, my breath hot on his neck. I not only had to ensure that Two Hearts did not escape into another physical body—animal, human or insect. I had to make certain he did not manage to evade the second death and survive to infest the living and steal their energy, like the other criminal souls that delude themselves that they are masters of the universe.

I caged him in a net of white fire. I shut the enduring part of him up and locked it behind seals he will not break until he has consented to walk the path of purgation and judgment. The judgment is likely to be the harshest possible, since it will be meted out by his true self, the big self he betrayed, though it will take many lives before Two Hearts understands what this means.

I dissolved his dreambody by pulling it into myself and turning the energy around. This made me crazy sick for a while, because I had to deal with all the evil Two Hearts carried with him. But when I got clear, I was stronger.

When Longhair returned from his reverie, Island Woman brought him a bowl of corn soup.

"A dreamer who can cook! Now, a woman like that is a jewel so bright it must soon call a husband."

"I am not interested in a husband."

"Ah, but you will be, soon enough. You took on a woman's body. You will live as a woman, in all ways. You will bear children. Your power will live on through your bloodlines."

"But you—"

"Me? I am beyond man or woman. But I remember a time when I was a man and used to enjoy myself with the girls." He cackled.

Island Woman wanted to talk more about the afterlife. He nearly said to her, *Don't forget to live in the body as well as out of it,* but caught himself. Her sense of humor had not evolved as fast as her other gifts. It was rather important *not* to be deadly serious about deathly subjects. But given the fearful experiences they had shared, he would allow her plenty of time before expecting her to crack any jokes about spooks and bodyhoppers.

The shaman told her, "The path of the soul after death, as in dreams, is in fact not one path but many paths.

"People do not go to the same places when they die, and they do not travel the same roads. The path *you* travel will be determined by your courage, your desires, the good or evil you have done to others, and your ability as a *dreamer*.

"Beyond death, as on this side of it, fear closes many doors. There are countless souls who cling to the living like drowning men because they are terrified to move on. Many of these people refuse to believe they are dead.

"When your soul leaves your body, in death as in dreams, it will follow the direction of your strongest desires. People who say they will no longer be driven by worldly appetites when they have died to the body are ignorant. People do not change all that much simply because they are dead. The same desires command them.

"Out of our desires and beliefs, we make heavens and hells. We create them, but they are nonetheless real. They may be inhabited by many who share the same beliefs, or the same appetites. One person's heaven is another's hell. I have seen people hurling themselves headfirst into places that looked hellish to me. I have seen a heaven of white men that, while not hellish, would be hellishly boring to me: a place where dead white men in green pants spend all day hitting little white balls with sticks.

"There is a path of trials, and a place of judgment. You will pass judgment on yourself. *You will answer to yourself.* But the self that will judge you is infinitely wiser and deeper than your little everyday self.

"One law is unbreakable: Those who have stolen the souls of others cannot pass into the light. I have seen many priests, as well as many sorcerers, huddled like bats in the houses of darkness where they seek to avoid punishment and to hold on to the souls they have taken."

The shaman broke off, because he saw Conrad climbing the steep rise.

"Sit down and eat," Longhair greeted him, as if they had parted company only that morning. "Did you know Island Woman is a pretty good cook?"

"I've noticed she's good at many things." He smiled but lowered his eyes. His shyness was not for Island Woman; their relationship had lost all its friction since they had agreed they would be brother and sister. His shyness was for Longhair, because of the decision he had come to share.

He began to explain that after all their struggles, the Palatines were losing their Promised Land in the Floodwood Valley. More and more were leaving. His own parents-in-law had gone. Many of those who remained had bowed to the relentless pressure from the Albany gang and signed leases with genuine names. Conrad and Eva had made their decision. They would take the children and a party of friends and family and push on down to Tulpehocken in Pennsylvania, where it was said a man could breathe a larger air. Swatana, who had been appointed by the Confederacy to watch over the southern tribes, had assured him they would be safe there.

Longhair heard him out patiently before reminding him, "I told you that you would be going Swatana's way."

Conrad looked into the shaman's shining eyes.

"It is like this," Longhair told him. "The spirits fall in love, just like people. The spirits are in love with you. They will find you again, maybe under different masks."

Island Woman looked troubled.

Longhair gave her a sharp glance, warning her not to speak what was on her mind.

"'There is something you need to remember," he told Conrad. "Spirits can lie, cheat and steal, just like people. You must never forget to challenge the spirits, to know exactly who you are dealing with. I gave you a place to see. Do you still have it?"

Conrad extracted the crystal rock from his pack.

"Keep this with you always, and use it. You will find guidance here."

"Will I find *you* again?"

"Look for me where the eagle flies."

PART THREE

THE

FALL

1729–1741

The wise man falleth seven times a day and riseth up again.
—William Blake

The Brother must take heed against the female sex.
—Warning to Conrad Weiser from Brother Friedsam,
in the *Chronicon Ephratense*

By what a man falls, he may also rise.
—Tantric maxim

CHAPTER 25

INTO PENNSYLVANIA

1.

Conrad led his family along the Mohawk path that ran westward through the forest to the north branch of the Susquehanna. Talldeer had volunteered to escort them as far as the rendezvous with Swatana. The Mohawk warrior flitted in and out of the shadows, scouting their flanks, hunting game for their supper. Eight-year-old Philip craned his head back, searching for a glimpse of sky through the dense canopy of the forest. When he finally found a patch of blue, it was smaller than his fist.

It was slow going, with so many small children and heavy packs and handcarts to haul over roots and fallen branches. They made frequent stops, when Eva changed the baby's native diaper of dried moss and suckled her at the breast before tucking her back inside the cradleboard. They were still an hour's walk from the north branch when Conrad loped ahead with Talldeer, leaving Freddie in charge of the women and children, eager for a glimpse of the river-road they would follow to Pennsylvania.

The canoes were still cached in the bushes below the stone heap, very near the place he had left them. They had been borrowed and returned somewhat the worse for wear. The canoe he had peeled from a chestnut tree had a rent in one side, but Talldeer mended it before the rest of the family caught up. It was simple work to lash together a raft for their supplies; the work was done by the time Eva had finished cooking a rabbit stew for supper.

Conrad watched the play of dappled light on brown water. He squinted along the river, trying to picture the shifting course of the long water-road that stretched before them like an inverted J: southwest to join the Susquehanna in its southward course toward the sea, then east-northeast up one of its tributaries toward the valley at the foot of the Blue Mountains where they would make their new home. A distance of perhaps four hundred miles. There were shorter roads, but none that matched the relative comfort and safety of the Susquehanna trail. They could float downriver most of the way; their main navigational problem would be to steer cleer of treacherous rips and fallen timber. As far as Otseningo, they would be traveling past Indian villages where the Mohawk language was understood and a friend of the Mohawk would be respected. At Otseningo—if he had remembered his promise—Swatana would be waiting to guide them into the country of the Shawnees and the Leni Lenape, whom the English called Delawares. Their route would take them far beyond the reach of old enemies in the New York colony.

Conrad looked back at the forest wall that stood between him and the home he had known. He had always felt himself a stranger there. He had been hunted as an outlaw. He had never been at ease under his father's roof, even on the day he and Eva were formally wed by the Reformed preacher in Johann's house at Weisersdorf. He had found a new identity among the Mohawks, yet he had been called from them by different spirits. Home was always somewhere else.

He squatted by the fire, where Eva was spoon-feeding two-year-old Maria. He cracked his knuckles and made rabbit ears with his fingers in front of the baby's face, and was rewarded with gurgles of joy.

This time, Conrad promised himself, he would make a home that could be relied on. He would put down roots and stand as a tall, sheltering tree for his family.

His night was restless. For most of it, he rolled on the cusp of sleep, alert to every creak or scuffle in the woods. He rose with aching bones and a broken shard from a dream: the strange image of a pyramid, set between a stream and a range of blue mountains. The thickly wooded landscape was surely American. Perhaps it was a glimpse of the country into which he was leading his family. But what was the pyramid doing in the midst of Pennsylvania hills? Was it a promise, or a warning of the arrogance of Pharaoh toward the Chosen People?

□

The long voyage down the Susquehanna was punctuated by a few days' rest at Swatana's village, and a briefer visit to the Delawares at Shamokin. The Leni Lenape, as they called themselves, were very different from the Indians Conrad had come to know. Their language was filled with clucking sounds, and they watched the newcomers with narrowed eyes.

"The Lenape are not your friends." Swatana confirmed what Conrad read in those stony faces. "This will not change. You can buy their smiles with rum and presents, but these smiles will come only from the lips. It is good that they know that you and I are brothers, because we have taught them to fear the Five Nations and made them our daughters."

Conrad noticed how the Delawares made room for the Oneida chief, receiving him with every sign of respect. He did not miss the edge of contempt in his friend's words. Swatana spoke of the natives of this country as if they were less than the Real People. There was something of King Hendrick in the way he strutted among them, and perhaps something of a Roman proconsul dealing with a subject tribe. Conrad observed without judging. There was a long history of bloodletting between the Five Nations and the Delawares, which had left the Iroquois with the upper hand. If he could stand apart from their rivalries, he would do so. If he could not, his loyalty was given.

"I told our daughters you are not one of the Sunrise People," Swatana translated his exchange with the Delaware chiefs. "I told them you belong to the Flint People, and wherever you go, you are under the protection of the Confederacy."

2.

Conrad shivered when he found his dream pyramid in broad daylight, between the Tulpehocken Creek and the Kittatinny Mountain, in a valley where a score of Palatine families had clawed homesteads from the forest. His family arrived hungry and exhausted, after paddling and poling up the Swatara and the Quittapahilla before the day-long trek through the foothills to the edge of the German settlements.

"There!"

Eva followed Conrad's pointing finger. Beyond Horst Wesselman's wheatfields and the deep woods behind them, she saw a strange, conical hill. Its sides were as straight as if drawn by a ruler, making a steep triangle against the sky and the distant blur of the Blue Mountains. Bald and solitary, it looked unnatural—a pyramid discovered in the wrong setting, a volcano that had erupted where lava did not flow.

A bird sailed above it, on flat wings.

"How do they call that hill?"

Wesselman shrugged. "I cannot get my tongue around the native words."

Conrad shaded his eyes with his hand to see the bird more clearly. It was a golden eagle. Its wings curved into a sickle as it broke from its glide. Conrad admired the fierce beauty of its dive, as it plunged toward unseen prey, talons outstretched.

"I think this is Eagle Peak," he announced. "I will build at the base of the hill. Will that be acceptable?"

Wesselman scratched his neck, coarsened by wind and sun to the texture of saddle leather. "We must put it to the elders. I am sure there will be no trouble. Out here, what a man is willing to work, he owns."

□

Conrad built a temporary cabin under Eagle Peak. Working in all weather, he was soon able to move his family to a square, solid stone house. The house was of the simplest design: one big room with raftered sleeping quarters up under the eaves. But it was warmed by an enormous fireplace, and Conrad built Eva's bake oven into the wall behind the hearth so she did not have to brave the elements to make her bread.

Here, in his own stone house, at the head of his own family, among neighbors from the old country, he was determined to fit in. On Sundays, he led his family to the simple stone church Rieth had put up on his land, for prayer meetings in the absence of a minister, and for sermons and services when an itinerant preacher came to the valley. Conrad was careful in his speech—careful, in particular, not to speak of Longhair or his teachings. Some of his neighbors believed that the Indians worshiped devils, and that their shamans were in league with evil spirits. There was a prevailing fear of witches, deeper even than Conrad remembered in Gross Aspach. On his first morning in church, he heard Wesselman's wife complain that her cow's milk had gone sour because someone had put the evil eye on her.

Yet his experiences in Mohawk country had left him with a hunger that could not be satisfied by sermons and scripture readings. It was a hunger to return to the other worlds that had opened to him—briefly but indelibly—in *dreaming*. He was astonished and thrilled to discover that, in the little German community in the hills of southern Pennsylvania, he was far from alone in this hunger.

Among the visiting preachers at Rieth's was a lanky man about Conrad's age called Peter Miller. Gaunt and bony, with undersized chin poorly masked by a scraggly beard, Miller's appearance was less than commanding. But when he took the lectern, his gray eyes sparkled into a cerulean blue, and his reedy voice gathered strength. Quoting his favorite authors, Jacob Boehme and Georg Gichtel, Miller insisted that a Christian life should be centered on the personal experience of death and resurrection.

"In his little, corrupted self, a man knows nothing," Miller insisted on a humid summer morning. "A man who believes in Christ on the authority of church and scripture is an incomplete Christian. To know the true nature of God and man, we must die to the old self and rise from the wasted flesh to see in the pure light of spirit."

Some of Miller's listeners dozed off in the drowsy heat, lulled by the drone of insects outside. Horst Wesselman snored loudly enough to rattle the glass until his wife jabbed the roll of fat under his ribs. But Miller engaged Conrad's rapt attention.

He invited the wandering preacher home for dinner, and they sat up long after Eva and the children had retired to the sleeping galleries.

"The Indians believe it is a man's duty to study the fate of the soul after death," Conrad said when he felt that a bond of trust had grown between them. "They say that we can learn such things through dreaming. I have heard reports of native dreamers who claim to have unsheathed their souls from their bodies and visited the Otherworld."

"Some of this may be true," Miller said curtly. "But heathen sorcerers travel between the worlds with the help of their devilish familiars. The realms they visit are the home of illusions and evil spirits. Nothing that belongs to the astral planes can be trusted. Gichtel is quite clear on this point."

Conrad was stunned by this attack, and very relieved that he had not referred to his personal experiences in broaching the subject of soul travel. He found himself unable or unwilling to contradict Miller's brutal dismissal of Indian practices. Doubt crawled in his marrow. The memory of what he had *lived* in his time as Longhair's student had dimmed with each day he spent clearing his land and tilling his fields. His adventures were fading like a dream. He no longer dreamed the way he had done before. He woke fogged with sleep, to stagger back to the fields or the barn to put in two hours' work before breakfast. Had he been duped by a native sorcerer? Or oppressed by an unclean spirit?

His hand twitched toward the gold medallion he wore under his shirt. This was the one piece from Captain Kidd's treasure he had kept for himself. It was etched with strange designs, Moorish or African. The metal under his fingertips reassured him that if all he had lived in Longhair's country was a dream, part of it was yet *real*.

"I am but a humble student of these matters," Peter Miller continued. "I myself am in search of a teacher. I have heard of one such, a true servant of God who casts out demons and restores men to the knowledge of the Master."

"Who is this man?"

"He shares your Christian name. He is called Conrad Beissel. A baker of Eberbach, it is said, whose calling was announced by an angel who drew him out of his body and showed him the wonders of the universe. A man who instructs his pupils in good German, and inspires them with the power of his breath. No more talk of conjurers draped in feathers and bones, Conrad. We are Germans and we are Christians, and we will not find salvation outside of what we are."

For an instant, Conrad recalled his vision of the Peacemaker as a

universal force of love who wore the face of Christ but also the faces of
many others. The vision wavered. He so much wanted to *belong*, not to
be forever a stranger among his own kind.

"Where is this Conrad Beissel?"

"I mean to find him," Miller declared. "I will tell him there is a
vineyard here that needs a gardener."

3.

While Peter Miller, a solitary bachelor, set off across the hills in search
of a spiritual teacher, Conrad was called to work that was of more immediate concern to the farmers of the valley.

Swatana came to the homestead on horseback, magnificent in a scarlet cloak and feathered headdress, accompanied by his Cayuga wife and
several Oneidas and Senecas. Conrad was disappointed that none of his
Mohawk friends were in the party, but glad to see the Oneida chief and
to trade metaphors in a language he had not employed in many months,
except in his dreams.

"I have placed a tree across my brother's path," Conrad announced
formally. "So he will stay by my fire."

"I am glad my brother remembers how Real People talk. I need him
to dig up the words and plant them anew in front of Onas."

Onas—meaning Quill—was the title the Iroquois gave to the rulers
of Pennsylvania; it was a rough translation of the surname of William
Penn, the colony's first Proprietor.

Conrad remembered his manners, and invited his Indian guests to
eat before talking business. Eva served them fresh-baked loaves from
the oven, with thick slices of smoked ham, and fresh vegetables from
the garden. After the meal, Conrad lead Swatana up onto the lower
slopes of Eagle Peak, where they shared a pipe and watched the silver-
white flash as a hawk rode a warm current of air toward the South Mountains.

"*Wanniserio*," Swatana nodded. "A beautiful place. A beautiful valley. You chose well. But I hope you keep your powder dry and your
flints ready to hand. You may be required to fight for this land."

Conrad tensed. He had heard evil reports of fights between settlers
and natives in other parts of the Pennsylvania border country: of a Delaware family slaughtered by Scotch-Irish over near Minisink; of the massacre of traders west of Tioga by Shawnees who had gone to Detroit to
join the French. So far, the violence had not touched Tulpehocken, apart
from the periodic complaints of a stolen cow or a pig, or a brush with
Delawares who had been drinking too hard.

"The Lenape say this valley belongs to them," Swatana continued.

"They say they never sold it, just as they never sold the land at the forks of the river the English call the Delaware."

"That cannot be!" Conrad said hotly. "When Onas invited my people here, he told us the land is free and clear, and that we would be given deeds at the proper time." Conrad paused. The Onas in question—the Pennsylvania official who had encouraged the Palatines to settle this region—was Governor Keith, long since retired. Conrad remembered the promises another governor, Robert Hunter, had made to the Palatines and what they had proved to be worth.

"Besides—" Conrad's gesture embraced the whole sweep of the valley "—the Delawares and Shawnees have gone west. There is only a remnant. Surely this land is ours by right of use."

Swatana shrugged. "The Lenape are not to be trusted. Each man speaks for himself. There is none who speaks for all. You pay one for something, and another comes to demand to be paid also, claiming it was his. Then another, and another. They are raising their prices, because the French are stronger among the western nations, and they think this will sow fear among Onas and his people."

Conrad set his chin between his fists. It was too hard, to think of all that his family and neighbors had endured in the province of New York—only to find themselves ensnared in another web of graft and deception.

"Onas is alarmed the Lenape do not fear him," Swatana continued. "But he knows the Lenape fear *us*. He has put these matters into our council fire. We go to Philadelphia to give him the judgment of our men of good minds."

"And you wish me to be your interpreter."

"We know you will give us your best words. You will keep a record for us, of the kind white men keep, that will rule in any disputes that may arise after this council. Onas will accept you, believing you to be half his, half ours. *We* know you belong only to us and to the spirits."

Swatana chuckled. "James Logan does not know you yet."

4.

Conrad Weiser, an outlaw and fugitive in New York, rode into Philadelphia along the Germantown Road at the side of the ambassadors of the Five Nations. He inspected the tall ships in the harbor, the prosperous houses crowded onto deep but narrow lots, the whir of Ben Franklin's printing press, the stir and bustle of carts and carriages driven at breakneck speed through the streets. It was a booming town, but his Palatine countrymen seemed to be at the bottom of the heap, crammed into low wooden shanties, airless and fetid in the oppressive summer heat.

It was cooler in the statehouse where James Logan, the provincial secretary, received his guests. Logan had ordered doors and windows opened to make a breezeway, and was flanked by servants batting fans. Logan was courtly and cultured, peppering his speech with Latin tags from Cato and Cicero, whom he had personally translated. Beneath the Irish-born Scot's civility, Conrad marked a cold, appraising eye. He guessed that Logan knew his way to a profit, or an adversary's soft spot, as surely as Robert Livingston. And had to remind himself that he was not dealing with a second Livingston: the provincial secretary was to be counted a friend, unless he showed himself in a different guise.

Still, there was another unsettling echo from the past when Logan referred to Swatana, in his welcoming speech, not only as "Shickel-lamy"—the Oneida chief's Delaware name—but as "the Half-King."

"We are honored by the presence of the Half-King, the viceroy of the great empire of the Five Nations that hold sway over all lesser Indian nations, from the Delaware River to the setting sun."

Swatana listened to these words, and Conrad's efforts at translation, without facial expression.

The English had called the Mohawks who visited Queen Anne kings, though there were no kings among the Real People. Now Logan hailed Swatana as a half-king. Clearly, more than casual flattery was at work here, and a different set of calculations from those that had led Hendrick's promoters to make him a king. Logan was not seeking to promote one Iroquois chief above another. As the public gatherings were followed by private sessions, Conrad began to grasp the deviousness and ambition of the deeper strategy that was in play. Logan had declared the Five Nations to be kings over other Indian nations so he could trade with the Iroquois for disputed lands. The Iroquois were likely to be more accommodating than Delaware or Shawnees since they were not living on these lands, though they claimed ownership by right of conquest.

Logan offered Conrad a glass of canary wine in his private study.

"I am impressed by your command of the Iroquois tongue, Mister Weiser."

"I lived with the Mohawks for a time, and learned their language. For a Mohawk to converse with an Oneida is as easy, or as difficult, as for a Scotsman to speak with a Londoner."

Logan chuckled. A little of the Scots brogue echoed in his speech, under the veneer of expensive schooling.

"I noticed you seemed troubled by some aspects of our interview."

"Not troubled, sir. Perhaps somewhat startled. I was surprised to hear the Five Nations declared to be owners of so much property beyond the province of New York."

"Perhaps you would care to read the situation on a map."

Logan unrolled a large, newly inked map. Conrad stooped over it.

He was astonished to see that on this Pennsylvania chart, half the continent of North America was attributed to the Five Nations of the Iroquois. The Shawnees, the Delawares and half-a-dozen other nations had simply disappeared, or were described as subjects of the Iroquois.

"Pax Iroquoia." Logan smiled.

"But, sir—" Conrad pointed at the vast expanses of prairieland south of the Great Lakes. "These lands have never belonged to the Five Nations."

"Right of conquest, man. How do you think William got England? It is the way of the world. Swatana agrees. I have already showed him this map. You may be glad to know he approves. Why should he not approve? We have made him a viceroy!"

"Have you shown the map to the Delawares? Or the Shawnees?"

"Come, come, Mister Weiser. If they have any complaint, they can take it up with the Iroquois and see if they keep their scalps."

"You have appointed the Five Nations your policemen, then."

"Do you know any superior to them in forest fighting? Why do you suppose the Delawares have left you in peace in your valley? They know the hand of the Confederacy is over you. Swatana has told them."

Logan replenished their glasses. "You are no raw youth, and you do not have the stamp of a carping moralist. You are not even a Quaker. I have admitted you into my confidence because you are Swatana's man, and already wedded to the cause of the Five Nations. I wish to give you reasons to add the government of Pennsylvania to your allegiances. We do not forget to reward those who serve us well. I know a little of your people. You Germans are a sturdy, hard-working, God-fearing lot, who value property. You cannot be unaware that one of the first fruits of our arrangements with the Five Nations is that you will get legal title to the lands you are working. As soon as the Five Nations release their claims to Pennsylvania lands, we are free to deed them or sell them to whomever we choose."

It dawned on Conrad that he had been made privy to a land fraud that might beggar even those engineered by the likes of Robert Livingston.

"We must look after our own," Logan said soothingly. "Our families, our neighbors, God and country. Do you not agree?"

"You are right," Conrad acknowledged. But at the moment he said this, he felt something leave him, as a bright spark flies from the fire.

□

Conrad got his land deed, which included a generous clause that allowed him to expand his property boundaries to the summit of Eagle Peak. Even before the deed was notarized, he was placed on Logan's payroll and awarded the title of Provincial Interpreter. He made the long trek north to Onondaga to sit with Swatana at the Fire That Never Dies, in the presence of the traditional chiefs of the Confederacy in their antlered crowns.

He was becoming "a man to be reckoned with," as Logan had promised, already awarded several mentions in Bejamin Franklin's newspaper. Yet he felt a hole inside him that yearned to be filled.

CHAPTER 26

BROTHER ENOCH

1.

"Conrad," Eva whispered in order not to rouse the children. She pressed her lips to his cheek again, drawing him gently from sleep.

Conrad opened his eyes, not certain where he was, as he lost the memory of where he had been.

"Conrad."

He blinked at her, remembering her sweet, strong yielding the night before. He touched her belly.

"There are strangers in the woods."

The warning brought him fully back to his body. Had the Delawares come to claim revenge for Logan's land fraud?

Cattle rustlers. This was his second thought. He had lost a heifer only a month ago. He suspected the thieves were Delaware youths looking for the price of a bottle.

He hauled on his shirt and breeches, and snatched up his firelock as he hurried to the door. He stopped short at the threshold, amazed by what he saw at the foot of Eagle Peak. A column of lights, too bright and too orderly to be fireflies. They had to be men, armed with blazing torches. There were dozens of them, moving in a curving line around the edge of the cleared land. They were singing, though the words were lost to him in the distance. Their chant was punctuated by whooping cries.

Conrad cocked his gun. If Logan and Swatana had been wrong, in their insistence that the Delawares would never dare to attack the settlers of this valley, he was ready to fight for what he had built with his own hands.

A gust of song floated in on the breeze. "*Nach Himmel.*"

Conrad's hand relaxed from the trigger guard of his gun, but his puzzlement increased. What were his neighbors—sober German farmers—doing singing in the woods in the middle of the night?

He caught his breath as a death's head figure loomed out of the dark. For a moment, he did not recognize Peter Miller. The face inside the monkish cowl seemed almost fleshless, the skin drawn tight against the skull. Peter's coarse black robe, tied by a rope, hung almost to his ankles. He was barefoot, and he gripped a massive staff.

"God in heaven, man. I did not know you. Have you become a Jesuit?"

"No papist, Conrad. But a true Brother. I have taken my vows at Ephrata. I have brought Brother Friedsam to spread his light in this benighted valley."

"Brother Friedsam?"

"We spoke of him by his birth-name, Conrad Beissel."

"The baker from Eberbach."

"Now he leavens souls. He is a true prophet, Conrad. I have told him about you, and he is eager to meet you. Come with me now."

Eva joined them at the door, having pulled a mobcap over her tousled hair. "Does your Brother Whatsit hold all his conventicles at night?"

Peter Miller recoiled from her rounded pink warmth, accentuated more than concealed by the loose nightgown. It was no great hardship for Peter to take monkish vows, Eva thought; he was terrified of women.

"There are many Sisters in our Order," Peter said primly. "There are some that have left their husbands, even at the marriage altar, to follow Brother Friedsam."

"Wait for me while I get dressed," Eva told her husband. She wished to see these prodigies for herself.

□

Conrad and Eva joined the swaying procession of torchbearers that was threading the woods at the edge of the cleared lands. Someone handed Conrad a pine torch and he held it aloft, falling into the rhythm of the shuffling feet. Soon he was joining in the hymns. He kept craning forward for a glimpse of Brother Friedsam, but did not see him clearly until the marchers had trooped into Horst Wesselman's big new barn.

Conrad was surprised that Wesselman—who rarely seemed to see farther than the furrow he was plowing—was hosting this gathering. The marchers, many of them robed like Miller and strangers to Conrad, doused their torches in the trough by the barn door. Conrad followed suit. He and Eva took their places in the outermost of the concentric circles that formed inside the barn. Men and women he did not know embraced him and murmured encouraging words. At first embarrassed by all the hugs and shining eyes, he soon felt buoyed by the raw energy that seemed to flow between these people. Their faces were flushed. More strangers hugged and patted him. "Welcome home," they greeted him. Part of him resisted, trying to set boundaries. Part of him wanted to flow with them, to merge with their force.

"We must make a place for the spirit to enter."

The voice spoke softly at first, then swelled to fill the whole space.

"Let us kneel before the living God."

They fell to their knees, Conrad among them.

"Let us cast out sin and the weakness of the flesh. Open yourself now to the power and might of the living God. Open your heart to the mercy and wisdom of the Virgin Sophia. Let the light of the Holy Ghost move into you and fill you, washing away all that is fleshly."

Brother Friedsam spoke with his eyes closed. His hands were never still. He shook his clenched fist, flapped his arms like wings, tugged at his long patriarchal beard. The words streamed on and on. He seemed to gather force from the crowd as he spoke, and to send it ricocheting back among them, with extraordinary effect. He set people shaking and sobbing.

A middle-aged farmer, thick and hairy as a boar, rolled and groaned on the dirt floor.

"Are you ready to be saved?" the preacher boomed.

"Yes!" The cry was echoed again and again.

"Are you ready to cast off the old Adam? Are you willing to expel the filth and corruption that infests you, to make room for the Holy Ghost?"

"Yes, Brother!"

"Do you renounce the serpent of lust and give yourself to holy matrimony as brides of Christ and bridegrooms of the Virgin Sophia?"

"Yes!"

"Who wishes to be healed tonight?"

A chorus of voices responded. But the person who first came forward was a frail old woman, dragging along on a stick, half-carried by her bull-necked son.

She fluttered to the ground like a wilted leaf at the feet of the preacher. Conrad peered between the heads of the people in front of him, trying to follow Brother Friedsam's actions as he made several passes with his hands over the old woman's body. She began to shake more violently. She buckled and convulsed, like a thing tugged by strings.

There was a gasp from the crowd as Brother Friedsam reached into the folds of his robe and pulled out a sword. He drew a sign in the air with the sword, then brought it down close to the old woman's head in a powerful slicing motion.

"I cast out the root of thy corruption!" Brother Friedsam boomed. "I shut it up in its true form, which men will spurn and kill."

A woman screamed as a small black snake darted for safety under a bale of hay.

"Now you are a vessel for the Holy Ghost. Walk in its power."

Brother Friedsam raised the old woman, first to her knees, then to her feet. She reached for his arm to steady herself, but he avoided her.

She got the shakes again, and seemed about to fall. As she trembled in front of the preacher, Conrad noticed for the first time that Brother Friedsam was tiny, shorter even than this bent old woman. Yet his presence was huge.

The old woman took one step without the aid of her stick or a supporting hand, then another. She broke into a jerky stride. It was a man's stride, almost military. She walked as if a soldier had jumped into her skin.

"God be praised," Horst Wesselman said hoarsely, and Conrad realized the old lady must be his mother.

She marched to the door at a quickstep. Then she roared and broke into a run. Many of the faithful ran after her. Conrad hurried to catch up. He was just in time to see the old lady hurl herself headlong into the creek. He feared that she had lost her mind and intended to drown herself. But Brother Friedsam, seemingly unfazed, waded into the cold stream and dragged her up by the scruff of the neck, to pronounce words of baptism.

"Do you renounce Satan and all his works?"

The old woman's mumbled assent was barely audible.

"Are you willing to die to your old life, and renounce all fleshly things?"

"Do you give yourself, body and soul, to the Holy Ghost who has entered you?"

"Yes, Father."

□

Eva, hanging back from this scene, was deeply uneasy. She was Lutheran enough to be shocked at the way the word "Father"—redolent of the church before Luther—had crept in. She was repelled by the drama that was being played out in black water under the sepulchral, pre-dawn light. Wesselman's mother looked half drowned and more than half crazed, staring up at the tiny bearded zealot as if she saw her Saviour. The cowled men and women who crowded together at the water's edge, chanting hallelujahs, seemed to have given up all individual identity. The power that moved between them was strong, but Eva did not trust it. She could see how the voluble little man in the creek was feeding on it. She did not care for him, even if he was a wonder-worker; he drew the devotion he inspired toward himself and exulted in his power. Besides, some of his disciples smelled *bad*.

She saw Peter Miller, accompanied by another monkish figure with the shoulders of an ox, push through the throng and signal to Conrad.

"It is your time." Miller's words came like the tolling of a bell.

Conrad hesitated. Eva laced her fingers through his, and saw Miller wince.

"Thou shalt leave thy father and mother—" the bull-like Brother intoned.

"This is the Prior Onesimus," Miller explained. "He speaks the truth of the Lord."

Conrad pulled away from his wife. He was trembling. "I must do this thing," he told Eva. "I have been missing something of myself and I must have it back. A man is nothing without his soul."

She begged him to wait, but he was off to the creek, his arms interlocked with those of the two robed men.

Perhaps a cold dunking in the water would bring him to his senses, Eva told herself. She remembered another baptism, when Island Woman had led them in sacred song at the falls, and they had been cleansed by fire and water to join in the dance of Making. How different that had been! Then, all of nature had been their church, and they had entered the rhythms of life itself. Here, though the faithful met in the open air and were bathed in the millstream, the natural flow of life was denied. Brother Friedsam ranted against sex—even against marriage—and urged his followers to turn their natural vitality into a different channel, a channel he controlled. Though Brother Friedsam spoke of light, Eva saw darkness here, like a great water-snake that lay in hiding in a sewer.

"I have been waiting for thee," she heard Brother Friedsam declare, as Conrad knelt before him in the water, submitting himself to the ritual dunking. "I will make thee the bridegroom of the Virgin Sophia."

Eva was not amused at this obscure but offensive talk about sacred weddings. She wanted to protest, *Conrad is already married! And he's mine, not your Sophia's!*

She touched her belly, where it was beginning to swell with a new baby. She smiled a little at the memory of her lovemaking with Conrad the night before. He had been absent from her these last months, troubled by things he chose not to share with her. She had welcomed his return as an ardent lover. He had always had a lusty sexual appetite, and she told herself now that this would keep him out of the clutches of a man who preached against the joys of the flesh.

She turned from the scene at the creek to watch the pink rays of sunrise breaking over Eagle Peak. She felt suddenly cold, and wished she had worn a wrap over her plain cotton dress. When she looked for Conrad, she found Brother Friedsam staring at her. The little monk's robe was sopping wet. A robed woman Eva recognized—Anna Eicher— knelt at his feet to wring out some of the water. Brother Friedsam's mouth was set hard, his eyes unsparing.

Close up, he did not look much like a saint. There was unnatural brilliance in his eyes, but it was a cold fire. The image of the serpent concealed in a dark tunnel returned to her. Brother Friedsam called on his followers to spurn the flesh, yet he was stripping her with his eyes. There was contempt in his gaze, but also the potential to take and use without warmth, without heart. Was she the only one present who saw this?

2.

When Conrad crossed the hills with Brother Friedsam and his acolytes, he told Eva he would return in a week, two at the most.

"You know I have been lost to myself, for long months past," he told his wife. "I believe Brother Friedsam is the teacher I have been waiting for."

"I don't trust him."

"How can you say that?"

"He is obsessed with sex."

"He calls us to follow a higher path."

"He despises women. He uses them like bondwomen. You saw how they kissed his feet and hung on his robe."

"Be careful how you speak, woman!" There was a deep burr of anger in Conrad's voice that stung Eva like a hornet. Seeing her expression, he tried to resume a normal tone. "You hear how he invokes the Virgin Sophia. He reveres Woman, but lifts her up to a spiritual plane where she is exalted."

Words, words! Eva had glanced at the difficult theological texts that Conrad had ordered from Philadelphia and hoarded in his personal chest. Böhme's *Aurora*, Arndt's *Paradies Gärtlein*. She had been able to fathom one sentence in four. All this talk about the divine Woman left her cold if it neglected the needs of women of flesh and blood. Spiritual marriage was fine, but what about the marriages that produced babies, like the new one stirring in her womb?

Yet she wondered how much she was to blame for Conrad's fascination with the strange mystagogue who spoke of creating an order of *Engelsbrüder*, Angelic Brothers. Conrad had found inner light in his seasons with Longhair, the native shaman. Had the confinement and responsibilities of marriage thrown him back into darkness? Had she somehow helped him to lose his wings, so that now he stumbled blindly after another man's visions? Had she been wrong to urge him to leave Mohawk country to follow her father's trail to Pennsylvania? Or was Conrad's folly simply the foolishness of men, who when seized by a vision forget to live on the earth, drifting away like dandelion fluff?

"You are in charge of the farm," Conrad told Philip, who puffed himself up, proud to be nominated the man of the house. Conrad had already arranged with Freddie and Horst Wesselman that they would help Eva with the running of the farm.

He turned his horse's head south, toward the valley the Lenape called Cocalico. Brother Friedsam and his followers had renamed the site of their cloister Ephrata, but this did not entirely cancel out the resonance of the Indian name, which meant Den of Serpents.

Eva seized the reins, delaying her husband's departure. "If you don't come back to us soon," she promised, "I shall bring you back."

3.

Prior Onesimus showed Conrad the space that would belong to him. It was outlined in chalk on the stone floor of a large, unfurnished room: the silhouette of a human body. There were eighteen sets of these chalk marks, radiating out from the center of the room like the spokes of a wheel. Neophytes and probationers were required to take their rest here, without mattresses or blankets.

Though used to sleeping rough, Conrad found sleep impossible that first night, lying on the hard floor, listening to the snores and grunts of the other men. Two hours after lights-out, the whole community was roused by the tolling of a bell. Conrad jumped up at once, fearing an Indian attack, only to notice the other men robing themselves and filing out the door, as if moved by a single will. He followed them to the meeting house, where Brother Friedsam proceeded to deliver an endless harangue that left Conrad nodding. He went reeling back to the dormitory, confident that fatigue would bring some measure of rest—only to be roused by another bell for morning prayers almost as soon as he had closed his eyes.

After three nights like this, never permitted more than an hour or two of uninterrupted sleep, Conrad's boundaries collapsed. He dozed on his feet, and jerked awake within minutes of lying down. He dreamed with his eyes open, and blacked out when he closed them. He caught glimpses of Eva and Longhair many times during the night, and even of the hawk that had lent him its wings, but these were fleeting phantasms. His diet was bread and gruel and water, and the flesh began to fall rapidly from his bones.

"You are being tried for a purpose," Brother Friedsam told them in one of his midnight sermons. "The fire that melts the butter tempers the steel. Out of the dirt of your bodies, we will forge the philosophers' stone."

Come back to us, Eva whispered when he lay inside his ghostly outline. He yearned for the warmth of her body.

But he seemed deprived of decision. The words of the Brotherhood's monotonous chants ran over and over inside his head.

On the morning of the fourth day, Prior Onesimus spoke to the neophytes, who were all required to wear coarse woolen robes that chafed the skin.

"Your rule here is silence and mortification of the flesh. You will speak only if addressed by one of *die Volkommen,* the Completed, or if called to join in prayer and hymn singing. You will rest only during the allotted hours, and only in the space permitted. You will eat and drink only what is provided for you in the refectory. You will *never* set foot in the Sister's dormitory. You will eliminate bodily wastes only when told to do so. You will observe the discipline of our Order without question until the Superintendent has decided the stages of your further purgation and perfection. You will search your conscience now to determine whether you can live by these laws. If you cannot, you must depart this place at once. If you remain, there is no turning back. You will belong to the Order and be bound by its laws for the rest of your days."

You can't even shit without permission? a voice like Longhair's cackled in Conrad's mind. *Get away from these people. They're crazier than you are.*

But something else had seized command, something beyond Conrad's personal volition: a collective will. He volunteered for the harshest austerities, drawing pleasure from pain. He felt the relief of no longer needing to choose and to reason for himself: of accepting his place as a spoke in the wheel.

□

He had lost count of the days by the time the bell tolled for him alone. This happened in the last watch of the night, in the vampire hours Brother Friedsam preferred.

Brother Onesimus came for Conrad, drawing him from his brief sleep with the tinkling of the small bell he wore on the cord of his robe.

The Superintendent of the Order received Conrad in a tower building overlooking the valley. The walls of the room were covered with intricate diagrammatic paintings. Some represented the human body, overlaid with colored designs at the genitals, the solar plexus, the heart and other centers.

"Leave us," Brother Friedsam instructed Onesimus. He sat on a carved, high-backed wooden chair, thronelike on its platform. There was nowhere for Conrad to sit, so he stood waiting for guidance.

"Take my place." Brother Friedsam bounded from his perch, throwing a huge shadow against the wall.

"I cannot."

"Sit, sit. I will wash thy feet, as our Lord washed the feet of his disciples."

Conrad took his place uneasily on the raised seat, while Brother Friedsam brought a bowl of lukewarm water and sweet-smelling oils. He palpated Conrad's feet, horny from going without shoes or moccasins.

"The Brother must take heed against the female sex," he muttered. "It is through his weakness for the female sex that he is fallen into the penitentiary of carnal man. *Ist in Kinder gefallen.* By having children he is fallen."

Brother Friedsam rushed on, speaking faster and faster, as was his way in his sermons. Hurrying after the spirit, he called it. The way he constantly referred to Conrad in the third person gave the younger man the sense of being inspected by a member of a different species.

"I have the entity," Brother Friedsam galloped on. "He needs further cleansing. He has been prey to unclean and pagan spirits. He must be prepared to unsheathe his soul from his body and be filled by the Holy Ghost."

He reached under Conrad's coarse robe and clutched at the gold medallion, breaking the chain—and with it, one of Conrad's links to his past.

Brother Friedsam was sweating when he finished. He dried Conrad's feet roughly with a towel, then brushed them with his lips.

He put the wash things aside. "Hast thou had a bowel movement today?"

"No, Brother. I have been clogged."

"Worry not about it. The elimination of body wastes, like the act of coition, is not necessary to perfected man."

Get out of here now, whispered an inner voice. *You are in a madhouse.*

But Conrad was restrained by the force of Brother Friedsam's stare, and the sense of something immense that moved with him.

"I can show thee wonders. I can open the door to all the heavens. Look there." He pointed at the ceiling. Conrad saw a pattern of smudge marks that looked very much like footprints. "I can unsheathe my soul from my body and prove this by the marks I leave. This is evidence of the power of the Lord that works in me. Who but He can accomplish such marvels? Only his imposters, who have truck with the Dark One."

With these last words, he silenced the answer that had begun to shape itself in Conrad's fogged head.

"I have watched and waited for thee, Conrad Weiser. Thou knowest the English, and the savages, and they converse with thee as if thou wert one of their own kind. I have need of such as thee to be our sentinel in this den of serpents. *Du bist Schmiere stehen.* Thou art to be my lookout man. To serve the perfected, thou must die to thy former self, which was a plaything for demons.

"Conrad Weiser." Brother Friedsam laid his hands on Conrad's shoulders. *"Art thou ready to receive the Holy Ghost?"*

"I am." The words were no more than a croak. Conrad had lost focus. The room swirled into a blur around him. He felt buffeted by massings in the air. The exhaustion born of all the sleepless nights, the incessant prayer and chanting, the food fit for a scarecrow, bore him down. He was ready to drop. He hardly noticed the stronger hands that pulled him from the chamber and hustled him down the stairs to a vault-like space under the earth where, for the first time in many nights, he was allowed to rest on a surface other than the hard floor. He did not realize for a time that he had been placed in an open coffin.

"Leave thy body," Brother Friedsam commanded. "Leave this vessel of putrefaction, and be filled by the Holy Ghost."

This is an abomination, said that inner voice.

But Brother Friedsam was relentless. "I conjure thee in the name of the Lord, Iao. Leave thy body and receive the Holy Ghost."

Conrad felt the lightening, the blessed relief as he slid free from his body and flew across the valley, back toward his wife and children. What he was leaving behind already seemed like a dark dream, a parody of religion and the sorcerer's art.

Go back.

He had heard this warning before. Its urgency made him waver in his intention of hurrying home to Eva. He turned back. What was this thing that was being committed in the name of the Holy Ghost and the Virgin Sophia?

He saw his body, wasted and deathly pale in the open casket. Brother Friedsam, with a sword or wand in his hand, was drawing something into it. But this was no being of light. It looked like a carrion bird.

"Thou shalt serve only me," Brother Friedsam intoned. "I am thy Saviour."

Like a man waking from deep sleep, Conrad realized the depth of the deception that had been worked against him—and how many others? With recognition came memory and anger: the memory of the arts he had studied with Longhair, and the righteous anger of one who has followed a false prophet. He hurled himself at Brother Friedsam, and the thing that was attempting to take possession of his body.

He banged up against a lead wall. Somehow they had shut him out. Conrad tried many ruses, and invoked help by many names. He called on Longhair for guidance and protection. He called on Jesus Christ. The leaden wall remained.

Brother Friedsam's magic was stronger. *How else could he have brought me under his spell?* But surely not because of the names he invoked in his sermons. There was only darkness here.

He saw how far he had fallen. Why had he forgotten Longhair's warning that he must challenge the spirits? Now he was drifting like a rudderless ship in a fog. He must find a pilot before he was lost to his body. Where was Longhair?

Look for me where the eagle flies.

4.

Eva kept her promise. When Conrad did not return from Ephrata, she went after him.

Prior Onesimus came to meet her.

"I have come to see my husband."

"What is his name?"

"Look at me. Don't pretend you don't know me. You were at Tulpehocken, when my husband was baptized."

"Name."

"Conrad Weiser."

"There is no one of that name in this community."

"When did he leave?"

She looked wildly around. She saw a line of cowled women, moving like clockwork dolls toward the chapel. And a man toiling up the hill under the weight of wooden buckets suspended from a pole across his shoulders. A gaunt, almost skeletal figure, the Adam's apple protruding like a goiter from his scrawny neck.

"Peter!" she called to him, "Peter Miller!"

Miller continued on his way without responding to her cry.

"That is Brother Jabez," the Prior said, stony-faced.

Something of what had happened began to dawn on Eva.

"Have you taken my husband's name?"

Onesimus would not look her in the eye.

The bell tolled, and more men came marching up the hill in single file.

"You must leave." Onesimus stretched out his thick arm, the long sleeve falling like a curtain.

She slipped past him.

"Conrad?"

Her husband swiveled his head slowly, and gave her the blank stare of a blind man.

"Conrad!" She ran to embrace him. She felt the angles of his ribs against her bosom and the abrasion of the stubble he had allowed to sprout on his face, but no answering warmth. And no recognition in those

eyes. "What have they done to you, my love? Come and sit with me. Come and feel our baby."

When she pressed his hand to her distended belly, his lower lip quivered and something passed across his face, as if a veil was lifting. Then his features reformed into a mask she hardly knew.

"Conrad Weiser is dead."

Eva turned toward the new voice, which resonated like footsteps inside a vault.

"This is Brother Enoch," Friedsam informed her. "His name is well chosen. Like the Enoch of scripture, his body is on earth while his spirit walks in heaven."

"Oh, my love." Eva touched her husband's hollow cheeks. "Will you leave me a widow and your children orphans?"

She thought she saw an answering glow of recognition, but it soon faded.

"My husband is not well," she told Brother Friedsam. "I must care for him."

"You cannot stay here while the fruits of carnal lust are in your body."

"Are you talking about our child?" Eva's jaw dropped open. "You dare—you *dare*—to profane the fruits of holy matrimony?"

A cowled woman intervened, kneeling at the Superintendent's feet. "Father, forgive me for speaking out of turn."

"What is it, Sister?"

"This daughter of God has made a wearisome journey over the mountains. She should rest with us overnight. I will watch over her, and make sure she does not pollute the other Sisters."

"As thou wilt."

Brother Friedsam turned impatiently away, herding the other men—including Conrad—ahead of him.

Eva was torn between gratitude toward the Sister who had spoken up on her behalf, and contempt for the way she abased herself before the tiny religious despot. This was the same woman she had watched wringing out the hem of Brother Friedsam's robe after the dunkings in the mill creek.

"It is Anna, isn't it? We have met before."

"You must call me Sister here. Come quickly. The Father has shown you mercy, but the wrath of God is in him, and he wields the sword of the Lord's judgment."

□

Over a frugal dinner at the women's table in the refectory, Eva watched and waited for a chance to speak to her husband. It was strange to her to eat sauerkraut and potato pancakes without meat. Anna Eicher whispered to her that the Perfected were not permitted meat and the *fleisch-lichen*—the "fleshly" members of the outer Order, who had not yet renounced their families—were strictly prohibited from consuming pork or goose, since Brother Friedsam had pronounced these staples of the German diet to be unclean.

After the meal, Eva sat through two hours of prayer and meditation, guided by the menacing Prior Onesimus.

"If you wish the Lord's peace," Onesimus proclaimed, "you must oppose the world in all things."

Eva was glad when the meeting was dismissed and she was able to stretch her limbs in the evening air.

"Is it like this every night?"

"Brother Onesimus cut it short. The Perfected have important work tonight. Do not tarry. You will be able to speak with your husband only if you submit to our rules. We must go to the cloister now."

The women slept softer than the men. They were allowed mattresses and some of them occupied their own cell-like rooms. Anna shook her head at the sight of Eva's ripening belly inside her shift, and handed her a long, uncomely garment that covered her like a tent.

Eva lay in the dark, listening to the breathing of the other women and the rumble of men's voices from another building. Despite her worry and confusion, she soon found herself drifting off to sleep. She was ripped from her slumber by an eager, whinnying noise close at hand. She peered around the darkened dormitory, looking for its source. She saw one of the younger Sisters—a pretty, fair-haired girl—bucking and gyrating on her pallet, her knees raised high in the air.

"Oh yes, Lord," the girl panted. "Make me your vessel. Take this body."

Eva stifled a snort of laughter. What hypocrites these people were! The young Sister was pleasuring herself, and called this a spiritual marriage.

Yet there was strangeness here. The blond girl's hands moved in the air, as if stroking a lover and pulling him deeper inside her. And when she groaned with the pleasure of completion, Eva saw something move across the room at shoulder height and fly out the window. It was a grayish-blue blur, with the substance of cloud or smoke.

The girl's breathing reverted to the rhythms of deep sleep. Had she actually been awake?

A chill ran up Eva's spine. What was happening here was against nature.

She resolved to leave the women's cloister and see if there was some way of getting to Conrad. But as she began to gather up her clothes, the door creaked open and a corporeal visitor stepped across the threshold. Eva pulled the blanket up to her eyes when she recognized Brother Friedsam, carrying a taper.

"Let us praise the Lord together," he said in his carrying voice.

The Sisters rose at once, as if used to such visits. They kneeled at Brother Friedsam's feet while he preached to them, eyes closed.

Did he ever allow his followers to sleep?

At last he stopped talking. He opened his eyes and announced, "It is time to mortify the flesh."

The women preened themselves in front of him, shaking out their hair. Eva was shocked to see how they transformed themselves. They now looked less like nuns than like whores who were vying for a customer with deep pockets.

Brother Friedsam reached for her with his eyes.

No.

Eva was grateful when he turned back to his Sisters, hugging each of them in turn. He held the pretty blond nun in a lingering embrace.

"To master the flesh, we must submit ourselves to the ordeal of every temptation," he intoned. "In this way, we raise the serpent energy to the heavens, and ready ourselves for the spiritual marriage." He took the young Sister by the hand and drew her into one of the private cells.

The light was extinguished. Eva lay on her back, hardly daring to breathe. After a long time, she heard a deep animal grunt and the single word, "Good."

Sleep carried her off for a little while before the morning bell. In her dream, she struggled to free herself from a nest of serpents that writhed between her legs and slithered over her breasts.

When she woke in a cold sweat, she found Anna Eicher sobbing. Was this jealousy, or something more?

"What is the matter?"

Sniffling, eyes reddened, Anna said to her, "Get out while you can. *Save your baby.*"

□

Eva dressed quickly, ready to leave the cloister but not to give up the man she loved. She would find a way to bring him back. Her touch, and the feel of her unborn child, must surely be more powerful than the sex magic Brother Friedsam was working among his acolytes.

She saw Conrad among the men who were feeding a bonfire behind the meeting house, apparently burning trash. She seized on her opportunity.

She ran toward him, then paused, appalled by what he was doing. He was tearing out the pages of his beloved *Paradies Gärtlein* and feeding them to the flames. All the men were engaged in burning books, scores of them.

She clutched at Conrad's arm.

"Look at me."

His eyes were like muddy water. To look into them was like looking into a clouded fish-tank, waiting for something to swim to the surface.

"Look at yourself," she urged him. "You are burning the books you love. This is shameful."

"The Father has taught us that revelation will come only through him." Conrad spoke in a monotone, as if reciting a text.

"Will you destroy everything you love, because of this tyrant? Will you kill *this?*"

She pulled his hand to her belly.

Something floated toward the surface, a gleam of the Conrad she knew.

"Come with me now. Come back to your family."

Conrad hesitated, letting the ravaged book fall from his fingers.

Prior Onesimus loomed up between them. "We are Brother Enoch's family. You are the one who must go."

Onesimus moved as if to push her away.

"No." Conrad sheltered his wife with his body. "I will see this woman safely home."

"It is not allowed. You will remember your vows."

"Conrad, our babies cry at night because they miss you. If you no longer care for me, think of them."

Brother Friedsam came over to inspect the cause of the commotion.

"I was wrong to let you stay with us, even for one night," he told Eva. "You bring the disturbance of the outside world. But I will permit Brother Enoch to escort you home. In this way, you will see that he is not kept here against his will, but because the Lord has shown him his way."

CHAPTER 27

EAGLE PEAK

1.

Though only a few miles of hilly ground separated Tulpehocken and the Den of Serpents, the road home was a long one, for both Conrad and Eva. He greeted his children and neighbors like a visitor from another land. When Eva finally coaxed him into her bed and kindled fire in his loins, he made love to her mechanically and perfunctorily, and knelt on the floor afterwards, asking forgiveness for the weakness of the flesh. He returned to Ephrata before the new baby was born.

When he reappeared, he was wearing a new robe and carrying a staff, like the one Brother Friedsam used. He announced that he had been ordained "a priest after the order of Melchizedek" and would be engaged in missionary work among far-flung settlements.

After the night he used her like a rough stranger, and then scourged himself with the lash, Eva stopped trying to lure him into her embraces, but found it less easy to stop crying herself to sleep.

Where was her splendid lover, the man who had lived as if he were born with wings?

Others were disturbed by the change in Conrad. James Logan missed the man he had valued as an interpreter, and sought to revive his interest in Indian councils. Brother Friedsam did not forbid his renewed involvement in provincial diplomacy. Though his community had renounced the world, he had picked Conrad as a "lookout man" who would bring him intelligence of what was going on in it. When Conrad traveled to Philadelphia, he was charged with missions for the Brotherhood, such as negotiating the purchase of printing paper from Ben

Franklin (who had established a virtual monopoly of this valuable re-
source) for a hymnal, one of the few books countenanced under the new
order at Ephrata.

Conrad's mastery of Indian languages had survived his spiritual up-
heaval. But his friend Swatana missed the man he had known almost as
keenly as Eva.

After journeying to Onondaga, to report on how Logan had dispos-
sessed the Lenape of the vast, fertile territory between the forks of the
Delaware River through the ruse of the Walking Purchase—without
Conrad's assistance—Swatana headed east to consult with Conrad's first
mentor.

"Longhair has gone the long trail," Island Woman told him.

"But I think he speaks to you still."

"Sometimes the great ones stay close to the earth, to watch over us."
Island Woman avoided giving a direct response. But she led Swatana to
the ancient tree that belonged to the shaman's dreaming.

"I am troubled by our friend," Swatana said to her. "He is no longer
Skycatcher. He speaks words from the mouth, not from the heart. What
is inside him hides from me. Can you help him, even at this great distance?"

"I do not know. I must dream on it."

"I brought you something that belongs to him. His wife gave it to
me. She said he no longer values it."

Swatana carefully unwrapped the object from the folds of soft doe-
skin. Sunlight falling through the leaves struck its facets and made crystal fire.

Island Woman received the rock with cupped hands. It was Longhair's see-stone, his last gift to Conrad.

She told her visitor, "Whatever can be done, I will do."

□

By moonlight, she watched for shapes to emerge within the crystal. She
found two figures. One was Conrad, stooped under the weight of a great
burden. The second was a winged being, who also resembled Conrad,
but stood behind him, close yet separate.

She focused on the burden the first Conrad was carrying. Now it
resembled the body of a dead man.

She saw the nature of the sorcery that needed to be undone. Somehow she must release Conrad from the weight of the dead stranger that
was riding him, so his bright soul—his winged spirit—could live inside
him again. She was not certain she had the power to accomplish this.
Conrad had been snared by a sorcerer of great skill, far stronger than
Two Hearts, and this man used arts that were foreign to the Real People.

The distance between them was also great, and if she journeyed across it in her dreambody for the work of healing, she risked attack from the sorcerer, who would surely have watchers posted.

She could not do this alone.

But as she rekindled the fire, she saw bear and panther moving in the shadows. When she shook her rattle, they were joined by many more guardian spirits.

You are never alone. Longhair walked through her mind. *And when your work is the care and guidance of souls, the whole universe supports you.*

2.

In Brother Friedsam's cloister, Conrad jerked from sleep before the morning bell. His stomach was churning. The spasms set his ribcage heaving and brought sour bile sloshing up through his esophagus. He rushed outside to vomit on the grass. He was amazed by the quantity of foul liquid that gushed out of him. Particles of food came with it. One of them was disgusting, fat and sheeny, like a black worm. It seemed almost alive.

It *was* alive.

His eyes widened as he saw the thing slither toward the cover of high grass. He rushed after it, stamping on it again and again with his calloused heel until he had reduced it to a small, messy puddle.

All that retching should have left him weak and depleted. Instead, he felt stronger. He stretched his arms high and wide and enjoyed the vital energy that streamed through all his body. It moved like waves of light, rolling down through the crown of his head, moving through every part of his being. He felt a ball of light growing at his heart like an inner sun. Its rays spread to the surface of his skin and shone beyond it like a golden aura.

It felt so good to be alive!

He turned in the direction of the rising sun and said aloud, "Thank you for the morning, thank you for the day. Thank you, Brother Sun, for bringing light and life into my world."

In that moment, a scene from his dream came back to him. He saw himself flying above Eagle Peak, on the wings of a red-tailed hawk. He had been startled when a larger raptor made a lightning descent from on high, rushing straight at his head, talons outstretched. In an amazing show of acrobatics, the eagle had flipped upside down, to offer him what it was holding in its claws.

What was this gift?

He was trying to remember when he saw a woman creeping around the side of the Sisters' dormitory.

Now he recalled all he had suffered and accepted in this place, against nature. The memories were strangely detached from him. It was like viewing scenes from the life of another person. Was it really possible he had willingly caged himself here, under the law of Brother Friedsam and his dark divinity?

He stepped toward the woman, and she recoiled from him.

"Keep away!" she hissed.

"It's Anna Eicher, isn't it?" He remembered they had briefly been neighbors, before she had put on the robe of a "spiritual virgin."

"Keep off," she warned him. "None of you will hold me now."

He saw that she had a kitchen knife in her hands, as well as a cloth bundle.

"I won't hurt you, Anna."

She changed, as she noticed the change in his speech. She crept closer to him, peering into his eyes.

"You're not the same."

"No," he agreed. "I came back."

"Quickly. There is something I must show you."

Anna led him down the rough slope beyond the meetinghouse, past the graveyard on the hill. Down in a damp hollow, she pointed to a small mound of stones where someone had placed wildflowers.

"The bastard wouldn't even give her a decent burial. Dumped her like a heathen. And he calls himself the perfected of God."

Anna was crying. Conrad put his arm around her, and she cradled inside his warmth.

"Who is buried here?"

"He killed my baby. He fathered it on me, telling me we were mortifying the flesh. Then he made me go on retreat so nobody would notice my belly. Said he would make all things well. Then he tied her up in a bag like an unwanted kitten. Said he'd make me Mother Superior if I kept quiet. He dishonored that promise too."

Conrad bent down and added another pile to the stone.

He murmured, "May your paths be open. May your spirit find peace in the Upper World."

Anna grabbed at his arm. "You won't let him get away with it, will you? Someone must right this wrong."

"Someone will." He promised himself he would find a way to settle accounts with Brother Friedsam, the thief of souls.

3.

When Conrad rode back to Philadelphia, James Logan was greatly relieved to see that he had shaved off his beard and was dressed like a prosperous farmer, with the embellishment of an Indian bracelet and beaded pouch.

"You were a puzzle to me for a time there, Mister Weiser. I have little leisure for the contemplation of first and last things, apart from what I glean from the Roman authors. The world is too much with us, eh? It is more than enough for me to contend with the natives, who are forever prating about dreams and spirits. Your German theologies leave me hopelessly at sea."

"I would like to speak to you about that."

"Presently, if you must. Have you heard in your border marches that we have a new governor? A capable man, Governor Thomas. Quite alive to the machinations of the French, who are meddling with some of our restive tribes. I have persuaded His Excellency that you will be of great service to us in a time that portends war, if only you will give a larger part of yourself to our Indian diplomacy."

"It is my calling."

"I am glad to learn we are of the same mind. Nonetheless, I am pleased to report that I have induced Governor Thomas to offer you a small inducement to stand with us. He has approved your appointment as a Justice of the Peace. I know your Brother Friedsam does not hold with our laws, but they must be enforced willy-nilly. And I believe you are the man we need for the back settlements, if you are minded to accept this charge."

"I have renounced the rule of Conrad Beissel's Brotherhood. I will be your Justice. In that guise, I may even be of service in the criminal matter I have come to report."

He reported Anna Eicher's accusations against Brother Friedsam.

"Rogered the poor wench and then smothered the baby?" Logan summarized. "Well, that will knock Brother Friedsam off his pulpit when it gets out. You will have all the assistance you need."

☐

Conrad climbed the summit of Eagle Peak on a crisp, breezy morning in early spring. He moved carefully as he neared the top, because he saw that hawks or eagles had built a nest high among the rocks. He crouched down and watched one of the parents bringing food to the nest. It was a red-tailed hawk, the female of the pair if he was not mistaken. It seemed the father had remained, to guard the eggs and help incubate them with his warmth.

A lesson from nature he had neglected, when he was under the spell of the Brotherhood.

As the sun rose in the sky, he set the crystal rock Swatana had returned to him on a ledge, to catch and refract the light. He reached into his pouch and retrieved a twist of native tobacco, which he stuffed in his pipe. When he had gotten it alight, he offered the smoke to the sky.

He followed the wisp of smoke that spiraled upward toward the zenith. A golden eagle turned a slow circle high above him, and Conrad's heart soared with it.

SOURCES AND CONSEQUENCES

ABBREVIATIONS

DCB   *Dictionary of Canadian Biography*. Toronto: University of Toronto Press, 1966–79. vols. 1–4.

DH   Edmund N. O'Callaghan (ed.), *The Documentary History of the State of New York*. Albany: Weed, Parsons, 1849–51. 4 vols.

JR   Reuben Gold Thwaites (ed.) *The Jesuit Relations and Allied Documents: Travels and Explorations of the Jesuit Missionaries in New France, 1610–1791*. Cleveland: Burrows Brothers, 1896–1901. 73 vols.

LAFITAU   Joseph François Lafitau, *Customs of the American Indians Compared with the Customs of Primitive Times* [1724]. ed. and trans. William N. Fenton and Elizabeth L. Moore. Toronto: Champlain Society, 1974. 2 vols.

NYCD   Edmund B. O'Callaghan (ed.), *Documents Relative to the Colonial History of New York*. Albany: Weed, Parsons, 1853–87. 15 vols.

NYHS   New York Historical Society.

NYSL   New York State Library.

WRAXALL   Peter Wraxall, *An Abridgment of Indian Affairs Contained in Four Folio Volumes, Transacted in the Colony of New York from the Year 1678 to the Year 1751* [1754]. ed. Charles H. McIlwain. Cambridge, Mass.: Harvard University Press, 1915.

ON THE FOUR KINGS AND THEIR VISIT TO QUEEN ANNE:

The most complete historical account of the 1710 visit is Richmond P. Bond, *Queen Anne's American Kings*, New York: Octagon Books, 1974. John G. Garratt, *The Four Indian Kings*, Ottawa: Public Archives of Canada, 1985, reproduces the portraits of the Four Kings and the broadsheets and playbills devoted to them. Maurice Ashley, *England in the Seventeenth Century*, Harmondsworth, U. K.: Penguin, 1952, provides a concise view of the condition of Queen Anne and her court. The most readable account of Queen Anne's war in North America remains Francis Parkman, *A Half-Century of Conflict*, Boston: Little, Brown, 1902, 2 vols., though the great New Englander is rarely friendly to the Iroquois or fair to New Yorkers.

The etymology of Hendrick's Mohawk name is discussed in Floyd G. Lounsbury, *Iroquois Place Names in the Champlain Valley*, Albany: State Education Department, 1960, a pioneering attempt to use tools of linguistic analysis to recover Iroquois traditions. A fascinating clue to Hendrick's physical size is a sketch that I found in the scrapbooks of Rufus Alexander Grider, a popular nineteenth-century illustrator, in the New York State Library. The sketch depicts the "thigh bones of King Hendrick," allegedly retrieved from his place of burial after the Battle of Lake George in 1755 (described in my novel *The Fire-keeper*). Each thigh bone was nineteen and a half inches long, suggesting that Hendrick was about seven feet tall. Hendrick described his own Mahican origins in a 1745 speech reproduced in NYCD 6:294. Hendrick was born around 1680, and by 1698 was a nominal convert to Christianity; cf. NYCD 4:345. The agent of his conversion was the Dutch minister at Albany, Godfrey Dellius, who worked with a female interpreter and was a moving spirit in the most notorious land swindle of the day; cf. NYCD 4:364, 533. Further biographical information on Hendrick may be found in Milton W. Hamilton, "Theyanoguin," in DCB 3: 622–624 and (with varying reliability) in William L. Stone, "King Hendrick," in *Proceedings* of the New York State Historical Association 1:28–34 and in Nathaniel S. Benton, *History of Herkimer County*, Albany: J. Munsell, 1856, 20–24.

Within a few years of his return from London, Hendrick suffered a major personal breakdown and was stripped of his authority as a Mohawk leader. Hunter was complaining about his unreliability as early as 1713; see *Calendar of State Papers, 1712–14*, 159. Peter Schuyler's role in his political resurrection at an Albany conference in 1720 is reflected in NYCD 5:569, where it is noted that Hendrick had been "suspended from being a Sachim by the Sachims of the Maquase about four years ago."

With the help of his white supporters and his own considerable gifts, Hendrick recovered from his disgrace and reemerged as the dominant Mohawk leader in the second quarter of the eighteenth century. Hendrick lobbied hard and successfully for the appointment of William Johnson as King's Superintendent of Indian Affairs, believing correctly that this energetic young Irishman could be persuaded to represent Mohawk interests at least as much as those of the Crown. Together, Hendrick and Johnson swung the Mohawks and their sister-nations behind the English cause in both King George's War (known in Europe as the War of the Austrian Succession) and the French and Indian War.

It was Hendrick Forked Paths who advised Ben Franklin—during a famous encounter at a conference in Albany in 1754—that the American colonists should follow the example of the Iroquois by uniting in a confederacy.

Conrad Weiser's own view of Hendrick was unflattering, perhaps for reasons reflected in this story. He described him as late as 1754 as "that Proud and Impudent Henery Dyionoagon" and cited him as an example of how the Mohawks had become "apostates as to their Old Natural Principle of Honesty"; see Julian P. Boyd (ed.), *The Susquehannah Company Papers*, Ithaca, N.Y.: Cornell University Press, 1962, 1:66.

Hendrick died on September 8, 1755, when he was shot off his horse in the opening skirmish of the Battle of Lake George at the ripe old age of eighty.

Colonial records state that the Mohawk Indian called Sayenqueraghta, or Vanishing Smoke, died on September 24, 1710, in the Moon of Shining Leaves.

The cause of his sudden death, within months of his visit to the Court of Queen Anne, was not established. However, the Reverend Thomas Barclay, rector of the Anglican church at Albany, reported to the Secretary of the Society for the Propagation of the Gospel in London two days after the event that rumors were rife in Indian country that Vanishing Smoke was the victim of witchcraft. Curiously, within a few years, Barclay himself fell prey to a condition that his Albany Dutch neighbors also believed to be the result of native sorcery. The minister ran screaming through his house, trying to set fire to drapes and hangings with live coals plucked from the fire. To avoid scandal, Barclay's friends and family were obliged to confine him to a small, airless room with a sturdy beam across the door.

The name—and in Indian belief, the spirit—of Vanishing Smoke was re-quickened in the person of a Seneca Indian who became a celebrated war chief, siding with the British during the American Revolution. His name is usually rendered as Kayenqueraghta.

A modern medical opinion about Vanishing Smoke's illness, based on his appearance in the Verelst portrait, is that he may have developed gynecomastia, which can be a symptom of liver disease, when the liver fails to detoxify the female hormone, estrogen. See Roderic H. Blackburn, "Indian Kings at Queen Anne's Court," Albany: Exhibition Guide, Albany Institute of History and Art, 1985. Brant Vanishing Smoke may be the grandfather or great-grandfather of Molly Brant, the Mohawk consort of Sir William Johnson, and of Joseph Brant, the famous leader of Tory and Indian rangers during the American Revolution, who was fond of stories of ghost warriors; cf. Carl F. Klinck and James J. Talman (eds.), *The Journal of Major John Norton, 1816*, Toronto: Champlain Society, 1970.

There is scant documentary material on the two remaining Indian Kings: the Mahican, Nicholas Etakoam, and the Mohawk known as John and de-scribed in the inscription on the Verelst print as "Ho Nee Yeath Taw No Row, King of the Generethgarich." Etakoam may mean Both Sides or Two Sides (as in "both sides of the river"). Patrick Frazier, *The Mohicans of Stockbridge*, Lincoln and London: University of Nebraska Press, 1992, provides some information on Etakoam's family. "Generethgarich" may be a colonial garble for Canajoharie, the Upper Castle.

Etakoam's family was living at Stockbridge, Massachusetts, in later years.

His grandson Jacob was baptised by John Sergeant and delivered a timely warning in 1754 to settlers in the Hoosic Valley about an impending raid by French Indians. He succumbed to the familiar problems of men who struggle to live in two worlds and was jailed for debt at Albany in 1763; a black man from Stockbridge bailed him out.

The fact that none of the Four Kings was a *royaner*, or traditional chief, can be readily confirmed by scanning the chiefly titles analyzed in William N. Fenton, *The Roll Call of the Iroquois Chiefs*, Washington, D.C.: Smithsonian Miscellaneous Collections 115/15, 1950. The classic account of traditional Iroquois society is Lewis Henry Morgan, *The League of the Ho-Dee-No-Sau-Nee, or Iroquois*, New York: Dodd, Mead, 1902, 2 vols. An early history, valuable despite its inaccuracies, is William M. Beauchamp, *A History of the New York State Iroquois*, Albany, N.Y.: New York State Museum Bulletin 78, 1905.

ON CONRAD WEISER AND THE PALATINE GERMANS:

I am greatly indebted to Paul A. W. Wallace's massive biography, *Conrad Weiser: Friend of Colonist and Mohawk*, Philadelphia: University of Pennsylvania Press, 1945, which describes Conrad's youthful wildness, his lifelong feud with his stepmother, and his extraordinary double life as Brother Enoch, the frontier mystic. Needless to say, as a novelist I have taken full advantage of the fact that precious little has been recorded about Conrad's early life in the East Camp and among the Mohawks. Weiser provided a sketchy version of his early life in his *Autobiography*; the Historical Society of Pennsylvania has a copy of the original German manuscript. Something of the quality of his mind, and his keen interest in native spirits, can be gleaned from two of his travel journals from later years: the *Narrative of a Journey from Tulpehocken, Pennsylvania to Onondaga in 1739*, printed in Henry R. Schoolcraft, *Historical and Statistical Information Respecting the History, Condition and Prospects of the Indian Tribes of the United States* 6 vols., Philadelphia: Lippincott, 1851–57, 4:324–341; and the recently translated *Journals of Christian Daniel Claus and Conrad Weiser: A Journey to Onondaga, 1750* trans. and ed. Helga Doblin and William A. Starna, Philadelphia: American Historical Society, 1994. The etymology of Conrad's first Mohawk name is discussed in Wallace, *Conrad Weiser*, 32.

The covenant the Palatine emigrants were required to sign is reproduced in NYCD 5:121–2.

My principal sources on the conditions of the Palatines in the tar camps and their confrontation with Governor Hunter are the colonial documents preserved in vol. 3 of DH and vol. 5 of NYCD. These include letters from Jean Cast describing the quality of the food supplied by Robert Livingston in stomach-churning detail; cf. DH 3:659–60. The Earl of Clarendon wrote the following observations about Livingston in March, 1711: "I think it is unhappy that Col. Hunter at his first arrival in his Government fell into so ill hands, for the

Levingston has been known many years in that Province for a very ill man, he formerly Victualled the forces at Albany in which he was guilty of the most notorious frauds . . . The consequence will be that Levingston and some others will get Estates, the Palatines will not be the richer"; see DH 3:656–7.

On the Palatine migration to the Schoharie valley, and their encounters with the law, there is much vivid material in John M. Brown, *Brief Sketch of the First Settlement of the County of Schoharie*, Middleburgh, New York: Middleburgh News reprint, 1975; and Jeptha R. Simms, *The History of Schoharie County*, Albany: Munsell & Tanner, 1845, and *The Frontiersmen of New York*, 2 vols., Albany: George Riggs, 1882. I found further useful material in W. A. Knittle, *The Palatines of New York State*, Johnstown, NY: Palatine Society/Baronet Litho, 1953; Wanda E. Burch, "History of Stone Arabia, 1711–1792, MA thesis, Cooperstown, 1974; and Rev. Wolcott Ellsworth, "The Palatines in the Mohawk Valley," in *Proceedings* of the New York State Historical Association 14:295–311.

Magdalina Zeh's treatment of Sheriff Adams is recounted in Judge Brown's *Brief Sketch*.

The character of Blackheath at the time of the Palatine tent colony is well described in Neil Rhind, *The Heath*, London: Bookshop Blackheath Ltd, 1987.

ON JONCAIRE AND INDIAN AGENTS:

The fullest accounts of the French agent's career are Frank H. Severance, "The Story of Joncaire" in *Publications of the Buffalo Historical Society*, vol. 9, 1906, 83–209; and *An Old Frontier of France*, New York: Dodd, Mead, 1917, 2 vols. Joncaire's reminiscences of the Denonville campaign in chapter three follow the "Memoir of the Voyage and Expedition of the Marquis de Denonville" in NYCD 9:358–369. On the names and locations of Seneca villages, I am indebted to a paper entitled "Ethnology, History and Seneca Origins" presented by George R. Hammell and Hazel Dean John at the 1987 Annual Conference on Iroquois Research at Rensselaerville, N.Y. My account of the council between Joncaire and the Onondagas is based on Lawrence Claessen's minutes, in NYCD 5:217–218.

ON THE MOHAWK PATENT AND COLONIAL LAND FRAUDS:

Governor Hunter reported to London that he got his deed to the Schoharie land. In documents preserved in the New York Historical Society, Hunter claims that Hendrick and other Mohawks conceded all the land in the Schoharie valley, reserving only flats and woodlands near "Onitstachragarawe" (Corn Mountain) for native use; see "Letter from the Maquas Indians to Governor Hunter and His Reply," August, 1710, in Miscellaneous Indian Manuscripts, NYHS. In my opinion, this version is highly suspect. Peter Wraxall, who worked with all the extant Indian records under the direction of Sir William Johnson to prepare his

Abridgment, found that when Hendrick and the Mohawks left Hunter's 1710 Albany conference, they had failed to sign a land deed. Even more telling (as in my version), they had failed to collect the valuable gifts the governor had assembled for them; Wraxall noted that this was without precedent. An excellent study by Georgiana C. Nammack, *Fraud, Politics and the Dispossession of the Indians,* Norman: University of Oklahoma Press, 1969, sets this episode in the context of other colonial land swindles.

ON SHAMANS AND IROQUOIS DREAMING:

Longhair appears once in the colonial documents: in an account by Father Lafitau, who was superior of the Jesuit mission at Kahnawake during this period, of a duel between a shapeshifting sorcerer and a renowned Mohawk shaman called Shonnonkouiretsi ("The Very Long-Haired One"); cf. Lafitau 1:247–248. Other missionary reports contain rich material on Otherworld journeys by Iroquois and Huron shamans; see, for example, Father Brébeuf's account in JR 10: 149–153.

On the Iroquois view of the dreamsoul, see J. N. B. Hewitt, "The Iroquoian Concept of the Soul," in *Journal of American Folk-Lore,* vol. 8, 1902, 107–116. From his mission among the Hurons, Father LeJeune described the native belief that some people have "two or three souls" and the case of a woman who ran after her escaping soul; cf JR 16:191 and JR 11:117. For tales of the double, see Arthur C. Parker, *Seneca Myths & Folk Tales,* Lincoln and London: University of Nebraska Press, 1989, esp. 159–70. Ake Hultkrantz, *Conceptions of the Soul among North American Indians,* Stockholm: Ethnographical Museum of Sweden, 1953, places these beliefs in a pan-American context. A Lakota spiritual leader is remarkably open about operations involving different aspects of the soul in Thomas E. Mails, *Fools Crow: Wisdom and Power,* Tulsa: Council Oaks Books, 1991.

J. G. Frazer, *The Golden Bough,* New York: Macmillan, 1951 (abridged edition): 208–20 contains ethnographic observations of soul-loss, soul-theft and soul recovery in many tribal cultures. For experiential insight into what may be going on, see Michael J. Harner, *The Jívaro,* Berkeley: University of California Press, 1984 and Sandra Ingerman, *Soul Retrieval,* Harper San Francisco, 1991, a practical guide by a gifted and generous shamanic teacher.

On the traditional dream spirituality of the Iroquoians, see my essays "Blackrobes and Dreamers" in *Shaman's Drum,* No. 28, 1992, and "Missionaries and Magicians: The Jesuit Encounter with Native American Shamans" in Peter Benes [ed.] *Wonders of the Invisible World: 1600–1900,* Boston: Boston University Press, 1995.

Medicine Grizzlybear Lake, *Native Healer,* Wheaton, Ill.: Quest Books, 1991, is a powerful account of the role of dreaming in the practice of a contemporary Iroquois healer.

For an experiential guide to the techniques of shamanic dreaming, see my book *Conscious Dreaming: A Spiritual Path for Everyday Life,* New York: Crown, 1996.

ON FALSE FACES:

The *akakon'sa*, or "face in front of the face," is an ancient power tool of Iroquois shamanism. In relatively recent times—perhaps in the period of *The Interpreter*—False Face Societies were created to harness and contain this power. An imposing guide to the whole subject is William N. Fenton, *The False Faces of the Iroquois*, Norman and London: University of Oklahoma Press, 1987. On dream callings to join the Seneca False Face Society, see Jesse L. Cornplanter, *Legends of the Longhouse*, Philadelphia and New York: Lippincott, 1938.

There is archeological evidence that False Face masks were made and used in Mohawk country since early times. A Mohawk pipe from the Otsungo site, dating from the early 1500s, is decorated with what is clearly a mask; the False Face covers and overlaps the front of the trumpet-shaped bowl. In his journal of his 1634–1635 journey, Harmen Meyndertz van den Bogaert refers to Mohawk "idols," a possible reference to the False Faces; see van den Bogaert, "Narrative of a Journey into the Mohawk and Oneida Country," in J. Franklin Jameson [ed.] *Narratives of New Netherland*, New York: Scribners, 1909. Two of the earliest (and most haunting) False Faces that survive in modern collections are Mohawk masks probably dating from the eighteenth century. One of them, collected by Harriet Maxwell Converse at Grand River in 1892, was represented to her as having belonged to Joseph Brant, who may have been the grandson of Brant Vanishing Smoke. A sketch of the second Mohawk mask, described as a "Mohawk Wolf Clan" mask, is among a striking collection of "portraits" of Iroquois Faces by Rufus Grider in the Newberry Library in Chicago.

ON CAPTAIN KIDD'S TREASURE:

I have profited from a recent scholarly account of Captain Kidd's career that analyzes his business dealings with Robert Livingston: Robert C. Ritchie, *Captain Kidd and the War against the Pirates*, Cambridge, Mass. and London: Harvard University Press, 1986. Livingston chronicles some of his dealings with Kidd in a journal he kept from August to October, 1695, that is in the Journal Mss. of the New York Historical Society. Governor Bellomont's suspicions of Livingston's "jiggling" are reflected in NYCD 4:583–6. Livingston was still defending himself against these charges several years later; cf. NYCD 4:883–4. A rousing early account of Kidd's adventure is Captain Charles Johnson [probably a pseudonym for Daniel Defoe], *Lives of the Most Notorious Pirates* [1724], London: Folio Society, 1962, 165–81.

Although there is no record of Kidd calling at Martha's Vineyard, he lingered for many days in the near vicinity, in the waters between Gardiner's Island and Block Island, on his last voyage on the *Saint Antonio*, and distributed part of his treasure to sloops and smaller vessels that made rendezvous with him there. He landed twice on Gardiner's Island, leaving a box containing 52 pounds of gold with its proprietor, John Gardiner; cf. Ritchie 230–1. On the condition of the Indians of Gay Head in Weiser's time, the sending of Wampanoags as indentured servants to Long Island, and the service of Nicodemus in the Port Royal campaign, see Arthur R. Railton, "The Indians and the English on Martha's Vineyard, Part V: Gay Head Neck and the Farm" in *The Dukes County Intelligencer*, vol. 34, no. 3, 1993, 109–164. For a vivid description of the clay walls of Gay Head by an early German visitor, see Albert C. Koch, *Journey through a Part of the United States of America in the Years 1844–1846*, ed. Ernst A, Stadler, Carbondale, Ill.: Southern Illinois University Press, 1972. On early life on Long Island (including the profusion of peach trees), see Jaspar Dankers and Peter Sluyter, *Journal of a Voyage to New York . . . in 1679–80*, trans. and ed. Henry C. Murphy, Brooklyn, N.Y.: Long Island Historical Society, 1867.

In the Palatines' 1720 schedule of complaints against Governor Hunter, they reveal that they paid "300 pieces of eight" to Schoharie Indians in a private land transaction—a very considerable amount for a community of only 150 families who were frequently forced (in their first years) to beg for flour and other necessities from Albany and Schenectady traders on credit; cf. DH3:709–14. There is no indication of how this money was raised.

Adventurers are still searching for Captain Kidd's gold, from Nova Scotia to the South China Sea, where two treasure-hunters were arrested by the Vietnamese coast guard in 1983.

ON THE PEACEMAKER:

The *real* Hiawatha story—the Iroquois legend of the Peacemaker—is one of the great sacred teaching stories of humankind, and an object lesson in the possibility of overcoming our adversaries through healing instead of aggression. Because it springs from an oral tradition in which it is used to encourage direct visionary exploration of its spiritual truths, it has not yet been translated into a written version that conveys its full wisdom (and perhaps never will be). An accessible version is Paul A. W. Wallace, *The White Roots of Peace*, Philadelphia: University of Pennsylvania Press, 1946. For a beautiful re-interpretation with guided meditations, see Jean Houston with Margaret Rubin, *Manual for the Peacemaker*, Wheaton, Ill.: Quest Books, 1995.

Handsome Lake, the Seneca prophet, had an important vision of Christ during his Otherworld journeys; cf. Arthur C. Parker, *The Code of Handsome Lake, the Seneca Prophet* Albany, N.Y.: New York State Museum Bulletin 163, 1913.

TOBIAS'S LADDER:

Tobias is studying Hayyim Vital's account of a sixteenth-century exorcism in his *Sefer haGilgulim*; a modern translation appears in Raphael Patai, "Exorcism and Xenoglossia among the Safed Kabbalists" in *Journal of American Folklore* vol. 91, no. 361, 1978, 823–33. On Enochian Otherworld journeys, see I. P. Couliano, *Out of this World: Otherworldly Journeys from Gilgamesh to Albert Ein-*

stein, Boston and London: Shambhala, 1991. On the experience of the spirit worlds in Jewish mysticism, see Ithamar Gruenwald, *Apocalyptic and Merkavah Mysticism*, Leiden: Brill, 1980, and Moshe Idel, *Studies in Ecstatic Kabbalah*, Albany: State University of New York Press, 1988.

INTO PENNSYLVANIA:

On Indian paths in Pennsylvania country, I have chiefly relied on Paul A. W. Wallace, *Indians of Pennsylvania*, Harrisburg, Pa.: Pennsylvania Historical and Museum Commission, 1961. On the Delaware Indians, the indispensable source remains John Heckewelder, *History, Manners and Customs of the Indian Nations who Once Inhabited Pennsylvania and the Neighboring States* [1876] New York: Arno Press, 1971. See also C. A. Weslager, *The Delaware Indians: A History*, New Brunswick, N.J.: Rutgers University Press, 1972. On the imperial claims advanced for the Iroquois, see Francis Jennings, *The Ambiguous Iroquois Empire*, New York: Norton, 1984.

The naturalist John Bartram, who met Swatana in 1744, reported that he was "a Frenchman born at Montreal, and adopted by the Oneidoes after being taken prisoner." There is an important brief biography of the "half-king" by William A. Hunter in DCB 3: 606–7.

BROTHER ENOCH:

The principal source on Conrad Weiser's involvement with the spiritual community founded by Johann Conrad Beissel is the *Chronicon Ephratense; a History of the Community of Seventh Day Baptists at Ephrata*, by Lamech and Agrippa, trans. J. Max Hark, Lancaster, Pa., 1889. The sections on Weiser appear to have been written by his friend Peter Miller. The Order's bizarre practices—including the proscription of bathroom visits for long intervals, the book burning, and the boasts of leaving "footprints on the ceiling"—are fully documented, as are Beissel's nocturnal visits to the Sisters. Some of Brother Friedsam's followers feared him as a powerful magician whose influence survived physical death. The diary of Christopher Marshall contains a chilling account of how Brother Friedsam allegedly returned after death to attack two of his disciples whom he believed to have betrayed him:

> Christiana being in her own room by her Self was Visited . . . by the Deceased Conrad Bysall and he in a very angry and violent rage fell upon her, taking her by the throat. So that She was almost strangled.

Beissel's ghost allegedly returned later the same night, accompanied by a small army of spirits, and attacked Christiana and her husband again, until repelled by fervent prayer (cited in Wallace, *Conrad Weiser*, 52).

For scholarly accounts that set Beissel's movement in the context of

German pietism and Bohmist theology, see Arthur Versluis, *TheoSophia: Hidden Dimensions of Christianity*, Hudson, N.Y.: Lindisfarne Press, 1994, and Chauncy David Ensign, "Radical German Pietism (c. 1675–1760)," Ph.D. diss., Boston University, 1955.

Conrad Weiser's denunciation of Brother Friedsam for having murdered a bastard child he had sired by Anna Eicher, one of his "spiritual virgins," is recorded in the *Chronicon Ephratense* 82–6. Two years after Conrad reported the matter to the Pennsylvania authorities, Anna withdrew the charge under relentless pressure from the Brotherhood; she died under mysterious circumstances soon afterward.

PERSONAL NOTE

This book has been borning for a long time. I wrote the first draft of chapter one in what was literally the "borning room" of the colonial Dutch settlers on a farm in upstate New York, the place where they brought both their women and their livestock to give birth. This seemed like a propitious place to deliver books, and I turned it into my study. The scene in which Vanishing Smoke steps into the bearpit and asks the bear who is torn and bleeding for permission to release him from the pain of this life remains substantially unchanged. I wrote it on November 15, 1987. The date is indelible in my mind.

Immediately after writing this scene—a deeply emotional experience, both powerful and exhausting—I lay down to take a nap. Two hours later, I was roused by a phone call from my mother in Australia. She told me that at the moment Vanishing Smoke sprang to life on the page and put his knife into the bear's heart, my father died in hospital in Southport, Queensland. Like the bear, he had been through a hellish season of pain and impairment, following a botched operation on his carotid artery to prevent further strokes. "The doctors don't know why his heart stopped just now," my mother reported, torn between grief and joy that my father had been released from his suffering. "But I know he was ready to go. He called me to say good-bye."

In the year that followed, my father returned to me and to other members of my family in dreams and in dreamlike experiences, with both practical and spiritual guidance. He left us in no doubt that there is life after life. He helped to recall me to the path of heart and to ways of being and seeing that are shared by *all* our ancestors.

This book is for you, Dad.

ABOUT THE AUTHOR

Robert Moss is a teacher, historian, best-selling novelist, and a lifelong dream explorer. He has been a university professor of ancient history and philosophy, an actor, a magazine editor and a foreign correspondent. He became interested in the Iroquois Indians and the history of America's first frontier when he moved to upstate New York in the mid-1980s and started dreaming in a language not his own, which proved to be an archaic form of the Mohawk language. Both *The Firekeeper* and *The Interpreter* have flowed from these dreams, as well as nine years of intensive historical research. Moss's previous books include popular suspense novels; the American historical adventure *Fire Along the Sky*; and *Conscious Dreaming: A Spiritual Path for Everyday Life*, which is both a personal odyssey and a practical guide to dreamwork and shamanism. Moss lives with his family in the upper Hudson Valley of New York, in what was formerly Mahican country.